WITCHES
GET
STITCHES

JULIETTE CROSS

UNION
SQUARE
& CO.

NEW YORK

UNION SQUARE & CO.
NEW YORK

UNION SQUARE & CO. and the distinctive Union Square & Co. logo are trademarks of Sterling Publishing Co., Inc.

Union Square & Co., LLC, is a subsidiary of Sterling Publishing Co., Inc.

Text © 2021 Juliette Cross

All rights reserved. No part of this publication may be reproduced, stored in a retrieval system, or transmitted in any form or by any means (including electronic, mechanical, photocopying, recording, or otherwise) without prior written permission from the publisher.

This is a work of fiction. Names, characters, business, events, and incidents are the products of the author's imagination. Any resemblance to actual persons, living or dead, or actual events is purely coincidental.

ISBN 978-1-4549-5364-7 (paperback)

For information about custom editions, special sales, and premium purchases, pleasve contact specialsales@unionsquareandco.com.

Printed in Canada

2 4 6 8 10 9 7 5 3 1

unionsquareandco.com

Edited by Corinne DeMaagd
Cover design by Jenny Zemanek
Cover images by Shutterstock.com: Dancake (mystic symbols); javarman (ombre); Kate Macate (ribbon, herbs); Nadeya_V (wolf)

For my beloved husband and best friend.
Thank you for being persistent and patient like
Nico and for waiting me out.
And for giving me the nudge I needed to wake up,
just like Violet did.
Love living my HEA with you.

PROLOGUE

~VIOLET~

"Okay, Violet's turn!" Clara squealed, bouncing excitedly beside me. Aunt Beryl had just done her reading using the divining bowl.

This was our 16th birthday present. My twin sister scooted over in the grass so that I could take the spot directly across from Aunt Beryl for my reading. I leaned forward to get a better look in the bowl, hemmed in with wild-growing flowers and herbs that had been manicured to look like an English garden in Aunt Beryl's backyard.

"I'm a Seer, too, you know." I swatted a piece of grass off my bare knee. "I could've done this myself."

Aunt Beryl, our mother's best friend who practically raised us alongside her, was one of my favorite people in the world. Not simply because she was cool as hell, but because she was outspoken enough to put people in their place and made no apologies for it.

"You're only sixteen." She arched a superior eyebrow. "Like a newborn babe in diapers when it comes to your magic."

See what I mean? I smiled. "I've read Jules's fortune with the new tarot cards Mom gave me. Said she would be head of New Orleans one day. Mom said that was definitely true, so I'd say not too bad."

She rolled her eyes and tilted her head, her long dreads sliding over one shoulder. "Or you have common sense and a lick of intelligence in that head of yours." She reached over the divining bowl and tapped me on the forehead. "Anyone could tell you that Jules will lead the coven one day." She put both palms on the outside of the wooden bowl filled with water from the first rain this spring. "Now, hush up and focus on your future. Never smart for a Seer to divine for herself anyway."

Placing my palms on my bare kneecaps, I settled into a relaxed pose and closed my eyes.

"Why not?"

"Too close to it. Some Seers, no matter how tight their psychic line is with others, can't see properly when it comes to themselves."

"But I—"

"Shh!" she snapped.

So I shushed. I felt Clara wriggling next to me, but she was better about obeying orders than I was, already quiet so Aunt Beryl could concentrate. The sharp snap of her magic swirled between us, tugging at my chest with a wash of sizzling energy. I loved Aunt Beryl's magic. It felt like a cool, comforting breeze on a summer's day.

"Hmm." Aunt Beryl's quiet contemplation sparked a little anxiety.

2

"What?" My eyes snapped open as I peered forward, unable to make out the blurry images of witch sign floating in the divining bowl.

Aunt Beryl's hands glowed white where she hovered them over the water before she placed them in her lap and stared down, her brow pinched.

"What do you see?" I asked, more eager than I thought I'd be.

"Stark independence."

"Shocking," whispered Clara with a soft snort. I elbowed her.

Our styles were already diverging. Where I wore torn jeans and rock-and-roll T-shirts, she wore willowy dresses that accentuated our elfin features, looking like a fairy stepping into the world of humans.

"Your dream career will take some time, but it will come. I see success. Struggle there, but also success."

"Awesome. Would love to know what that dream career is, by the way."

She gave me a withering look. "That's not how divination works."

"And what about her one true love?" asked Clara excitedly, the only thing she was really interested in.

Aunt Beryl whispered something under her breath and waved a palm over the divining bowl, the water swirling faster at her verbal command. I tried to pretend I wasn't that interested in knowing about my *one true love* as Clara liked to put it, but the truth was that I was a sappy romantic beneath my gruff exterior. I leaned forward anxiously.

"Oh." Aunt Beryl sat back, frowning down at the bowl.

"Well, that doesn't sound good. Can you elaborate please?"

She hit me with a sharp look. "Your true love is broken inside. Like all of his kin." She glanced back down at the bowl.

Of all the men in the world, that's the true love I would get. Still, my heart leaped at the realization Aunt Beryl saw anyone at all.

"But Violet can heal him?" Clara frowned down at the bowl.

"Maybe," said Aunt Beryl. "Wait, yes. You can. If you think with your heart, not your head."

Something more aligned to Clara, not me.

"How will I know him?" I asked, anxious about this new revelation in my future.

"By his eyes."

"That doesn't tell me anything, Aunt Beryl. What color will those eyes be? What is so special about them? Is he short? Tall? Blond or brown hair?" I scoffed in teenage frustration at her cryptic response.

She simply smiled in that knowing sort of way, then used her maternal, hear-my-words-you-silly-child voice. "You'll know by his eyes."

CHAPTER 1

~VIOLET~

"A LITTLE LOWER."

I pulled both sleeves of my loose-fitting tank top down to my elbows so he had better access.

"Lean forward more." Zaire eased closer behind me, his long legs straddling the short stool I sat on.

"I feel like we're about to have sex."

He chuckled. "Are you too cold out here?"

I glanced down at my black bikini top. I'd worn it since it tied around my neck and would keep all straps out of Zaire's way while he worked.

"I'm currently sporting nip-cicles, but no pain, no gain, as they say. Besides, I promised a favor for a favor, so keep going."

"Don't make me laugh unless you want this tattoo all fucked up." The rhythmic vibration of the tattoo needle settled into my skin, a welcome pain. "The favor was just to let me put this tattoo on you, not to put on a show for every male in the bar."

"You did want new business, right? What better way to attract business than to tattoo a witch in a bikini top in thirty-degree weather on New Year's Eve?"

I was a little numb from the cold by now, even with the outdoor space heater radiating warmth sitting next to us. Besides, the needle was giving me a heady buzz of pleasure-pain. He'd already outlined the orchid on my shoulder on my last visit and was now adding the blue shading tonight, which would advertise his artistic skill best. It was that exact skill I'd been practicing as his apprentice with the intent of opening my own shop in the future. Hopefully, the near future.

I'd met Zaire at last year's Witch Coven Summit here in Austin, Texas. He didn't normally attend those things, but since his grandmother was a high-ranking witch in the local coven, she forced him to go to find himself a good witchy wife. Unfortunately, he just found me, a fellow Divine Seer, also wishing she was anywhere else besides the witch marriage market.

A friendship sparked immediately. It was his scowling face and broody manners that had me zero in on him from the second I'd walked in the door. A kindred spirit. But it was the full-sleeve tattoos on his dark skin that had me beelining toward him at the bar. I was an ink whore and could never help myself from checking out other people's tattoos. I should've known then that my love of the art form would eventually lead me to become a tattoo artist myself.

Supernaturals strolled through the rooftop door. The beefy bouncer nodded them through as they flashed their wrists, signaling they'd been approved and stamped downstairs.

I winced as Zaire's needle stung the edge of my shoulder blade, the skin thin there. "Does giving a tattoo give your magic a buzz?"

He shifted closer, his long fingers curling over the outer curve of my shoulder as he worked the needle lower. A few partygoers filtered around our quiet corner of the rooftop bar, Mickey's. It was closed to the public for New Year's Eve so the witch who owned it could open it to supernaturals, invite-only.

Since Zaire was trying to build up his own clientele, he was using me as a walking advertisement at the party. I readily agreed as part of the exchange for tattoo lessons. "What kind of buzz?"

"You know. Like a tapping on your line."

I'd always felt like there was a direct link, like an electrical circuit, that lit up inside supernaturals when their magic woke up for whatever reason. Whether we called it forward or it turned on all by itself. Whenever I tattooed someone while apprenticing for Zaire, my body hummed with magical energy.

"No," he finally answered. "I've never had that happen." He lifted the tattoo needle away from my skin. "Have you?"

"All the time," I answered honestly, now frowning since Zaire didn't experience this same sensation.

"Doesn't surprise me. You've got more magic in your little pinkie than any Seer I've ever met."

"Stop it." I batted my eyelashes, then turned serious. "Even your grandmother?"

"Don't you dare tell her I said so."

"Wow," I whispered all sultry. "Is this some witchy ploy to seduce me?"

He gave me that rock-star smile before settling back to work. "Tempting, but no."

"Do tell." I loved flirting with Zaire. I'll admit I'd thought more than once about crossing that friends-only line, but he was smarter than me and never let it happen. "Not on your life." See? Party pooper.

"I want to keep you as a friend," he added. "I've seen the broken hearts you leave in your wake."

"You say the sweetest things."

"That last kid. What was his name?"

"Ben?"

"No."

"Darius?"

"No."

"Hopper?"

"No." He lifted the needle from my skin again. "How many guys have you dated this year?"

"Define *dating*."

"Exactly. So, no. As tempting as it is, we will not be leaving the friend zone, Ms. Savoie."

"You're smarter than me, so I'll agree with you."

I glanced around at the young people of Austin, drinking and carrying on. An indie band—two vampires and a grim reaper—had started up about an hour ago, their cool vibe setting the scene for a good time.

"Hmph," Zaire grunted.

"What was that noise for?"

"Was just thinking about something my grandmother said when I first told her I was going to use my art degree to become a tattoo artist."

"She didn't like that idea?"

"The opposite, kind of. Said a lot of witches and warlocks were called to it."

8

"Why's that?"

"Because of our ancient ties to enchanted tattoos."

A zap of electricity surged through my veins. I sat up straighter. "How do you mean?"

"Something about the ancient druids and shamans . . . In the early days, some of the witches and warlocks used their magic to permanently spell supernaturals."

"Wow," I breathed airily, wondering at the sudden hum of magic just beneath my skin at Zaire's mention of enchanted tattoos. I could actually feel my psychic line tapping me on the shoulder. It was a light premonition, a sign for me to look and listen. I was so attuned to my magic as a Seer that I knew what each surge of power meant. My ability made itself known on a giant sliding scale. Everything from full-on visions of the future to tiny tap, tap, taps on the psychic line telling me to pay attention. Like right now.

"So when are you going to do it?" Zaire wiped the excess ink from my tattoo before settling in again.

"What's that?" I asked, having drifted far away for a minute.

"Open your own shop."

"Oh, I'm not ready yet. I started saving, picking up extra shifts at the Cauldron and stuff.

"And I've been apprenticing with a local artist, though he's not as good as you, of course."

"Of course," he agreed smugly.

"But I need to find the right place and the right people. Make sure everything is just right."

A skinny warlock and two witches strolled up to watch. Zaire was chitchatting with them when the energy on the rooftop bar suddenly shifted. For most supernaturals, magic pinged along our radar with various degrees of energy. Depending on whether it was a witch of significant power or a vampire with very little, the pulse of magic varied. For me, it was different. I couldn't just feel magic; I could taste it. And right now, danger was settling evenly on my tongue.

The ones giving me the vibes were the four men walking onto the rooftop. Werewolves, actually. Hot as fuck werewolves to be super specific.

The two in front, with easy smiles and younger than the two behind them, strode straight for the bar. The other pair eased in with more awareness, more experience. Werewolves weren't always welcome, you see. Their volatile reputation made them pariahs among most supernaturals. But the bouncer at the door had just fist-bumped the tallest of the four and let them on through.

The tallest one was a smoking hot, five-alarm fire. His black hair and bronzed skin were a turn-on, but it was more about the way he moved and assessed the place with predatory stealth that sent a delightful shiver along my skin. All the same, there was a sensitivity and gentleness in the lines of his face. I could taste his dominance from here, and yet he was also giving off cinnamon-roll vibes. What a paradox this werewolf was.

Though quite chilly up here, the long sleeves of his button-down were rolled up, revealing intricate black tattoos extending down to his wrists on both arms. That alone piqued my interest.

"Don't even think about it," Zaire whispered close behind me.

"Why not? Out-of-town hookups are the best. No strings attached."

"Not that one."

"You know him?"

"A friend of mine does his ink. That's Nico Cruz, a member of the Blood Moon pack."

"Oooo. He's in a werewolf gang. Delicious."

"Your sister Jules would kick your ass if she were here."

He'd lifted the needle from my skin to wipe my shoulder again. I made a show of looking around the bar. "Hmm, don't see Jules anywhere, do you?"

"Sit back, smartass."

"Seems harmless enough to me." I kept my voice low. The gaggle of witches were still watching, sipping their beers and chatting while leaning against his display table where Zaire had set out photographs of his work.

Zaire huffed a laugh. "There was a rumor he lost it one night," he whispered low. "Clawed the hell out of a sixteen-year-old. One of his own pack."

"Ouch." The tall one, Nico, stood off to the side of the bar, waiting on the others, watching the party scene with a kind of wary calm. "Did the boy recover?"

"Don't know. Never got the details. Best to stay away, Vi."

"That may be kind of hard, Z."

"Why's that?"

"He's coming this way."

Zaire heaved out a sigh, continuing to work on the tattoo as he mumbled, "Leave it to you to draw the most dangerous super in the room."

"I'm gifted like that."

Nico and his friend strode over at a leisurely gait. A casual, indifferent amble. All the same, the flash of electric green in his eyes made me fully aware his wolf was present, front and center.

Those watchful, hypnotic eyes checked me out while I noted the cut of his sharp jaw angling toward a beautiful mouth.

He carried a bottled import in one hand, his other tucked into his pocket. I loved it when werewolves tried to look tame. I might've laughed if Zaire hadn't just warned me about this one.

"Zaire. Doing some moonlighting?"

Oh my. His voice was the perfect combination of raspy and warm.

"Nico." I couldn't see him, but he must've done that head-chin-lift thing guys do in greeting.

"Damn," said the other guy, a handsome, brown-eyed blond, coming around close to my left shoulder. "Nice ink."

Werewolves were always pushing into people's space. This one was no exception. If you ever meet a close-talker, they're probably a werewolf. They just can't help but push boundaries. Maybe that's why I liked them despite the fact my sister Jules had told us our whole lives to stay away from them. Also, rebellion was stamped into my DNA.

Nico edged closer in front of me, watching Zaire work. Now I could see that his eyes were a deep green, the tiniest starburst of gold ringing his pupil, which flared the slightest bit when he settled his heated gaze on me.

"The blue orchid. That's interesting."

"How so?" I quirked a brow. "Do you even know what it means?"

His sensual mouth quirked up on one side. Coupled with the hot look he was aiming at me, I would have known this one was trouble without Zaire's warning.

"I do," was all he said, still giving me that devastating, crooked smile.

"What? I don't look like the spiritual, deep-thinking kind of girl?" Because that's basically what the blue orchid meant—the deep thinker. Though I was aware that I was an overthinker, I really chose it because it was just so damn pretty, and blue was my favorite color.

The big, bad werewolf moved even closer, tilting his head down. He whispered almost intimately, "The blue orchid is also the rarest of them all." His gaze narrowed, smile widening.

"I'll bet you're a one-of-a-kind witch, aren't you?"

While holding his intense gaze, I didn't miss the expanding of the gold starburst in his eyes—a sure sign his wolf was sniffing around at the surface. I was about to make some snappy comeback if I could get my mouth to work when Zaire interrupted our flirty little exchange.

"All done." Zaire turned off his cordless tattoo machine. "Wanna look?"

Blinking away the intimate connection, I glanced over my shoulder. Zaire handed me a handheld mirror while holding his own so that I got a reflection of the reflection.

I was well aware that my tank top hung half off. The girls were fully covered in the bikini top, but I was showing quite a bit of skin for a rooftop party in winter rather than sunning on the beach. Still, I was getting a kick out of Nico's mixed expression of shock and arousal.

I took a good look, completely spellbound for a moment, forgetting where I was. "Damn, Zaire. Your skill is so amazing. Sure you don't want to move to New Orleans?" I caught his bright smile in the mirror and gave him a wink.

"Glad you like it." He went to work with the final ministrations of wiping the excess ink, cleaning with antiseptic, then spreading the transparent, waterproof tape to cover it all. He didn't bother to answer me for the hundredth time that he wasn't moving. But a girl had to try.

"Same price as last time?" I asked, scooping my tank top back up onto my shoulders. "Two blow jobs and a steak dinner?"

Blondie coughed out a laugh where he was leaning against the table. The witches giggled. I swear I heard a deep-throated growl from the big werewolf still standing in my private bubble.

Zaire arched a brow at me and shook his head.

"You know what the payment is."

"*One* BJ and dinner?"

"Jesus, Violet. Stop it." He looked at the two werewolves, shaking his head and chuckling.

"She's joking. That's just her way."

"Oh, look." I nodded toward the door. "You have impeccable timing, Zaire. Josie's here."

The petite witch with a pixie cut and hair dyed every color of the rainbow practically skipped toward our little corner. I was experimental with my hair color—currently a peacock blue—but Josie took it to the next level. She was his second walking advertisement for the night.

"Can I buy you a drink?" Nico hadn't moved from my personal space the whole time I'd lifted my gray jacket from my lap and slipped it on.

"Sure thing." I tucked my hands in my pockets and glanced over my shoulder, winking at Zaire's scowling face. Since he would be busy for a while, I saw no problem in hanging with the werewolf till he was done.

This guy wasn't dangerous. I mean, he certainly wasn't the loose cannon Zaire had heard from his little witch sewing circle. My magic was strongly attuned to warning me of danger.

Okay, maybe he was putting off the bad-boy vibes when he walked in, but up close I knew there was no sign of *danger* danger. And my, how I enjoyed this close-up view of his pretty face.

We found two stools at one of the bars, of which there were three spread out over the rooftop. Trellises with fairy lights set the ambiance and, in this lighting, his face looked like it was cut out of a magazine.

"What is it?" he asked, a small smile teasing his lips, which only drew my attention back to them.

"You've got an awfully pretty mouth."

He laughed, then surprised me with his next question. "Zaire didn't scare you off?"

"How do you mean?" Though I knew exactly what he meant. I was just caught off guard at him going straight for the sensitive topics.

"Surely, he told you stories about me."

"Singular. One story."

"Mm." He nodded, wide mouth quirking on one side.

"Is there any truth to the story?"

"Don't know what he told you."

"That you lost control. Went wild wolf on a sixteen-year-old and hurt him."

He swallowed visibly, his Adam's apple bobbing once, but he didn't wince or look away.

No. He held my gaze, as if transfixed.

"There's truth to it. It was an accident."

"Honest. Wow. That's interesting."

"You thought I'd lie?"

"No. But I thought you might evade, since I'm pretty sure you're trying to impress me."

"You're wrong. I'm not trying to impress you. I want you to see me."

"Why?" I reached out with my magical senses. "We just met."

"And when we did, the earth opened up beneath my feet."

That's when I tasted a shift of energy, my psychic line tapping into his emotions. I wasn't as adept at reading emotion as Clara— my twin who was an Aura and could read feelings like words on a page—but I still could catch a whiff on the air. Like a passing breeze. And a magical wind had just wafted waves and waves of sincerity through me. It was heady. And aggressive. I'd even say seductive.

This werewolf was unique.

"So he didn't scare you off then," he stated as a challenge more than a question.

"I'm still here, aren't I?" That earned me a great big smile. "My, what big teeth you have."

He stared at me a few seconds before asking, "So, what do you do?"

"No, no, no." I shook my head, my blue hair brushing over my shoulders. "Let's not do that. That's boring."

"Okay." He grinned wider. "Tell me what we should talk about."

I exhaled a deep breath and rolled my eyes. "*Entertain* me, wolfie."

That all-observant gaze flared for one second before his brows shot up and he recited in a rather formal voice, "There once was a werewolf from Kent, whose cock was so long it bent. So he found him a witch, to scratch his big itch, and with a great howl, he spent." I tossed my head back and burst out in throaty laughter.

"Your turn," he said after a soft chuckle.

"We're having a limerick war?"

"You started it." He held up two fingers to the bartender and pointed to the whiskey. "If you can't think of one in ten seconds then I win." *Shit!* He was good. Naughty wolfie.

Clearing my throat, I sat up straight and, with a haughty air, did my best. "There once was a grim from Liverpool, who was caught playing with his tool." I paused. Nico arched a superior brow, which made me laugh before saying, "But then he met Paul, who played with his balls . . . aaaand they both went to ball-juggling school?"

"Are you asking me if they went to ball-juggling school?"

"No!" I swatted him on the biceps. Ooo, nice. "It just came out that way."

"Oh, sweet Violet," he said with a playfully condescending air. "I think you just lost."

"What are you talking about? That was a perfectly good limerick."

"Actually, it was near-rhyme only with *Paul* and *balls*, not exact rhyme. So, *not* a perfectly good limerick. You obviously aren't as expert at this as I am."

"Fine, fine. If you can come up with a next-level limerick, better than mine—"

"Shouldn't be hard."

"Shut up. As I said, better than mine, then you win."

"I want a prize when I win."

"*If* you win. Presumptuous much?"

"Confident." He tilted his head to the side, cocky smirk on his lovely face. "And werewolves like tangible prizes for their achievements. We're visceral creatures."

I ignored the rumble of his words on that last part. "I'd hardly call creating a dirty rhyme an achievement."

"You haven't heard it yet," he challenged as the bartender set two whiskeys on ice in front of us.

"And what makes you think I like whiskey?" Pushy bastard, this one. I liked him.

"Am I wrong?"

"No, dammit." I took the glass and knocked back a swallow. "I know you already have something in mind, so what do you want if you win?"

"A kiss."

I huffed a laugh. "I don't even know you." Not that that's ever mattered.

"You know me enough."

We'd literally just met within the last half hour, but somehow he was completely right. I felt like I knew him well enough for a little tongue-tangling.

"Fine. I'll give you a full minute to think one up because this has to be super epic." And I was hoping he'd win so I could give him that prize. "And just so there's no question about it, we'll have a guest judge alongside me, of course."

When I waved at the bartender and she came over, I explained our need for an unbiased judge. "I'll be glad to help," she said, setting both forearms on the bar top.

"Nervous?" I asked, because he suddenly looked that way.

Then he didn't, his superior expression returning tenfold.

I pulled out my phone from my jacket pocket and found the timer. "Your minute starts now."

After I clicked the start button, only five seconds passed before he said, "There once was a wolf from the city, who met a witch who was *stunning* and witty." His voice was low and luscious and gruff. "She charmed him at a glance, making him wish he had a chance, to kiss her sweet lips and her kitty."

Most girls might slap a guy for being so bold, for saying exactly what they were thinking. Specifically that he wanted to eat her out, even if he did say it with pretty words. All I could do was bite my lip and shake my head, recognizing my equal.

"Well, fuck," I muttered under my breath.

"Yep, he won," said the bartender before sauntering off.

"What do you say, Violet? Do I get my prize?"

Before I could launch myself into his lap, a guy I'd seen with the band earlier approached and tapped Nico on the shoulder. "They're ready for you, man."

His smoldering expression evaporated as he glanced over his shoulder. "Shit, I forgot."

"You forgot?" asked the guy. "Isn't that the reason you came?" Then the guy looked at me, realization dawning on his face. "Oh, right. Well, you still comin'?"

The music died down to just the vampire on vocals speaking into the mic. "I have a special guest here tonight. You guys have surely seen him around town. Please welcome Nico Cruz to the stage for a few songs."

Nico gripped my hand in his as he slid off the stool. He gave my hand a good squeeze, the sensation pinging down to my lady bits. He leaned forward, close to my ear. "Don't go anywhere." He leaned back a few inches, catching my gaze. "Please." Then he grinned wider. "I want my prize."

As he followed the other guy through the crowd toward the stage, I got a good look at his fantastic ass. "I do too," I murmured to myself while sipping my whiskey.

I leaned back against the bar, ordered an old-fashioned for my second round, and enjoyed the show. This werewolf was full of surprises. Nico didn't do any grandstanding or make any cute, quippy remarks into the mic, he just picked up a guitar, slung the strap over his shoulder, and began to play. And sing.

Fucking hell. His voice. Rough and smooth and smoky with a direct line to my pussy.

He played "Feel Like I'm Drowning" by Two Feet, then some Kaleo and some indie song I'd never heard. But when he sang his own masculine rendition of Skylar Grey's "I Know You," his attention riveted on me, I actually started to shake. Me! Shivering on that fucking stool.

Here's the thing about werewolves. Once upon a time, a seriously pissed-off witch cursed a man who became the first werewolf. The curse divided him in half. Gifted him with the most sublime magic of creativity and cursed him to become a beast upon the full moon. So when a werewolf created art, there was magic in it. And when Nico sang to me, he *sang* to me.

My heart pumped faster, blood rushing to tantalizing places, and his voice vibrated straight to my bones, keeping my ass on that stool and my eyes on the sexy-as-fuck man serenading me from the stage, breath frosting the air.

When he poured the last lines of the song out in a desperate plea, directed at me, the vampire singer stepped up beside him. Nico pulled back from the mic and lifted the guitar away as the guy said, "Let's give Nico a big round of applause!" And so they did. "Almost to countdown time, everybody."

While the vampire roused the crowd, Nico stepped off the stage and headed toward me with fire blazing in his eyes.

"Oh boy."

I knew that look. And I was 100 percent ready for it. I popped off the stool right as he made it to me. He grabbed my hand and laced our fingers, then tugged me away from the crowd. I didn't ask where we were going. I didn't give a damn. As long as he put his mouth on me.

He hauled me behind the bar where there was a thin partition between the back-door entrance and the area for customers. Cases of beer were stacked in rows, leaving a tiny corner vacant in the shadows. He backed me into the corner and pushed his fingers into my hair, tightening his fist before his mouth crashed onto mine.

He parted my lips with deft precision and a bit of desperation. When his tongue touched mine, I couldn't help but rock my hips up, bending one leg to wrap at his hip.

His deep groan was heavenly rumbling against my chest. "Fuck, you're so fine, Violet," he whispered against my mouth before he bit my lip with a little sting and thrust his hard cock between my legs. The friction was divine.

"Keep talking, wolfie"—I leaned up and bit his neck—"or put that mouth to better use."

He froze. His otherworldly gaze was locked on mine, a question hanging in the air. Holding his focus, I started unsnapping and unzipping my jeans to answer it, not giving a damn that anyone could walk up on us.

Needing no more encouragement than that, he was on his knees, curling his long fingers into the sides of my jeans and panties and dragging them down my legs. He pulled off the sneaker on my left foot then freed my leg of clothes and draped it over his shoulder.

I might've whimpered when I combed my fingers into the black waves of his hair, fisting my hand to give him a little of the pleasure-pain he'd given me.

His wolf-green eyes flickered up at me as he eased forward, sliding the tip of his middle finger along my slit.

He nuzzled my inner thigh with his nose. "I want to drown in your scent," he said, voice having dropped several octaves.

"Be my guest."

So he did. He gave me one long slide of his hot tongue while holding my gaze. My fingers clenched tighter in his hair on instinct, dragging a growl from deep in his throat. I whimpered as he went to work. Lapping at me with fierce licks and sucks, driving me like a freight train on fire toward climax.

"I don't know where you learned to use your tongue like that," I panted, riding his mouth with feverish agony.

I couldn't even finish my sentence, forgetting what I was about to say. I had to get there, and I needed him and only him to do it. This semi-stranger werewolf with a poet in his voice and a devil in his tongue.

The distant laughter and raucous cheers of the crowd skirted the periphery of my focus. The in-unison countdown began—*ten, nine, eight, seven!*

Then Nico slid two fingers inside me and pumped hard and fast, playing my clit like he played that guitar.

Six, five, four!

"Damn, you're so good," I mumbled.

Three, two!

His answering growl vibrated against my clit before he curled his fingers slightly as he stroked out, hitting my G-spot and sending me over the edge.

One!

Fireworks went off in the distance with a loud, modern chorus of *Auld Lang Syne* as I came on Nico's mouth, my head back against the partition wall, staring up at the night sky. He continued to lick with leisurely strokes and a satisfied hum, lapping all of me up. The cold night air, his hot mouth, the skyrocketing endorphins and ecstasy-like orgasm wouldn't be something I'd soon forget.

Slowly, I came back to myself, vaguely aware of Nico slipping my leg back into my panties and jeans, zipping and snapping them.

He stood, wrapped his fingers around my nape, and pressed a soft, slow kiss to my mouth, letting me taste our mingling scents together before he pulled apart, green eyes fiery and smoldering.

"Happy New Year, Violet."

I didn't respond other than to give him one last, lingering kiss. Because I knew what would happen next. I'd hurry a goodbye, then duck out the door and haul ass back to New Orleans as fast as possible. Because whatever this werewolf was, it was my brand of addiction. Zaire wasn't wrong when he said my sister Jules would kick my ass.

Lucky for me, I'd never see this werewolf again.

CHAPTER 2

10 months later...

~NICO~

For the first time since New Year's Eve, my wolf had chilled the fuck out. My body was at ease. Not because I'd done gigs like this a hundred times before, but because *she* was in the room. Muscles relaxed, breathing steady, I watched her greet her first table as I slipped the strap of the guitar over my head.

She frowned, sensing a new supernatural in the pub. I stared, enjoying my fill of her, as I strummed a few chords. It had been too long since I'd soaked her in, enjoyed her stark beauty. Her gaze swept to me, widened in surprise, then narrowed. That only made me smile as I leaned close to the mic.

"Good evening, everyone. I'm new here to New Orleans, so I hope you'll be gentle with me tonight."

"Come over here! I'll be gentle!" called one of the young women at a high-top table with her friends closer to the stage.

I gave her a smile, then glanced down at my guitar, adjusting a string before strumming again.

"Thank you." I nodded at the table of ladies, playing to my small audience. "I heard that New Orleans had fantastic hospitality. Glad to see that was true." A few whistles and a sputtering round of applause from the Cauldron's customers. "Well then, my first song goes out to a girl who took my breath away the first night I met her." More whistles. "Then she bailed on me."

"I wouldn't do that to you, baby," said the brazen woman at the high-top.

With a low chuckle, I played the first chords of "Ain't No Sunshine," glancing over at Violet now at the bar where she stood there slack-jawed and staring. I couldn't help but grin wider, then I started singing. She carried on with her business, throwing me not-so-pleasant glares as she served her customers, a pretty blush high on her cheeks.

After several songs where Violet tried to pretend I wasn't in the room, walking with undisguised hostility, I was positive she'd thought she'd never see me again. I had no problem with hard-to-get. I was a patient man. And my wolf, he'd have no other, so she was in for a rude awakening.

I wasn't going anywhere, and I wasn't going to give up until I got what I wanted. Her.

After ending my current song, I slipped the strap of my guitar off my shoulder. "Taking a five-minute break, guys. Be right back."

I set my guitar on its stand, then meandered through the tables. The place was pretty packed. Stopping at the end of the bar, I nodded to the beefy bartender JJ at the other end. He waved as he took the order of the woman in front of him. I'd met him when Violet's older sister Jules gave me a brief tour right before the dinner rush. I'd been elated to discover that Violet would be waiting tables on my first night.

I'd been pleasantly surprised that her sister, the Enforcer and head of all supernaturals in New Orleans, had given me the time of day, much less given me a weekly spot at her family's restaurant and pub. I wasn't surprised she'd asked if I knew anyone in town.

When I'd said that my cousin, Mateo Cruz, lived here, she'd taken all of five seconds to hire me. That was this morning, and I hadn't had time to even text Mateo yet. I was too busy shopping for a place to live and dealing with a real estate agent.

A fantastic house with a business attached had caught my eye. It was at the end of a dead-end street a few blocks from here. I didn't have need of commercial space, but the fact that it was so private appealed to me, especially in a busy city. No one would hear and complain if they heard animalistic growls and howls if I lost control of my wolf.

The image of Ty's anguished—and scarred—face flashed to mind again, piercing me with a sharp sting of bitter and painful regret. Yes, a large lot with secluded privacy was just what I needed.

I closed on the property tomorrow, then I'd be a permanent resident of the city where Violet lived, whether she liked it or not. Right now, it looked a lot like *not*.

"What'll you have?" asked JJ.

"Killian's Red." I pulled out my wallet.

"Nah. On the house." He pulled a longneck from the cooler and popped it open for me.

"Thanks, man."

"You want a mug?"

I shook my head. "This is good."

"You know what isn't good?" asked Violet, suddenly there beside me, her scent snatching my senses captive with unnatural speed. "This werewolf who's stalking me."

Smiling, I tipped the beer bottle back and took a swallow, noticing her noticing me.

"Stalking?" I swept the room as if looking for the culprit. "That does sound like a problem." JJ gave us both a quizzical look, then sauntered off down the bar to another customer.

"Don't play with me, Nico. Why are you here?"

"Well, you see, my mom and dad met and fell in love. Then they got married and fucked each other and—"

Unamused, she interrupted, "You think you're funny, don't you?"

"Just stating facts."

"The fact I want to know is why you're here"—she pointed at her feet—"in my city, in the Cauldron."

"You own this city? Had no idea."

"Stop playing." She tilted her head, hair still a vibrant blue as it slid over her bare shoulder, her tank top exposing the blue orchid, reminding me yet again of the electric night we met.

"Thought it was pretty obvious." I glanced at the stage. "I moved here. Got a job."

Those sapphire eyes assessed my expression, looking for lies. There wasn't one there. That was all true.

"Why New Orleans?"

"Why not?" Leaning forward into her space, I inhaled a divine whiff of her scent as I growled, "I have a better question. Why'd you bail on me five minutes after I made you come on the rooftop in Austin?"

All her bravado vanished behind wide eyes while I took a casual sip of my beer. I practically purred at the sight of her surprised and sputtering for an answer.

She crossed her arms. Defensive move. "I had somewhere to be."

Biting my bottom lip, I let her squirm uncomfortably beneath my gaze before I said, "That was rude."

She winced. "I know."

"Pretty immature too."

"Look, I know. You're right. I'm sorry."

"Are you? Or sorry that I showed up to remind you of it?" She actually did look fairly remorseful.

"Forget about it," I said. "Listen, I was looking for different scenery. Austin was getting too crowded." And hostile. "So I decided to move. My cousin lives here in town, and I thought New Orleans seemed as good a place as any."

She tensed a little, a frown puckering between her brows. "Your cousin? What's his name?"

"Mateo Cruz. Know him?"

Since her sisters were the head witch coven in New Orleans, they'd likely know most of the supernaturals in the city, personally or not.

"Yeah." She nodded her head, seeming disappointed. "My sister Evie and him are friends." She gestured toward the young woman swishing out of the kitchen, her ponytail swinging.

Violet blew out a heavy breath, lifting a strand of blue hair. I wondered what her natural color was. "I really am sorry for bailing on you that night." She closed her eyes in misery for a second.

"That was seriously shitty of me." She then lifted her gaze to me with a questioning look.

"I'm not going to argue," I said playfully but meaning it.

And I sure as hell wasn't going to tell her how it had left me in agony for months. Not because of the blue balls she'd given me, but because I knew the second I kissed her what she was to me. One taste had sealed her into my flesh and bones.

She glanced over at her tables before she straightened and flashed me a small smile. "I've gotta get back to work."

"How about a drink later? After I finish?"

She eyed me warily, and I wasn't sure where that was coming from. She didn't seem to have had a thing against werewolves on New Year's Eve. But then I hadn't known her intentions were to have a little fun, then vanish into thin air. Maybe werewolves were only good enough to toy with. Not date.

"Not tonight," she said with no further explanation. "I'm sure I'll see you around." Then she turned on her heel and returned to her tables.

I was suddenly relieved I'd already found a place and was putting down some long-term roots because, apparently, this conquest was going to take some time.

~VIOLET~

I TRIED TO PRETEND THAT NICO'S PRESENCE IN THE CAULDRON DIDN'T rattle the living shit out of me. But it so did. That werewolf was fine as fuck, and it would take a freaking miracle for me to keep my ass out of his bed. Especially after I knew how talented the man was with his tongue.

My psychic magic had flat-out given me a vision of Evie and Mateo living blissfully together one day, whether they knew it or not, which also told me I needed to keep my thirsty thoughts off Nico Cruz.

I'd done a reading on Evie privately and was well aware that she and Mateo would be together forever. But it was better she didn't know right away. Not that she'd rebel and toss the guy before their romance ever took place, but sometimes interference from a Seer could muck things up. So I typically only interfered when necessary.

What that did mean was that Nico was a permanent fixture in our lives. And my usual MO of love-'em-and-leave-'em wasn't going to go over well with Nico. Unless . . . ?

I stopped at a table where my customers had just left. After pocketing the tip, I slowly bused the table, stacking empty glasses and plates onto my tray while watching Nico croon an old Nirvana song. His smooth but smoky voice did things to my insides. Melty, wonderful things. He'd been singing with his eyes closed. When they opened, his burning gaze landed directly on me.

Ever heard that phrase *when time stood still?* I'd never felt it myself, until that moment. His eyes locked on me, paralyzing me on the spot. A feverish frenzy of adrenaline flushed through my blood. Magic tingled along my skin. A bare caress of it lifted the hairs on my arms.

Was he the one?

Swallowing hard against the exhilarating possibility that the man of my dreams could very well be the devastatingly handsome werewolf singing a soft ballad with a sexy voice and staring at me with those hypnotic eyes, I got my ass to the kitchen. Then I kept myself busy all night.

Mateo and Evie had shown up at some point. I sneakily watched Mateo talking to Nico on another break later in the night. Then I smiled to myself when Evie danced with Mateo before the two of them disappeared down the hallway to the storage room.

All that did was draw my attention back to Nico. I needed to know. Before my shift was quite over, I took off a little early, knowing my sisters and I would be doing our monthly witches' round later. I had something I wanted to do first.

I slipped through the back door, then headed down the short alley between the Cauldron and our metaphysical shop, Mystic Maybelle's. Clara had closed it up hours ago, so the place was full dark. I made the short walk down the side street to our two-story bungalow, up the driveway, and to the stairs leading to the carriage house loft where Clara and I lived.

We still hung out in the main house, but we had two bedrooms and a small kitchenette and living room of our own in the carriage house. Clara wasn't home and must've been in the main house. Good. Because I didn't want to explain to her why I was doing a late-night reading.

"Okay, okay." I shook out my arms, the adrenaline shooting like wildfire through my veins.

"Calm down."

Easier said than done. I rummaged in my desk drawer for my oldest deck of tarot cards, the one Mom had given me when I was sixteen, the same year Aunt Beryl gave me the premonition about my one true love.

I'd pretended that her words hadn't sunk in. That her psychic vision hadn't jarred something loose inside me and had realigned the way I moved about in my adult life. It was no secret that I enjoyed the hell out of men. But if I didn't get the sense that they could be *the one*, I'd moved on pretty damn quickly. To be honest, I hadn't thought about it in a long-ass time. Not until tonight when Nico looked at me in a way that turned my legs to pudding.

After finding my well-worn deck in shades of cream and gold, I sat cross-legged in the middle of my bed and blew out a shaky breath.

"Ten of Cups, Ten of Cups," I chanted, closing my eyes and hoping like hell.

Ten of Cups was the epic happily-ever-after card. It meant divine love, blissful relationships, harmony, alignment. That was the card I longed for when I'd done this reading in the past.

I'd only done a reading about this twice before now. For Paul, my first college romance that went nowhere. However, when we first met, I'd been dazzled by his striking blue eyes, which immediately made me think of Aunt Beryl's vision.

I'd also done a reading for Hayden, this warlock who sat in my section at the Cauldron three days a week till he finally asked me out. There hadn't been anything special about his eyes or the way he looked at me or the way I felt when he looked at me, but I really liked him for a while there and thought, *what the hell*. Of course, the reading didn't give me the Ten of Cups because here I sat. Single as ever.

Inhaling a deep breath, then exhaling slowly, I spread the cards out on my mattress facedown, conjuring my magic as I mixed them up. When I felt that certain rightness, my magic in sync with my mind and body, I sat straight and whispered into the room what I asked for. A three-card spread would be more thorough.

"First card is for me."

I hovered my palm over the cards, then flipped the one that spoke the most to me.

Death stared back, smiling from a death's head. The most prevalent meaning of the Death card was *endings*.

"Fuck." I pushed down the anxiety, remembering that maybe it was the ending of my single life. "That could be it," I muttered, hoping for the best. "Okay, the second card is for Nico." My hand snatched a card quickly, almost as if it was someone else's.

"Are you kidding me?"

The Three of Swords. I stared at the card with the bleeding heart stabbed through with three sharp swords, making my chest ache. It meant heartbreak.

Great. So Nico is going to bring me heartbreak and emotional pain?

"Last one. Third card is for our relationship."

I flipped over the last card and laughed bitterly at the Tower card, a crumbling one with flames shooting out of the windows and the spire. It meant upheaval and chaos.

"Definitely not the Ten of Cups."

My chest pinched with disappointment. Especially when I remembered the way the man could make me feel with one glance of those deep green eyes.

If Aunt Beryl was right—and Aunt Beryl was always right—he wasn't the one. "Ah, hell," I mumbled, flipping over the cards and mixing them up again.

One more time.

I repeated what I wanted before I flipped over three cards in quick succession. Again, in that order, came Death, Three of Swords, the Tower.

Leaving the cards on the bed, I cursed my way through a hot shower, then came back to them and tried *again*. The same three cards stared back at me. The skeleton of Death seemed to grin wider.

Finally, I gathered the cards and put them away, accepting that I'd been wrong. Wasn't the first or the last time. But it was more than apparent that endings, heartbreak, and chaos were not the cards that would lead to my happily-ever-after.

I stretched out on my bed and sighed at the ceiling, lamenting that Nico wasn't the one. And knowing he was Mateo's cousin and now employed at the Cauldron, that put him firmly in the friend zone.

No matter how badly my libido told my brain to fuck off, I wouldn't put myself through all that turmoil. Nor would I put him through it. And if those green eyes made me weak again, I'd just think of burning, crumbling towers, three sharp swords stabbing my heart, and that wicked fiend Death grinning back at me.

"Sorry, Nico." And *sorry, self.* "Friends it is."

CHAPTER 3

Present day...

~NICO~

Yes, I was a masochist. I enjoyed pain. Why else would I lay here shirtless beneath Violet Savoie with her hands on me and unable to move a muscle? She leaned closer, her nearness, her scent, threatening to choke me. I wanted to touch her. What's new? I always wanted to touch her. But I couldn't, so I kept my arms and hands limp at my sides—claws threatening to come out—while she tattooed a crescent moon surrounded by mystical stars at the top of my right pec.

Nope, I just lay there dormant as fuck like every brush of her hand and fingers wasn't utter agony. The pain of the needle while she detailed the shading was a mild but welcome distraction.

I congratulated myself on becoming a fantastic actor since I'd moved to New Orleans.

Seriously, I could kick the shit out of some Broadway if I wanted to.

Partnering with Violet was my idea, so no one was to blame but myself. Regardless of the fact that she pretended New Year's Eve two years ago had never even happened, this was still a great idea. Partnering and investing in Empress Ink allowed me to finally put down roots somewhere.

Sure, I could still move on and monitor the business remotely, but I liked it here in New Orleans. My cousin Mateo, who was more like a brother, was close by. Empress Ink already had a wait list for clientele, and we hadn't even officially opened yet. The Savoie family had welcomed me like I was one of their own.

Then there was Violet. Pretty, foul-mouthed Violet. My unhealthy obsession was tempered only by the brick wall she'd erected when I'd moved to New Orleans. Despite the fact that I could tell our attraction was mutual, she'd solidified our status as friends pretty damn fast. But my patience was starting to run out. Becoming her business partner was my newest tactic to get closer to her.

So here I sat, letting her put her hands on me in a very non-sexual way that had my dick harder than a hammer. Still, I was happier here in this chair in our shop than I could ever remember. Just having her near me was a sweet torture I couldn't live without.

"What happened there?" she asked, sapphire-blue eyes meeting mine as she touched a gloved finger on the side of my rib cage.

Glancing down where her finger had brushed a two-inch scar, I cleared my throat and tried to halt my wayward thoughts. "Happened in Austin." I didn't want to admit my flaws, but I wanted there to be honesty between us. To be closer to her. "I got in a fight with this asshole at a bar. Another werewolf. His claws snapped out when he shifted unexpectedly."

She sat back and scowled at the scar. "He turned wolf and hurt you?"

A tension eased behind my sternum, noting the sincere compassion in her voice. For me. "Well, I did the same. And though I'm not proud of it, I left him with a limp. A bit worse than a little scar."

Her frown softened, then she smiled. "Good. I'm glad you got payback."

"Bloodthirsty," I teased. "I like it."

She settled back to shading the crescent moon. "If he lashed out first, then he deserved what he got."

While we stayed in silence, I basked in her concern for me, though I could tell she was mulling this over. Violet liked to analyze things to death, so I knew there'd be a question for me soon enough. I was right.

"So," she finally said, "your wolf can shift without you really wanting him to?"

I laughed. "Hell yeah. He's a fucking beast, Violet. If a werewolf gets angry too quickly, he can shift on a dime. Even when he doesn't want to."

She nodded, taking this in. When she stopped to wipe some excess ink away with a cloth, she glanced up at me before returning to her work. "I remember once around the full moon last year you got upset about those guys outside the Cauldron, remember? You half-shifted right there on the street."

She wasn't accusing me of anything, but I felt the shame of it nonetheless. I remembered that night. I'd done a gig at the Cauldron and offered to walk Violet home since she'd closed. Usually, JJ did that, but I told him to go on and I'd do it. Obviously, I had an ulterior motive just to spend a little private time with her.

Some dicks, vampires who'd come from the direction of Ruben's vamp den, the Green Light, were drunk and passed us by. As they did, one muttered he'd like to *fuck that witch* as he eyed Violet. Pure rage surged through my blood, and I'd snatched the guy by the collar and threw him against the wall before he could blink, my claws out and skin prickling with the fur just beneath, my beast ready to break through and tear him to shreds.

"I remember," I finally said as she turned off the cordless tattoo machine that was no bigger than an electric razor. "Wish I didn't."

"No worries." She set her machine aside and rolled back to me, then wiped the last of the excess ink. "They were being total dicks. But I guess I shouldn't provoke your wolf?" she teased.

The thought of her trying to draw my wolf out both terrified and aroused me beyond reason. "Hell, Violet. I wish you could come up with a spell to calm him down."

I was smiling at her when she jerked, her fingers clenching around my forearm.

"Vi, you okay?"

She didn't respond, her eyes falling half-closed, her body perfectly still as she seemed to stare at nothing. Then the hairs on the back of my neck stood up, recognizing the presence of magic. Violet always seemed to hum with energy, but this was stronger, more potent.

I waved a hand in front of her, realizing immediately what was going on. She was having a vision. Something about this vulnerable state, that she was here but unaware of her surroundings, raised my hackles. Not liking her in any unsafe situation, an involuntary growl rumbled in my chest.

She'd told me she had visions sometimes and they came unbidden, but I'd never witnessed it. I didn't like it. I wanted to haul her into my lap and guard the door at the same time. If anyone walked in, I was sure I'd rip their head off. Metaphorically speaking. Now, if someone tried to hurt her, then I'd *literally* rip their head off.

But I did neither. I waited, watching her as patiently as possible, taking advantage only once to run the pad of my finger along her cheek as I tucked a loose tendril of hair behind her ear. I took a moment to admire her sleek hair she was letting grow longer than usual. This was the first time I'd ever seen her natural color. Her hair was pale blonde down to just below her ears, then dyed pale purple to the tips. Yeah, I knew her real color would be the same as her twin sister, Clara, but for some reason it looked different on her. The blonde softened her hard edges. She came out of it with a sudden, sharp inhale, blinking quickly. "Are you all right?"

She had a lost look on her face. "Yeah, sorry." Her voice was gruff, as if she'd just woken up from sleep. "Sorry about that."

"No need to apologize. Your visions are part of who you are."

Then she blinked up at me with a look of complete elation. "Nico," she whispered like she had a secret, "my vision was about you."

"Me?" My heart galloped three times faster.

"Werewolves. What you said about coming up with a spell." She glanced over her shoulder, then rolled over to her table and poured some disinfectant onto a gauzy pad. As she wiped my new tattoo clean, she kept her voice low as she said, "I've been experimenting."

"With what exactly?"

"My magic and charmed tattoos. It's experimental right now." She frowned as she dressed my tattoo with the clear waterproof tape to protect the new ink for a week. "I mean, I can't promise anything, but I've had a little success so far."

The excitement in her voice mesmerized me. "And you think you can do what? Tattoo a spell for werewolves?"

"Maybe." She gazed at me hopefully. "I'd never really thought how bad it was for werewolves and the issue of control. But when you said that, I immediately fell into a vision."

"What did you see?"

"It sounds crazy." She laughed. "But it was floating witch sign surrounding a full moon in the clouds. Sometimes, my visions are of actual events to come. Like premonitions. Sometimes they're messages."

"Magic messages."

"Yeah." She nodded, smiling.

The very idea that she might have the ability to help me control my wolf punched me with a lightning bolt of hope. Ty flashed to mind and what I'd done to him. If Violet was right and she could do this, I wouldn't have to worry about losing my temper and permanently maiming someone—or worse—ever again.

"If you want to experiment on me, you're more than welcome to." I glanced down at my shirtless chest. "I still have quite a bit of available canvas."

She laughed, her gaze sweeping over my chest. Then the mirth shifted to something darker, sweeter. And there it was again. The same lust I'd seen in her eyes before. It was there for a second, then she blinked it away as always. I wasn't sure why she was fighting this so hard, but I'd let her fight it a bit longer before I took matters into my own hands.

The outer door opened and the animated voice of Violet's sister Livvy filled the front lobby. She'd been helping us with the promotion of Empress Ink. The entire shop, which was connected by a courtyard to my own place, was completely open, separated by partitions that didn't quite reach the ceiling. It had once been a hair salon. Sound carried, but the partitions gave customers some privacy while getting their tattoos.

My major contribution to Empress Ink was the use of this part of the building I now owned. How fortunate that when Violet was actively seeking a place in our neighborhood to lease or buy for her new business, I happened to have one. I stepped in without giving it a second thought. I might've had an ulterior motive, but she wasn't aware of that. For now, that's how it had to remain.

I also split the monthly expenses, while Violet handled most of the costs for equipment and furnishings. We felt it all evened out so that we could split the profit fifty/fifty once that started. As of now, we were still in the red, but Empress Ink had only been open for two weeks. Our soft opening. We hadn't even had our grand opening celebration.

Something semi-heavy thumped as it hit the floor in the lobby.

"Let's go see what's up." Violet stood, shucked her latex gloves, and washed her hands in the sink installed along the exposed brick wall.

I picked up my shirt, carrying it loosely as I smoothed a thumb over the transparent tape covering my new tattoo. I was only a few steps from the front lobby, following behind Violet after she sprayed and wiped the chair and equipment down with antibacterial cleaner.

"So how about we have dinner on Saturday night if you're free?" Sean Blackwater, all 150 pounds of his tall, lanky seventeen-year-old self, was draped over the front counter on his forearms, making sexy eyes at Livvy. Or trying to, anyway.

"Give it a rest, Sean," grumped Violet. "She's got a girlfriend."

Livvy turned, wearing black tights, a purple faux leather miniskirt, and a black blouse that had some kind of sheer fabric over the deep V back and neck. She was a curvy woman who knew how to dress to enhance all her assets. The signature red lipstick didn't go amiss either.

She was the kind of woman that turned heads on the streets.

Sean frowned. "Damn. It's like that, is it?"

"Actually," said Livvy to her sister, "Mary and I broke up last week."

"Oh, sorry to hear that." Violet gave her a hug. "I haven't seen you at the house in a few days. I didn't know."

Livvy waved a hand in a blasé manner. "No worries. She was sweet. Just didn't work out."

"So I don't stand a chance?" asked Sean, still trying. Poor guy. "I don't tempt you, even a little?" He waggled his eyebrows and gestured to his wiry adolescent body.

She smiled. "Darling, though I am attracted to men, too, your grim mojo doesn't work on me." Grims were a secretive lot, but one thing everyone knew was that their aura called to a person's darker urges and impulses. "Grims don't appeal to my baser instincts. Not usually, anyway." She mumbled the last under her breath. "Besides, you're not quite a man just yet."

"Will you wait for me?" he asked, completely unruffled.

"Not likely," she said, opening the lid of a large box at her feet. "I'm not very patient."

Livvy pulled out a black T-shirt from a large stack of the same, then held it up to herself and faced us. "Well, what do you think?"

It was the Empress Ink logo she'd designed, a stylized, crowned empress from the tarot deck. She was winking, her hand gesturing toward the name of the shop in cool script lettering at her feet.

"It looks amazing," I got out before Violet squealed and launched herself across the room, snatching the T-shirt from her. "Livvy! I *love* it."

"I hope so, because I ordered a shit ton of these T-shirts. I got you a much better price in the larger bulk. I thought we could use them as giveaways for the grand opening or sell them cheap at cost, which would then turn around and act as promo when people wore them around town."

"Brilliant," said Violet. "We need pictures!"

"My thoughts exactly." Livvy held up the camera around her neck before looking at me. "Nico looks like he needs a shirt." She rummaged in the box and glanced back at me. "Extra large, I'd say." She tossed it to me. "Don't get me wrong, the view is lovely, but I need some shots of you both out front in these."

"I could take my shirt off for you, Livvy," offered Sean.

"Don't bother, darling. You just sit behind the counter and look pretty. And talk less. It'll bring in more customers."

"You think I'm pretty?"

"For fuck's sake, Livvy," said Violet, "stop teasing him."

"But it's so fun." She winked at Sean as she headed out-side. "Hurry and put that on, Violet. I've got a thing in forty-five minutes."

It took Violet about thirteen seconds to disappear behind the partition, remove her shirt, and put on the logo T-shirt. Yet again, I lingered and listened to every slight sound of the material moving over her skin as she removed one and slid on the other. Why? As we've discussed before, I enjoyed self-torture.

She popped out, seeming surprised to see me, still standing there with the T-shirt in my hand like an idiot.

"What's wrong? Is the tattoo hurting?"

I sighed, pulling on the logo shirt. "Not the tattoo."

Sean's infernal grin as Violet passed out the door caught me by surprise. "Got it bad, eh, wolfie?"

"Shut it, Sean," I growled, "before you never make it to manhood."

He cackled, then went back to tapping the computer keyboard. I pushed open the door and sidled up to Violet standing right underneath our shop sign. The air was a biting thirty degrees today, a colder day for January in Louisiana. But I shook off the chill for the photo op. And the opportunity to get close to Violet.

"Where do you want us?" she asked, her eyes flashing over her shoulder at me as I drew up behind her.

A sudden spike in her pulse had my wolf fully awake and alert. Now, that was interesting.

As if he wasn't alert whenever she was around anyway.

"Right where you're at is good," said Livvy. "Nico, move closer up behind her and a little to the right so more of the logo is show-ing. Good. Now put your left arm around her shoulders."

Not a problem. I was really starting to love Livvy. Her photo ops for the social media pages somehow kept throwing Violet and me into close proximity. I anchored Violet to me with a heavy arm over her shoulders.

"Okay. Big smiles." *Click, click, click.* "Bigger." *Click.*

Livvy pulled the lens down and arched a brow at her sister. "Can you try to not look constipated? You're happy. You just opened a business. Your dream career, remember?" I felt Violet's sigh more than I heard it.

"Yay. I emptied my life savings. So excited. Go, me." She waved an invisible pom-pom with zero enthusiasm.

"So what you're saying," I murmured down to her, still smiling for the camera as Livvy moved to different angles and clicked, "is that you're now indebted to me forever."

Violet looked at me over her shoulder, amusement softening her features. "Only until our business takes off like a rocket and I buy you out."

"Who says I'd sell?"

"I could make you."

"What? With witch magic? That's illegal, Miss Savoie."

"Nah. I'd just get you drunk, then gamble you for it. I'm a shark at poker."

"Then I'm definitely not playing poker." I smirked down at her. "I'd think of another game."

"I'm not playing *strip* poker with you, if that's what you're thinking."

I pulled her close and bent to her ear, peeking up at Livvy as she still snapped shots.

"Limerick war."

Violet burst out laughing, tossing her head back. I laughed with her, hugging her a little closer. For the camera, of course.

"Oh yeah. That's perfect," said Livvy, snapping a few more.

Violet shook her head and posed, simmering her laughter. "There's no way I'd bet in a limerick war with you."

"Because you'd lose." I tugged on a lock of her light lavender hair.

"So I guess we're at a stalemate then."

"Yep. You're stuck with me."

"All good, guys. Thanks," said Livvy, putting the lid back on her camera and sliding it into the case she had dangling from her shoulder. "I'll have these up on social media ASAP." She glanced at her Smartwatch. "I've gotta run," she called as she click-clacked on her stiletto boots back to her car at the curb.

Violet glanced up, her expression unreadable. "I'm okay with that." She pulled out of my embrace and backhanded my abs. I tightened just in time to take the punch. "You're not so bad." I followed her back inside, glancing around for my T-shirt. I'd dropped it on the black sectional sofa that took up the lobby waiting room. I stripped off the logo shirt, careful of my bandage, and picked up the one I was wearing earlier.

"You can keep it," Violet said with a smile. "You own the place. Or half own it, you know."

I cleared my throat. "I have to wash new shirts before I wear them," I grumbled.

"Oh wow." Violet beamed like she'd just garnered a state secret. "I had no idea you were a germaphobe."

I pushed my arms into my long-sleeved T-shirt, pausing to glare at her. "Just because I don't like to wear shirts that have been handled by machines and ten T-shirt shop workers makes me a germaphobe?"

"This is such an interesting facet of Nico Cruz." The shop door opened.

"Whatever." I scoffed at her mocking tone and pulled the shirt over my head.

A feminine gasp, then a plunk.

A pretty brunette stood in the doorway staring at me, a French Truck Coffee to-go cup at her feet, the contents spilling across the floor. Glad we went with the dark stained concrete floors when we remodeled.

"Oh my God! I'm so sorry." She squatted quickly to scoop up the cup. That's when I noticed that her black pencil skirt revealed a leg tattoo of exotic flowers winding beyond her hem. She had another tattoo peeking out of her neckline and a cuff bracelet of ink around her left wrist.

"You must be Lindsey," I said, stepping forward to shake her hand.

Her mouth dropped open, then closed, then opened and closed again like a guppy, while she passively shook my hand, her entire neck and face flushed pink. And damn, if her pulse wasn't racing like a rabbit.

"You okay?" I asked, knowing full well that I flustered the hell out of her, even though I was trying not to.

She was a young witch, a Conduit, like Violet's sister Isadora. Her healing magic gave her the perfect temperament for soothing clients as she worked on them. Violet had told me she came highly recommended by Zaire, who'd met her at a trade convention.

"Let me help you," said Sean, already there wiping up the mess and taking the empty cup.

"Name's Blackwater." I bit back a smile as he dropped his voice a few levels.

"His name is Sean, and he's underage," said Violet, offering her hand. "Hi, I'm Violet. We spoke on the phone."

"Lindsey Farmer." She nodded and beamed a nervous smile. "So nice to meet you in person."

"And this is Nico Cruz. My partner."

Her gaze swiveled back to me. "You're my boss?" she breathed out in disbelief.

Her pulse triple-timed. Oh, right. It wasn't my being a werewolf that had her heartbeat racing. She licked her lips nervously and kept darting her gaze away.

"We both are," said Violet more emphatically.

"Nice to meet you, Mr. Cruz," said Lindsey, beaming a smile at me.

"And you." I nodded, returning a polite smile.

"Nico, I've got this. I'll give her the tour. You can be on your way." If I didn't know better, I'd say Violet was trying to get rid of me.

"You sure? I could stay and help out. Show Lindsey how to use the new stencil machine." I'd bought the latest high-tech machine for the shop and had trained myself on it first.

"I can show her," she snapped before haughtily turning away toward the partition. "This way, Lindsey. I'll show you to your station. You can meet our other artist, Tom, tomorrow," she continued, walking away.

I ignored Lindsey's lingering stare as she slowly followed after Violet. My attention was riveted on the perturbed set of my partner's shoulders. And that fine, perky ass of hers that somehow looked even better when she was irritated or pissed off.

"You need me for anything else?" I asked, pushing her buttons on purpose.

"Nope. You can go," she called over her shoulder.

"Cool. I've got a gig at the Cauldron and want to rest and get cleaned up."

"You're in a band?" Lindsey had stopped following Violet, which Violet finally realized, spinning around and propping a hand on her hip.

"Not a *band*," she spat like it was a criminal idea. "He plays acoustic guitar at a few spots around town. No big deal."

"You do?" she asked, all breathy and still focused on me, not Violet, who walked back over to her and was growing more annoyed by the second. "I'd love to see you play. I'm free tonight."

I turned to Violet, enjoying the tension around her eyes as she glared at Lindsey. "Violet, why don't you bring her to the Cauldron tonight? She's new in town and could use some friendly faces."

Violet's fiery blue eyes snapped to me, then she cleared her throat. "Sure. Sounds good." Then she turned back toward the stations, all business. "Follow me, Lindsey, and I'll show you your setup."

I shook my head as I left through the back hallway that connected to my private courtyard and led to my two-story house. I had no idea why but that entire scene had me smiling. Perhaps it was because underneath all of Violet's rough handling and no-nonsense attitude toward Lindsey, I detected a tiny spark of jealousy. If that were true, then maybe the torture wasn't one-sided. That would be a revelation. There was only one way to find out.

CHAPTER 4

~VIOLET~

"This was a bad idea."

I glanced down at myself as I walked alongside Clara. I'd upgraded my ripped jeans to dark skinny jeans and a blue long-sleeve pullover that hugged my breasts.

"To hang out with your sister? Someone needs an attitude adjustment." Clara tapped my arm with that all-patient expression, jolting me with her happy juice.

"Not to hang out with you," I added, moving over so a couple headed in the opposite direction could walk between us. "But to waste a night out when I have receipts to go over from last week's shipment and new inventory I haven't even unboxed yet."

I was making up excuses, and I knew it. I honestly just didn't like the way Lindsey had ogled Nico like the prime piece of meat that he was. Nor did I like his response to be overly helpful with her settling in.

"Well," added my twin with infinite patience, "you look very pretty."

I shook my head on a laugh. "Thanks." I blew off a strand of my long bangs that had strayed over one eye.

"Now let's tackle the real issue."

"Which is?"

"Why don't you like your new hire?" She flipped her long braid over her shoulder. Clara always let her hair grow out much longer than me, now past the middle of her back.

"I like her fine."

Clara laughed in that way that screamed *liar* without her saying a word.

"According to you," she continued kindly, "she was Zaire's top recommendation, and you practically begged him to help persuade her to uproot her life in Texas to move here. And now you're complaining about having to show her a little hospitality on her first night in New Orleans."

"Damn, C." I stopped right outside the doors of the Cauldron and faced her, the acoustic strings of Nico's guitar speaking to me in that intimate way his music always did. "Am I really that much of a heinous troll?"

"Yes." She beamed, squishing my cheeks between her palms and saying in baby-talk, "But you're my heinous troll."

Rolling my eyes, I pushed past her to open the door, unable to hold back my smile. I swear, I wondered sometimes if it was her magic as an Aura—a positive-energy pusher and emotion reader—that made her so damn likable. Or if it was just Clara herself. It was impossible to get angry at her.

"Hey," I said suddenly, stopping at the entrance before we stepped inside. "Do you still feel like the tattoos are enhancing your Aura ability?"

Her eyes twinkled. "Yes! I swear. The auras are more immediate and the emotions more intense. Even the other day, this sweet old lady came into the shop, looking depressed, said she was looking for a tea to help with stress. Her aura was this super sad gray. I hadn't even touched her, just *thought* about zapping her with my happy spell, and it was like a ray of sunshine swept over her, transforming her mood and her aura. That's never happened before."

Biting my lip, I studied my sister. "And you really think it was one of the tattoos I gave you?"

She nodded, reaching to open the door. "Sure of it. I felt the tingle along my hip where you put the last tattoo. That was the winner, I know it."

Feeling a bit happier, I sighed with relief. Especially after having that vision today when I tattooed Nico. It was like my magic was giving me the solution to the wolf problem with a vision of witch sign. I still needed to think on it, but my intuition told me this was good.

Clara had been letting me practice my tattoo charms on her using ultraviolet ink, which was invisible to the naked eye. She didn't want to be covered in ink, but she'd wanted to help me, so the UV ink was our solution. And thank goodness because I'd had to practice a lot until finally reaching what I believe now was the right spell for an Aura witch.

The pub was pretty packed. Thursday nights were half-off imports and our cousins' beer, Witch's Brew. Cole and Drew couldn't make it for the Empress Ink grand opening coming up but said they'd be visiting soon and would be bringing a special new microbrew with them to add to the party.

While I was excited they were coming to town, I also dreaded it. No one could do peer pressure like my cousins and their roommate/business partner, Travis. They lived perpetually in party mode, and my mind was too preoccupied with getting Empress Ink off the ground right now. Somehow, I knew that would be no excuse to them.

Belinda was waiting tables along with my replacement, Finnie, who had been promoted from dishwasher. Finnie was a college kid and easy on the eyes, so he was doing well for himself. I told Jules I'd still work busy weekends and holidays when she needed me. After all, I still owned a sixth of the business.

Jules had congratulated me on my new venture and didn't once make me feel guilty, but I did anyway. I was devoted to my family, and leaving this place had taken a lot longer than I'd planned.

I wove through the tables to the bar, catching a glimpse of Nico out of the corner of my eye.

Fucking hell. That damn man.

His black Henley was pushed up to reveal the tantalizing ink on his forearms, his long fingers strumming wickedly as he sang his own sultry rendition of Lynyrd Skynyrd's "Simple Man." His voice was achingly soulful, which apparently had a direct line to my libido.

And now I realized why I really hadn't wanted to come tonight. Because Nico at work was distracting. But Nico in his natural habitat—a dimly lit bar where his voice resonated in the air like a dark angel—was temptation incarnate.

Thoughts of the first night we'd met flashed to mind, the kiss he'd planted between my legs that haunted me in my wettest dreams. There was no question that the man would likely overshadow every lover before and after him if I'd let myself go there, but I was also aware that he was practically family now besides being my business partner.

Whenever I got the urge to say *fuck it* and jump his bones, I remembered those three fateful cards—Death, Three of Swords, the Tower.

Having magic was a responsibility. If I ignored my magic and did whatever the hell I wanted, I wouldn't just hurt myself. I could hurt Nico too. I might be selfish sometimes, but I wasn't that selfish. The man felt things deeply, and I wasn't about to subject him to the burning Tower of chaos that would be our relationship if we went there. So I had to be the stronger one in this scenario. I was the psychic.

So I ignored the urge to grab a table right in front of him and swoon like a fan-girly teenager and forced my way to the bar where Lindsey was already waiting, smiling at something Charlie was saying.

Charlie was JJ's best friend, and also one of mine. JJ had been tending bar for us for years. They were part of our "human" family who knew who and what we were and kept our secrets.

Charlie and JJ were also the kind of best friends who should've crossed the friend zone into manland a long-ass time ago. But they were stubborn bastards, both pretending they didn't want to tear each other's clothes off on a daily basis. Or perhaps JJ was in deep, deep denial.

Sounded a little like me. My gaze instinctively found my own temptation, crooning into the mic with his eyes closed.

Fucksticks! Why was he so hot?

It might be easier to ignore my craving for the man if I didn't know what his mouth felt like on my pussy. But unfortunately— or actually SUPER fortunately—I did know. That, in addition to everything else, including his perfect hard-jawed, wide-mouthed, green-eyed face, made resisting him so much harder.

I was the kind of woman who typically followed my instincts and spontaneous desires, never denying to sit on a pretty face when I wanted to. And let's be real, Nico had a face worth sitting upon.

But! I couldn't go there for all the reasons previously discussed. Also, everyone knew it wasn't smart to mix business with pleasure. I mean, I wasn't saying I had a magical pussy or anything, but men had been known to stalk me a time or two after a night in my bed.

Sex complicated things. And Empress Ink was my brainchild, my little dream taking flight. It didn't need complications. It needed simplicity and success. So there would be no sitting on Nico's fuckable face.

"Hi, Lindsey." I greeted her with a warm smile, feeling like an ass for being a bit rude to her earlier in the day. What could I say? I wasn't fond of her immediately falling in love with Nico.

But I couldn't blame the girl either. "This is my sister Clara."

"Hi, nice to meet you." Lindsey beamed sweetly.

"And you too," said Clara, shaking her hand. "Lindsey, I have to tell you this. You have the prettiest pink aura I've ever seen."

"Do I?" Lindsey blinked rapidly at Clara. "I hope that's a good thing."

"Definitely. It means you have an optimistic spirit." Clara sat on a stool next to her while I meandered to the other side of Charlie and leaned on the bar.

"How are you doing, new business owner?" he asked, sipping his Blood Orange Old-Fashioned, one of our most popular drinks at the Cauldron.

"Tired."

"Well, sit up here next to Uncle Charlie and take a load off. Enjoy the scenery." He put his hand on the crown of my head and twisted it to check out the stage.

"Ugh. Stop, Charlie!"

JJ sidled up with an old-fashioned for me as well.

"Thanks." I took a sip. "Hey, tell your bestie to stay out of my sex life."

"Interesting, because I thought the problem was you had no sex life." Charlie sipped from the cocktail straw, his blue eyes blinking all sweetly. I wondered if he was taking lessons from Clara.

"Why do I tell you guys anything?"

"I don't understand what the big deal is." JJ planted his hands on the bar, arms straight, which flexed his biceps nicely. I wasn't the only one who noticed. "I mean," JJ continued, "so what if you work together. Scratch that itch and get it over with."

"Interesting advice coming from you." I glanced at Charlie, who suddenly had found the ceiling very interesting, then over at Lindsey, who was still immersed in conversation with Clara.

"What does that mean?" JJ wore a perpetual scowl. With his broad brow, deep-set eyes, and super masculine jaw beneath his beard, it made him look rather menacing. So opposite of clean-shaven, neat-as-a-pin Charlie. Also, JJ was an idiot.

"Nothing." I rolled my eyes, noting that Charlie had gone silent. Not the norm for him at all.

I promised myself I wouldn't interfere, so I wouldn't.

JJ left to serve a customer. Charlie decided to take that moment to stare at me with his stop-kidding-yourself-and-fuck-the-werewolf face.

I shrugged. "It would just make things weird and awkward once it was over." *Plus, grinning skeletons and stabby swords through hearts and burning towers!*

"If you say so. Then again, maybe it would be more than sex."

I scoffed, turning around to lean back against the bar and face the stage. "You mean, like a relationship?"

He swiveled on his stool to face the room with me. "Foreign concept for you, I realize, but these things do exist."

Yes, I knew. And I wished he was the one, but that asshole fate had other plans apparently.

"You should take up stand-up comedy, Charlie. You'd do so well."

"You should stop sowing your oats and plow some fields. Maybe something would grow."

"I thought the guy did the plowing."

"Depends on the guy." He surreptitiously glanced over my shoulder at JJ before resuming watching Nico onstage.

I narrowed my eyes on him. "You are such a hypocrite."

"What?"

I laughed. "You do know that I'm a psychic, right?" I tossed my cocktail straw on the bar behind me and took a big swallow. "I've done a reading for you, ya know."

"You didn't!" He looked excited and terrified at the same time, which was the typical look I got when people wanted a certain something to show up in the cards.

"I did. On my own. Because I had to know if I was right. I was, of course. And I know good and well that you two"—I gestured between Charlie and JJ serving beer at the other end— "need to get the party started."

His brow pinched together into a frown. "You're deflecting again, darling. The topic was whether or not you have big enough balls to *actually* engage in more than a one-night stand."

"I'll have you know I've dated a guy for a solid month before. And my balls are plenty big, thank you very much."

"A whole month?" Charlie gasped in wide-eyed exaggeration, clutching his invisible pearls.

"Well, then. What was I thinking? Call Dr. Phil. You're the relationship expert."

"Dr. Phil?" I snorted. "Is he even on TV anymore?"

"Personally, if I knew that someone I was hot for was hot for me, I wouldn't be waiting around and wasting time." Charlie's gaze on the stage grew dreamy. "I mean, just look at him."

Nico was singing a slow and smoky rendition of "Lovely" by Billie Eilish, the tenor of his voice wrapping my chest in a vise. It made me agitated. And horny.

"Well, you're not me, now are you?"

"Thank the heavens." He turned to face me, brows raised, eyeing my head. "I wonder if I gave you a good whack if it would slap the stupid out of you."

"Harsh, Charlie."

"You can take it. But also, I mean it. So what if you run a business together? Even if you give it a go and it doesn't work out, you're both mature adults. You'd just go back to being friends. I'm sure you could still work together without too much awkwardness." He glanced at Nico, then back at me. "Well, one of you is mature. I see the dilemma now."

I couldn't help but laugh. "You're just mad that I know you're in love with your best friend."

"Need another one, Violet?" JJ asked from behind us.

Both of us jumped like we'd been caught with our hands in the cookie jar. "What's got you two spooked?" JJ grinned, eyeing both of us.

"Nothing," we said in unison. Then I added, "No, I'm good."

"Killian's Red," said Belinda, sidling up to the side of the bar where the waitstaff placed drink orders.

JJ slid a Killian's Red onto the bar top in front of Belinda right as I heard Nico telling the audience he'd be taking a break. My psychic magic pinged me, letting me know I was right. "Belinda, that for Nico?"

"Yeah."

"I'll take it to him."

"Awesome. These tables are running me ragged." She slid it my way and dashed into the kitchen.

I took the beer as Charlie leaned over to me and whispered, "Proactive. That's my girl." And that was when something happened that never ever happened to me. I got nervous.

My heart skipped a beat, and a cold sweat flushed the back of my neck. What was going on? It was just Nico. I was just bringing him a beer . . . after Charlie had bullied me into agreeing to act on my attraction. I'd ignored it this long, so why would I do this? It was like my instincts had just grabbed the wheel, yelling at logic in the back seat to shut the fuck up.

I pretended I wasn't mulling over life-changing decisions—like ignoring the cards and Aunt Beryl's vision—as I paraded around the tables to bring him the beer. When his eyes landed on me, they stayed there, luring me like the moon to the tide. Maybe moon metaphors were cliché where a werewolf was concerned, but that was damn sure how it felt. An undeniable, magnetic pull. A cosmic force.

Still, I kept it calm and casual as I handed him the beer. "Nice set."

He swigged the longneck, and I couldn't help but watch how his throat worked as he gulped it down. Why in the fuck was that so sexy?

"What's the special occasion?" he asked as he balanced the beer on one knee, the other holding his guitar.

"Pardon?"

He chuckled, his brow pinching in confusion. "I've never heard you use that word in my life."

"Sorry," I said, propping a hand on my hip, trying desperately to look casually cool and feeling like an imbecile for some reason. "What special occasion were you referencing?"

Referencing? How did being nervous suddenly alter my vocabulary to formal librarian?

"Bringing me a beer." He glanced down, peering inside the bottle. "You didn't spit in it, did you?"

"Why would I do such a thing?"

He shrugged one shoulder and took another gulp, my eyes zeroing in on the cords of muscle in his neck. Apparently, I had a neck fetish I wasn't aware of till this very second.

"You were so pissy at work this afternoon. I didn't expect kind treatment. I'm assuming you're being friendlier to your new hire too." He looked at Lindsey at the bar with Clara. I'd totally forgotten about her. Damn, wasn't I the hospitable host?

"Of course I am," I snapped.

"There's the Violet I know and love," he teased in a low, sultry voice.

He didn't mean the words for real, but suddenly I was infatuated with that sentence. And terrified for some reason. Those giant balls I bragged about to Charlie were shrinking by the second. They'd be dried-up raisins by the time I got out of this conversation.

"You okay?" he asked, concern etching his brow.

"Just a long week, ya know."

I slid both hands into the back pockets of my jeans, needing to do something with them before I started biting my nails. That would be a travesty.

I'd finally broken the habit by making damn sure I wore nail polish 24-7. FYI, nail polish didn't taste good. On top of that, I spent inordinate amounts of money on my OPI nail color collection. This was my logical reason I shouldn't be biting my nails since I'd be wasting money.

And who wants that? Isadora said my logic was faulty, but it worked for me.

"Mmm. And you'll have to do some training tomorrow."

His gaze swiveled to Lindsey again. A flash of irritation flushed through me. Not because I had to train Lindsey but because that was the second time I'd seen his gaze wander to her in this conversation.

"Hopefully, she'll live up to the reputation Zaire painted of her and won't need handholding."

"I can help you out if you need. Give her the ins and outs of the shop."

"You'd like that?" I asked, knowing full well my aggravation bled into my voice.

He glanced at her again. "Sure." Then took a swig of his beer, watching me.

Okay, time for a little investigative exploration. "She's pretty, huh?"

He took a long moment to respond, his gaze skimming my throat before meeting mine again.

"Fucking gorgeous."

Ouch. Why did hearing him call another woman gorgeous make me want to hurl right on his size thirteen shoes? My nausea quickly turned to anger. "Nico, must I remind you about the company policy that there will be no fraternizing with employees?"

"Is it policy, though? Or just your personal opinion?"

"You can't sleep with the new girl," I practically hissed, my face flushing with heat.

Whoa, Violet. Pull back the aggressive reins.

"I think she's attractive, so now you're assuming I want to sleep with her?"

I scoffed. "That tends to be the usual progression for most guys."

Maybe that was a little rude and presumptuous, but the idea of Nico being interested in the *gorgeous* new hire had me nearly hyperventilating.

He took another gulp of beer, examining me like a bug under a microscope. I even felt the sizzle of magic in the air. His wolf was near. Strange. Well, not so strange. The full moon was in a few days. There was a pressure, a push of dominance, rolling off him, yet his demeanor was all cool and composed.

"That's all you're going to give me?" I shifted to my other foot nervously.

"What else do you want, Vi?"

"I want you to say you won't badger the new girl. She needs time to get acclimated to the new job, the city. Give her space." *Don't fucking sleep with her.*

"Time and space." He chuckled low before downing the rest of his beer and handing the bottle back to me, his long fingers brushing over mine. "I'll keep that in mind." Then he shifted back toward the mic and dragged it in front of him, introducing his next set.

I wandered back to the bar, a little off-center and confused. Then I looked back at the empty beer bottle in my hand, wondering why in the hell I'd decided to bring him a beer. It felt like a girlfriend move, not a business partner move.

Girlfriend?

Had I truly lost my mind? Why was I thinking things like this?

We were business partners. And friends. Who'd once had oral sex under the stars on a rooftop nightclub. A moment that I couldn't get out of my head no matter how hard I tried. "What—?" Charlie started to ask.

"Shut it. And good night."

I made excuses to Lindsey, letting Clara take the lead. I needed to get out of this room filled with his intoxicating voice and my crazy ideas that included words like *plowing* and *relationship* and *girlfriend*.

Clara was right. I needed an attitude adjustment. Nothing some good ol' masturbation, refined whiskey, and a good night's sleep couldn't handle. Tomorrow, everything would be back to normal.

CHAPTER 5

~VIOLET~

I'D ESTABLISHED EVERY OTHER THURSDAY AS OUR REGULAR STAFF NIGHT. Even though we weren't officially open to the public yet, I thought it would be a good idea to meet regularly, to discuss new ideas or share opinions.

At our first meeting, Tom reported that the plug in his workspace didn't work to recharge his cordless tattoo machine. So we'd gotten an electrician over to fix that and do a check on the rest of the building, finding a few other electrical outlets that needed an overhaul.

At the last Staff Night, Sean had complained that our bookkeeping program was too antiquated and suggested something his cousin used for his businesses. At first, I thought Sean was a bit out of his depth and wouldn't know a good program from a bad one. After all, he was only seventeen. I realized I was wrong after conferring with Ruben, the vampire overlord and family friend, who owned several successful businesses himself.

So thus far, our meetings had been productive and fruitful. This would be our first one with the newest employee, Lindsey. I'd given myself a stern talking-to about how I'd been a bit short with her and possibly a little rude yesterday when she'd first arrived.

So I swanned into the shop, all smiles and bearing gifts. The bakery across from the Cauldron, Queen of Tarts, was Clara's favorite place to buy sweets for her High Tea Book Club gatherings, so I picked up some lemon berry petit fours and chocolate raspberry tarts.

Lindsey and Sean were already seated in the lobby area on our comfy sectionals, which was the best gathering place since our office was pretty small. Besides, Nico had bought soft, plush furniture for our lobby.

"Whoa. Whatcha got?" Sean was already up and in front of me, helping with one of the pastry boxes.

"Thought we could have some refreshments to welcome our final staff member of Empress Ink."

"Oh wow. That's so sweet." Lindsey sat forward and peeked in the bakery boxes as I opened them.

"I'm going to get some coffee first." I started backing to the hallway. "Anyone else?" Lindsey raised her to-go cup from French Truck Coffee.

Sean muffled, "Nah. I'm good," around a full mouthful.

"Chew, Sean. Don't choke yourself," I told him as I went to the kitchen and popped a pod into the Keurig.

"Meeting time?" asked Tom, coming in and grabbing a water out of the fridge.

"Yeah," I told him. "Nico isn't here yet, but we can go ahead and get started."

Tom Bounyasang was the first artist I'd hired after my cousins Drew and Cole had introduced us when I was on a visit to Lafayette back in April. He was another warlock friend of theirs. Drew and Cole had invited me to the Laotian New Year celebration, a party that gave Mardi Gras a run for its money.

The best thing about that night, however, had been meeting Tom—tall, lean, and covered in artistic tattoos. When I learned that he'd been freelance tattooing for family members and friends, I snatched him up, offering an annual salary plus a generous percentage on his client's work. I'd never seen such unique skill on tribal tattoos like his. He also could do portraits, which was something I could never do.

I wanted to cover my bases in offering a variety to our clientele, humans as well as supernaturals, which meant having a wide array of artistic ability. Tom also had that mysterious, badass quality that made women want to keep coming back. He was an Influencer warlock after all, like Livvy. But rather than have that effervescent personality that lured people in, he had that quiet, sexy charisma that magnetized people without him saying a word.

By the time I made my way to the front, Nico was there. Sitting right next to Lindsey and making her laugh about something. To be honest, they looked so adorable together, I thought I was going to be sick.

He was also eating a petit four as I walked toward the lounge area. Glancing up at me, he sucked a smear of raspberry off his thumb. The sight of his tongue as he swiped it across the pad set my panties on fire.

"These are delicious," he told me all casual while my heart raced ridiculously. He scooted over toward Lindsey, creating a space for me between him and Sean.

I almost took a seat in the overstuffed chair across from him, but then he'd know I was pissed or jealous or turned on or whatever the hell I was feeling, so I casually sat next to him.

"Glad you like them. I wanted to celebrate finally having our first full Staff Night now that Lindsey has joined us."

She beamed brightly on cue as they all gave her a nod and smiled in welcome.

"So," I started, "anyone have something they want to share?"

"Yeah," said Tom, "I was wondering about our artwork you wanted for matting and framing. I found a good deal at a printer over on Prytania Street. He works with local artists so his printing and framing is better than just some random place. He also said he'd cut us a deal since we want quite a few done in lots of sizes."

"Oh, awesome." I pulled out my phone. "What's his name? I'll shoot him an email this week. I'd definitely like to get those up by the time we have the grand opening celebration. I have a feeling we'll be pretty busy after Livvy works her magic." Tom gave me the guy's name and contact information.

"Sean, how's the new bookkeeping program working?" I asked.

"Awesome. Just like I told you. It provides a much more detailed breakdown of ingoing and outgoing expenses, but also gives projections on what we should be aiming for in profit margins."

To hear the kid talk about profit margins was a little surreal, but also comforting. We'd hired him as a favor to Ruben, who'd asked on behalf of Sean's brother, Henry Blackwater, a grim who worked for him. Turns out, the favor was no favor at all. Sean was kind of a whiz kid.

"How about you, Lindsey? Need anything in your workspace that you don't have?"

"Not at all. Seems that everything has been accounted for." She looked as if she wanted to ask me a question but bit her lip.

"Something else?" I raised my brows.

"It's totally unrelated to work, but Clara told me you were a Seer, and I was kind of hoping you might do a reading for me. You know"— she shrugged a shoulder—"for my new life here in New Orleans."

Her gaze drifted to Nico, who'd been sitting back with both arms across the sofa behind both me and Lindsey. But his gaze was on me. Heavy and watchful.

"Uh, well, maybe after we've covered all the business stuff if we have time." I glanced at my phone. "I do have to meet Clara at Maybelle's to talk about something." That was a lie, but for some reason I didn't want to do her reading right now.

"Anyone else have business to discuss?" asked Nico.

No one said a word. He moved his gaze back to me. "Looks like you've got time."

"Okay. Sure. Sure thing."

I stood and walked over to my workspace, uncertain why I was hesitating. Maybe because I'd never done a reading in front of Nico. Still, why would that make me nervous? It was like my magic knew something that I didn't. Yet.

I grabbed a pack of tarot cards I kept in my drawer, because honestly I had a deck stashed everywhere I spent any length of time, then strode back out to the lobby. Rather than sit next to Nico where I'd been, I knelt on the opposite side in front of the coffee table.

"So do you mind if we keep it simple? A single card reading?" I set my phone off to the side. My nerves were jittery, and I still wasn't sure why. My psychic line was already tapping along my bloodstream, pouring a shot of adrenaline through my body like an electric volt. "I need to get going soon."

"Thanks! I haven't had a reading in forever. My cousin in Austin used to do them for me, but she moved last spring so it's been a while." She leaned forward excitedly, arching a perfect brow with a tiny hoop piercing, dark hair falling forward in a silky wave.

I spread the cards out on the table, facedown. "So we're just going to focus on one card today." I stared down at the pile of cards. "Your future here in New Orleans. Go ahead and pick."

She reached out and hovered her hand over the pile, moving to one side then the other, then finally pulled one half-hidden beneath another and flipped it over.

You've got to be kidding me.

"Ten of Cups," I said with a smile and through gritted teeth.

The card I'd been wanting to pull forever. Specifically when it came to the man sitting next to her. *Oh no.* Please don't let the card be about her and Nico. Please.

"Is it a good one?" she asked, her pretty eyes bright with excitement.

"Yeah." I laughed. "It's a great one actually." I cleared my throat, staring at the card and not her or the man boring a hole into my face with his gaze. "It means divine love and complete joy in relationships. Harmony in romantic love. So it looks like you'll be finding your true love here in New Orleans."

"Seriously?" She laughed sweetly.

"Damn. My last reading wasn't that good," sniped Sean.

"You're a teenager. I'd hope not," Tom added dryly.

"That's right," said Sean playfully. "Still got oats to sow."

Ignoring Sean, I went on to add to Lindsey, "It also means bliss at home and true emotional fulfillment. So I'd say life looks good for you here."

I forced a smile on my face as I glanced up at her and started to gather the cards. Nico stopped my progression by placing his giant paw on top of mine. I flinched and met his gaze across the table. "Do mine."

Gulping, I glanced at my phone. "No, seriously. I've gotta go." My heart pumped faster because I was flat-out lying and because his touch, even as slight as this, set my skin ablaze. It had me imagining all the places his hands would feel so damn good on my body.

"You have time to pull one card."

"Um." I moved the cards around to get my hand out from underneath his. "Um, I really have to get going."

"What's the emergency? A crystal shortage at Maybelle's?"

He knew there was no emergency and was calling me on it, dammit.

His gaze narrowed. "Why don't you want to do my reading, Violet?"

The way he said my name—a mixture of familiarity and dominance rolled together—made me freeze and stare like a dummy. He clasped his hands together, leaning forward the way Lindsey was a minute ago. He arched a brow at me, the slightest tilt to his mouth, challenging me.

"Fine! Okay. One card. No problem. Would you like your reading to be about your future too?" I tried to sound not-so-aggravated but knew I'd failed when Tom and Lindsey turned my way where they were chatting about something together.

"My near future," Nico clarified.

Shuffling the cards, I focused my eyes on the deck, trying to ignore my racing pulse and the thrumming of my magic streaking like wildfire through my body. It was the kind of channeling of magic I usually only felt when in the witch's round with my sisters to recharge our energy. I was surprised I wasn't glowing like a lightning bug.

I stopped mixing the cards and told him, "Go ahead," without looking at him.

In less than a second, his hand snatched and flipped a card. The gasp that escaped my throat was like something out of a sitcom.

"Lovers," said Nico, his voice so deep and rough I couldn't help but look up at him, unsurprised to catch a flash of gold in his eyes.

"Oh," said Lindsey next to him, blushing.

"Sweet," said Sean with a cackle.

Tom said nothing per usual, unruffled by just about everything in life.

Clearing my throat nervously, I straightened the card and stared down at it, the naked lovers entwining. "So this card means, um, obviously physical love and harmony in relationships."

"In my near future," added Nico.

"Right, it—"

Sean was making some other quippy remark, but a sizzle of magic froze me in place, flashing a vision into my head.

Nico was laid back on a sofa I didn't recognize with me lying beside him, my head at the other end. I was massaging his feet that were in my lap, and then I said something that made him laugh. Then his gaze turned molten hot, and he licked his lips and—

What the hell? I wasn't even the lovey-dovey type, much less the kind to massage a guy's nasty feet. *Hell no, Spirit! You can take that vision right back and shove it up your ethereal ass.* But then a niggling little voice whispered how good it could be. Would be.

"You okay?" asked Lindsey.

I was scattering cards like crazy and had already turned over the Lovers card because I couldn't look at it a second longer. Nico just sat there, grinning at me like a fiend.

"You know what? Lindsey, could you pick these up for me and y'all just put the pastries in the fridge." I was on my feet and running out the door. "Gotta go!"

"Violet!" Nico called at me as I opened the door.

He strolled to me, his movements smooth, his gaze focused. "You forgot this." He held out my phone.

I reached out to take it from him. "Thanks."

But as I tugged, he wouldn't let it go, pulling my gaze back up to his. He didn't smile or laugh or look like he was teasing at all, but rather he wanted my attention. I stood there, breathless, eyes wide, and my mouth unable to say a word. He trailed his index and middle finger over the underside of my wrist, surely feeling my pulse, before he finally let me go.

Somehow, I felt branded by that featherlight touch. He was telling me something without saying a word. Stubborn as I was, I didn't want to listen, but my body sure as hell got the message loud and clear. I took my phone and ran like the coward I was, though I was pretty sure he wouldn't let me run forever.

CHAPTER 6

~VIOLET~

THE NEXT MORNING, I SHUFFLED INTO MINE AND CLARA'S KITCHENETTE in our loft above the carriage house and frowned at my French press coffeepot. Well, I thought it was my French press coffeepot. It had been yesterday. *This* morning, it was a purple nightmare.

"Clara," I mumbled under my breath, trying to decide whether I was amused, irritated, or grateful.

If I could be all three at once, I suppose that's how I was feeling while staring at the coffeepot cozy made of various shades of purple. This was Clara's newest obsession. Knitting. One of the widows who was in her historical romance book club had brought her knitting to their group meeting a month ago. That was it. Clara was hooked. Ever since then, Clara had been on a mission to cover anything and everything with yarn.

Thankfully, she left the handle free. As I lifted the pot, I noted that she was really good. Not that I was an expert in knitting, but there were no gaping holes or lopsided lines. All tight stitching, nice and neat rows.

After setting up the coffee, I sat on the sofa in our little living space and waited for it to percolate. And sighed. Heavily.

I'd thought I'd be back to my carefree self by now. I wasn't. If anything, I was more agitated by the other night's brief but unsettling encounter with Nico. I wasn't the jealous type, but clearly my green-eyed monster showed her ugly face when I'd seen his interest in Lindsey. I wasn't the relationship type, but for a hot minute I was considering what that might look like with him. I was accustomed to moving through life with confidence and conviction. Today, I just felt . . . icky.

The sound of the coffee finishing its percolating pulled me off the couch. I poured myself a cup with the perfect amount of my almond milk creamer and savored the bliss of the first sip.

Ahh. This should bring me back to myself. I was simmering in the warm buzz of caffeine on the sofa when a shriek and a squawk and a bark startled me.

"Shit." I spilled my perfect cup of coffee all over my boob.

I ran over and swung open the door to see Clara in her pink-and-white striped pajama shorts and tank top chasing Isadora's dog, Archie, who was chasing my rooster, Fred. Zombie Cat was perched on the top of Fred's chicken coop watching the mayhem, his tail swaying leisurely.

"Not again!" I jogged down the steps in bare feet, the steps freaking cold with the lower temps this morning. "Corral him this way!"

Clara glanced at me, then tried to get Archie running in my direction, but he was a crafty little thing. He stopped, his ears perking up, all while Fred puffed himself up, wings flapping, try-ing to look intimidating. If a dog could laugh, Archie was howling with laughter.

"Come here, you little fiend," I muttered. He dodged away again, now playing chase with me. That's it. I stopped dead cen-ter in the courtyard, about to use magic to lift his ass up and bring him to me. A spark of energy sizzled in my bones.

"Don't you dare, Violet!" Clara shouted, knowing full well what I was about to do.

"I'm gonna do it."

"No, you're not!"

"It won't hurt him."

"It will. It'll scare him."

"We won't catch his little ass if we don't."

"Archie!" Isadora in a short nightgown and long robe streaked toward us from across Devraj's yard on the other side of the wrought iron gate. Her hair was sleep-mussed—or probably sex-mussed with those two—but she still looked like a fairy queen dashing across his yard. I should probably say Devraj *and* Isa-dora's yard since she lived there more than at our house now.

"Your spawn of the devil is stressing out Fred," I called over, shivering in the morning air.

As soon as Archie saw his mama, the little fucker pranced away toward the fence happy as could be.

"How did he get over there?" Isadora called from across the fence.

Clara walked over while I scooped up Fred, removing his newest bow tie, which was dangling and askew. It was Star Wars themed with tiny X-wings. Evie had bought it for him.

"I just don't understand," Isadora was saying as I made my way over.

Clara lifted the little orange monster and handed him over the fence.

"Devraj has checked for holes and weak spots in the fence." Is looked exasperated.

"I don't know either," Clara commiserated while scratching the fluff-ball's head.

Isadora looked genuinely stressed. "I'm so sorry, Violet. Is Fred okay?"

My boy's beady eyes narrowed at his nemesis through the bars, a steady, deep clucking in his chest.

"He's okay," I assured her, not wanting to make her feel any worse. As I said it, another feather fell from his throat and drifted to the ground.

"Oh no." Holding Archie on the hip farthest from us, she reached through and placed her palm on Fred.

I kept him still, knowing she was sending him her healing magic. Instantly, his agitated clucking eased as a hum of energy washed over him and my arm.

"Dev said he'd set up a camera so we can figure it out. I swear, I think the dog might be magic." Is huffed out a laugh. "So sorry, Vi."

"Again?" came the deep voice behind Isadora.

Devraj stalked across the yard in loose joggers and nothing else, his long black hair in a messy bun. Not that I had ever wondered, but this was visual proof why Isadora spent so much *alone* time at his house. The man—or rather, vampire—looked like a walking sex god.

He stopped midway to us, propped a hand low on one hip, and surveyed the yard, checking the fencing for holes where Archie may have escaped.

"No idea either," I said when he made his way over to us and scratched Archie's head even as he scowled at him. "How the hell are you doing it?" Then to me, "Sorry, Vi. I'm going to buy the cameras *today*."

"All good." My gaze strayed from the large mandala tattoo that fully covered one shoulder to the smaller mandala with shades of green and blue just below on the side of his rib cage, the one I'd given him about a month ago.

"So what's the word?" I nodded toward the tattoo I'd given him. "Anything new to report?"

His expression morphed into utter joy. The man was beautiful on any occasion, but that smile made him lethal to all of womanhood.

"It's unbelievable. It'd been a month since I fed when you gave me that tattoo. We're going on two months, and I haven't had any cravings at all."

His dark gaze slid to Isadora, then his hand disappeared behind her back, where he was obviously caressing her. "Well, I still have cravings. Just not for blood."

"Aww! Y'all are so cute," cooed Clara, practically beaming heart-eyes at them.

Isadora turned the brightest shade of pink, but while they were getting all gushy and red-faced, I was marveling at the fact that my spelled tattoo was legit working on him.

To be honest, I'd tried twice before, simply spelling the outline of the new mandala I tattooed to his rib cage, but it didn't work. I enchanted the blue ink and shaded in the mandala with my second incantation, but it still hadn't worked. Apparently, third time's a charm.

Devraj happened to be a vegetarian, which totally sucked for a vampire—no pun intended—who had to drink blood in order to stay alive. He was also a three-hundred-year-old, powerful as fuck vampire, so he'd gone over a month without feeding before.

Most vamps couldn't go near as long. He'd told me that after two months, he'd be pretty ravenous. Except now he wasn't. Because of my charmed tattoo.

I wanted to jump up and down and do cartwheels, but since that was more Clara's style, I just beamed excitedly, letting out a relieved laugh.

"I can't believe it." I caught Clara's eye. "It's working!"

"Of course it is. You're a brilliant, gifted witch."

"You know," said Isadora, cutting in warmly, "this type of magic has the ability to heal, Vi. You could do so much good with this."

A new kind of thrill ran through me, my thoughts instantly jumping back to Nico and his werewolf problem. Actually, all the werewolves' problem with control.

"Again, sorry about this little guy," said Devraj. "I'm headed to the store now." He leaned over, brushing Izzy's hair aside, and planted a kiss high on her jaw. "Be back soon."

She gave him those lovey eyes and nodded before turning a concerned frown at Fred.

"Stop worrying. It's okay." I glanced back at the chicken coop, thinking of ways to fortify his pen. "I just hate to close him up in his pen. He's gotten used to having full reign of our courtyard."

"And trust me," added Clara, "he thinks this whole yard is his territory." Fred clucked louder at that as if to agree.

"I just feel awful," Isadora added. Archie tried to lick her face, wagging his stubby tail and proud as he could be of himself.

"I think I've got an idea," I said. "Let me check on something, and I'll get back to you."

Then I headed back in, dropping Fred by his coop on the way back to the carriage house. I dressed quickly, having a heavy debate with myself on whether or not this was a good idea, then I picked up my phone and texted Nico.

Me: Are you home?

Nico: Yes.

Me: I'm coming over.

A brief pause, then . . .

Nico: Come on.

I almost forewarned him with what I wanted but thought better of it. Better to ask forgiveness than permission, I always said. Actually, that advice came from our grandmother, Maybelle. She was always a rule-bender. I was fairly positive I carried more of her genes than my mother's.

After a quick shower, I dressed fast and twisted my damp hair on top of my head. After grabbing a new black-and-white polka-dotted bow tie from my pantie drawer and one of Clara's reusable grocery bags out of the kitchen, I headed downstairs. I put a small sack of feed inside my bag and swung it over my shoulder.

"Come on, boy." I put Fred's new bow tie on, which had him puffing up arrogantly, looking more like himself. Then I carried him out the gate and headed toward Magazine Street.

It was a pretty big hike since Nico's place and our shop was a couple of blocks toward City Park, but I needed the exercise.

You might think that a woman carrying a bow-tie-wearing rooster down the street might seem odd, but this was New Orleans. Much stranger sights have been seen, which was why I only received friendly smiles as I passed those sitting at the outdoor tables of the Ruby Slipper Café and Red Dog Diner. The smell of sausage, eggs, grits, and biscuits reminded me that I'd skipped breakfast. My stomach rumbled, but I ignored it. I'd grab something before I opened the shop.

By the time I reached the dead-end street that housed Nico's place and Empress Ink, I was rethinking this plan. And wondering why my first thought was to go to *him*. What I should've done was call Aunt Beryl.

Since our parents were now enjoying retirement in the Swiss Alps, Aunt Beryl was our go-to person when we needed help with something. She also happened to be the Dr. Doolittle of witches. But no, I hadn't even thought of her at all until I was on Nico's doorstep.

I opened the tall wrought iron gate that opened to his private courtyard from the street and crossed the brick pavement courtyard that separated our shop from his private residence, while examining the large grassy area tucked away on the right.

A high brick wall completely enclosed this space for privacy, which also made me think Fred would be fine here. While he liked to prove he was head cock of his domain, he honestly was a total chicken when it came to venturing beyond his grounds. Also, he was kind of fat, if I were honest. He couldn't fly very high, and I was pretty sure he'd look at that brick wall and think it wasn't worth the effort.

The grassy area in the back looked sufficient for him to peck around in.

Oh! A pretty rock garden and a fountain. I paused at the sight of a sculpture. One obviously created by Nico's cousin and Evie's boyfriend, Mateo, who happened to be a metal sculpture artist. It was a naked fairy about three feet high. She had one knee bent and was dipping a toe into the water fountain. Her hands were on her hips and her wings were dangling leisurely behind her, brushing her bare ass. She looked . . . sassy. Even from behind.

I couldn't help but laugh. Leave it to Nico to commission a feisty fairy and to Mateo for having the talent to fill the order.

Walking toward the back door to his home, I admired the portico that jutted out over the first floor, Greek columns giving it some sophistication. There was a comfortable-looking bench on the small porch. A side table held an empty beer bottle, and an old guitar leaned against the brick of the house.

"Okay. Now mind your manners," I told Fred as I knocked on the door, my nerves jittery after our last encounter. Putting thoughts of his Lovers card and that hot look he gave me away, I plastered a friendly smile on my face.

Within ten seconds, Nico was opening the door, looking heavenly as always. His hair was freshly washed, still damp, the longer strands sticking to his neck. In jeans and a black T-shirt, no shoes. At the sight of his bare feet, a rush of heat flushed my cheeks. The vision of us on a sofa and me massaging his feet hit me like a sledgehammer.

That vision was wrong. *Had to be.* First of all, they were feet, for fuck's sake!

Although to be honest, they were nice feet. Long and wide with a sparse dapple of hair, high arches, and that second toe longer than the big toe, which I'd read meant you were a dominant. I knew this because I also had a second toe longer than the big toe.

And he smelled, damn, like citrus and man soap and, wait, I sniffed. "What's that smell?"

"Bacon. Good morning to you too."

Clearing my throat, I glanced down. Fred was twisting his head about, obviously taking mental notes of his new realm. "Can I leave him right out here while we talk?" And for the foreseeable future until we can contain the orange demon next door?

Nico frowned, but rather than protest, he stared over my shoulder into the yard. "He won't fly over the wall?"

I scoffed and set Fred on the porch. "Nah. He's way too lazy for that."

"If you say so." He opened the door to let me in.

As I passed by him, I had the strangest urge to drag my nose across his T-shirt on a deep inhale, maybe circle his nipples while I was at it. Thankfully, I rarely gave in to my stranger urges.

That's a lie. I typically gave in to all of them. But this, whatever the hell it was with Nico, had me second-guessing myself and reining in those typical instincts that pushed me to do all manner of questionable things.

Nico closed the door and headed into the kitchen. I was surprised to find the indoor space entirely open. A large living room with fireplace overlooked the courtyard and garden. Right off the living space was a modern kitchen with gray stone counters and white cabinets, stainless steel appliances, and fitted with a small dining room table and tall black stools at a bar top.

"Wow. I didn't expect this." Most of these older homes were finished in a more classical style or still bore the old bones of when it was built with a touch of new paint here and light fixture there.

He was already at the stove, forking bacon out onto a napkin.

"Wish I could take credit, but it was newly remodeled when I bought the place."

"Suits you, though."

I glanced around. No, also a lie.

I categorically *examined* in hyper-speed every single thing I saw. A bookshelf with pictures, books, and what looked like journals that I wanted to study closer.

A soft gray throw on the sofa—my heart thudded—the *same* sofa from my vision of us snuggled together. I forced myself to move on.

I'd learned visions were only possible futures. Different decisions had different outcomes. So I wasn't going to ogle that couch and dream of snuggling with the werewolf. Especially when my original reading of us together haunted me daily.

Moving on, there was a coffee table with an open notebook and pen set aside. I could just make out on the page that there was writing and scratched-out words. A guitar on a stand in the corner. Several guitar picks in an ashtray on another end table with a pretty silver lamp. And yet another guitar, but this one mounted on the wall carefully in a place of honor. "Is that one special?"

Nico glanced up from where he was whisking eggs in a bowl. "My dad gave that one to me for my twelfth birthday." He kept his eyes on the bowl as he poured in a little milk, then kept whisking. "It's a Gibson Les Paul once owned by BB King."

"Whoa. That must've cost a pretty penny." I sat on a stool at the bar.

He nodded distractedly. "I started playing when I was about nine. Dad knew that music was my thing." His voice slowed and softened with affection when he spoke about his dad, then he glanced up. "You want an omelet?"

"Love one." I beamed, which got me a smile. "And by *thing*, you mean your insane talent at music."

He huffed a laugh. "Yeah. That."

I shouldn't, but I couldn't help it. We'd always steered away from too many personal things, but I needed to know. "What happened to your dad?" I stood and walked around the counter to wash my hands.

"He died when I was thirteen. That's when I went to live with Mateo, my uncle, and my grandfather."

I rinsed the soap from my hands and dried them on a towel, leaning back against his sink. "Sorry, Nico."

"It's okay." He gave me a smile that was small but genuine. No pain there. Or, at least, none too deep. "It was a long time ago. He'd lived a nice, long life for a werewolf. His heart just gave out."

"Really? How old was he?"

"Seven hundred and two."

"What?" Most werewolves were lucky to live to five hundred. "Shit on a cracker, how old are you?"

"Only a hundred and three, Violet."

I wrinkled my nose. "Old fucking man. Why didn't I know this about you?"

"You never asked." He poured some of the egg mixture into his hot pan, then dropped mushrooms, cheese, crumbled bacon, and purple onions on top.

"How do you know I like all that?"

He looked at me like I was dense and rolled his eyes. "You order a double bacon cheeseburger, add mushrooms, from Red Dog Diner every Friday." Oh yeah. I did.

"So what's going on with Fred?" He folded the omelet, then slid it onto a plate. He handed me the plate and tapped my hip, nudging me toward the dining table. "Go sit."

I did. "Mmm. There is nothing that smells better than bacon and melted cheese."

His gaze slid to me. Hot gold rolled through his eyes before he focused back on the skillet where he was making his own omelet.

"I figured you liked savory for breakfast."

"I like anything for breakfast. Love sweet too. Chocolate chip pancakes is a particular favorite."

"I'll remember that." He watched me take my first bite. "Tell me about Fred." There was a tad of a growl in his voice now, and I wasn't quite sure why he was getting wolfie at the moment. Not because I'd brought Fred, I hoped.

"So you see, Devraj got this dog—"

"Archie, yes, I know."

"How did you know?"

"Devraj and I see each other every week at Sunday dinner. Or didn't you notice?"

True. Jules had started a tradition of hosting Sunday dinner at the restaurant for us and the Cauldron family, if they weren't gathering with their own families. And now that included significant others like Mateo and Devraj. Nico had been invited one Sunday by Evie as an extension of Mateo's family, so he was kind of a permanent fixture there too.

"Violet." He said my name with force and emphasis.

I startled, sitting up straight, my heart pumping just a wee bit faster at the aggressive mention of my name. I knew in that very second that he would be super dominant in bed.

Stop it! I'd already nearly sniffed his nipples and was now conjuring images of him on top of me, saying my name with that deep, husky voice of his, talking dirty and making sexy demands.

He sat with his plate on my left at the head of the table and gave me an expectant look.

"Okay." I took a sip of juice he'd set on the table for me. "Archie keeps mysteriously escaping their yard into ours and chasing Fred and making him lose his fucking feathers. I don't want to close him in the pen with his chicken coop because he'll get depressed, and Fred is a very old rooster. He's delicate, even with Isadora's healing sessions, so I was hoping you might possibly allow him, because you love and adore me so much, to stay here in your courtyard while we figure out how the hell that Tasmanian devil is getting out of the yard." I put my hands together in begging style and did just that. "Pleaaase, Nico. Just for a few days. They're getting cameras and crap to catch Archie in the act, then we can solve the problem. And I'll bring him right back home."

For a minute, he simply stared at me, soaking in every part of my face, roving with painstaking slowness.

Shit! He was going to say no.

"Of course he can stay."

"Really?" I may have squealed.

"Sure. But I'll be gone a few days around the full moon. You'll have to come and check on him."

"Oh, I'll be checking on him every day." I shoveled more of his delicious food in my mouth.

"You're a nice guy, Nico."

His brow pinched. "You say that like it shocks you."

"Nah." I smiled and wiped my mouth with a napkin. "I just feel like I've been a total fuckface to you lately, so I guess I expected . . . I don't know."

"That's what friends do. Help each other out, right?" His expression was even, blank, though a muscle jumped in his jaw. He was so strangely serene and yet tense at the same time this morning.

There'd been weird vibes between us for the past week, and I was well aware that a good part of that was my fault. The strangest was that moment after the reading when he handed me my phone. "Handed" being a loose term here because he'd all but captured my wrist and screamed with his eyes that I was the other one involved in his *Lovers* premonition.

And don't think for a second that I hadn't jumped to the same conclusion. We'd built a solid friendship over the past year. And even though I knew because of my readings of us that we'd only crash and burn, the fight to keep from tying him to a bed and having my wicked way with him was becoming increasingly difficult.

I'd managed to restrain my lusty thoughts and longings before we went into business together. But now that I was with him so often, he was all I could think about. And let's not even get started on the wet dreams.

But then, there were moments like now when I wasn't getting any sexy vibes. Only Nico vibes. Usually one and the same, but he was radiating more walled-off aggression from behind a calm veneer. It was almost creepy.

"Yes, definitely," I finally answered him. "Friends." I smiled, then leaned over and punched him in the biceps. Those tight, muscular biceps. "You're the tits, Nico." Then I dove back into my omelet.

"You're so odd," he said with more lightness than earlier. "If that's a thank-you, then you're welcome."

"It is," I said around a mouthful of deliciousness. "Tits are great, right? Possibly the greatest body part on man or woman. So if you're THE tits, then you're like the best of the best."

He eyed me with those raised brows, and hell no, I didn't miss the fleeting glimpse at my boobs before he muttered, "You're the strangest girl I've ever known."

"But also the coolest. And most badass. And amazing."

"Absolutely," he agreed with too little enthusiasm for my taste, though his lips quirked with amusement.

He finished his omelet before me and took his plate to the sink. Then he returned and set a single key on the table next to me.

"What's that?"

"A key to my place. You'll need to store that bag of feed you left by the door in here."

"How did you know—?" I shook my head. "Werewolf olfactory senses, I presume." I took the key and looked at it. A single thread of magic zinged along my skin. Not sure why. It was just a plain, silver key, but my psychic abilities were stirring as I held it in my palm. "You knew what I wanted when I came in the door," I accused.

"Pretty much." He was leaning back against the counter, legs casually crossed at the ankles, arms crossed over his fine chest.

"I could leave the feed in the shop and bring it over."

"You may need something. Keep the key, Violet."

It was a command that saturated my pores and lodged somewhere in the middle of my chest.

"Okay." I licked my lips and put it in my back pocket as I stood, pretending I hadn't just been punched with werewolf dominance that was now buzzing sweetly between my legs. I picked up my plate. "If you insist."

He stepped forward and took the plate from my hand. "I do," he said nice and low, his fingers grazing mine. A wave of tension rolled between us in those two seconds, his gaze hot and hard, then cool and distant in a flash.

"Guess I'll see you in the shop." I backed up a step.

"Sure thing." He was at the sink, rinsing our plates.

"Thank you, Nico," I said sincerely as I stopped at the door. "I really do appreciate it." He looked over his shoulder, soaking me in with a brief flicker of sharp green eyes.

"Anytime."

The word was soft and deep, but also hard and smooth. How? I have no fucking idea. It wasn't the words that Nico said, but how he said them. How they sounded coming out of his mouth that made me weak-kneed.

I'd tried like hell to ignore my attraction for the man, but it was getting impossible to pretend I didn't have a huge crush. Infatuation. Borderline fixation.

But let's be real here. Any warm-blooded woman, or man for that matter, would be attracted to Nico. Take Lindsey, for instance. A flicker of a noticeably green flame burned at the center of my chest at the thought of her all googly-eyed, batting her lashes at him. Especially after he admitted he found her pretty. She was also really nice and a very talented artist, which I loathed to admit.

Wait! Was the Lovers card for Nico and Lindsey?

I buried an overwhelmingly nauseous feeling behind a layer of fuck-it-all. Swallowing the painful thought of Nico and Lindsey together, I strode to the shop to submerge myself in work where I could try to ignore all of these unwanted *feelings*. That niggling voice told me I wasn't going to be successful.

CHAPTER 7

~VIOLET~

I FILLED IN THE FINAL WHITE TOUCHES ON THE FACE OF THE BARN OWL on the hip of my client Tia. She was Isadora's best friend as well as Aunt Beryl's niece, a Conduit witch, a healer like Isadora.

"I was going to work on a spell for Conduits next, for you and Is, but I can't help but feel like I have to work on the were-wolves first."

"And by *feel*, I assume you mean your magic is telling you so." From her reclined position, Tia stretched her neck to watch my progress on her tattoo. Her shoulder-length black curls were pulled back with a red bandanna folded as a headband. The white ink on her taupe skin was a beautiful contrast. And though the white ink would fade some as it always did, it would remain a striking image on her smooth skin. "Then that's what you have to do," she stated as fact.

"I'm working on it. I've been meditating on a vision I had earlier this week. I had it while tattooing Nico and talking about a scar he got from his wolf losing control."

"Interesting. What was the vision?"

"It was all witch sign." I paused, wiping the excess ink from her hip. "Like my magic was trying to voice the spell but through witch sign. And it wasn't completely clear, so I was hoping to recapture it, but I haven't yet."

"Hmm. Does Jules have any books on witch sign?"

My head snapped up. "I'm an idiot."

"Not most of the time."

"I can't believe I didn't think of it." Sitting back, I shook my head at my own stupidity. "We only have the rarest book of witch sign ever recorded. *The Etymology and Definition of All Known Witch Sign* by Marigold Lord. It's a compilation of ancient knowledge and rare, even forbidden, witch sign. Ruben acquired it through Devraj when Mateo had that spell put on him and we needed help."

"Well, there you go. Pull that sucker out and comb it till you find the answer. Aunt Beryl's talked about that book, though she doesn't own a copy. Your answer should be there."

Feeling relieved, I finished Tia's tattoo, then cleaned and taped her up and wiped down the chair while she checked it out in the mirror.

"So cool, Violet. Your shading skills are killer."

"Thanks." I was really proud at how far I'd come from when I'd first started. It was good to hear her say that. "Let me walk you up front."

I gave Tom a little wave as I passed the doorway of his partition. He'd come in after I'd already started on Tia. He was working on his artwork on his Mac for the website, which Livvy had asked for.

Livvy said a soft opening with family and friends as clients while she got our website up and running would be best. Let us get our feet wet slowly, then make a big splash on social media to reel in new clientele and line up the calendars. We were of course listening to Livvy, the PR expert.

As we ambled to the front, Sean was already eyeing Tia. "Where's the tat?" he asked, dark eyes roving all over Tia. "Let's see what you got."

Tia laughed but pulled down the waist of her loose sweatpants anyway to show him.

"Ooh, nice." He grinned, leaning forward on the counter. "So you're a witch, right?"

"What makes you think so?"

Narrowing his eyes, he assessed her carefully. Or seemed to be anyway. "You've got that aura of mystifying beauty."

She smiled wide, then licked and pursed her lips. "Bullshit."

"What do you mean?" But he was laughing as she pulled out her credit card and set it on the counter.

"You're a fucking grim. And you're also a Blackwater, which means not only do you know every basic thing about everyone within a hundred-mile radius, you probably know every deep dark secret about them too."

Henry Blackwater worked for Ruben. He was Sean's older brother and seemed to collect every minute piece of information on every person living in the lower Garden District. He had his hands in everything but was also tied to no one.

I'd given his little brother a job here as a favor to Ruben, who'd asked on Henry's behalf. I was pretty sure it was paying back the favor for Henry's help in that whole blood trafficking ring debacle.

And the fact that I knew Henry's name made me utterly gleeful. Grims didn't even like people knowing their names. They were . . . odd. The strangest of the supernaturals by far. They collected info like data-drive hoarders and yet wanted no one to know anything about them at all.

Sean rang Tia up, still grinning to himself. To be honest, he wore a perpetual grin. He reminded me of a jackal toying with his prey. I had no doubt that when he grew older he'd become less scavenger and more predatory.

"Tell me, Tia." He handed back her credit card. "What does my aura do to you? What does it make you think about? Naughty things, right?" He winked.

Tia took the card and slipped it back into her bag, then signed the receipt and asked me, "He's not even eighteen yet?"

"Nope."

"Get ready, Violet. You're gonna have your hands full."

"I already have my hands full. He's more trouble than he's worth."

"That's a lie," interjected Sean, completely amused. "I talked two girls from my class into getting their bellies pierced when only one did at first. Doubled that sale."

"Bye, Tia." I waved her out the door. "Maybe you are useful," I told him. "When you aren't being a pain in the ass."

"Maybe?" That perpetual smirk suddenly dropped, and his eyes darted toward the entrance.

"What?" I glanced toward the door, but no one was there.

"I think you should go get Nico," he said steadily, his voice gone stone-cold.

"Nico isn't home. Said he had errands to run before he came in today. What's going on?"

But before Sean could say a word, the door opened, and four werewolves walked in. The guy in front was the blond I'd met with Nico that first night in Austin, the one he'd shown up at the party with. All four were covered in denim and leather and dripping with dominance.

Nico and I had never talked about his time with the pack in Austin or why he left. But something about the cold look in the blond's eyes and Sean's distinctly defensive stance had me labeling this little encounter an immediate threat.

Still, I wasn't afraid. Sure, werewolves could rip out a witch's throat faster than she could blink, but he'd have to actually reach me first. These guys had no idea what I was capable of, and I preferred it that way. Let them think that they were the actual threat and not me. Made things easier.

Blondie might've been putting off ultra-alpha vibes, but his aggression didn't seem to be projected at me. I was suddenly thankful Nico was out of the office, running errands.

"Hello, there. Can I help you? We're not open to walk-ins yet."

His smile widened, reminding me how handsome he was. If he wasn't stalking through my door, seeming to be looking for trouble, I'd say he was charming. The big werewolves behind him didn't bother smiling or playing it cool. They stood at his back, searching the place as if waiting for someone to jump out and attack.

"Guys, this is a tattoo parlor, not an ambush. Is there something I can help you with?"

Blondie whispered something over his shoulder, then turned back to me, ambling closer. "Don't mind them."

All three of them took a seat on the sectional, stiff as boards and on full alert.

"Name please?" I asked again.

"It's Shane. And you're Violet Savoie." His smile was sincere even as his gaze flicked around the room searchingly before returning to me.

"Nico isn't here, Shane. Would you like to leave him a message?"

He stepped forward, stopping inches from me, a little closer than I'd like, but I wasn't about to show unnecessary aggression. Not unless I had to.

"I'm not here for him. I'm here for you." His gaze swept over me, the brown of his eyes ringed in gold. "Is there someplace we can talk?"

"Want me to call Nico?" Sean butted in.

Damn. That kid didn't scare easy. These guys could rip him apart if they wanted to, but he didn't bat an eye at their menacing stares.

"No need, Sean. We'll be in my workspace."

I led Shane into my room and toward a table with two chairs on either side. This is where I'd discuss the details of the tattoo my client was looking for. But rather than follow me, Shane stretched out in the reclining chair where I gave the tattoos, crossing his arms behind his head. Since it would've been stupid for me to sit at the table so far away, I sat in my rolling chair next to the recliner.

"What do you want?"

He chuckled. "Is that how you greet all your clients?"

"You're not a client. You're a former friend of my business partner who's pissing all over my tattoo shop."

"Not pissing yet," he said, all teeth, his canines a tad long.

I crossed my arms. This dickweasel had his wolf half ready to shift while he had the audacity to sit and smile in my fucking chair.

"Look, Shane. I'm aware that you think you're a big bad wolf and your coming in here with your pack of dogs is meant to be some sort of intimidating display of prowess. But I'm not intimidated. Or impressed. What the fuck do you want?"

His charming smile slipped. *Good, dickhead. Now get to the point.*

He sat up in the chair, dropping one leg to the floor where he hooked his boot on the bar of my rolling chair and hauled me closer. He was so damn lucky he'd done that slowly. I would've knocked him across the room if he'd reached out too fast. But this was strangely slow and . . . seductive? What the hell was all this alpha fanfare about?

"Word is," he said, easing a hand onto the arm of my chair, "that you're giving special tattoos to supernaturals."

What the hell? How did he know that?

An incredulous "excuse me" was all that came out of my mouth.

"Don't play dumb."

"Where'd you hear this?"

He gave me a not-so-nice smile. "On the SuperNet. Where else?"

I stared at him, dumbfounded. The Supernatural Net, often called the SuperNet or SuperWeb, was an underground network that only supernaturals had the codes and access to. It was highly protected from hackers by the most brilliant grims in computer tech. If humans ever leaked through, they'd get a swift visit from a vampire who'd wipe their memories. And their hard drives.

"Oh no." It finally dawned on me. *Livvy.* We'd talked about advertising on the SuperNet, but not this soon. I wasn't ready! *What the hell?* Shit, I needed to text her to pull that down.

I jolted as Shane stroked his index finger over the back of my wrist. He'd reached out while I'd zoned out, trying to figure out how the hell he knew.

I arched a brow at him, pushing my rolling stool a few inches back.

"Is it true?" he asked unflinchingly, golden eyes watchful.

I wasn't sure why his wolf was on full alert or pushing him so hard right now, but that was another reason to make slow, calming movements.

"It's not a big secret," I finally said. "Though I didn't know my sister had advertised yet."

"So these tattoos are permanent spells, right? They can help supernaturals with what they want?"

"Look, I've only just perfected the charm for Auras. Each spell is specific to the supernatural and their magic. It's not like I can permanently spell love potions or some shit like that. It doesn't work that way."

I was more than anxious to know what kind of charm a werewolf with that look of menace in his eyes might want.

He laughed cynically. "It's not a love potion I want."

"What is it you want exactly?"

He swiveled his legs around and planted them on the floor, leaning closer with his elbows on his knees.

"Have you created a spell for werewolves yet?" Before I could answer, he curled his lip with a touch of disgust. "Probably not. I'll bet we're lowest on your priorities."

Offended, I crossed my arms and scowled back at him. "You don't know anything about me."

His expression went cold, rigid. "Known enough of your kind. The only way to get something we need from witches is to take it."

The harsh words and icy tone rose the hairs on the back of my neck.

"Listen, Shane," I said as calmly as I could, knowing his wolf was riding him hard at the moment. The last thing I needed was this guy and his buddies shifting into werewolves right now. Werewolves had to shift at least once a month at the full moon, but they didn't need the moon to shift. One more reason they were feared and ostracized by most supernaturals. "This isn't just a potion in a bottle you can take. It's a complex incantation and a kind of magic that hasn't been practiced in decades, maybe centuries."

"And you're the only one practicing it?" He lifted his brows, the menace leaking away with a note of amusement. This guy's Jekyll and Hyde mood swings were giving me whiplash.

"I'm actually trying to figure out the right spell for werewolves right now. That's what I'm currently working on." I almost added *jackass* but was trying to keep him calm so I refrained from my normal name-calling. "Nico has volunteered to help me."

Well, he never said as much exactly, but I knew he'd let me experiment on him till I got it right. Nico seemed to always help me when I needed it. My heart clenched at that thought.

"I'll bet he has." The darkness faded from Shane's gaze, but it was still hard, unrelenting.

Wow, if I could bottle the amount of disdain in that sentence, it would fill twenty jars.

"I'm working on it," I assured him. "It's not easy, these spells. I have no one to teach me, so I'm figuring it out."

"How long?"

"I don't know."

"Give me a time frame."

"I can't do that."

"Because you're lying," he accused and stood abruptly.

"I'm not *lying*."

"Need help in here?" It was Tom. Even though Shane had fifty pounds of muscle on him, Tom looked like he could and would take him if necessary. But I could take him and his pups up front if I needed to. Still, the heroic gesture made me want to hug Tom, even if he wasn't the hugging type.

"We're all good. Shane was just leaving."

The werewolf latched his hand around my wrist, not to hurt but to get my attention. "I'll be back."

"Sure thing, Terminator. And I'll be right here when you do."

"You're not afraid of me." He actually sniffed the air. Probably was using his wolfie senses to detect my heart rate and so forth.

"Not at all." I glared right back. "You should probably be afraid of me."

An ancient vibration thrummed through my body, packing electricity in my pores as if I had a one-way connection to a lightning bolt. A shift in the air, emanating from me, billowed my hair off my shoulders. I popped my neck and exhaled slowly, willing the primal pulse of my magic to simmer. The tarot empress tattoo on my forearm heated my skin.

Glancing down, I caught the slightest shift of her head and eyes, moving mystically, the inked moon above her brightening under my skin.

This was the first tattoo I'd given myself using charmed ink. It wasn't until after I'd given myself the tattoo that an incantation came to me in a dream. It was the same night I'd held that book by Marigold Lord. Ever since then, the empress on my arm had become like a guardian, warning me when I needed to heed a particular vision or premonition. Or when danger was near.

Like now.

Shane released my wrist with a huff, staring down at my arm with a bit of shock and surprise. This wolf had no idea who he was dealing with. That became more obvious when he belted out a cynical laugh, probably thinking his eyes were playing tricks on him or that I was only joking that he should be afraid. Or both. I wasn't, but whatever.

With a clenching of his jaw and another death glare, he marched for the lobby. I followed him out, then waited by the register until he and his goons had left the shop.

"Is that something we need to worry about?" asked Tom, appearing in the lobby.

"Nope," I assured him.

"Good." Then he returned to his workspace.

Sean glared at the door where they'd left, the stern expression so foreign to his usual demeanor. He looked a lot like his brother when he did that.

"You sure about that?" he asked.

"Nope."

"Want me to get Henry to watch the place?"

"No need. I can take care of it myself."

"A single werewolf is dangerous," he said, like I didn't already know this. "A whole pack is lethal. I can guarantee you that those four aren't the entire pack. There'll be more."

It was true. While all of the other supernaturals—witches, vampires, and grim reapers—had a solid governing body with hierarchy of heads of houses and covens, the werewolves did not. They were mostly loners except for those who traveled in packs, which was about as organized as they ever became.

"You can ask Henry to find out how many are in town. I'll report to Jules."

"On it." He pulled out his phone and started texting.

While I was positive I could take on any number of werewolves all by my little self, I was also aware that a pack roaming New Orleans with trouble on their minds was not good. Jules was going to be pissed about this, and I could only imagine how Nico was going to react.

CHAPTER 8

~NICO~

I'D MADE MYSELF SCARCE. I HADN'T LIED TO VIOLET. I HAD ERRANDS TO run but, honestly, I could've gone grocery shopping for my full-moon trip later. I'd found reasons to stay away from Empress Ink all day, because having Violet in my home had upset my entire being.

I'd grown accustomed to being around her and ignoring my attraction. It had become easy to tell my dick he wasn't getting any whenever he perked up around Violet.

But hell. Having her wander through my private domain, eat my food, sit on my furniture. It had made me want to lock the door and never let her leave. Now that was a crazy thought.

So wandering the neighborhood and doing any possible little miscellaneous thing, like browsing the liquor store to stock up for my couple of days in the woods, seemed the right thing to do.

After putting the box of six bottles of whiskey in my trunk, I thought maybe I was going overboard for a three-day trip.

The bottles rattled in the back of my Jeep as I pulled into my driveway behind the shop.

Mateo had texted and said he was coming by, which I'd totally forgotten about. He hadn't been by since we'd made renovations to the shop, and I wanted to commission a piece from him, a metal rendition of the logo, to stand in the center of the lobby.

Besides, I was being preposterous, I realized as I opened my door. There was no reason to be so territorial over— *Who in the fuck was that?*

A feral growl rumbled in my chest as the distinct whiff of werewolves hit my nostrils.

Leaving the back hatch of the Jeep gaping open, I followed the scent in long strides all the way to the front door of the shop where it was the strongest.

My wolf raged and pushed me to shift and rip open the door, but I shook my head, knocking some sense into him. For now.

Still, I was less than gentle when I swung it wide and stepped into the lobby. Sean was the only one up front, his gaze shooting to mine. He held up his hands in a calming gesture. "It's okay, Nico. Nothing happened."

But I could barely hear what he was saying over the raw ache to shift. The buzzing of rage heated my blood and filled me with the need to bite and claw.

Interlopers. Invaders. Frenzied fury burned through my blood. I wandered along the sofa, smelling the familiar scents of the guys from the Blood Moon pack. Then a very distinct one hit me, and it was coming from . . . Violet's workspace.

A guttural growl vibrated in my chest, my sight and other senses intensifying in a blink. I knew good and well my eyes were glowing when Sean murmured "oh shit" under his breath as I stormed by him.

When I stepped into her workspace, she was alone, but his scent was still there. She was sitting at her desk in the corner, sketching. Her eyes rounded when she saw me.

"Nico?"

I strode toward her in three long steps, narrowing in on the source. Grabbing her hand, I leaned over and lifted it to my nose, then skated up to her wrist.

There. That motherfucker.

"Nico."

Her voice was low and soft as I tugged her forward and smelled her hair, along her neck, across her shoulder. I needed to be sure he hadn't touched her anywhere else.

"You need to calm down."

No. Just the wrist. I swept my nose along her skin, the silky texture barely distracting me as I double-checked that it was indeed Shane touching my territory.

"*Nico.*"

I snapped my gaze to hers, realizing my wolf had taken over. Even so, I couldn't peel my fingers from around her wrist, subconsciously swiping my thumb across the delicate webwork of veins, needing to wipe away his scent.

"When was Shane here?"

Oh *fuck.* My voice was so deep. I was riding a razor's edge, literally about to shift right then and there. Glancing at my hand, I saw my nails had already transformed to black claws and were now abrading her silky skin. I flinched and dropped her wrist, then backed away.

She stood slowly. "It's all right. No need to go wolfie," she teased, even though her expression was a touch hard and grave.

Magic saturated the room. And not my kind. It was hers I tasted in the air, ready to erupt if necessary. I was aware she was a strong telekinetic on top of her clairvoyance, and I was pretty damn sure she was preparing to use her magic on me. Against me.

Pain, sharp and piercing, cut through my chest.

"Fuck," I growled, backing all the way to the wall, pressing the heels of my hands to my closed eyes, willing my blood to stop boiling to the surface.

The image of Ty flashed through my mind. His wide eyes, his fear, the bloody wound opening up his throat and shoulder.

"It's okay." She was close now, but I didn't dare open my eyes, afraid I'd grab her and bite her.

Because that's all I could think about right now, marking the fuck out of her so no other wolf could come walking in here, thinking he could touch her.

I was truly lost. This was so bad. We weren't even dating, but my emotions were a roaring avalanche of *mine, mine, mine.*

"Easy," she whispered.

I winced when her hands brushed up my arms to my shoulders, then back down. Then up again. Soft and slow.

"Everything's okay," she said again in that breezy, lovely way.

Almost immediately, I felt the raging heat retreating. She had no idea how close I'd been to losing myself entirely. Nor did she know how quickly she'd calmed the beast.

My claws retracted, while my heart slowed to normal. It took intense concentration to beat back the trembling urge to shift. Her gentle voice soothed the beast.

That was another thing about Violet. While her words were often crass and hard and profane, the timbre of her voice resonated with a raspy, musical quality that penetrated through centuries-old beastly DNA. If there was such a thing as a werewolf whisperer, she was it. Or maybe it was just me who responded to her in this way. The idea of other werewolves finding pleasure in the sound of her crooning voice lit another flame of fury in my gut.

"You're okay," she went on, murmuring soft assurances that all was well.

Still, I waited with eyes closed, sucking in deep breaths, fighting my wolf, swallowing the need to stake a claim that would prove to Violet that I was the wild animal all supernaturals thought us to be.

"It's all fine." Her lovely hands drifted up to my shoulders, her thumbs pressing at the base of my neck, a massaging squeeze before sweeping away again. The smell of her so close was doing the trick as much as her hands on my body and soft words, gentling the beast.

If I could open my eyes, grab hold of her waist, and pull her into me, hug her slender frame to mine, that would be the greatest feeling in the whole wide world. The sweetest balm to my overheated brain and body.

But we were friends, right? I'd said it this morning at breakfast because it was true.

It was also true that I wanted us to be far more than that, but I was afraid of losing this right here if I crossed a line she didn't want to cross with me. I'd rather have this than nothing at all. It needed to be her who made the first move. Not me.

I finally opened my eyes to find those gorgeous blue ones peering up at me, the most tender expression of concern on her face. I couldn't help but smile.

I'd never seen her look worried about anything. Pissed off, yes. Frustrated, yes. Furious, lots of times. But anxious about someone? Never.

"I'm okay," I said. The rustiness of my voice proved I'd nearly transformed, the internal shift having partially completed before I could stop it.

I reached up my hands to place them on her hips but then thought better of it. Straightening, I shifted sideways slowly, letting her hands drop from me. Again, a tiny stab to the solar plexus jarred my senses.

"You sure?" she asked, her expression still soft but now a little smile twisting her lips.

"Mm-hmm." I nodded, tucking my shaking hands into the front pockets of my jeans.

"I need to figure out that werewolf spell quick, don't I?" This softer side of Violet had me weakening further for her, wanting to cradle her close.

"Yeah." I cleared my rusty throat. "You can see now why that would be really helpful." I tried not to sound sardonic, but I did anyway.

She propped a hand on her hip and teased, "Thought I was going to get to see what the real-life *American Werewolf in London* looked like."

That was the Violet I knew. Each word was edged with a hint of playful sarcasm. Though I didn't like that the soft Violet had retreated, I was also glad she was treating me like normal. Not some bomb about to spontaneously combust.

Then she asked, "You okay?" Her brows raised high and her head tilted, sincerity etched in her expression.

"Completely fine."

"Completely, huh?"

"One hundred percent."

"So I can talk to you about your buddy, Shane, without you losing your shit now?" The door in the lobby opened. Sean greeted someone.

"He's not my buddy. Not anymore."

"I got that feeling. He—"

A sudden snarl from the lobby. *"Where are they?"*

"What the hell now?" Violet turned toward the door.

"Mateo," I answered on a sigh, following her back into the lobby.

Of the two of us, Mateo has always been the cool and controlled one. I should say *had* always been. Until this witch put a curse on him that had changed him permanently. Sort of.

When the curse prevented him from shifting each month, his wolf rose to the surface, speaking to him like his own personal little devil on his shoulder. I found it fascinating since my own wolf never actually spoke to me. We were much more aligned as one and the same, not separate entities. Which was why I'd always been cautious, especially after that tragedy with Ty.

The problem for Mateo was that after the curse was broken, his wolf, Alpha as he liked to be called, didn't go away. Mateo was still the thoughtful, sensitive artist, but Alpha often exerted his presence when he sensed a threat. Like he apparently did now.

He was leaning over the sofa, sniffing the back cushion. He jerked up, moved down the sofa, and did the same to the next cushion.

Evie was parked at the front counter where Sean watched in fascination, his eyes darting to Evie. Couldn't blame him. Her long auburn hair was pulled back in a ponytail, highlighting her pretty heart-shaped face. She was dressed casually, much like her sister Violet, in jeans and a T-shirt that read *The Dark Side made me do it.*

Mateo suddenly stood straight and turned on us, staring at Violet with raging intensity. He strode over, but before he could reach out and grab her hand to smell her wrist—because I knew exactly where this was going—I stepped in front of him and put a hand to his chest.

"Settle down, man."

"Where'd they go?" His eyes were full-on carnivorous gold, his voice barrel-deep.

"Christ. Is this what I looked like a few minutes ago?"

"Worse," said Violet, peeking around my shoulder.

"They're not here," I assured him, which eased his intensity by a single small notch. "Who are they?"

I heaved out a sigh, knowing he was going to rip into me. "It was some of the Blood Moon pack."

"Blood Moon?" Sean snorted. "Seriously? Can we be any more cliché?"

"Those assholes? I thought you were finished with them," Mateo accused.

"I was." Then, "I am," I clarified. "No idea why they're in town."

Evie hopped up to sit on the counter, completely unfazed by her boyfriend's frenzied behavior. "Alpha, they're not here, so cool your jets." Interesting that she knew when to address his wolf.

And just like that, Mateo relaxed, rolling his neck to pop it. But then he asked, still gruff, "What do they want?"

"That's what I was about to find out when you stormed in." I turned to Violet.

"Well?" She shrugged one shoulder. "He was asking about my charmed tattoos."

"How the hell did he know about your ability to do that?" I growled.

She sighed, looking a little despondent. "Apparently, Livvy posted something of an ad on the SuperNet about it."

"Already?" I snapped.

"It wasn't her fault really. I remember us talking about it, but I'd thought I made it clear I was still experimenting. I didn't want to promote it yet. Which reminds me." She pulled her phone from her back pocket and started texting.

A sharp tug of force pinched my chest as I thought of Shane returning and harassing her.

"You're not to be in the same room with him or any of them without me."

"Don't worry about them," she said swiftly, still texting Livvy.

I clenched my jaw so tight I heard something pop. My urge to dominate the situation—and her—was overriding all reason.

"They're dangerous," I added.

She huffed out a laugh. "I can handle them."

Then I dropped my voice low, taking a step closer to her. "But I don't want you to."

She put her phone back in her jeans pocket. A pinch between her brows was the only response as she soaked in my words.

Mateo stepped up between us. "I don't want a pack of fucking werewolves in our neighborhood, sniffing around my—"

Evie's laugh filled the lobby. She was leaning back on her hands, looking at Sean and laughing at something he was saying. He had that usual Sean smirk as he propped his upper body over the counter really close to Evie, whispering in a far too intimate way.

A growl rumbled in Mateo's chest.

"He's just a kid," I assured him.

But, apparently, in Mateo's state, or rather in Alpha's, that didn't matter. He marched across the lobby and took Evie's hand, then tugged her gently and firmly off the counter, shooting a death stare at Sean, who didn't seem to mind at all. Then Mateo scoured the lobby before he marched toward the partitions.

"Do you want a tour?" asked Violet.

I sighed. "He doesn't want a tour."

"What's he doing then?"

He returned from Violet's workspace in two seconds, then headed up the hallway toward the office area in long strides.

"We'll be right back," Evie called over her shoulder lightly, still being pulled around behind him as he stormed down the hall.

"What are they doing?" Poor Violet was so confused. There was a lot she didn't yet understand about werewolves.

The music that usually played over the speaker system I'd installed throughout the shop was on Violet's nineties playlist, currently pumping out Pearl Jam.

"Sean, turn the music up."

"Why?" asked Violet just as Mateo opened the storage closet, pulled Evie in behind him, and slammed the door. "Are werewolves always this weird?"

It wasn't strange at all if she understood our true nature. When a pack of werewolves came wandering into our territory, we wanted one thing. To enforce our dominance over what was ours. Short of pissing a circle around Evie, he was doing the next best thing.

There was a bump of something falling in the storage closet, then a rhythmic bang against the wall and Evie's somewhat stifled moans. But with my hearing, it was clear as day.

Violet snorted. "You're kidding me."

Sean turned the music up, but her moans got louder. So he turned up the music again.

"What's going on?" It was Tom, standing in the lobby. "I can barely hear myself think in there."

"Sean." Lindsey walked up the hallway from her workspace, the farthest away from the lobby. "Can you turn that down a little?"

Then all of us looked down the hall as a crescendo of moans peaked and the pounding against the storage room wall sped up with loud thumps. Something else crashed to the floor but the banging—literally—kept on going. Then it stopped altogether, the sexual groans subsiding.

Sean turned down the music, his grin saying everything. "Epic."

Lindsey, wide-eyed and blushing nearly purple, turned around abruptly and headed back to her room.

The closet door wrenched open, and Mateo stepped out holding Evie's hand and guiding her back to the lobby with a swagger.

Evie's ponytail was askew, her lips swollen, and there was a reddish bite mark on her neck.

She looked sex-rumpled and sated.

I was so damn jealous my head was about to pop off. Not that Mateo had fucked Evie and marked his woman in the closet, but because I wanted to do the same to Violet.

"Fucking werewolves," muttered Tom with a shake of his head and headed back to his workspace.

"Sorry," Evie said to Violet with a somewhat penitent expression.

Mateo didn't look remorseful at all. That smug son of a bitch let out a satisfied sigh and said casually, "Ready for the tour."

"Well"—Violet cleared her throat—"you know where the supply closet is, so why don't I show you where the magic is done?"

"We just saw that too," said Mateo, his voice back to its usual smooth timbre.

Evie snickered. Mateo smiled down at her, lascivious as ever, tugging her close to wrap a hand around her hip.

Violet stepped close and pointed a finger at them. "No more fucking in my shop," she hissed. "This is a place of business. You're not some damn teenagers. You can wait till you get home."

"Yes, ma'am." Mateo's smile hadn't slipped one single millimeter.

When Violet's gaze slid to mine as they walked away, I was struck with an unusual and awesome discovery. There wasn't just anger and aggravation gleaming from those bright blue eyes, but another emotion that punched me with devastating force. Lust.

Was it because that little display triggered her arousal in general? Or was it because she was imagining us doing the same thing? Like I was. Sooner rather than later, I was going to find out.

CHAPTER 9

~VIOLET~

"D<small>ID HE ACTUALLY START TO SHIFT</small>?" <small>ASKED</small> J<small>ULES</small>.

Ironically, Jules was the oldest of my sisters and the most powerful, but also the smallest in stature. Her bobbed hair, a deep shade of auburn, perfectly haloed her heart-shaped face.

"No," I said emphatically for the second time.

Ruben and Devraj sat on our living room sofa while Nico stood leaning against the shelving on the wall with our flat screen, hands in pockets, and not even remotely coming off as calm and collected as I thought he was trying to.

"Seriously, I'm sorry," said Livvy, looking as penitent as was possible for her from her spot on the love seat next to me. "If I had any idea it could've endangered you, I wouldn't have posted it on the SuperNet."

"I think you're all blowing it out of proportion." I ignored the huffing sound Nico made. "Yes, they were werewolves, and sorry to offend, Nico, but sometimes werewolves can behave aggressively. But that doesn't mean they intended to harm."

"We don't always intend it." Nico's gaze burned into me. "But it happens anyway."

Ruben had been listening in complete silence as I'd recounted my encounter with Shane at the shop. He sat in his typical three-piece suit, charcoal gray and expensive looking. He'd come over to the house as soon as I'd made Jules call him. Devraj arrived without warning at the same time.

"Nico's right," said Ruben, combing a hand through his perfectly styled blond locks, a silver skeleton ring winking in the candlelight. "Though I'd trust Nico and Mateo with my life, a pack of werewolves roaming the city with dubious intent isn't something we can simply ignore. They need to be watched."

Clara had started burning her happy candles infused with her Aura magic in the hopes to keep this conversation civil. So far, it actually seemed to be calming everyone's nerves.

Well, everyone except Nico, who looked like he was about to burst into flames at any moment.

"Nico," said Ruben calmly, "what are your thoughts? Is this pack a threat?"

"Yes," came his emphatic reply. He dragged his burning gaze from me to Ruben, clenching his jaw.

"Did he ever say what kind of spell he wanted?" asked Jules from her quiet place in the chair next to the love seat.

"No, he didn't." Which had bothered me. Frowning, I went on, "The thing is, these tattoos aren't like spells witches can do that can be for anything they want. The way this magic works is that it targets the magic-bearer and what he or she needs the most. That's why I didn't want to advertise yet. I want to be able to clearly define what this is before I start telling everyone."

"I'm *sorry*." Livvy looked despondent.

I reached over and squeezed her hand. "It's okay. I'm not saying that to make you feel bad." I turned to Devraj. "Like for Devraj, the tattoo I gave him works to quell his craving for blood. Because it's the one thing that works against his magic of vampirism. He's not like most vampires who enjoy that craving."

Jules shot Ruben a look, who merely lifted an eyebrow at her. I'd often wondered if she'd ever let him feed on her when they were together way back when. She looked back to me, her steel-gray eyes cool.

"And so now you're working on one for the werewolves?" she asked.

"With Nico's help, yes. If he's willing."

His grave expression softened a fraction. "Of course I will. It's you that would be helping me, anyway. Not the other way around."

"Do you think that Shane might want the same thing you do?" I asked.

I didn't want to expose Nico's vulnerability in front of everyone—his obvious shame about his lack of control—but I thought this was important information everyone needed to hear.

"Possibly," he said, a line crinkling at the center of his brow. "When I was a part of their pack, Shane seemed to relish the fights with other gangs. Other packs. But then there were times he'd admit he didn't . . ."

He bit back his words a moment, obviously struggling with confessing this weakness. I wanted to reach out and tell him not to, hating the look of anguish crossing his features. But he went ahead anyway.

"He didn't always enjoy the lack of control either. The instant violence that could come over us when the wolf was stirred up about something."

Jules sat straighter in her seat, hands clasped neatly in her lap. For one who coveted her self-control, she should have empathy more than anyone for their problem.

"Mateo struggled with this as well before Evie broke his hex," she said softly, seeming to remember something about that time.

"All werewolves struggle with it," Nico said, his voice gone deep, his wolf rising to the surface. A flash of electric green rolled over his eyes that he then blinked away. "It's part of the curse," he said with sad finality.

"The curse put on the first werewolf by a witch," I added with a hint of bitterness. "So it only makes sense that a witch be the one to finally help them."

"You can't make a werewolf no longer a werewolf," said Jules. "That ancient curse will never be broken."

The one put on them to curse every male descendant with werewolf blood in their veins.

"I know that," I snapped back, not angry at Jules but at the whole fucking situation. "I'm just saying that they suffer unnecessarily. And it's because of a witch that they do suffer. One of *our* kind. And this whole *no werewolves* thing has ostracized them to the point that no witch has ever helped them. It's fucking ridiculous."

I was aware that my voice was far louder and more aggressive than I'd intended. And it definitely wasn't Jules's fault. She was only following protocol of her higher-ups in the Guild and advice from our own mother who'd learned it from her predecessor when she'd spouted the same rule. Before Mateo came along anyway.

Ever since that first witch used dark magic to curse the first werewolf and every one of his male descendants, there had been a long-standing prejudice against them. Even in our enlightened age, it was still quite prevalent.

"Violet," Jules said softly, "it's not that we don't agree with you, but this prejudice has been going on for centuries. It's not like we can wave a wand and make it go away. Even if you're able to help Nico and others."

Not that witches used wands, but I got her meaning. Still, I was enraged. "I understand that. But just because something has been wrong since the dawn of existence doesn't make it fucking okay."

The silence thickened with tension. Livvy reached over and squeezed my hand for comfort this time. Clara, who'd been standing behind me and ghostly silent the entire time, reached forward and placed a hand on my shoulder. I was so ornery, I almost shrugged her off, wanting to hold on to my anger.

But rather than hit me with her happy juice, she let me feel my righteous anger and simply said, "Violet's right. This prejudice against werewolves only hurts the whole supernatural community. Not just werewolves. And Violet has the power to change all of that." I glanced over my shoulder, a little shocked.

She smiled sweetly. "Don't you?"

I nodded to my sister, then locked on Nico's gaze, which burned with intense adoration. My heart tripped faster.

"I think so." Clara squeezed my shoulder, sending me the confidence I needed. Sitting up straighter, I said with conviction, "Yes, I do. Once Spirit gives me the incantation I need." Jules spoke with perfect calmness as always, as if I hadn't just called our entire kind a bunch of self-righteous bigots moments before. "Your spells have always been innate. A few words, a little flirting with the new moon, and the right divination charm just falls into your brain."

At her words, a powerful pulse of magic rocked through my body. A vision of the slivered new moon popped into my mind, hanging above us at a witch's round in our back courtyard. Then a flash of Nico's face, his eyes electric green, his canines extended from his half-open mouth, a vicious expression reflecting the pain of his wolf transformation.

"Damn, why didn't I think of that before?" I whispered to no one.

"Think of what?" asked Jules.

"The ink for werewolves needs to be spelled on the new moon." I stood suddenly. "I need to go and check something."

Ruben stood as well. "I'll get my men on the lookout for this pack," he told Jules.

As the overlord of vampires in this region, his only immediate supervisor was Jules, so he reported to her.

She stood too. "Thank you. I'll alert my channels as well."

I left the room, quickly heading for Jules's library, needing to get my hands on that book by Marigold Lord. It was the physical connection I needed to confirm the vision I'd just had.

The book was a treasure trove of witch sign. Witch sign were markings we used in casting circles and spells, to channel our magic to do what we wanted it to do.

Think of our magic as being like a remote control, and the witch sign was like flipping the channels. The problem was, I didn't know what fucking channel to flip to for helping werewolves control their rage issues.

Maybe that was the problem. I was too focused on controlling their highly emotional nature, when their passion—whether it was violence or lust or something even stronger—was part of their nature. Maybe that couldn't be changed, even by strong magic.

Because that's what it came down to, I learned after a little light reading last night. If the wolf is threatened or someone they care about is threatened, then the only response is shift, then maim. Not even in that particular order.

There were hundreds of historical examples on the SuperNet. Since Jules was, well, Jules, I was able to study up on what others had found could help werewolves.

Know what I found?

Nothing.

Because no one seemed to have ever given it a shot. I supposed it all went back to the fact that the one who actually cursed and created the first werewolf was a witch hunted by the hunter she cursed. And since every generation of witches had kept werewolves on the outer perimeter of the supernatural circle, werewolves had never had access to the kind of magic they needed.

Witch magic.

Not until me anyway. Because I was going to fix this. I didn't give a shit if every witch and warlock snubbed their noses at me for doing it. They could all suck a bag of dicks. It was ridiculous that in the twenty-first century, they were still clinging to old prejudices that not only spread hatred but also danger and violence. The only way to heal old wounds was through mercy and kindness. And one thimbleful of fucking compassion.

Nico's face appeared in my mind. His expression was guarded despite his easygoing nature. I wanted to wipe that look from his face permanently. I didn't want him to doubt himself. To *fear* himself. How horrific to even contemplate that what lived inside you could do irreparable harm to a loved one against your own will.

I plucked the book off Jules's shelf, knowing exactly where it was since I'd been reading from it excessively lately. The book fell open in my palms to a page with a passage entitled *Black Moon*. This was another name for the new moon when it was fully in shadow, and the witch sign to call upon cleansing and transformation.

A rightness hummed through my body, magic singing through my veins. My psychic power whispered reassurance. "Yeah, that's it."

As for the incantation, my magic never failed me when the time came.

"Thank you for that."

I turned at Nico's voice in the doorway. His face was blank, but his rigid stance told me he was riddled with tension.

"For what?"

He blinked, a flare of tenderness sweeping from him. "For saying something no witch ever has." He glanced down at the book in my hands. "For trying to help us."

Swallowing the sudden well of emotion that tightened my chest, I said softly, "I'm not going to try. I *am* going to help you." My breath quickened. "I promise."

His gaze roved from my eyes down my cheek to my mouth, then back up, his haunted but grateful expression keeping me frozen on the spot. With a sad lilt in his voice, he said, "You already have."

Then he quietly left, leaving me with a hammering heart. But also new determination to use every ounce of magic I had to forever wipe away that look of painful despair from Nico's beautiful face.

CHAPTER 10

~NICO~

Mud boots. Rain slicker. A case of water.

I mentally checked off my list as I lined up the last items I'd need for my monthly trip. I'd pick up a few snacks on the way out, but I kept the cupboards stocked with canned soup if I needed. I rarely did, letting my wolf eat his fill of the wild game in the swamplands of Bayou Sauvage.

I rented the place from an old Cajun whose hunting days were long gone, but he wanted someone to still use the property. Of course, he had no idea I wasn't going out to take advantage of duck or deer season. I used it year-round, every month. The perfect place, far from prying eyes. And from innocent people.

As I chucked my hiking backpack onto the bed, my ears pricked. A soft voice and familiar scent drifted up from the courtyard. My senses knew who it was immediately. A prickle of awareness skated over my skin, drawing it tight. My adrenaline spiked and my cock twitched.

Combing my fingers through my hair, I shook off my body's natural reaction to her nearness. Or tried to anyway, then headed downstairs and into the courtyard.

There she was, sitting in the grassy side yard, her pretty head bent over Fred. For a second, my heart rate spiked. I glanced over at the fountain, but then realized she couldn't see the sculpture from where she was sitting.

Would it matter if she did? Maybe it would clear things up. Or maybe she'd think I was a creep.

I strode forward, trying to figure out if she was actually doing what it looked like she was doing.

"What in the world are you putting on him?"

She didn't glance up but kept on painting. "OPI nail polish, Aurora Berry-alis."

"No. I mean, why are you putting pink nail polish on a rooster?"

"He likes being fancy."

I paused a second before taking a seat in the grass across from her, stretching out my legs and leaning back on my hands. "You don't think he might want a more masculine color?"

"Real men wear pink, Nico. Haven't you heard?"

This woman. She was half crazy. And I loved it.

"Must've missed the memo."

"Well, that's why you have a well-informed and supersmart business partner."

"Of course it is."

She finished off a—a what? Toe? Talon?—then set Fred free. Rather than run to get away, I swear the damn bird strutted past, eyeballing me as he went. He puffed up his feathers, then meandered toward the fountain, pecking in the grass.

"How did you come to domesticate a rooster?"

She laughed. "He's not really tame."

We both watched him strutting through the grass.

"Well, he apparently enjoys pedicures and bow ties. I'd say that's pretty civilized." Her smile grew warm.

"What are you thinking?" I couldn't help but ask. Longing to discover everything about her, I always wanted to know what she was thinking. What she liked, what she disliked, what made her laugh and smile. What made her angry or upset so I could avoid doing any of those things.

"About how I got him. Jules had this call from a witch friend of hers. Her friend told her there was definitely some black magic being practiced in the house next door. So Jules, Livvy, and I went to check it out. We found evidence of animal sacrifice and some witch sign of blood spells. Dark magic."

My pulse lurched at the thought of her in the vicinity of danger. "Did the witch resist?"

Husky laughter bubbled out of her slender throat. "No way. Jules nulled her the second we walked through the door. The aura of black magic was heavy, and since it's a crime to practice, Jules didn't wait to ask questions. When we checked out the house, I found Fred in this cage on the back patio. He was so scrawny, but he was pissed off and still haughty as ever." She huffed another laugh. "Reminded me of an old aristocrat in one of those historical romance movies that Clara watches all the time. The ones that bluster about all snobbishly. His feathers on his head waggled furiously as he clucked at us. Anyway . . ." She sighed. "I took him home and fell in love with him."

Chuckling at that, I asked, "He's old, isn't he?"

"Yeah. Like way older than any rooster should be. Isadora's magic keeps him going, though."

Fred pecked at a bug or something in the grass in the corner of the yard. "So you and Fred have had a long relationship," I teased, still watching him.

"Look. I'm well aware that it's a sad admission that my longest-standing relationship has been with an ornery rooster."

When I turned back, I caught Violet staring. Interesting. I wish I was an Aura like her sister.

Then I could read her emotions and know what she felt for me.

Was it the same dizzying desire that I felt? Doubtful. I expended an inordinate amount of energy restraining my thoughts and feelings for her. I'd become adept at hiding behind casual friendliness. But Violet wasn't like that. Her emotions spilled out of her eyes and her mouth.

Her mouth. My brain took a detour to catalog all of her lovely features. This was nothing new, of course. If she actually knew how often I covertly stared at her without her knowing, she'd have put a restraining order on me by now. Stalking doesn't even cover my obsession with this woman. I've been coveting her from afar so long the ache in my chest has become an old familiar friend.

Still, I couldn't stop myself from taking advantage when I could. Like now.

At the moment, she seemed to be contemplating something quietly. I let her so that I could drink her in. The perfect slant of her jaw, rounding at a strong, feminine chin, was smooth perfection, reminding me of the sleek slope of the neck and headstock of my favorite guitar. The sharper jut of her cheekbones just a little too high on her face elevated her from pretty to striking.

Her smooth forehead and those feline eyes always alight with mischief. And that fucking mouth.

I could dedicate lines, pages, entire journals of poetry to the pouty curve of her lower lip when her expression was relaxed, and how those lips transformed into the most carnal seductress when they ticked up into a half-smile. If she would ever give me the green light to cross the friend zone, she'd have to beat me off her.

Her curious gaze traced the lines of my face, then flickered away, focusing on her lap while she twisted the top of her nail polish.

"I'll be gone a couple of days." I switched subjects, pretending my mind hadn't wandered onto a lusty path.

"I know." She rolled the bottle of nail polish between her palms, thinking. "How long exactly?"

"Be back Friday. But I'll have the shop looked after while I'm gone."

"I can watch the shop just fine."

Clearing my throat, I clarified, "No, I mean, should Shane and the others come back. They should be out of the city, too, but just in case."

She tilted her head, the lavender ends trailing over her breasts.

Fuck, don't look at her breasts.

It was hard enough to not get a raging erection whenever we were close like this, when I could smell the faint scent of body wash—lavender and lemon—and could feel the warmth of her body and hear the beat of her pulse.

"Nico." She jarred me out of my sensory overload. "I don't need anyone looking out for me." She smiled patronizingly. "You do realize I could beat the shit out of you and any other guy who came waltzing through my door unwanted, right?"

I nodded. I knew she had strong telekinetic powers, though I'd never actually seen her in action. "Still, Devraj and Ruben said they'd take care of it." My fingers drummed on my thigh.

"Just for my peace of mind."

Rather than make a big deal about it, thankfully, she rolled her eyes and said, "Fine. Whatever."

"You still have my key in case you need something for Fred, right?"

"Mm-hmm." She picked at the grass distractedly for a second. Then her gaze dropped to my forearms covered by long sleeves. "I'll need to give you the tattoo when you return. After I have a chance to spell the ink with the new moon. So think about what you want."

"I will. I'll have nothing but time to think while I'm out there." I blew out an exasperated breath, not meaning to sound cynical but knowing I did.

Her blue eyes flicked to mine before settling back on my covered arms.

"Did you want to see my sleeves?" Referring to the ink.

"Uh, yeah. If you don't mind."

She'd never asked before, but she'd stared often enough, always trying to get a better look. I scooted closer, my legs stretched out and crossed at the ankles, then pulled my sleeves up to show her.

She dropped her polish, then jumped up to kneel, sitting back on her heels. Leaning over, she grasped my right wrist first. "Wow." She trailed a finger along the blank line of evergreens, towering high, then around the full moon enveloped in wispy clouds and the eyes of the wolf woven into the trees like an optical illusion.

I had to swallow the moan of pleasure from just the tip of her finger trailing along my skin, igniting electric currents in my blood.

If she had any idea what she was doing to me, she didn't let on. She just let that arm go and grabbed the other, leaning even closer to the second scene, a continuation of the first arm with a cabin in the woods, a flock of ravens lifting off, and yet another wolf hidden among the trees. "This was Zaire's cousin's work, right?"

"Mm-hmm," I managed.

"He's so talented. Maybe I should've tried to steal him," she said on a laugh before tracing the eyes of the larger wolf again. "He looks sad."

I couldn't comment. Her loose hair had fallen forward and brushed against my skin at the wrist. I imagined what it would feel like brushing over my thighs with her head bent over my lap when she took me in her mouth.

Then her words drew me out of the gutter with a softly whispered, "I'm sorry."

Reining in some seriously lascivious thoughts, I asked, "About what?"

She sat back on her heels, hands back in her lap. "I guess I just never put myself in your shoes. The way it must be for werewolves. Until recently."

Here's the thing about Violet. She never held back her thoughts or opinions on any topic. Not once since the second I met her, except for the obvious monster of sexual frustration sitting between us. Usually, her thoughts and opinions were delivered with a heavy dose of sarcasm or mocking humor.

But the look on her face right now—soft sincerity—was gutting. It tore something open inside my chest. It made me want to curl around her, strip her naked, and fuck her on the lawn.

Then hold her close till the stars came out while I whispered words of adoration in her ear.

But she was still talking, and I kept perfectly still, willing myself not to reach for her.

"I did a lot of research, and I've just become so aware of how insanely stupid the supernatural society is."

"Come again." I couldn't help but smile.

"Bunch of goddamn pisswizards." She rolled her eyes disgustedly, a face I was familiar with but not when referring to the entire world of supernaturals. "I mean, sure, okay, I understand that the first, second, and maybe third, fourth, fifth generations of witches following the curse of the first werewolf would be total bigots about the whole thing. But we live in a modern age where people are supposed to be more self-aware. You know what I mean?"

"Maybe. Not sure. No." My grin grew as she blew out a breath of exasperation at my density.

"Someone should've helped werewolves by now. Witches should've made amends by now. You can't curse an entire species just because their great, great, great, whatever-the-hell grandfather was a complete fuckface, making life a shit show for all of his descendants."

"Actually, that's exactly what she did." I was amused, not upset by her tirade. Somehow, her anger lightened my mood. "Hence, the reason I'm shuffling off to the middle of nowhere for three days every month."

The pinch between her brows became more pronounced. She swallowed hard as she examined my face before clearing her throat.

"Well, I'm going to fix it," she said in that haughty way of hers. "Don't doubt it for a minute."

"You're making fun of me?"

"Never."

"Then why are you grinning?"

I shrugged a shoulder, unable to tell her that I couldn't help but smile when she said she was going to conquer the world because, one, I believed her and two . . . two . . .

I wanted Violet Savoie with every leaden beat of my besotted heart.

Before I could answer, my phone vibrated in my back pocket. When I pulled it out and saw who it was, I had to make a quick decision. Violet glanced at the screen, my phone flat in my palm. When her eyes widened and a frown puckered her brow, I knew what I had to do. I answered. "Hey, Layla."

"Hey! You've been busy lately. I can't seem to reach you these days."

"Sorry about that. We've been slowly opening the new business, and it's taken a lot of my time."

"Well, I wouldn't bother you, but Gigi misses you. And she's been begging to talk to you. Hang on."

A shuffle, then that sweet angel's voice said, "Hey, Uncle Nico."

I softened my own voice as I always did when talking to Gigi. "Hey, sweetheart. How was your week?"

"Awful. Mr. Bobo got dropped in the toilet and Mama had to wash him in the washing machine and his eye popped off."

I chuckled, very aware of Violet's gaze on me as I stared down at my lap.

"Sorry to hear that. But all good now, eh?"

"Yep. When are you gonna sing for me? I need it so bad. Mama tries, but she just doesn't sound so good."

"Soon. I promise."

"'Kay!"

Then the phone was quickly passed back to Layla. "So I guess you'll be off the radar for a few days, right?"

She knew I was unavailable around the full moon but never pointedly talked about it. She also knew it was the reason she never saw me in person. Nor did Gigi.

"Yeah. But I'll call as soon as I get back and make it up to her."

"I know you will. Gotta get going to dance lessons! Love ya, bye!"

"Love you, too." Then I clicked it off.

Most people would've been polite and casually explained why they'd had to take a call. Especially if it was someone important to them. Someone they obviously loved. And by the questioning look on Violet's face, she damn well wanted to know. I also knew that she wasn't going to ask because she was one stubborn woman.

I should've been nice and told her who it was, alleviated any misunderstanding, but I was done playing nice. Violet had already put me safely in the friend zone, keeping me at a far distance from where I wanted to be. The only way to get closer was to make her come to me.

And I had no problem playing dirty to get what I wanted.

"I better go finish packing." I casually stood and offered her a hand.

For a second, she just frowned at my hand.

Go ahead. Ask me, Violet.

But she didn't. Just stuffed her nail polish in her back pocket. I could feel the anger vibrating off her as she cleared her throat.

"Guess I'll see you when you get back then," she snapped, looking up at me.

It took everything for me not to laugh. But then she took my hand, and I pulled her up, keeping her close. She peered at me, a storm of emotions sweeping those ethereal eyes. I caressed my thumb over the back of her hand and across her knuckles.

"Be back as soon as I can."

"No worries," she said lightly, covering the anger, the envy I'd caught a glimpse of a moment before. "I'll manage any inventory issues till you get back. You go do your thing. Run wild and kill animals and such." Her expression turned thoughtful. "Do you actually eat raw meat out there? Like animals that you kill?"

"You really want to know?" She didn't seem the queasy type, but I wasn't sure.

"Yeah."

"All the time when I'm the wolf. We get really"—I tilted my head in thought—"primal this time of the month."

I recognized my voice dropping several decibels and the low growl rumbling against my rib cage. I also realized that she hadn't pulled her hand away and I hadn't let her go. She studied my face, gaze darting from my eyes to my jaw to my lips, then back again.

"Guess you can't help it," she said rather low. "Kind of part of the whole wolf package."

"Does it bother you?" I stroked my thumb over her inner wrist.

"Uh-uh." A shake of the head, her silky blonde/lavender hair sliding over one shoulder, reminding me how badly I wanted to wrap it around my fist, hold her down, and fuck her senseless.

Damn. Too close to the full moon. My impulses were running riot with my fantasies of taking this woman and making her my own.

"Good thing," I said. "Don't think a spell can change that."

"I wouldn't want it to."

Raising an eyebrow, I asked, "No?"

"You can't help who you are, and I—" She shrugged, slowly pulling her hand out of mine as she dropped her gaze. "I like who you are."

That was no small admission from the tough girl who rarely showed emotion of any kind.

But here she was, being vulnerable. For me.

"Good to know," I finally answered, voice rusty. And it was. Not everything I wanted to hear, but definitely an admission that would warm me over the next few days in that cabin in the freezing-ass woods.

I was about to reach up and squeeze her shoulder in farewell when her phone buzzed.

Swiping it on, she checked the text and blew out a sigh. She texted back with quick fingers.

"What is it?"

"It's Livvy. Our cousins and Travis just got in."

My entire body tensed. Their cousins were cool. Actually, so was Travis. But Travis was also a serious player, and I never knew if his playful flirting with the Savoie sisters was real or not.

"They're in town for a while?" Okay, that sounded completely casual. No territorial vibes were in my voice even though my wolf was already bursting at the seams.

"Just tonight. They had some business with a liquor distributor in town about their new microbrew line."

The three of them owned Bayou Brewery located in Lafayette, Louisiana, farther west in Cajun territory. Any time they were doing business near New Orleans, they stopped in to see their cousins.

She tapped a few more lines in a text, then sent it. "Guess my afternoon of organizing that damn supply closet is out."

"Y'all going out?"

She snorted a laugh. "Yeah. Every time they come here they demand we take them out even though they sure as hell know more nightclubs in the city than we do. Well, maybe not Livvy, but still."

"You don't have to go," I offered all nonchalant. Or at least I thought it was till she glanced my way, that simmering smile of hers making me weak in the knees.

"You wanna go? Because I could totally use some help wrangling these asshats. They can get ridiculous when they drink."

With a microsecond's time to think it over, I nodded. "Sure. I wasn't planning to head out of town till the morning. I can even be designated driver tonight."

"Great!" She walked away backward, grinning. "But don't be mad at me when their shenanigans aggravate you. With the exception of Drew, who typically plays the role of cackling voyeur, Cole is the devious one and Travis is just a big man-child."

I smiled back, pretending I wasn't already riddled with anxiety about going out with these guys. I was feeling the pull of my wolf as the full moon drew closer, but I also knew that I wasn't about to sit at home and let Violet go out with these guys alone.

If they were truly reckless, then I needed to be there. This wasn't a city to be too carefree in, especially with the tourists pouring in for Mardi Gras.

"Text me the details," I called as she turned and walked back across the courtyard toward the back entrance to the shop. She gave me a wave, and I watched her go, one of my favorite pastimes.

I hated leaving her for even three days every month. And something told me that this month it was going to feel colder and lonelier than ever out there by myself.

CHAPTER 11

~VIOLET~

"Violeeeeet!" Three gregarious, masculine voices sang my name as I entered the Cauldron. I couldn't help but laugh at the doofuses at the bar, apparently already a couple of drinks in.

"There's our girl. Where ya been?" Drew pulled me into a tight hug first, squeezing the life out of me. His positive vibes seeped into me.

He was an Aura like Clara and had that same magnetism, just on a masculine level.

"Yeah, we've been waiting forever." Cole pulled me in with one arm, his other clinging to his half-empty mug of draft beer.

"Y'all do know that I just started my own business, right?"

"That's why we're here, gorgeous," said Travis, spinning me around and bear-hugging the life out of me as he lifted me off the ground. He smacked a kiss on my cheek before releasing me. "We had to come celebrate since we can't be here for that street party thing."

"Y'all look like you've already been celebrating awhile."

"You took too damn long," said Drew, his brilliant smile in place. "Livvy, Is, Jules, and Clara already came and ate dinner with us. Livvy and Clara just went home to change."

Jules never went out with us when the boys came into town, always proclaiming to be too old for that crap. Well, I was feeling a bit old myself these days, working so much. But here I was anyway. And I can bet Isadora made excuses to slink away to Dev's house. She'd rather swim laps in a vat of acid than go to a crowded bar, and the guys knew it. So they never pressured her to go out.

"Sorry. I had to do a few things before I left the shop. Where's Evie? She didn't meet y'all for dinner?"

Travis rolled his brown eyes, combing his auburn hair back away from his face. "That witch broke my heart. Shacking up with a werewolf, I hear."

"Yeah, Jules said she left town this morning with him for his monthly."

For some reason, the mention of Evie going with Mateo on his full-moon trip sent a tingle down my spine. And a little longing I pretended I didn't feel.

Travis snickered like a child. "Sounds like you're talking about their period or something." Cole leaned back against the bar. "Might as well be. They get all temperamental and mean. Just like chicks do when—oof!"

I punched him none too lightly in the stomach. "First of all, stop making fun of werewolves. And second, stop making fun of women. Without women and their periods, you wouldn't even exist on this planet."

"Okay, okay." Cole raised his palms in surrender, then his eyes twinkled as he whispered, "Do you happen to be on your period?"

Cole set his empty mug on the counter.

"Want another?" asked JJ.

"Naw, man. You can close out our tab."

Narrowing my gaze at Cole, I then pointed at each of them. "Behave tonight. Nico is joining us. As a matter of fact, he's playing designated driver, so be nice."

"Awesome. I like Nico," said Drew in his ever-pleasant voice.

"Here you go, man." JJ slid a credit card to Cole and the ticket.

"You want to come meet us out?" I asked JJ. "You'll be off soon."

JJ glanced at his Apple Watch, checking a text or something. "Um, no. I've got plans." When he glanced back at me, there was a distinct flush of pink on his cheekbones above his beard.

"Really? A date?" I leaned over, elbows on the bar.

He tossed a bar towel over his shoulder. "None of your business."

"Since when? You've always told me everything." He chuckled nervously, glancing down at his shoes.

My eyes bugged out. "JJ, you're *nervous*." Which could only mean one thing. "Does your date happen to be about six feet tall with dark blond hair and devilish blue eyes and the snarkiest mouth in the South?"

JJ's complexion turned crimson, and I burst out laughing in complete shock. But before I could demand more answers, he shooed me away with a flick of his bar towel.

"Go have fun tonight. Be safe!" Then he walked away to another customer with a shit-eating grin on his face.

A giddy thrill shot through me that JJ and Charlie might actually be moving out of the friend zone. It also made my thoughts stray to Nico, wondering about our situation. And if I should be considering the same thing.

"Okay, boys! Let's go." Livvy and Clara burst through the kitchen door, having come through the back alley exit, which was closest to our house.

"Hot damn!" exclaimed Travis, pressing a palm over his heart and pretending his knees buckled. *Drama queen.* "You Savoie women are a full-blown smoke show." No doubt, Livvy and Clara would turn some heads tonight.

Livvy had on a tight black minidress with black thigh-high boots and a red leather bolero jacket that ended above her narrow waist. Her silky black hair and red lipstick alone would be drawing eyes.

Clara was her complete contrast in a pale pink minidress that showed a vee of creamy skin and lots of leg. Her brown leather boots made the outfit more casual, though she typically wore cute flats most of the time.

"Oh hell," I exclaimed, realizing their footwear signified where we were headed. "We aren't going to the Quarter, are we?" Boots were protective gear for the filth on the streets of the Quarter, which was highly trafficked by drunkards.

Travis barked out a laugh. "We always end up in the Quarter."

I rolled my eyes. "Y'all. It's Mardi Gras season. It'll be packed with tourists. Let's stay on our end of town."

"Your werewolf is here," said Cole with a tilt of his head toward the door.

Before I could ask why Cole would call Nico my werewolf, my head swiveled to the door as the man himself stepped into the bar, looking fine as fuck. Dark jeans and shirt with a brown leather jacket. Nothing out of the ordinary there. But the disheveled, wild look about him, the intensity of his gaze as he found me across the bar, was wreaking havoc on my body parts.

Specifically the ones below my waistline.

He walked up with confidence and gave each of the guys a manly handshake. "So where are we headed?"

"I've got a cool new place for us." Livvy grinned far too excitedly. A pulse of magic radiated from her, followed by the sudden urge to agree with whatever she said.

"Stop using magic to try to make us follow your plan," I ordered.

"No worries," said Travis, grinning. "I'll follow you anywhere, Livvy."

Cole slapped the back of his head. "Stop looking at my cousin that way."

"I always look at them this way. They're gorgeous, man."

I'd noticed Nico easing closer to my side. Right now, he was partially behind me, his chest pressing into my left shoulder. I was getting all the possessive vibes even though there was no need. I mean, they were my cousins. Travis might not be, but I looked at him like a brother. Still, I was enjoying his proximity, so I'd just let it roll.

"Who's with me?" asked Livvy, ignoring the boys' bickering.

"Me!" yelled Travis.

Cole shoved him in the chest toward me and Nico. "No, you're not. I am. I want to talk to her about some social media stuff anyway."

Cole was an Influencer like Livvy. Even as his broody self, he still wore an aura of magnetism just like she did. What he didn't have was her skill set in promotion on social media, so every time we were together, he liked to pick her brain for the brewery.

"I'm parked out front," said Nico, nudging my hip toward the door.

"Come on, beautiful," said Travis, offering an arm to Clara, "come keep old Trav company." She laughed, looping her slender arm through his as they headed toward the front.

"I sent you a text where we're going," Livvy called to me.

We strolled out into the brisk night air. Nico made a point to open the front passenger door and nudge me into the seat with a palm to my back. I didn't comment, even though I knew he was trying to corral me farther away from good old Trav.

Once we were buckled in and headed out, I checked the address and plugged it into Google Maps.

"Where we going?" asked Nico.

"The Brat Pack? Never heard of this place. Keep going straight."

I stayed focused on the road while Travis carried on loudly in the back seat. "Seriously. Give me your hand."

I twisted around. "What are you doing?"

"Reading her palm."

Clara gave me a questioning look. "Can he really read palms?"

Travis was a Seer, but what worked for one seer might not work for another. "I don't know. Can you?"

144

His aggravated look was amusing because the man never looked serious and he was trying so hard to look stern and offended. "I can. I'm a fucking psychic."

"I'm a psychic, but I don't read palms," I argued.

"You're better at scrying in water," he admitted. "And I'm not good at that, so it is what it is."

Turning back to my phone and the road, I directed Nico on the next turn even though my Google Maps chick gave the audible directions right after me. We were heading toward the central business district while they gabbed in the back seat.

"This must be a new place because I've never heard Livvy mention it before." Nico was quiet. Tense. Broody.

"You okay?"

He glanced my way, unable to remove his scowl quickly enough. "Yeah. Just, uh . . ." He peered up through the windshield and pointed a finger upward. "Getting close, you know?"

I nodded, because I actually did. The closer it was to the full moon, the stronger the wolf was, urging the man to let go and let him take the reins.

"You sure you can handle coming out with us?"

That earned me a condescending look. "I'll be fine."

My Google Maps chick said in her robotic voice, "You've arrived at your destination."

We were outside a high-rise with a long line wrapped around the corner. The Brat Pack was illuminated in a neon sign over the black double doors.

"There's a parking garage right down here."

Nico zoomed ahead, turned into the garage two blocks down, and stopped to take a ticket at the gate.

"No way!" Clara's laughter pulled my attention to the back seat while Nico found us a parking spot.

"What?" I twisted around.

Travis held her hand, grinning at Clara's laughter. "Damn, you give much better happy drugs than Drew."

He was obviously referring to the blissful feeling people felt when they touched Clara. She couldn't help but exude her magic when someone touched her, like it was innate to zap them with joy. Just in case they needed it.

Ignoring his comment, Clara beamed as she told me, "Travis said I'm going to live a very long life."

"Like how long?" I asked.

"Over nine hundred years!"

"Travis! Stop making shit up."

"I'm not!" he defended himself.

"Witches only live like three or four hundred years on average."

"Doesn't matter." He shrugged, letting go of her hand. "The palm don't lie."

"And," she emphasized, "I'm going to be happily married to one man and we're going to have seven kids together. Six boys and one girl."

I burst out laughing and shook my head at Travis. "I think you got a drunk reading, Clara. Don't listen to everything he says."

"I ain't drunk," he protested. "On the happy side of tipsy, maybe, but I'm telling you. I'm right."

"Whatever, Nostradamus." I gave Nico a disbelieving look. "Let's go check out Livvy's new hot spot."

CHAPTER 12

~NICO~

THIS NIGHT NEEDED TO END. SOON. I NEEDED TO GET OUT OF HERE and get out of town, let my beast take over and hunt for blood.

After three hours of watching Violet, her sisters, cousins, and Travis drink and dance in this crazy-ass place, my patience was teetering on the edge.

I'd lied to Violet when I told her I was perfectly fine going out so close to the full moon. I wasn't fine. I was being clawed and maimed from the inside out.

Every time a man looked at Violet or touched her or tried to dance with her, my claws would slice out, and I'd have to close my eyes and do a Zen-like countdown to slide them back into my skin.

Devraj had encouraged me to try yoga to try to reel in my impulsive anger, but that wasn't for me. Still, I'd tried the breathing technique along with blocking out whatever was triggering the rage. So far tonight, I'd counted to twenty multiple times.

The club was showered in bright colors, neon lights, and eclectic memorabilia from the eighties on the walls. For example, in a place of honor, in glass cases against the back wall of one bar, in between rows of expensive liquor, was Duckie's shoes in a blue-lit shadow box and Andie's prom dress from *Pretty in Pink*.

Scattered around the floor-to-second-story ceiling were popular quotes from films. They were scrawled on large art boards in different handwritings to match the character they came from. One from *Sixteen Candles* read, *Can I borrow your underpants for ten minutes?* Another was from *Ferris Bueller's Day Off*: *Life moves pretty fast. If you don't stop and look around sometimes, you could miss it.* But the one that made me laugh the most was from *The Breakfast Club*: *If you mess with the bull, young man. You'll get the horns.*

This was a place for a specific audience. But eighties retro was in, so whoever came up with the branding and marketing was clever.

When Violet headed toward me where I stood next to the bar, watching their jackets—basically, I was the coat-check guy for the night as well as chauffeur—the knotted tension in the center of my chest eased.

Reaching for her jacket, she grabbed hold of my shirt, clenching her fingers into the fabric when she stumbled a little. She was a bit drunk. "We're leaving?"

Please, heaven above, let us be leaving.

"Yep." She emphasized the *p*, grinning up at me. The knot loosened further when she looked at me like that. "Headed to the Cat's Meow next."

"You're kidding."

The Cat's Meow was on Bourbon Street and would be packed as fuck with rowdy tourists.

Now I was more than glad I'd suffered through the night so far.

No way could I let her enter that cesspool without being there to protect her, especially after she'd been imbibing all night and Shane and the Blood Moon pack were somewhere in this city. Unless they'd already left for the full moon. All werewolves sought out remote, rural areas for the monthly shift.

Laughing, Violet shook her head, glassy gaze roving over my face. She lifted a hand and pressed a finger into the divot at the center of my chin. "I like this dimple thing."

"How much have you had to drink?"

"I only had four Molly Ringwalds. No, five."

I'd watched them make every one of her drinks, making damn sure nothing got dropped in it before it found its way into her hands. So I knew what she'd had already. I was just trying to emphasize to her that she'd probably had enough.

"It was five," I confirmed.

The others crowded over, snatching up their jackets.

"Oh no! I love this song!" screamed Livvy, drunker than I'd ever seen her, as "Fire Woman" by the Cult started pounding through the place.

Her level of inebriation didn't surprise me. Probably because the bartenders didn't skimp here. They used quality liquor too.

"Come on, Livvy," crooned Travis, pulling her close. "Time to sing me a lullaby." Cat's Meow also happened to be a karaoke bar. Great. Couldn't wait.

"Dammit," Livvy grumbled, watching some guy approach our group. "Not him."

Before he'd even gotten within fifteen yards, my senses pegged him as a grim. Dressed professionally in black pants and a white button-down with a jacket, he marched right up to Livvy, ignoring the not-so-welcoming looks of the men around her. He had dark hair and eyes, pale skin. It was a gut instinct to want to protect her since it was obvious the hellfire coming out of her eyes meant she didn't like this guy.

"Livvy," he said softly, still ignoring the fact that she was surrounded by three big warlocks, two witches, and a grumpy werewolf. "I didn't know you came to this club."

"Why would you? It's not your place to know my comings and goings." She fought to sound haughty and condescending, but her slight sway and slur from the drinks took off that edge.

"Just thought you might've mentioned it." His mouth lifted into a crooked smile. "This club has some high-end marketing. Would've been something to add to the PR group."

"I'll add what I think is relevant to our group discussion," she snapped back.

What the hell were they talking about?

"Excuse me," said Violet. When she went to lean forward, I gripped her hip to keep her close to me. "Who are you?"

When he turned to introduce himself, Livvy planted a hand on his chest and pushed off him toward the door. "No one. Let's go!"

"Fine by me," said Travis, trailing after her, the rest of us following.

Grims were an odd bunch. I was even more convinced of the fact when I glanced back at him to see him chuckling to himself rather than simmering with anger at her insult.

Once outside, we made a quick decision to taxi our way into the Quarter rather than drive. We hailed a minivan cab and crammed inside. The parking was hell down there, especially at this time of night. Much easier to get a cab in, then make our way back here later.

He dropped us on the edge of Jackson Square along Decatur Street. From there, we meandered down Chartres to intersect with Bourbon.

The drunk partygoers were out in droves, flooding in and out of bars. I didn't know what Violet thought when I grabbed her waist and pulled her close after a hulking guy stumbled out of a pub and nearly rammed into her. I didn't let go afterward, and I didn't care if she thought I was being too handsy. The only way to keep from losing my temper and slicing people with my claws was if I kept her close to me. Where she was safe.

As the cousins and Travis took the lead, pushing through the crowd and parting it like the Red Sea, I stayed in the rear with the ladies.

Yes, New Orleans was a fun party town. But when you mix shitloads of alcohol and thousands of people in a matchbox of space, it's always a cocktail for violence. I just wanted to be sure I'd be ahead of it and keep all of them safe if it came to that.

A prickling of my senses made the hairs on the back of my neck stand on end as we made our way to the entrance of the Cat's Meow. I surveyed the crowd meandering down Bourbon but didn't see anything out of the ordinary. Still, my wolf senses were on high alert.

"Come on!" Violet grabbed my hand and yanked me toward the entrance.

"How'd we get in that fast?"

Violet snorted. "We have two powerful Influencers working their magic."

Sure enough, Cole and Livvy were dazzling a waitress who not only squeezed us in ahead of a few others but found us a nice table dead center of the karaoke stage. I'd complain about that being cheating if I wasn't so glad to get inside. The sooner we got in, the sooner we could leave. Or so I hoped.

As we found our seats, Clara was already listing songs she wanted Drew to go up and sing with her.

The MC on the stage thanked the burly guy closing out a country song. "Let's give him a hand! Never heard a Garth Brooks impersonator quite like that."

The crowd laughed, so he must've been pretty bad. The burly guy stumbled back up the steps and took another bow to rowdy laughter.

"Next up, we've got a nineties fave. Please welcome Rosy and her sister Talullah singing 'No Scrubs' by TLC!"

Cheers erupted as the curvy women did their thing. They seemed to have practiced a few dance moves for this one, even as they half-laughed, half-sang into the mics.

"Hurry and pick your songs so we can get on the list fast!" yelled Clara over the noise.

Violet grabbed my forearm and shook it. "What are you singing?" she asked excitedly.

Shaking my head, I nodded toward the rest of them. "You guys enjoy this. I'm not getting up there."

I wasn't afraid of the stage, obviously, but I didn't like crowds like this. I preferred laid-back and mellow. That was the reason I'd decided not to pursue a life in the limelight when I had the chance. Well, one of them anyway.

"Booo! Party pooper," Violet teased.

Travis was on her other side and started rattling off some songs that he wanted her to do.

"No, not that one," she complained.

"Oh, come on," he begged. "I want to hear you sing that again like you did at our party in Lafayette."

"Why?"

"Because it was fucking hot!"

She laughed and shook her head at him. "Fine, fine, whatever."

Now that was interesting. They'd had a karaoke contest at the Cauldron not that long ago, but Violet didn't participate.

Leaning to my left, I asked Livvy, "Can Violet sing?"

She blew out an exasperated breath. "Can she sing? Just you fucking wait, werewolf." She grinned lasciviously.

The night rolled on. Clara and Drew sang a horrific rendition of Rihanna and Eminem's "Love the Way You Lie." There was heckling and laughter from the audience when neither of them could hit the right key to save their lives. And still, they were brimming with laughter the whole time.

Livvy managed to belt out a very decent version of "When Doves Cry" by Prince. She had the deeper register for it. Then there was a highly entertaining performance by Cole, Drew, and Travis to the Beastie Boys' "Fight For Your Right to Party," which practically set the place on fire.

When it was finally Violet's turn, that twisted knot returned tenfold. Not sure if it was because I was feeling anxiety about her performing in front of a wild, drunk-as-fuck audience like this or that she was on display and I just didn't want her to be.

She smiled and waved to the whooping catcalls that greeted her when the MC called her up.

She was perfectly at ease.

She wasn't dressed up like the others, wearing her usual faded jeans and a long-sleeved lavender top. But the woman was fucking gorgeous regardless. The lights highlighted her creamy complexion, her vibrant eyes, and soft, wavy hair. When she took the mic off the stand and turned her back to us, displaying her perfect, heart-shaped ass, the crowd erupted some more. "And here we go," howled the MC. "Violet Savoie to perform Beyonce's adaptation of 'Fever.' Take it away, Miss Savoie!"

The song began with nothing but that simple guitar strumming with snapping fingers. Violet snapped to the beat, bending one knee to the tempo. She began singing the lyrics all husky and slow, keeping her back to the audience.

My heart climbed into my throat and lodged there, threatening to choke me. My entire body went rigid and tight with arousal.

She turned her head, her hair covering half of her face as she sang about kisses and arms around her and a fever through the night. To say the audience, especially the male half, was engaged would be an understatement.

"Yeah, baby!" howled Travis, but it didn't pull my gaze away for one fucking millisecond.

I was riveted. Frozen. Utterly entranced as she swaggered across that stage in denim, singing like a goddess, her voice filtering into the air, all sex and smoke.

For a while, her gaze roved the crowd, landing on no one, till she found me. Then that tilted smile and raspy voice poured out the rest of those taunting lyrics directly at me. Her free hand slid up her body along her hip, waist, and to the side of her breast before coasting back down.

I thought I was going to have to pour a bucket of ice water on every man in this fucking place or force myself out of my seat so I could beat the shit out of all of them for catcalling and ogling her.

But I wasn't going anywhere. I couldn't move, just sat there dumbfounded, soaking in every word, every flicker of those blue eyes, every sensuous movement of her lips, and trying hard not to swallow my own tongue.

Her voice resonated on some primal plane of mine. Man and beast in the very heart of me cried out to hold the siren on that stage, to clutch her tight and never let her go.

By the time she sang the repetitive chorus at the end, I agreed wholeheartedly. *What a lovely way to burn.* I'd light the match myself and set myself on fire if it meant I could finally have her.

I was glad that Mateo and the vampires weren't with us because they'd have detected my heart rate tripping at alarming speeds. Not that Mateo didn't already know how I felt about Violet, but I was trying to keep my obsession under wraps as best I could. I hoped we'd stay at least a half hour because I'd need that much time to get my dick under control.

The place erupted in roars of applause. I joined them, watching her take a demure bow and rush off the stage, laughing with that wild, throaty sound I'd come to love so much as she returned to the table.

She avoided my gaze until right before she sat down. What she saw there, I have no idea. I'd done my best to keep it neutral, but there was no way I was pretending that seeing her sing that song hadn't decimated me.

She might as well have taken a knife and cut a heart-shaped hole in my chest to remove the organ that already belonged to her.

She high-fived everyone at our table before she rounded back to her seat next to me. When she plunked down, I grabbed the back of her chair and hauled her against my side. Leaning into her ear, I whispered low, "That was . . . fucking amazing."

That was me. The wordsmith. Poet. Spouting lame words for what I'd just witnessed.

Blushing, she smiled at me, but said nothing.

"You've been holding out on me." I tugged a lock of her hair. "How come you never told me you could sing?"

She sipped her beer that had been delivered while she was onstage. "You never asked."

Chuckling, I added, "But, Violet. You can really sing. I mean, you could have a career in it if you wanted." I had no idea she had an affinity for music like me. Perhaps that's why she always watched me when I was onstage and seemed to listen intently.

"Thank you." She seemed to think for a minute while I stared at her in wonder. "I really do love music, and I like singing, but it isn't what I want to do with my life."

I nodded, understanding what she meant. While I enjoyed singing, making some extra money with gigs, it was actually the songwriting I loved far more. What called to my soul, compelling me to pour myself into words?

After that, Clara and Travis did another number, but our group was winding down. Much to my complete satisfaction.

I'd withdrawn from conversation, content to keep my arm across the back of Violet's chair and rewind her performance over and over in my head.

What a song for her to sing. That's exactly what she was. A fever in my blood, wrapping me in heated need. I wondered how much longer I could keep this pretense, how much longer I could resist taking her in my arms and showing her what it truly meant to burn.

"Let's go, y'all!" called Livvy, half-stumbling to her feet.

Cole helped her, looping her arm through his. We all ambled through the crowd toward the door.

It was nearing two a.m. I was going to be exhausted tomorrow, but it would be a short drive out to the cabin. Then I'd sleep all day anyway and run the woods all night as I typically did at the full moon.

When we stepped outside, gathering at the corner of Bourbon next to the Cat's Meow, that same prickly sensation assaulted my senses.

Snapping my head to the right, I saw him. Shane. Two blocks down, leaning against the corner of a bar. He held my gaze for three heartbeats, smiled, walked toward us. Four other werewolves appeared, flanking him in vee formation, weaving through the drunk crowd who were oblivious to the predators stalking around them.

"That motherfucker."

"What?" asked Violet at my side, then followed my gaze. "Oh shit."

"What's going on?" Drew growled at my side, sounding more like a werewolf than a warlock.

"Those assholes." I turned to Violet. "Stay here."

She opened her mouth to protest but I'd already stepped off the curb toward Shane. When he saw me coming and the warlocks right behind me, Shane smiled, then ducked down a side street.

The other werewolves followed him at a quick clip.

By the time I'd pushed through the crowd and followed them, they were halfway down the darkened street, barely populated like Bourbon Street. Shane glanced over his shoulder, laughing. I took off, sprinting toward him like mad. Travis, Cole, and Drew weren't far behind me.

Though witches and warlocks didn't have the super-speed that werewolves and vampires did, these guys were in good enough shape to remain only a few yards behind.

The street that bisected the one up ahead showed cars and people crisscrossing. Must be Royal Street, a busier thoroughfare than this side street.

When I came out at the end, chest heaving, I looked both ways, then caught sight of Shane and the others climbing into a big black SUV at the curb at the corner. Sprinting through the crowd, I dodged a couple, almost knocking them over.

"Hey!" shouted the guy, but I kept going.

The SUV sped away from the curb right as I reached them. When I stopped running, the SUV suddenly braked, red taillights glowing in the dark.

Frowning and panting, I watched as the SUV reversed, the front passenger window lowering halfway till Shane's grinning face peered from the dark.

"What the fuck do you want?" I growled, knowing if I leaped forward to grab at him, they'd only take off before I had time.

"So you left us for a girl?" His tone was belittling. "You were never one to follow your dick around, man. Thought more of you."

My leaving Austin was more complicated than that. I wasn't just following my dick, but the organ that pumped the blood through my veins.

"I left the pack long before I left Austin."

His face tensed. He never did like hearing the truth. Though I hung with him and some of the guys once in a while, like I had on New Year's Eve, I'd officially left the pack long before that.

The pack's former leader, this dick named Mason, had led them into a fight with an MC gang that had almost killed a few of them, including Shane, who'd gotten a crowbar to the head so hard it fractured his skull that night.

I'd kicked the shit out of Mason and left the pack for good. I'd stayed in Austin, playing music and hanging with some of the guys here and there, until I had good reason to leave.

"You're right," Shane bit out bitterly, "you abandoned us long before you chased after the witch."

"Where's Mason?"

"Gone."

"You're in charge now?"

He grinned. "Don't look so surprised."

I wasn't. "What the fuck are you doing in New Orleans?"

"Not here for you." His gaze slid sideways right as the guys ran up on us, standing at my side.

"You really are a witch lover, aren't you?" Again, that condescending tone, underlined with menace.

Shane had been my best friend for a long time and obviously had hang-ups about me leaving, but I couldn't help his ego. It seemed our friendship might be beyond repair by the look of disgust on his face.

"You wanna talk this out?" I asked, throwing out an olive branch, knowing he sure as fuck wasn't going to.

All I got in return was a curl of his lip. "No, I don't wanna talk this out. I'm not here about you."

"Why are you here then?"

"None of your fucking business."

I stepped off the curb but didn't lunge and reach for his throat through the window like I wanted to. "Tell me why you went to see Violet." I clenched my fists.

His grin spread wide, then he raised the window just as the SUV launched forward, tearing dangerously down the narrow street.

"Who is that asshole?" asked Cole.

"An old friend."

"Don't think he's your friend anymore," said Drew at my side, the four of us watching as the taillights disappeared around the corner of Canal Street farther in the distance.

"No, he's not," I agreed.

We made our way quickly back to the girls, who'd headed in our direction but at a much slower pace, mainly because Livvy and Clara were wearing heels and couldn't move very fast at all.

I was relieved to see the three of them safe and sound when we met them halfway down that darker side street.

"What happened?" asked Violet, looking much more sober all of a sudden.

Without answering her, I pulled out my phone and punched in Devraj's number. It only took him two rings to answer, even at this time of night. But I wouldn't expect anything less from a vampire like him.

"What is it?" he asked on the other end. There was rustling as if he was getting out of bed.

"I have to leave for three days, but I just had a run-in with Shane and a few of his pack."

"They'll need to leave, too, won't they?"

"Yeah. But I'd still feel better if someone was watching the shop. And the Savoie house."

I coasted a hand down Violet's back, a friendly brush I told myself, while she frowned up at me, obviously wondering what was going on.

The guys were telling Livvy and Clara about our incident. Violet half-listened to them, but her gaze kept coming back to me, concern etched on her face. Cole was scowling and Drew looked grave, but Travis said something lighthearted, probably to keep the ladies from worrying.

"Not a problem. I'll have my eyes on the Savoie sisters, and I'll talk to Ruben about the shop."

I breathed out a heavy sigh, frustration making me furious.

"Don't worry, Cruz. I'll take care of your girl."

Well, I guess Mateo wasn't the only one who knew.

"I owe you."

"No, you don't. Go take care of yourself, and everything will be fine when you get back." With a muttered "thanks," I hung up and followed the others, who were already to Royal Street again.

"Who was that? Ruben?" asked Violet.

"Devraj."

"What happened with Shane?"

"Nothing worth mentioning."

I grabbed her hand to guide her through the crowd across the street. I was glad she didn't pull away, letting me keep her hand in mine, after we wound into a less-populated space.

She was probably still a bit buzzed and would undoubtedly presume this was a friendly hand-holding.

Her other sisters and the guys were walking in a straight line, arms hooked together like children, Travis saying something that had them all laughing. I was right as rain where I was, tucking Violet's slim body close to me, her hand cradled in mine.

Never before had I wished I wasn't a werewolf as much as I did right now. Being away from her for even a day felt like pure torture. My desire was spiraling out of control, and I knew it.

Maybe the absence would help me get grounded and take control of this obsession so that I could come back and play like friends. I could only hope.

CHAPTER 13

~VIOLET~

From one of Livvy's many eclectic playlists, Kaleo crooned their Icelandic song "Vor í Vaglaskógi" in the kitchen.

I was snuggled on the sofa, waiting for Jules to come home with leftovers from the restaurant. She'd texted our sister chat group earlier to let us know it was slow at the Cauldron today and she had a pot of crawfish étouffée she was bringing home for dinner.

After the boys rolled off our sofas at the crack of noon, we'd devoured some burgers from Red Dog Diner, which Isadora had sympathetically picked up for us. Drew had told us to be careful with those werewolves around town, giving Jules another talking-to after running into Shane and those guys last night. Not that anything bad had happened. It was just kind of weird.

Then the boys hugged us with smiles on their faces and headed back to Lafayette like they hadn't consumed unknown gallons of liquor the night before.

As for me, I did *not* recover so quickly. I hadn't had a hangover like that in ages.

But I did have that "night after" fear of what I might've said or confessed or did in front of Nico. You know those moments after waking from a rowdy night full of way too much alcohol and your memory is spotty so you spend at least an hour recounting every event just to be sure you didn't do anything too embarrassing? That was me.

After going through the night, I realized I might've been a little touchy-feely with Nico, but that was about it.

Except for the karaoke at Cat's Meow. I distinctly remember sliding my hand over my breast and ass, while singing "Fever" directly to the man. I blushed now just thinking about it.

What the hell was in those drinks at the Brat Pack?

Truth serum, most likely. Because all it did was loosen my inhibitions enough to let down my guard and sing my feelings to Nico. I was so close to saying *fuck you* to the Death card and the Three of Swords and the Tower. My feelings and cravings for Nico were out of control. Maybe disaster and chaos and utter heartbreak were worth mind-blowing, skin-melting sex.

Who was I kidding? My feelings for him weren't just about sex anymore. Though I wanted to spend a solid week sweating in his bedsheets with him, I was very aware that my heart was wrapped up in this craving as well.

Which is why I kept rotating back to my psychic reading and the fact that this could potentially break both our hearts. I might risk mine, but I couldn't risk his. Not Nico.

Thank every angel in heaven that Nico had taken off for his full moon trip this morning because I wasn't sure I could face him properly. Even though he wasn't there, I called in sick to the shop.

Livvy was working on our Empress Ink website at the kitchen table on her MacBook while her friend Maya made suggestions over speakerphone. Though Maya was an experienced website designer, Livvy had a knack for aesthetic appeal and knew my clientele best. So she was overseeing the project, not to mention taking all of the photographs for the site.

The only reason I knew all of this was taking place in the kitchen was because she was being so fucking *loud*, even from an entire room away.

Also, I might be a little hangry. And still hungover. That's why I was so irritated. Or that's the story I was telling myself anyway.

My thoughts kept jumping back to Nico getting that phone call from some chick named Layla. Someone he told that he loved when he hung up the phone. And I could totally tell he was talking to her little girl too.

Did he have a daughter I didn't know about? He wasn't married. Or at least, not anymore. He didn't wear a ring. Did he leave Layla and the girl in Austin and come to live here to get away from them or something? Maybe it was one of those amicable breakups where he still loved the woman who bore his child, but they just couldn't make the relationship work.

A sickening feeling erupted in my belly that had nothing to do with being overly hungry or hungover. I decided to flip open the shop's social media pages that Livvy had been managing for us as well. For a fee, of course. My sister was crazy talented in this arena, and we didn't take advantage. Though she did say she gave us the relative rate.

When the Instagram page popped up, I sucked in a breath. The most recent post Livvy had put up was a picture of me and Nico in the logo T-shirts below our new sign.

Swallowing hard, I tapped the pic and zoomed in. I was laughing, my head half-tilted back while Nico grinned and stared down at me. You could only see his face in profile but, even so, the intensity of his gaze zapped me right through cyberspace. It was electric. I wanted to reach through the phone and touch that hard-edged jaw.

Below the pic, Livvy had captioned it: *This business duo is NOT all work and no play. Don't miss the Grand Opening Street Party for Empress Ink. Details to come!*

"Holy shitsticks!"

"What?" Livvy called from the kitchen.

"There are three hundred comments on this freaking post." And 1,200 likes.

"Uh. Yeah. I know." She went right back to her conversation with Maya.

I stood and ambled into the kitchen. "Damn, Livvy. Didn't you just open our account last month?"

"Hey, Violet!" Maya yelled from the speaker of Livvy's phone. "Congrats on your new shop."

"Thanks, Maya. Sorry to interrupt you guys, but, Livvy, we already have five thousand followers! How did you do that?"

Livvy turned away from her laptop to peer over her shoulder at me with her silly-sister look.

"Who exactly do you think you're talking to?"

"You're not using magic to get them, are you?"

Livvy's pretty eyes narrowed to slits. "If you mean, am I using magic in how it naturally affects my ability to make the best promotion and marketing decisions? Then yes, I am," she snapped. "But if you're accusing me of spelling people illegally to gather your clientele, then *no*, I am not."

"Whoa. Ease up on the angry eyes."

Maya laughed from the speaker. "It's not you, Vi. She's just pissed at some guy who was harassing her at the PR contest thingy she's doing."

"Harassing is a kind word." Livvy was calm again. Like an ice pond on the darkest night of winter calm. "That asslick better step off the next time I see him. Hopefully, he'll be cut from the contest in this next round, though. If there is a goddess watching over us, he will be."

I remember Livvy saying something about a PR contest she was doing, sponsored by some local bigwigs. But I honestly couldn't make myself care right now because my attention was snagged on another photo on our IG page with twice as many comments and likes.

It was one of Nico and Mateo installing the wrought iron chandelier in the lobby. It shouldn't be so sexy, but it was the way Nico balanced himself on the ladder, one foot higher on the step, his muscles straining against his threadbare T-shirt as he used a screwdriver at the top of the fixture. Oh, and Mateo who was assisting was hot too. But I couldn't drag my eyes off Nico.

Nico, Nico, Nico. My brain needed to give it a damn rest already!

My stomach growled, and I blew out a frustrated breath. "Stepping outside a minute," I told Livvy, though she was already back to tearing this nameless guy from that contest thing a new asshole.

Once in the quiet courtyard, I ambled over to the bench while scrolling through my favorites, then tapped Evie's number. It rang a few times, and right when I was about to hang up, she answered with a breathless "hello."

"Hey. Sorry to bother you."

"No bother. What's up?"

"Where are you guys anyway?" I knew they left town but wasn't sure where they'd gone for the full moon.

"We're in Mississippi." I heard something brush against the mouthpiece, then her light laughter. "Mateo found this cabin out in the middle of nowhere near the Natchez Trace. So beautiful out here!"

"That's awesome." I gazed upward, finding the moon full and bright through the silhouette of the bare tree branches. I couldn't help the pang of jealousy I felt that Evie got to go with Mateo. They were a couple, so of course he'd take her. Why did that make me suddenly feel sick and empty?

"Is something wrong?" Evie's voice turned serious. "Is everything okay?"

"Of course, it is. I just had a question for you, but I guess you're busy." Because I could totally hear Mateo wrestling her in bed or something.

"I'm not busy." Then another muffling of her phone before she told her obviously randy werewolf, "Mateo. Alpha! Go play."

"That's what I was doing," came a rumbly reply.

She laughed, then more rustling and a door slam.

"Okay, he's going hunting now." A heavy sigh. "How can I help you?"

"Um." And this was new for me. I didn't quite know how I wanted to ask what I wanted to know.

"If *you* are struggling to find the words or the balls to ask me something, then I'm kind of worried."

I laughed. Because she was right. I was known as the sister with zero filter about my thoughts and opinions. But this wasn't about either of those. This was about my emotions, and that's why I was struggling.

"Has Mateo ever told you what it's like? This monthly wolf thing?"

"How do you mean? Has he explained what it feels like to shift?"

"Not that. Has he mentioned what it's like having to go off alone every month? I mean, obviously he's not alone now, but before."

There was a pause before Evie replied. "Are you asking me if my boyfriend was lonely?"

"Kinda."

She snorted. "No, you're not. You're asking me if Nico is lonely out there in the woods all by himself."

"Evie."

"Look, I may not be psychic like you, but it's plain as day that you two want each other. Like *bad*."

"Since when?"

"Since the day I brought you up to Mateo's apartment with me that first time. Jeesh, Violet. It was so obvious."

"What are you even talking about?" I could barely remember that day. Except for the fact that I really loved the way Nico held a longneck beer, his pretty, masculine fingers all perfectly displayed.

She gave a deep, throaty chuckle. "You were defensive as fuck. Curt, rude, and mean as hell."

"You're exaggerating. If I was rude, it was because we were running late and I hate wasting time."

"Liar, liar, pants on fire."

"How does me being an asshole prove that I want Nico anyway?"

"Because that's what happens when you have a serious crush on a guy and you're trying not to. You become a supreme bitch." She paused, her tone turning secretive. "Anyway, Mateo told me something I probably shouldn't tell you."

"Tell me right fucking now, Eveleen."

"Hmm. Not sure I should. Seeing as you might just throw it in his face or something. You're a bit confrontational, Violet, if you hadn't noticed."

"Tell! Me! Or I'll put a potion in your gumbo or your beer at next Sunday's dinner."

"I'm a hex-breaker, so that wouldn't help you much."

"Evie!"

"Fine, fine." She laughed. "I was going to tell you anyway, but now you've proven to me how bad you've got it for him. So have you ever noticed how much he touches you?"

Heat instantly flared at how he'd touched me on New Year's Eve two years ago and how I'd love for him to touch me again. Anywhere.

"No. We haven't had sex or anything."

"Jesus, Violet. I don't mean that. I mean just light touches. On the arm, the body, casual touches."

I thought back, remembering how often he actually did do that. Passing behind me in the shop, leaning across me to fetch something, he always did graze my arm, my hips, my shoulder.

Even last night, he was exceptionally handsy. But so was I.

Warmth suffused my cheeks at how impossibly good it felt when he held my hand. Even though I was drunk, I could still remember that lingering lovely feeling.

"Yeah. But that's all innocent. Other guys have done that." But now that I thought about it, no one really did on the same level as Nico.

"Not for a werewolf." I could hear the smile in her voice as she went on. "To them, touch is a form of communication and, um, declaration."

"What is he communicating and declaring exactly?" A burst of butterflies scattered like buckshot in my belly, because I was pretty sure I knew what it meant.

She huffed out a sigh. "And I always thought you were the smartest of my sisters. When it came to men anyway. Gotta go. I'm cooking dinner just in case Mateo wants something other than raw deer."

"Ew."

She laughed again. "You get used to it." She said that as if she was giving me personal advice.

I was actually relieved when she hung up. And then aggravated. She'd never answered my damn question!

Was he lonely out there? I slumped down and let my head fall to the back of the bench so I could gaze upward. The moon pulled me again. It beamed brightly through the craggy, leafless branches, swaying in the gentle breeze. What was he doing at this very moment? What was he thinking?

I hugged my arms across my chest, remembering the many times he found a way to touch me in some innocent way in the office, the shop, even at the Cauldron. Was this some werewolf courting ritual to stake your claim?

Now that I thought about it, he had freaked the fuck out when that guy Shane touched my wrist.

I waited for it.

The outrage at some guy thinking he could claim me without my permission, exerting his caveman, possessive bullshit without even asking.

But the usual resentment I felt every time a guy had tried that shit before never came.

Instead, all I could do was stare up at the moon, remembering the sad look in his eyes when we talked about his tattoos. The forlorn wolf inked into his arm said so much about the man who bore it. For the first time in my life, I longed to soothe that ache, to share that burden, to wrap my arms around him and make it all go away.

"Fuck." I sighed.

Evie was right. I wanted him. Bad. So, so bad.

I stared at the endless glittering stars, winking at me as if trying to whisper their secrets. I pushed out my psychic magic, letting it hum an aura around me, thinking of the man at the forefront of my thoughts.

"Give me an answer."

But my magic wouldn't budge, wouldn't send me the message I longed for. And the stars only blinked in benign indifference, mocking my frenzied state. All I could do was wrap my arms more tightly around me and wonder what to do. And hope for a sign.

CHAPTER 14

~NICO~

THE RIPPING OF MY SKIN AND BREAKING OF MY BONES DIDN'T EVEN hurt anymore. Much. The shift was painful, yes, but fast. As soon as I'd become the nine-foot monster standing outside the cabin, it wasn't the physical pain that lingered. It was the hollowness echoing inside my chest, my heart. My lonesome soul.

Jerking my snout toward the sky, I howled up at the moon. An aching, long wail that went unanswered. That's where the true agony was.

We need her.

The gruff voice of my wolf in my head didn't startle me. His will became my own this time of the month. He also erased any pretense that I could hide from what we both wanted most. The one woman who would satisfy us. Complete us. Fill this hollow ache in my chest, my soul.

When I had been with the Blood Moon pack, there was a unity among us that kept the piercing emptiness away, the reminder that we might be monsters, but we weren't alone. Still, living with a pack was dangerous. *We* were dangerous. It was safer to be on my own. That way, no one got hurt. No one suffered. Only me.

A feral growl rippled through my chest. The beast was unhappy and restless.

Bring her to me.

That was impossible. Violet was still denying what we could be. While she did, I couldn't and wouldn't cross that line. No matter how gutting it felt when the wolf made our needs known.

Like now.

I ran. I fell to all fours, then whipped through the swamplands, relishing the sound of small animals skittering out of my way. I didn't want blood yet. I wanted to run. The cold wind on my face, caressing my fur, stinging my eyes, numbing me from the outside in.

I huffed and pounded my way up a small hill onto a manmade levy to keep the bayou water to one side, away from civilization. I galloped to the top, then watched the moon glistening on the water, fractured like white glass. Night creatures moved in the brush and trees. In the distance, the stealthy walk of a deer splashed in water. Still, I wasn't ready for blood.

Tilting my head toward the sky, I howled again. That deep part of me yearned for an answer. For some reply to the hopeless longing throbbing in my veins, pounding in my aching heart. The beast had full sway, snuffling the air for a scent of her. Man and beast sent a mournful cry up into the night.

Hoping.

Craving.

Longing.

But as always, there was no answer. There never was.

CHAPTER 15

~VIOLET~

AFTER A RESTLESS SLEEP, I CHUGGED TWO CUPS OF STRONG COFFEE and headed for the shop, deciding to check on Fred before I met my first client. It was early, and I doubted even Sean, Tom, or Lindsey were there yet, which is why the sight I found out in front of the shop had me stopping in my tracks.

There were parts of the sidewalk all along the lower Garden District where the concrete bordered a small section of soil for small trees and shrubs. It added to the homey garden-like aesthetic of the neighborhood.

Outside Empress Ink, we had a long, thin border of crape myrtle trees, which would be full of purple blooms in the spring. Right now, they were bare of any blooms or leaves at all. But they *were* wearing sweaters. I shit you not.

Clara stood next to the third and last tree, the only one without brightly knitted clothing. She hadn't noticed me because she was chatting away, while knitting, to the grim leaning against the brick wall next to our entrance. He wore faded jeans and a leather jacket, his jet-black hair hiding most of his profile as he lifted a cigarette to his lips. Henry Blackwater, Sean's older brother.

"So you're kind of on a stakeout but without hiding in a non-descript car around the corner?" asked Clara.

"Something like that." His voice was low and deep and soft but not gentle.

"You know, cigarettes are really bad for you."

"I'm a grim. I've got a long life."

"Doesn't matter. Supers can still get sick, which can take years off your life. Instead of living three hundred years—well, how long do grims live anyway?"

"Why are you doing that?" He gestured toward the crape myrtle in the last square plot of soil bordering the sidewalk.

"Yeah, what are you doing?" I asked, hands on my hips.

I ignored the brush of darkness radiating off Henry. Way stronger than his baby brother's aura. A grim's aura tended to make humans focus on their baser, darker urges. Right now, I was just getting more irritated. Not at Clara, really, but at . . . at what?

I'd become increasingly more aggravated since the day Nico left. And that was only two days ago. Dammit, what was wrong with me?

"Violet! Isn't it adorable?" She gestured wide to the colorful menagerie of covered tree trunks. "I'm yarn bombing you."

"Ah. Gotcha. And why are you yarn bombing me?"

She smiled brightly at my silly question in Clara fashion, her long blonde hair loose down to her hips.

I caught a pulse of magic. Not threatening, but . . . something. When I glanced at the grim, knowing full well it was coming from him, he remained casual as you please, blowing out a stream of smoke into the cold morning, dark gaze still on my sister.

"Because it's pretty, Violet. And your trees will now be nice and warm till spring."

"Of all the things I have on my plate, I wasn't really concerned about my trees."

"Which is why you're lucky to have such a thoughtful sister." She beamed at me as she continued knitting the last sweater onto its new owner. "Besides, Bernard was definitely getting too cold on that last freeze."

I knew better to ask, but I did anyway. "Bernard?"

She pointed to the skinniest tree on the far end. "That's Bernard, then Lucy, and this is Doyle."

"Trees speak to you?" Henry took another drag on his cigarette. Strangely, his question wasn't mocking in the least.

"Not with words." She slid a shy smile to him. "But they feel. Like all living things. I just prefer to give them names."

"Why?" he asked in a deep, indifferent tone.

"Because it makes me feel good."

Clara's need to coddle and nurture all living creatures, right down to the nest of sugar ants that set up a residence in our cupboard last winter, was nothing new to me. And yes, I'm serious about the sugar ants. Rather than allow me to spray them with insecticide, she reorganized the shelves to allow them to keep that one, providing a dish of brown sugar for them.

I wasn't in the mood to argue about this latest exploit of hers and, honestly, tree sweaters just made us look more bohemian, which was kind of an allure in this part of New Orleans. I turned to the grim. "Sean asked you to come?"

He pulled his gaze from Clara to me and stubbed his cigarette out on the concrete before standing. "Ruben."

Clara interrupted. "Are there really some werewolves bothering you?" She reeked of concern.

I shook my head. "Nothing I can't handle. But Nico is just"—I shrugged a shoulder—"you know, cautious."

"Mm-hmm." She smiled. "I know how Nico feels."

"What does that mean?" I stepped closer, then glanced at the grim, knowing he could hear our whole conversation. "Never mind. Let's talk later."

I stormed off, irritated that yet another sister seemed to recognize the simmering attraction between myself and Nico. I suppose we weren't fooling anyone. Not even ourselves.

By the time I'd unlocked and opened the door to the shop, Clara was already back to chatting up the silent grim acting as sentinel.

Honestly, I wasn't even sure how he could help if a whole gang of werewolves showed up. As far as I knew, all grims could do was appeal to a person's darker nature. And for werewolves, that wasn't anything we wanted. But if Ruben trusted him, then I was fine with it.

I flicked on the lights as I headed down the hall to the back entrance. After unlocking the door to his courtyard, I relocked it from the other side. I didn't want anyone traipsing back here to Nico's private residence. A place I now felt perfectly natural invading myself.

Fred clucked at me and pranced around the grassy area, which he'd apparently commandeered as his personal territory. I went over and petted him on the chest how he liked. After about three minutes of that, he was done with me.

I took my keys out and went inside Nico's house to fetch the feed he'd left in the closet in the foyer. After spreading some feed for Fred in the grass, I went back inside to wash my hands.

Afterward, I couldn't help but wander his quiet domain. I wasn't about to go upstairs to his bedroom because that felt too invasive, but I couldn't help but peruse his bookshelf to discover what books interested this man.

I didn't know what I expected, but historical biographies was not it. Napoleon, Winston Churchill, Queen Elizabeth I. The one I found most interesting was Lord Nelson, an admiral of the British Royal Navy in the 1700s.

"You are just full of surprises, Mr. Cruz."

I trailed my fingers along the spines till I saw a few photographs on one shelf. There was one of him and Mateo in front of a stone fireplace in what looked like a ranch house. Then another of them much younger, maybe late teens, sandwiched between two men, one who looked exactly like an older version of Mateo and a silver fox on the other side.

I remember Nico mentioning that he'd grown up with Mateo, his uncle, and his grandfather.

The last picture squeezed my heart for a different reason.

It was a pretty brunette woman taking the selfie of her and Nico. Nico held a precious little girl on his shoulders. She had chubby cheeks and brown curls and she held a stuffed bunny triumphantly over her head. Behind them was a carnival stand, a carousel in the distance.

I couldn't look at it long before my stomach flipped with that nauseous feeling again. If he had a daughter, that was great. Right? She looked adorable. And the woman looked, well, goddammit, she looked kind and lovely. I'd never been the jealous type. I never wanted a guy long enough that warranted envy.

I was *not* a fan of this feeling.

Pushing down the wretchedness, I moved on, finding a shelf with more books. Poetry?

Who was this man?

Here I'd thought he was just this broody, somewhat cocky, loner who liked to hop from town to town, playing barroom gigs and such. But just like everything else in the world, there was so much more beneath the surface.

There were some classic collections: Frost, Dickinson, Thoreau. Then some modern ones I didn't know at all. I pulled out one by a poet named Kahlil Gibran. There were sticky notes marking some pages. I flipped open to one of them.

The poem was about fear. A metaphor about a river, flowing on and unable to go back. Because going back was impossible. A profound and beautiful reflection on not allowing mistakes or regrets to guide you. Or fear. Nico had obviously read this one many times, highlighting a few of the lines. He'd even made a pencil notation. Three words. *Let it go.*

As I slipped the book back into its place, I saw the journals. The one he'd had open on the coffee table the last time I was here wasn't there. I really shouldn't snoop in his journals. But wouldn't it give me better insight into who he was? No harm in that, I told myself, biting my bottom lip.

I wanted to walk away, but I couldn't.

"Just one peek," I whispered to myself before snagging the brown, leather-bound one in the middle.

Taking a seat on the sofa, I flipped toward the beginning. I suppose I was expecting some kind of dated diary entries or something. But that wasn't what I was looking at. I scanned the first page, marveling at the lyrical beauty of the words in verse. Then the next and the next. I was hypnotized by this little glimpse into the man I was currently obsessing over.

And what a glimpse it was. Pages and pages of loveliness. Drafts that had been scratched out, then rewritten. But all ending in something utterly beautiful.

"Do you like them?"

I jumped right out of my skin, snapping the journal shut. Nico stood in the entryway of the living room, a backpack at his feet. He looked haggard, bags under his eyes and two-day-old scruff, almost a full beard already. Even so, he took my breath away. And not just because he scared the shit out of me.

"I'm sorry, Nico." I popped up and went to the shelf, putting it back. "I didn't mean to snoop."

"Yes, you did." But his mouth ticked up into a half-smile when I turned around. "Did you like them?"

There was a soft vulnerability to the question, in his voice. I nodded.

He moved closer until he stood beside me, staring at the neat row of journals.

"You're a poet," I said stupidly. For someone who was never at a loss for words, I couldn't come up with anything better than that.

"A songwriter, actually."

"You write songs?"

"I do." Now he was grinning down at me, only a foot away. "What did you like about them?"

"Fishing for compliments?" I arched an eyebrow, trying to play off some of the sexual tension ratcheting up like a fucking rocket at the moment.

"Yeah," he said evenly, leaning in even closer. "From you, I'd beg for them."

I gulped hard at that. His gaze dropped to my throat, skated a little lower, and then slowly rose to meet my own again.

I'd heard of werewolf hangover, the aftermath of a full moon excursion. And maybe I'd noticed Mateo or Nico act like this before, but for some reason, it was wreaking havoc on my lady bits this time.

There was a feral look in his eyes. And some other raw emotion that sizzled off his skin. It was said the wolf lingered following the full moon, just beneath the surface.

Today, I knew that was true. There was magic—wild and potent—pulsing in the air around him, now encircling me as well. His slow movements actually made me feel more nervous rather than put me at ease. I stared at the journals, a little afraid to meet his gaze though I could feel him staring at me. A blaze of heat licked along my skin.

"Why haven't you tried to sell them as your own? Your voice is amazing." That was the damn truth. "You could be a rock star if you wanted."

"I don't want to."

"What?" I finally turned my head to look up at him.

"I could've had that life. Had a contract offer with a studio in LA about ten years ago."

"A lucrative contract?"

"Very."

"Then what was so unappealing? People would kill for a voice like yours, a talent like yours. To get offered something like that?" It wasn't that I thought him ungrateful. I just didn't understand why someone would spit in fate's eye and say *no thanks* to potential success like that.

"Guess I'm just broken inside." His steady, unwavering gaze eased over me with torturous slowness. "A werewolf should never live in the spotlight anyway."

"Devraj did. He was a Bollywood superstar for years."

"He's a vampire. There's no chance of him suddenly shifting into a raging monster in front of a stadium of thousands."

I shook my head, very aware how close we were standing. "Is it really that bad? The lack of control?"

He looked away toward the living room window. "Sometimes," he admitted gruffly, pain flickering across his face. "It can be."

I looked back at the shelf, running my fingers over the tops of the journals. "Such a shame. Your writing is . . ." The right word wouldn't come, but "stunning" was what I finally said.

My heart screamed at the injustice of someone as talented as he was being forced into a more limited lifestyle because of his werewolf. Again, I felt the keen unfairness of his situation, more determined to help him.

He exhaled a heavy breath. "I sell my songs to indie musicians. But some of it I just write for myself." His eyes were back on me. "I didn't want that kind of life anyway."

"Like just being a loner, don't you?"

"I didn't say that."

He was standing in front of me now, so close. I flinched at the sudden contact of his fingers skating along the backs of my hands, sliding over the knuckles until they curled around my wrist. His thumbs glided back and forth across my pulse on each inner wrist. I gulped hard when I looked up at him, apparently having lost all saliva in my mouth. "What are you scared of?" he almost whispered.

"I'm not scared," I argued.

"Your heartbeat says otherwise."

I started to pull away, but he gripped me harder, easing closer. His body heat scattered what brain cells I had left. I stopped struggling. His hold loosened, but he didn't let me go.

He was right. I was scared. Terrified actually. Obviously, I was attracted to him, but what if we went there and it all went to hell like the cards had told me it would. Then it ended in heartbreak and he hated me.

"We're friends," I said stupidly, my odd protest sounding weak even to myself.

"No, we're not." His green eyes had gone deep-woods dark, an aggressive tint that had me hypnotized. I couldn't look away.

"You said we were friends." I think I even whimpered.

"I lied." His thumbs continued their slow sweep over my pulse, now with gentle circles.

"We can never just be friends. You know this. You're not stupid."

I did. *I did!* But dammit, he didn't have to go and say it aloud! Now I couldn't laugh off his flirting and pretend I didn't feel the blazing sexual tension anymore. You can't put that genie back in the bottle. Once it's out, it's out. Did I even give a fuck about the stupid card reading anymore? I wasn't sure.

"We work together" were the ridiculous words that came out of my mouth. There was a strange desperation in my tone. I didn't know where it came from.

"No, we don't. I'm an investor in your business. I check in from time to time with inventory and building issues, but we don't work together. I'm more of a landlord."

"Semantics."

"That doesn't make a difference anyway." He tilted his head, brow furrowing, his expression hardening.

"Could be a conflict of interest," I added, trying to find a way out of whatever the hell was happening right now.

His piercing gaze intensified and I could've sworn he was about to shift, his electric energy vibrating over my skin. His body whispered to mine, some kind of siren song, entrancing me with his nearly hostile and violent allure.

"It's not." His gaze dropped to my mouth, but he didn't lean the last few inches to kiss me.

Just looked and looked, his broad chest rising and falling. "You're just running."

"I'm afraid it will all go sideways." My voice cracked. "And it'll end in heartbreak. For both of us."

"It won't," he said with conviction.

"It's just that we're—"

"I *know* what we are," he snapped back, almost viciously. He curled his hands completely around my wrists, squeezing firmly but not to the point of pain. "What we could be," he growled.

"If you'd just let it happen." Then he let me go. His voice was rusty and grating, demanding that I listen. "I'm tired of waiting, Violet."

I didn't move. Didn't respond. Didn't take the opening he was offering me. Why? Because he was right. I was running. And I didn't fucking know what to do. His primal, possessive look screamed words like *heart* and *soul* and *forever.* But that psychic warning I'd received in that reading a year ago kept haunting me.

The intensity of it, of him, had me scared shitless. No one had ever looked at me like that. It was awesome and terrifying at the same time.

For once in my life, my confidence wavered. I just stood there, unable to form any kind of response, not knowing what to do. So afraid to make the wrong move that I made absolutely none instead.

He gave me a stiff nod, then fisted his hands at his sides and took a step back, dropping his gaze for a brief moment before he turned and marched toward the entrance to the foyer.

"I'm really tired, so if you'd excuse me." He gestured toward the door, a mixture of disappointment and irritation in his tone.

He was kicking me out?

He was kicking me out!

Was he breaking up with me? We weren't even together yet!

My mouth hung open for a few seconds before I snapped it shut. Then I pulled on my cloak of bravado and marched across the living room. Only when I glanced at his pack did I realize something. I stopped in front of him.

"You're back a day early."

The bags under his eyes seemed more pronounced all of a sudden, but the hardness of his gaze didn't falter at all. If anything, he drew his own mantel around himself, a cold, frosty one.

"I need to rest, Violet."

He wasn't going to tell me why he was back so early or why he looked like such hell. I knew for a fact that he and Mateo typically returned from their full-moon weekends looking more virile, more powerful than when they'd left. What was so different now? "You didn't have to return early because of those werewolves."

"I didn't."

"None of them have been around," I assured him.

His expression was completely unreadable, his gaze still hostile. "I know."

Yeah, of course he'd know. He'd been keeping tabs with Ruben and Devraj, who were obviously on the lookout for those guys.

"I guess I'll go then."

"That would be a good idea."

I frowned up at him, but still, his expression was grave, adamant, unmoving. A fiery tempest blazed deep inside those eyes.

I stormed out of the house and back across his courtyard toward the shop. He'd never been legitimately angry with me, but there was no mistaking the cold fury following in my wake. I walked straight through the shop and out the front doors in sort of a daze.

Clara was gone, but Henry was still there at his post. I didn't say a word but kept walking home, feeling somehow disconnected from everything. Sort of adrift.

I replayed our conversation on loop all the way home. My stomach fluttered at the thought of his soft, burning touch. I remembered how the hypnotic sweep of his eyes and fingers had held me spellbound so intensely, I hadn't even realized I'd day-dreamed the entire walk home till I was suddenly on the little sofa in our loft and staring out the window at Archie playing in Devraj's backyard.

Tears pricked my eyes with a sudden wave of emotion as I recalled the heartbreak already in Nico's eyes. Was the Death card already coming true because I was rejecting what we could have before it had even begun?

Laying onto my side, I hugged a throw pillow to my stomach, feeling so much self-loathing and pity I wanted to scream. My thoughts spun in my head, making me dizzy with fear and sadness.

I squeezed my eyes shut to will it all to go away but, instead, my mind drifted far back into my memory to a summer day long ago. Green, prickly grass. Warm summer sun. My twin sister laughing beside me. I fell asleep.

The dream wound in circles, only sensory images flashing in and out. A blue-breasted lark sang from the branch of a flowering dogwood tree. Then everything went silent; only the wise voice of Aunt Beryl resonated through my mind.

"Your true love is broken inside. Like all of his kin."

I snapped awake and sat up with a frightening jolt, the sun having slipped behind the houses. "Oh my God!"

I'd slept the entire day away, but that wasn't what had struck me like a thunderbolt. Nico's voice echoed right behind Aunt Beryl's. *"Guess I'm just broken inside."* "It's him," I whispered to myself, voice shaking.

Aunt Beryl's words slammed into me like a psychic whip cracking through my soul. *"Never smart for a Seer to divine for herself anyway."*

The magic didn't sizzle under my skin. It burned, punishing me for what I'd obviously gotten so wrong.

Unable to ignore my magic screaming at me to pick up my cards, I scrambled back to my bedroom and pulled my favorite deck from my desk, the old ones my mother had given me. The ones I'd used in my first reading.

With blinding speed, I scattered the cards upside down— hands shaking—and chose three cards within nanoseconds for Nico, for me, and for our relationship.

Death, Three of Swords, the Tower.

A tear escaped, trailing down my cheek, because now I could see what was there all along.

What I'd been too blind to understand. To *see*.

Death did mean *endings*. But what it also meant, which I'd failed to see, was change and transformation. Indeed, my life had been going through transformation. Even when I'd first pulled the card, I'd been on the path to opening my shop and changing things. But this wasn't even about that. This was about changing my life to include him.

"Nico," I whispered.

I'd wanted him for quite some time. Even as I'd denied us both.

The Three of Swords reflected Nico's heartache, which I'd caused by my constant rejection of him when he so obviously wanted me all along.

I sobbed, realizing I'd been breaking his heart by refusing him. My blaze of magic sung with the truth of it like living flame searing through my blood.

The Tower, the symbol for our relationship, could've meant chaos and upheaval as I'd thought all along. But my magic whispered that I'd misinterpreted that as well. The Tower also meant revelation. Awakening.

A starburst of powerful energy shattered with warmth inside my chest as it hit me. The awakening was happening right this very second. I opened my eyes to realize that Nico was the one. He was mine.

"My one true love." Laughing and crying at my sappy words and the pain I'd caused us both, I swiped angrily at the tears on my cheeks.

The cards had been true. I'd just misread them, thinking only disaster awaited us. When in reality, my denial was part of what put it all in motion.

The transformation began the night Nico arrived in town because that's when I'd stopped hooking up. I'd been focusing on opening Empress Ink and had put all thoughts of men and sex to the side. Except for my secret craving for Nico.

His heartbreak began when I set on a path to reject what we could be, thinking wrongfully that I was saving us both.

His words at his place echoed back to me. *I know what we are... what we could be.*

And now I was standing at the pinnacle of the Tower in the light of the awakening, the dawning realization that it was him all along. The one that was meant for me.

"Fuck."

I'd really messed things up. But I could fix them. There was still longing in his eyes tonight before he'd turned a cold shoulder and kicked me out.

I needed to gather my thoughts and my courage. Tomorrow, I'd pull him aside before Sunday dinner and tell him that he was right. We should go for it. Or I'd just kiss him and hope like hell he'd kiss me back. The rest would be easy, I hoped, because our bodies had been craving each other for a while now. I wasn't oblivious to his desire all this time, even if I'd pretended I was.

Sighing deeply, I headed into the kitchen and poured myself a glass of wine, even though it wasn't even five o'clock yet. I sat on the sofa and hugged myself under a pretty pink crocheted blanket I'd never seen before. Must be one of Clara's new creations.

Sipping my wine, a heaviness that I'd been carrying a long time suddenly floated away.

"Tomorrow," I whispered happily.

Tomorrow, I'd finally cross that bridge and tell Nico he was right. That I wanted him. And hoped he still wanted me.

CHAPTER 16

~VIOLET~

THE FIRST THING I NOTICED WHEN I WALKED INTO THE CAULDRON for Sunday dinner, late as usual, was that one person was not there. Nico.

For months now, he'd been at our Sunday dinners that Jules cooked for the family as well as our Cauldron extended family. Mateo had started inviting Nico since they were cousins and all, which hadn't bothered me really. Especially after we'd become business partners and we could use the time to talk about the shop in a relaxed environment.

I'd procrastinated today because I needed extra time to scrounge up enough courage to lay all my feelings on the line. To swallow my pride and tell Nico that I was basically an idiot who could see clearly when it came to everyone else. Just not when it came to myself. And also that I really wanted to lick him from head to toe if he didn't mind.

"Why are you scowling?" asked Clara, carrying a large salad bowl past me from the kitchen. "Your aura is all blurry."

"Please don't analyze my emotions today," I begged her, making my way to the table.

"Well, stop being all blurry then. And your irritation is bleeding over into our twin bubble."

"There's no such thing as a twin bubble," I snapped, following her to the table.

She laughed and shook her head. "Just because you've never been able to tap in to it doesn't mean it isn't real."

Clara set the giant green salad bowl on the buffet table parallel to the long dining table, which was basically a bunch of four-tops pulled together with tablecloths tossed over them.

Isadora and Devraj were at the far end, their heads bowed together as they whispered like the disgustingly-in-love couple they were.

Evie stood behind a seated Mateo at the other end, her arms wrapped around his neck while watching and listening to Livvy carry on about something. Really *loudly*. But that was the norm for Livvy.

Life of the party. She's a Leo.

Our line cook Sam and food servers Belinda and Finnie were listening to her rattle on about whatever. In the middle of the table was JJ and Charlie, a vacant seat to Charlie's right.

"Hey, Mateo," I said all casual as I passed him and Evie. "Nico isn't coming tonight?"

Mateo leaned back into Evie, grasping her behind the knees while turning his head to talk to me. "Not tonight. Said he had some work to do or something." Mateo's dark eyes scrutinized my reaction before he asked, "Why? You need him?"

"No, no." I cleared my throat. "Just thought we could go over some stuff for the grand opening thing, but it can wait." I waved it off like it was nothing, all the while my stomach twisting into a tight knot.

Nico wasn't the kind to miss a free meal, especially one prepared by the culinary grand master, Jules. The man liked his food. So I wasn't thinking it was just coincidence that he decided to skip today of all days. The one after we'd had a clash of sorts. One that had ended with him kicking me out of his house.

Suddenly, I was scared. Nico had never put distance between us. And maybe that was the problem. I'd gotten so used to his constant presence, enjoying our easy camaraderie, our flirty friendship, that I assumed he would always be there. We'd been dancing along the sexual high wire, circling each other for a long time now. And he'd never gotten angry with me.

Except last night, he'd called me out. Then told me he was tired of waiting.

The Tower card had hit me full throttle last night, and now I needed to talk to him. To tell him. Why wasn't he here?

I'd had it all planned out in my head. I'd pull him aside in the back courtyard behind the kitchen, explain about my reading a year ago but that I'd gotten it all wrong and that I wanted him, and then we'd make out like crazy before finally coming back inside to eat dinner calmly and everything. Then we'd go back to his place and fuck each other's brains out and officially begin this courtship.

Feeling ornery, I finally plunked down in the chair next to Charlie, immediately catching his deviant expression.

"What are you grinning at, bitch?"

"A little lost lamb. Looking for her wolf." He batted his dark eyelashes at me.

"Shut your trap, Charles." I slid my hand under the table and squeezed him on the thigh close to the knee.

He jerked hard and barked out a laugh, knocking the bottom of the table so hard the silverware and glassware clattered. Charlie was ticklish as fuck.

JJ leaned forward on his other side, scowling at the two of us.

"Daddy is mad," he whispered out of the corner of his mouth.

"Bet that's what you call him in bed, huh?"

He scoffed at the same time his cheeks flushed rose-pink. "You better behave or I'll tell the whole table you're boning your business partner." He tossed his head so that his blond bangs fell to one side. He was honestly so handsome he was almost pretty. "Or I suppose *he* is doing the boning. Right?"

"There is no boning going on whatsoever, and even if there was, I wouldn't be telling you, nosy britches." I poked him in the ribs and wiggled my finger, which had him squirming away and laughing.

He bumped into JJ on the other side, who then leaned back over and said, "Do I need to separate you two? We're trying to listen to Livvy."

I stuck my tongue out at Charlie, then followed JJ's attention down the table to Livvy sitting at the head, gesturing wildly with a cocktail straw in one hand.

"And if he thinks he can intimidate me with his big brain, that hot nerd has another thing coming."

"Wait, wait, wait." Finnie had been leaning back on two legs of his chair, but suddenly plopped forward. "You never called him a *hot nerd* before."

Finnie was the kind of guy who was always smiling, even when he talked. He had what some might call "careless charm." From what JJ had told me, it was working for him waiting tables. He was racking up those tips. As a nursing student at UNO, he needed the money, so good for him.

"He's right." Evie finally took her seat next to Mateo, quirking her brow in mock confusion.

"I think I heard you call him butt-munch and fuck-nugget, but never hot nerd."

"Don't forget cockwaffle," JJ added.

"Oh yeah. My favorite." Evie giggled.

"Hold up," I interjected. "I have no idea what's going on. You're gonna have to tell the story again. Who is a cockwaffle exactly and how has he earned this title?"

Also, I applauded Livvy for her creative profanity. We sometimes played a drinking game to see who could come up with the most unique swear words.

But I also noticed that when her emotions were running high about something or someone, she tended to come up with all manner of names.

Livvy rolled her big blue eyes. "First off, I have eyes, Finnie. He's using that grim reaper swagger to his benefit. I can see that. But it doesn't change the fact that he's also a—" She raised both hands, spluttering to find the right word.

"Thundercunt?" I suggested.

"Yes!" She clapped her hands together, laughing and winking down the table at me. "Nice one."

"Well, now I need all the details. Please start over."

"Okay." She took a deep breath and started from the beginning. "There's this marketing contest, and it's sponsored and hosted by Garrison Media Corporation."

"Should I know them?" I asked.

Finnie, Evie, JJ, and Sam all said in unison, "The biggest PR company in Louisiana." Livvy ignored them, giving Finnie the side-eye before going on.

"Anyway, there were some preliminary rounds, which I made it through. But on the semifinal round, we were grouped with two other contestants and given a panel interview. In my group, there was this guy Willard Thompson from Metairie and this grim, *Gareth Blackwater.*"

She practically spit his name out and hissed it with such venom there was no question who the cockwaffle was.

"You guys actually saw him at the Brat Pack the other night. He was the guy who walked up to us."

She glanced from me to Clara. I vaguely remembered someone talking to us before we left, but to be honest, I had been severely fixated on Nico at the time.

Devraj perked up, turning away from Isadora and tuning in to the conversation. "Gareth? What's he doing now?"

Apparently, I wasn't the only one distracted, but this was nothing new for Dev and Isadora. I swear, if we weren't all here, they'd probably be going to town on top of the table. Not that I was jealous or anything.

"You know him?" Livvy glared at Dev.

He chuckled. "Uh, yeah. He's done a few jobs for Ruben. As a matter of fact, he's the one who created the vampire tracing app. Helped us out when those girls went missing."

Livvy crossed her arms and seethed over this news. "He's created his own app?"

"He's created a couple. His most popular of course is iBite, the vampire app to find blood-hosts."

I swear, I thought there was steam rising out of Livvy's ears. "Are you kidding me right now? He doesn't even *need* the prize money!"

"Forget about that," said Evie. "Tell us what happened next."

Livvy inhaled a deep breath, getting hold of her temper. "So the interview seemed to be going well. Everyone was being respectful of each other, answering the questions. But then after I responded to the guy heading up the contest, I hear this not-so-subtle snort of derision on my left. The douchey grim."

"Not all grims are bad," Clara added with a bit of disapproval.

"I didn't say they were, Clara darling, but this one—" She wrung her hands in front of her, strangling the invisible grim, Gareth, apparently.

"It seems every grim you guys know is a Blackwater," said Devraj, his fingers combing through Isadora's hair trailing down her back.

"You want anything?" Charlie asked me in a low voice, starting to get up, nodding toward the bar.

JJ was suddenly out of his chair, a hand on Charlie's shoulder, gently pushing him back into his seat. "I'll get it. What do you want?"

Charlie settled back into his chair, that telltale blush sweeping his cheeks again.

Well, now, what was this?

"Another merlot. You, Violet?"

"The same."

I didn't miss the way JJ sensuously stroked his thumb across the nape of Charlie's neck as he walked away. And I couldn't help but grin like a fiend at Charlie, who avoided my gaze, still managing a "shut up" under his breath.

Oh, ho! Charlie boy had some explaining to do. He was definitely the one JJ went on a date with the other night.

"Are you listening, Violet?" Livvy had that you-better-fucking-focus expression on.

"Listening. But I still don't know what got your panties in such a bunch."

"Okay, so he makes that aggravating and rather condescending noise in his throat, so that only I can hear, every single time I answer a question for Mr. Davis. So afterward, when we're dismissed and told it'll be another couple of weeks before they choose the finalists, I stopped him outside the building and asked him what his problem was. Do you know what this ass said to me?"

I shook my head since she was obviously creating a dramatic pause for a big finale.

She leaned forward, narrowed her eyes, and lowered her voice as if mimicking the guy. "He gets up in my face and says, 'I'm onto you, witch. You better not use your magic, or I'll report you to the Guild.' Ha! Threatens me like I'm some kind of supernatural criminal."

I smirked because, although Livvy was vivacious and passionate, she rarely lost her temper.

"So what did you tell him?"

Finnie was already snickering behind his hand. He must've known what was coming.

Livvy lifted both brows haughtily. "I said, 'First of all, I don't need to use my magic to beat you, grim. I'm going to win on my talent alone. And second, you'd be reporting me to my own sister, dimwit, and I think I know whose side she'd take.' Then I left him there gaping like an idiot." She smiled victoriously and lifted her drink to take a sip.

We all laughed with her, but I was still a little confused. Sure, he might've been out of line a little, but that didn't seem to warrant this level of rage on her part. Then again, Livvy liked dramatics, so maybe that's all it was.

Jules walked in with a giant serving bowl of crawfish fettucine and set it on the buffet table so we could all serve ourselves. "Dinner's ready."

As we stood, I called out to Livvy, "So what happens if you're both finalists in this contest up against each other?"

"Then I guess I'll have to beat the knobhead and put him in his place for good."

Jules turned from the buffet, hands on both hips. "What contest? And who's a knobhead?" We all groaned, nearly in unison, while Finnie and Evie laughed. Livvy heaved out a sigh.

"Nope, nope, nope. I'm not telling it a third time. Later, Jules. Let's eat your fabulous food."

"Sounds like a plan," said Mateo, rubbing a hand over his flat abdomen, nudging Evie in front of him.

She wrinkled her nose a little bit. Fettucine had never been her favorite. The rest fell quickly in line.

After we'd all filled our plates and pulled up to the table, the conversation flowed freely as usual: multiple conversations overlapping, and voices rising higher and higher to be heard over everyone else.

Our family meals were a kind of organized chaos, but that's the way we liked it. Normally, these gatherings fueled me with joy and energy to face another long week as a new business owner.

But tonight, I couldn't help but glance at the empty chair where Nico usually sat, diagonally across from me next to Evie. A sharp pang pierced my gut.

Sometimes, he'd even bring his guitar and play a few songs that others could sing along to. We didn't even mind when Clara belted out a solo, sounding like a dying cat as always. It was family and friends and fun.

I wasn't sure if I was the only one who lamented the noticeable absence. But I was the person who was the likely reason he was avoiding dinner with us.

He probably just needed another day to rest, though. He'd come home a day early and looked worn out from going all wolf and stuff. That's what I told myself anyway.

After I cleared my plate, taking Evie's and Mateo's plates with me, I set the dishes in the giant kitchen sink, then pulled out my phone. It wouldn't hurt just to check in, make sure things were all cool between us.

> Me: Hungry? I can bring you a plate of crawfish fettuccine.

I stared and waited a minute or two. Just when I thought he must be asleep or something, he answered.

Nico: No thanks.

I frowned. Somehow I could see him scowling on the other side of the phone.

> Me: Okay, then. I'll bring it to the shop for your lunch tomorrow. Jules insisted.

Lie.

No response. A sickening feeling swirled in my stomach. When no response came again, and it was obvious he wasn't in a friendly mood, I slipped my phone into my back pocket.

I walked toward the kitchen door, then stopped, listening to the chatter and laughter on the other side. It just didn't sit right with me. Usually, our businessy/flirty texts ping-ponged back and forth for twenty or thirty minutes.

Huffing out a frustrated breath, I texted back quickly.

> Me: We need to meet first thing in the morning with Livvy to hammer out the details of the grand opening celebration. 8:00 a.m.

I sent it, murmuring, "There." When he didn't respond *a-fucking-gain*, I furiously typed an addendum. Deleted it. Typed it again, then sent it.

> Me: I expect you to be there. On time.

He was never late for our meetings, so I don't know why I felt it necessary to add that.

Actually, I did. I was pissed, and some part of me wanted to poke the bear. Or the wolf, in this case, to get some sort of reaction out of him. What did I get?

Nico: Can't. Won't be into the shop tomorrow.
Make it Tuesday.

"What's wrong?" Clara stood in the open doorway, a stack of dirty dishes in her hands.

"Nothing," I snapped, turning and heading toward the back exit, not wanting to try to lie my way out of this one. Clara knew something was wrong just by looking at me. "Tell Jules I headed home. Got some work to do."

Before anyone else could stop me, I pushed into the cold night air, turning my face up toward the moon. It was still mostly full, just starting to wane on one side.

After inhaling another deep, cleansing breath, I marched through the back courtyard and then down the alley between the Cauldron and Mystic Maybelle's toward our house.

I sent a text, telling him that was fine, though it didn't feel fine.

Where the hell did he have to go tomorrow? Why wasn't he coming into work? I wanted to know, but not enough to ask him. Then I shot a text to Livvy, telling her we had a meeting Tuesday morning since I'd made all that shit up just to get some sort of reaction out of the damn man. I had to make it legit now.

Rather than texting me back, she telepathed a quick message, *I'll be there.* As an Influencer, Livvy had the ability to telepath. But it was a one-way connection unless she was chatting with another Influencer with the same gift. Like Cole, our cousin.

That taken care of, I walked quickly home. The nausea in my stomach was swelling to new heights. There was only one thing to do.

After the meeting Tuesday morning, I'd pull him aside and tell him. Or maybe take him out to lunch. That would be better. But I wasn't sure if I could wait another whole day to get this off my chest, especially when my psychic magic tingled every single time I thought of him, warning me to make it right since I'd fucked it up.

But I'd respect him if he needed time to cool off after our last encounter. I wasn't an Aura like Clara, but he'd been pissed at me. I wanted him calm and open-minded when I explained things, because he'd likely be angry all over again.

I waited for the nausea to disappear now that I knew my definite course of action. After two Tums, a shower, and three gulps of Pepto Bismol, it hadn't gone away. So I took a sleeping pill to knock myself out.

I needed a good rest tonight, so I'd be ready to open up my stubborn heart and prepare for possible rejection Tuesday morning.

CHAPTER 17

~VIOLET~

"Good. That settles the food issue. I'll contact them today," said Livvy.

She'd had the fantastic idea of acquiring two food trucks for the grand opening. With a small after-hours fee, they'd set up on our dead-end street and work late for us.

"All we have left to discuss is the music. I had some ideas." Livvy was tapping her notes into her tablet.

I'd been avoiding Nico's gaze most of the meeting in our small office. He wasn't behaving angry at all. If anything, he was being exceptionally cordial, but it still felt off.

My heart had been jackhammering sporadically all morning, every time I thought of what I was going to tell him after the meeting. Though he gave me a few puzzled looks, he hadn't been rude or anything like I thought he might after our last interaction.

Forcing my focus back on Livvy, I said, "We're not going to have an eighties tribute band. I don't want The Cure and Depeche Mode on loop for this crowd."

Livvy arched a brow at me. "Are you hating on my music?"

"Not at all. I just think our clientele is more eclectic."

"So do I, which is why I hired Southern Sun. They play a mixture of old and new classics with more of a rock vibe."

"I know them." Nico had one ankle crossed over the knee of his other leg, his body leaning away from me in the chair at my left. "They're a good band."

Those were the most words he'd said all morning. I gave up on being nonchalant and turned my head to take him in.

He looked way better than he did two days ago. He'd shaved, and the bags under his eyes were gone. And while he looked cool and aloof, there was an edge to his demeanor. Nico was often broody, but usually with an easy smile. For me, anyway. Now he barely looked at me.

And if that didn't chafe my ass, the fact that he was being painfully professional did. No banter. No flirting. Nothing but pure professionalism coming from him. Not a single, solitary note of friendliness anywhere. This was going to be harder than I'd thought.

"Fine," I agreed. "That's good for me then."

"Who'll be manning the merch table?" Livvy asked while typing on her phone.

"Sean will do it," I said, realizing I hadn't even asked him to work the grand opening yet.

"Lindsey mentioned she'd help out however we need," added Nico. "I'll see if she'll relieve Sean when he needs a break."

That rubbed me wrong. "Don't worry about it. I'll ask her when she gets in later today."

Nico stood. "She's already here. Working on some sketches for the display portfolios we're putting in the lobby."

"I didn't even talk to her about that yet," I said to him.

"Don't worry about it." Then he finally looked down at me, hands propped loosely on his hips, expression blank. "I did." Then he turned his attention back to Livvy. "Are we done?"

It was way early for Lindsey to be here. We didn't even open till noon. And the fact he knew she was here had turned my breakfast into a nest of snakes in my stomach.

And when had he talked to her about the portfolios?

"Yeah. I think we've got it," said Livvy, popping out of the chair she was in. "You guys have a good day."

Nico and I walked toward the office door at the same time, but he backed away before our shoulders could touch, gesturing for me to go first. I glared at how he took a full step away from me to allow me to move ahead of him.

I didn't have the freaking plague.

Once we were back in the lobby, I meandered to the front counter to leave Sean a note about manning the merch table at the party. Nico didn't even glance at me, marching straight to the end of the hall where Lindsey's partitioned workspace was.

Dammit. I didn't even have a second to ask for a private conversation.

I heard her soft hello, then Nico's deep voice as they spoke, the conversation indecipherable. Then she laughed. So did he.

What the hell?

Two days ago, he was pretty damn clear about wanting to be with me. Had he moved on already? Wait, Lindsey had off yesterday. Did they go on a date? Was that where he'd been?

Suddenly, my neck was sweating, and my breakfast bagel was trying to come back up. I twisted my hair up and used the holder on my wrist to tie it in a messy bun.

The light laughter and murmurings continued down the hall for the next ten minutes. Twelve actually, because I was staring at my damn phone to be pretending to do something whenever he decided to come back to the front.

But he hadn't come back up yet. He was still flirting and laughing with Lindsey.

The front door opened, and Sean sauntered in, giving me that head-nod greeting guys liked to do. "What's up?"

I was sitting on his stool behind the counter. "Nothing," I snapped. "Why are you here so early?"

His brows popped up at my catty tone, but he kept on grinning as was his typical facial expression.

"Nico said he wanted me to enter inventory receipts into the system before we opened today. Something wrong?"

As he rounded behind the counter and I maneuvered out of his space, I caught a sudden wave of his dark aura. Usually, I pushed away his grim magic automatically, almost desensitized to his brand of wickedness. But today I was off my game. I had a one-track mind, solely on Nico and whatever the hell was going on with him. And her.

So when Sean's pulse of magic pushed against me, rather than push back, I drank it in, feeding on the ragey feelings. It incited a jealousy-fueled string of curses, which I somehow managed to only mutter under my breath as I stormed off.

Riding the envy train, I marched down the hall toward Lindsey's workspace, slowing only when I was near the door. And yes, I was tiptoeing. And eavesdropping. I didn't care how unprofessional or ridiculous, I couldn't control myself.

Lindsey giggled, her voice soft, like he was standing close to her. "I would just love something like that. A little edgier. Maybe across my back."

"I like your style just fine. It suits you."

"What do you think of this one?" she asked softly.

Peeking around the corner, I don't know how I managed to stay quiet when I saw that she'd slid her sweater off her shoulder, exposing the red strap of her bra and a tattoo, her adoring gaze fixed on Nico mere inches next to her.

A spike of adrenaline shot through my system like an arrow ripping through my chest. My knees buckled. If that wasn't enough, he lifted his hand and traced a finger along the curve of her shoulder before righting her sweater and leaning in to tell her something. *Or to kiss her!*

I couldn't watch. Whatever was about to happen next, I didn't want to see it.

I turned around and sped diagonally across the hall into the kitchen. I turned on the Keurig and started opening and closing, slamming actually, cabinets to find the coffee, a coffee cup, and possibly some whiskey.

What the hell was he doing? How could he imply he wanted something with me a few days ago and already be dating her?

I'm tired of waiting, Violet.

I winced at the memory and the stark pain in his eyes that I'd ignored right before he'd kicked me out.

Well, I can't say he wasn't a man of his word. He sure as shit wasn't waiting. I was shaking with fury. I'd finally gotten the message from my psychic eye that I should go for the asshat and he'd already moved on?! Was this some kind of cosmic joke?

I popped a K-cup of dark coffee into the Keurig, then pulled down my favorite mug that read *No one cares, work harder.* When I hit the on button, I felt him come into the kitchen behind me.

There was never any doubt whenever Nico walked into a room. His wolf energy buzzed along my skin, warning me that a hunter was near.

Normally, I got a little high from that sensation. Today, I wanted to swing the toaster off the counter and hit him across the head with it.

He walked behind me and opened the fridge. I tapped my spoon on the counter, possibly a little maniacally, trying to make my coffee percolate faster with wishing before I lost my goddamn mind.

When it finally finished, I moved my cup aside, then spun around to find him looking in the fridge. For what, heaven only knows, because it was only ever stocked with creamer, condiments, and leftovers.

"Do you mind?"

He glanced up, brows raised, looking adorable and innocent as fuck. I couldn't help but zone in on his lips, trying to determine if they looked redder, as if recently kissed. The rage returned tenfold. I clenched my jaw tight, pretty sure I tasted molar dust, refusing to spew out what I wanted to say right now.

He pulled out my Almond Silk creamer and passed it over without a word. I snatched it from him and went back to my coffee, pouring fast, then sloshing the coffee over the lip when I stirred too furiously.

"You're welcome," he said, sounding amused.

That motherfucker. I spun around, glaring daggers at his back as he finally pulled out a lowfat yogurt and reached into a drawer for a spoon.

Ha! Yogurt? What was he doing, trying to stay fit for his new boo?

Without even thinking, I telekinetically grabbed the loaf of bread sitting on top of the fridge and threw it straight at his face. It bounced off his big-ass head and rolled off his shoulder to the floor with a fluffy plop.

He froze in the middle of tearing the foil lid off the yogurt, his eyes flicking down at the floor, then up to me, his mouth open in complete shock.

"Did you just throw a loaf of bread at me?"

I stood there, fists balled at my sides, glancing at the bowl of apples on the table. I swear, I couldn't control myself. I lifted one with my magic and shot it at his chest. Hard. He deflected it, sending it slamming into a cabinet. His eyes narrowed, his expression hardening to granite.

Oh, he was pissed? I knew I was acting irrationally, but I didn't give a damn. I just wanted to hit him with something. Hard!

I looked at the toaster.

"Don't you dare, Violet." His voice was all dark and dominant and wolf.

My heart rate spiked with a mixture of fear and excitement, my anger boiling. I held his gaze and lifted the toaster with my magic, but before I could throw it at his stupid, fine-ass face, he dove for me.

I yelped and lunged out the door, throwing two dining chairs in his way with a flick of my hand over my shoulder. With no effort, he leaped over them. Then I was running.

"You better run," he growled, right on top of me.

I sprinted with all the speed my long legs would take me, zipping down the main hall, feeling his heat right behind me. I flew past all the workspaces on the right, then past the lobby that opened up on the left, trying to make it to the back door, yet knowing I never would.

Then I yipped as I was suddenly lifted off my feet, a strong arm banding my waist. The supply closet door opened. He swung us both inside, then slammed the door shut and pinned me with my back to the door, my wrists manacled above my head. I looked up into wolf-green eyes.

His head dipped low, and he bared his teeth. "Any reason you're trying to hurt me?"

"If I wanted to hurt you, I would've crushed you with the fridge."

He huffed out a laugh, though his mouth never formed a smile. "Semantics." He tossed that word back at me from our last conversation at his house. "What was that all about?" His voice was all growl.

I clamped my mouth shut, glaring at him with my pent-up anger at the thought of his mouth on hers, his body against hers.

As if he could read my mind, he pressed his full weight against me, chest to chest, thighs to thighs.

"I'm pissed at you," I gritted out.

Then he dropped his head lower and grazed his nose up the side of my neck, crooning, "I noticed." He retraced the same line back down my throat with his tongue. My insides liquefied, but I kept myself rigid, unyielding, even as he nuzzled my ear. "Tell me what made you go hellcat."

I whimpered but refused to open my mouth. That is, until he opened his own and bit the slope of my neck, hard enough to sting. I gasped before hissing, "Stop that." But the words sort of fluttered out of my mouth and fell to the floor. Like my self-control.

When he licked the spot, a helpless moan vibrated deep in my throat. Piercing me with predatory eyes, he grazed his nose along the side of mine. Soft, slow, petting. His wolf was caressing me, teasing me.

"Let me guess." His voice was all beast, ocean dark and fathoms deep. "You were spying on me and Lindsey."

I tried to jerk my hands free, gritting my teeth in my fury, but his strength was a powerful force. Well beyond me physically. I could've used magic, but I'd told him the truth. I didn't want to hurt him. And if I were totally honest, feeling the force of his brute strength had me beyond turned on.

"Did you kiss her?" I spat, seething.

His lips were a bare whisper away from mine. "No." The intensity of his gaze heated further.

"You really think I want her?" There was definite amusement in his voice.

I narrowed my eyes to slits. His smile widened.

"I don't care," I snipped like a petulant child.

"Such a bad liar."

"I hate you."

"Still lying."

"Stop talking and fucking kiss me."

"There's my girl."

He slanted his mouth over mine, taking zero time to push his tongue inside. Our moans mingled as he held my wrists with one hand and reached between us to clamp his hand over my breast with the other.

It was a possessive grip. Not a subtle or gentle touch, but a hard and domineering claim of ownership. That in itself shot a wave of heat between my legs. Nico wasn't wasting time. He was a visceral man of action.

I rocked up against him helplessly. I could taste his aggression, a hard pulse in the air that scraped against my skin. I wanted to swallow it down and let it rattle my bones.

While lapping fiercely inside my mouth, he kicked my feet apart and ground right between my legs, his dick a steel pipe inside those jeans.

My head spun, intoxicated on his pheromones, on the delicious friction between my legs. Hiking one leg over his hip, I rubbed my pussy against him, frantic to get him inside me.

He tweaked my nipple through my thin shirt and bra, swallowing my sexual sounds of desperation and pleasure, then he slipped his hand to the hem of my shirt and yanked it up. He released my wrists to pull the shirt off, then tossed it aside.

"Nico." I dug my nails into his shoulders, but he was already tugging my bra straps down and lowering his head.

When his mouth opened on my breast, his teeth grazing my nipple, the pulse between my legs became a constant throb. Heady. This was escalating at an astronomical pace, and I didn't care. I couldn't think past *fuck me, Nico, please fuck me.*

I clenched my fingers in his hair, pressing him closer, demanding him not to stop. He circled my taut nub with his tongue before latching on again, sucking hard. I moaned, nails scraping his scalp.

"Are we actually going to fuck for the first time in a supply closet?" I panted.

He lifted his head freakishly fast, his hand circling my throat, and froze. He didn't squeeze, just held me still, another sign his wolf was fully in charge. I loved it.

His gaze intensified as the caged animal behind his eyes all but declared victory at my admission we were about to have sex.

I might be a fumbling imbecile when it came to actual relationships with men, but I also knew that when my body wanted a man this badly, there wasn't anything that was going to stop me. Right now, I just wanted him in.

And what he must've seen in my eyes was reflected in his own. Stark lust—brutally raw and starving.

Easing close until his mouth was against mine, he whispered, "I'll fuck you wherever you want me to." His thumb grazed my pulse, his fire-gaze burning me up with feral hunger. "But it'll be my way."

I smiled a little at his super-alpha rising to the surface. Lots of supernaturals tended to be dominant, but I'd heard werewolves were intensely so in bed. Evie had even mentioned it a time or two, right before she blushed and got that dopey, drugged look in her eyes.

"Whatever you want, wolfie."

We had both been powder kegs waiting to go off ever since that first contact two years ago.

There was no mistaking that now. I don't even know how I kept us apart this long.

My hands were shaking as I pushed up his shirt, needing skin. He stopped long enough to strip it off. When I went for my pants, trying to unsnap and unzip as fast as possible, panting like I'd run a goddamn marathon, he lifted me by the waist and turned me around. There was a table for T-shirt folding with a box of the logo T-shirts sitting on top. He knocked it all off with one sweep and bent me over the table.

"Yes. God. *Please.*"

I started to lift up onto my arms, but he growled and pressed his hand between my shoulder blades, pushing me back to the table.

I wanted to touch him, to feel him, but he wasn't listening any longer. As soon as he'd stripped my jeans and panties down to my ankles, I expected to feel him plunge deep. But when his hot mouth opened on my slit, I jerked and cried out.

His vibrating groan as he licked and sucked added a layer of pleasure along with his tongue. He spread my lips apart with his thumbs and licked with long strokes, then he slid a finger through my folds before spreading a slick circle around my clit, still fucking me with his tongue. I grabbed the edge of the table, trying to hold on and not buck against him, the sensation so intense I was already about to come.

"*Dammit.* Get it in."

"So impatient," he growled and bit my ass.

I jumped when he slid two fingers inside me, and I came so hard and fast my vision blurred at the edges. I cried out while he continued pumping inside me, moaning his appreciation, whispering words of praise.

When he pulled his fingers out, he opened his hot mouth on me again, already stoking a fire that hadn't nearly died out. If anything, I was more eager to feel him stretching me, filling me.

I reached back and managed to clench my fingers into his hair. "Nico," I demanded.

He chuckled but lifted away. I heard the sound of his belt unbuckling, his zipper unzipping, and the distinct crinkle of a condom wrapper.

"Music to my fucking ears," I mumbled, pushing up onto my elbows.

He leaned over me, bracing one arm on the table by my head, and licked a line up my spine that made me arch and jut my ass up into the air.

"You taste so fucking good," he growled as he nipped my shoulder.

"Yeah? What do I taste like?"

He fisted my hair and turned my head so we were nose to nose, mouth to mouth. Something primitive sparked in those electric eyes before he rumbled, "Like *mine.*"

Then he sank inside me with one sharp thrust. I gasped at the sudden invasion, clenching my eyes closed. So thick. So full. He held still, not moving, his lips sweeping across mine, holding me still with his tight fist in my hair.

"Look at me, Violet," he whisper-rumbled against my mouth. "Open those beautiful fucking eyes."

So quiet, yet the power of his voice had me obeying him at once. Only then did he start to move, pumping in slow and deep, holding me captive with that feral gaze. Every slide of his thick cock was better than the last. The wet sound of raw sex heightened my arousal.

"God, Nico," I breathed against his mouth.

"And you kept us from this for two years." His fist in my hair stung when he tightened just a little more. Punishing me. I deserved it.

"I'm so fucking stupid."

He really had no idea how much, but I'd wait to tell him later. Right now, all I could think was *harder. Deeper.*

He grinned before giving me a quick, wet kiss. Then he straightened, released my hair, and gripped my hips, his long fingers digging into my skin.

"Touch yourself," he commanded. "Need you to come soon."

I glanced over my shoulder, shivering at the slits of green staring down at where his dick entered my body, flesh slapping flesh.

"Can't hold on much longer, huh?" I teased.

He lifted a hand and slapped my ass. Hard. When I jolted, my pussy clenching, he hissed in through his teeth.

"Fuck, Violet." He gripped my hips tighter and growled, "Do as I say."

I gulped hard at the sheer dominance in his voice. I was so goddamn turned on.

"Yes, sir." It came out sassy, and his answering growl catapulted me toward another orgasm.

I gripped the front of the table again with one hand and reached between my legs with the other, circling my slick clit with two fingers. Laying my cheek to the table, I moaned at the euphoric sensation of my wet fingers sliding and his driving rhythm and my nipples rubbing against the cold table with each thrust.

When I felt myself climbing fast, I reached up and held onto the edge with both hands, my moaning gasps filling the small room. He reached down and lifted one of my legs, bending my knee to rest on the table and opening me wider. Then he really started pounding me. He took over, stroking my clit fast and hard.

"Fuck!" I cried out as I came, my sex squeezing his dick.

He pinched my clit while continuing to fuck my brains out, sending me into one of those out-of-body orgasms. Before my moans had even died, he moved his hand from between my legs to my thigh, squeezing to the point of pain. I didn't think he meant to. He was lost to his own orgasm as he fell forward onto his other forearm and bit my shoulder—that was definitely going to leave a bruise—his animalistic groan vibrating from his chest to my back.

He shuddered then stilled, his dick swelling bigger as he came, the stretching sensation making me whimper with pleasure.

I couldn't move. Just lay there, panting and grinning like an idiot. He wasn't much better. His weight on top of me was heavy, but I didn't care. It felt so good. He felt so good. This was *so fucking good*.

"Damn," I muttered after a few minutes.

He laughed, his bare chest shaking since it was still pressed to my back.

"Yeah," he breathed into my ear before pressing a kiss below my lobe. With a heavy sigh, he lifted up and pulled out of me, helping me get my leg down and foot firmly planted on the ground.

Because, let's face it, my legs were jelly, my body completely useless in post-orgasmic bliss.

By the time Nico had disposed of the condom, zipped up, and got his shirt back on, I'd managed to straighten my bra and that was it. I stood there, still breathing heavy and staring at the sex god in front of me. He caught me looking, a sinful smile spreading across his face.

"Need some help?"

"Mm-hmm."

I wasn't proud. I could barely move, still stunned that I'd been cockblocking him all this time.

"Here we go."

He knelt in front of me, looking up as he eased my panties up my legs. That knowing smile—smug and satisfied that he'd made me explode like a nuclear bomb—remained on his chiseled face. There was also a touch of warm affection there.

He trailed his long, perfect fingers down the backs of my thighs and calves, a tender caress, to my jeans and pulled those back on too. After zipping and snapping, he leaned forward and brushed his mouth on my belly before pressing his forehead there as he wrapped his hands around my waist and squeezed. I couldn't help but comb a hand through his sex-mussed hair.

Something about this gentle gesture gave me a pinching sting at the center of my chest. It was so sweet, so tender, so serious.

To lighten whatever heavy emotion weighed the room down, I cleared my throat and clenched my fingers in his hair, then pulled his head back so he'd look up at me. "If you think you're getting this on all work breaks, you're out of your damn mind." He chuckled, then nipped the bare flesh on my belly with his teeth.

"Ow!" I jumped.

He soothed with his thumb but looked anything but remorseful. He got to his feet and found my shirt. He handed it over rather than helped me back into it, for which I was glad. We were in unfamiliar territory, and I wasn't sure how to behave.

It was sex, but it also more. I definitely understood that when I'd interpreted the tarot cards correctly. And I didn't know what to do with more.

He kept a hand on the doorknob while he waited for me to get my shirt back on. "Come to my house for dinner."

"Why?" I asked lightly.

"Why do you think?" He frowned, his gaze watching every move I made while I slipped on my shirt. "So we can do that again properly."

"What, like missionary style?" I goaded.

His scowl deepened, but there was amusement twinkling in his eyes. "Thoroughly," he corrected.

"Ah." I propped my hands on my hips, my shirt back on. "Should I make a list of what I consider thorough?"

His eyes darkened, heating again. A throb between my legs pulsed in response.

Holy hell.

My body was ready again. His nostrils flared, and he arched a brow.

"Yes," he finally answered, his husky voice telling me he knew exactly what was going on in my panties. "A detailed list."

He opened the door and gestured for me to go first. As I passed, he planted his palm on my stomach to stop me, leaning down close to my ear, his hot breath sending a shiver over my skin.

"Text me the list."

I stepped forward and glanced up at him. "Maybe." I was pretending I wasn't as affected as I was about sending him a list of what I wanted him to do to me tonight.

As I sashayed by him with a wicked smile, I turned to find Sean at the counter, leaning forward on his forearms, staring at us both. And the shit-eating grin on his face told me he just sat there and heard everything that had happened.

"Enjoy the show?" I snapped snarkily.

He winked. "Magical supply closet, eh?"

"Fuck off, Sean," I called before storming off to my workspace.

But then I heard Nico answer him as he headed across the lobby to leave. "Yeah, it is." My heart fluttered, and I grinned like an idiot the rest of the day, mentally making my list.

CHAPTER 18

~NICO~

FUCKING *FINALLY*! TO SAY TODAY WAS A GOOD DAY WAS THE understatement of the year. Of the last two years actually. I knew it would take a little push to make Violet give in to me. I felt a twinge of guilt for flirting with Lindsey and letting her think I was interested just to get a rise out of her.

But when I'd heard Violet hovering at the door while Lindsey was doing all the flirting, I couldn't resist encouraging it a little, hoping it would have the exact effect that it did.

As soon as Lindsey pulled her sweater down, I'd gently told her that we could only be friends. Was it an honorable thing to lead Lindsey on? Not at all. But I wasn't what Lindsey really wanted or needed. And winning Violet would take a little deviousness, and perhaps a firm hand as well.

I clenched my jaw at the thought of her moaning response when I slapped her ass with that firm hand. Not only did she not mind my overbearing dominance during sex, she seemed to love it. And truth be told, I was still restraining myself. Damn, that woman was made for me. The wolf rumbled in my chest, completely agreeing.

As of now, Violet might think this was just sex, but I was pretty sure the only way to get close to Violet's heart was through her panties. She was a sexual creature. *Christ.* So sensual and responsive.

I was half-hard just thinking about the look on her gorgeous face when she came beneath me. I finished setting the food I'd picked up for dinner aside, then glanced at my watch. Still thirty minutes before she'd be here. I set out the Old Smokey Salted Caramel whiskey, thinking she might enjoy this one.

Picking up my phone, I then flipped back to the list she'd texted me today, grinning at the screen like a fool.

1. Oral sex (reciprocal)

2. ~~Doggy style~~ (scratch that; don't want to offend your wolf)

3. Wall sex

4. Cowgirl

5. Reverse cowgirl

6. Sixty-nine

7. Shower sex

8. Whips (no chains, please)

9. Blindfolded

10. Tied up

11. Chocolate syrup (or anything you'd like to lick off me)

12. Sex swing (can save this for later; here's a link on Amazon)

She'd ended her list with nothing but a smiley face. I swear, if I wasn't in love with her already, I would be now.

My phone buzzed as I was holding it, Layla's name flashing on the screen. Video call. My sister rarely spontaneously video called.

"Hey," I answered hurriedly.

"Hey." She looked and sounded down.

My protective instincts kicked in at once. "What's wrong?"

"Oh, nothing too terrible. It's just Gigi. She had a bad day. I didn't realize it was daddy/daughter lunch day at her school, so I wasn't able to get my father-in-law to go and sit in for Daniel."

Fuck. My heart sank. This was the kind of thing I wished I could do for Layla. *Should* do for her. Especially since she lived in Baton Rouge, only an hour away. Other than her elderly father-in-law, who wasn't getting around so well these days, I was the only family she had.

After Daniel died, she relied on her father-in-law to help out. This was actually another reason I felt guilty for not visiting. Since the incident with Ty, I was terrified of something setting me off and accidentally hurting Layla or Gigi. "What's she doing now?"

"Moping. Curled up on the sofa with Mr. Bobo."

I was already heading upstairs to grab my guitar. "Let me sing her something."

Layla sighed with relief. "That's what I was hoping. Thank you!"

I saw her walking through her house as I picked up my guitar, then set the phone on my nightstand. I was tuning a string when Gigi's angel face popped on-screen.

Layla was saying, "He wants to sing you a lullaby."

Her sad blue eyes sparkled with joy when she saw me. The phone screen wobbled as she seemed to be getting comfortable on the sofa.

"Hey, Uncle Nico."

"Hello, my sweetheart." I gave her my brightest smile. "I've been missing you."

"Me too. When are you going to come and visit?"

Another sharp pang stabbed me in the chest. "I will as soon as I can." As soon as I could trust myself. "I promise. How about your favorite song for now?"

Her chubby cheeks puffed when she smiled wide. "Please, please!"

"You and Mr. Bobo settle down. Here we go."

I strummed the opening chords, then launched into "Somewhere Over the Rainbow," singing the words I'd sung a hundred times for her since she was a baby in the crib.

Her sweet smile and bright eyes melted my heart. Especially when she mouthed the words *where trouble melts like lemon drops* as I sang them. She squeezed Mr. Bobo tighter, his floppy ears bent as she squished her cheek against his. When I ended the song, I got close to the screen.

"Is Mr. Bobo asleep yet?"

She glanced at her bunny, then turned back to me and shook her head. "Not yet. One more!"

Knowing that would be the answer, I laughed and strummed some soft chords, moving into something slower.

"One more. Then you have to promise to go to sleep and dream about happy things."

"Okay. I promise."

I heard footsteps on the stairs and had actually smelled her as soon as she'd entered my house. I kept playing, feeling her draw closer. I sensed her leaning against the doorjamb, watching me. I glanced over and gave her a smile, still singing Gigi'ssong.

There was a surprised and sort of sad expression on Violet's face. A little stricken, I focused back on Gigi with a smile as I sang the final chorus.

"Yay!" She clapped, then made Bobo clap with his bunny paws.

"You feel better, sweetheart?"

"Way better."

"Here's a big kiss." I leaned in and blew her a kiss. "Now get to sleep and you better keep your promise."

"I will. Good night, Uncle Nico!"

"Sweet dreams, angel."

I ended the call and turned to Violet. Her expression had morphed into one I'd never seen her wear. If adoration had a face, it was the one Violet was giving me right now. My heart rate tripled in speed.

"That's my niece," I said quietly.

She glanced down and cleared her throat before saying, "You sing lullabies to your little niece."

"As often as I can." I stood and leaned my guitar on its stand in the corner.

"Layla is your sister?"

"Actually, she's my mother's granddaughter by her second husband. My mother was human."

"How's that?" she asked.

"You do know I'm a hundred and seven, right?"

"Old man. You're robbing the cradle with me." She smirked playfully.

"But yes, she is like a sister to me. Her husband died in an incident working offshore, so I try to help out and keep in touch when I can."

She took a step into the room and put both hands into the back pockets of her jeans, then huffed out an embarrassed laugh.

"What?"

"I, um . . ." She tilted her head to the side, a guilty smile on her face. "I saw the picture of y'all downstairs and her name on your phone when she called the other day and thought she was maybe an ex-girlfriend. Or wife."

My brows shot up as I stalked closer. "You thought I had an ex-wife and a child I didn't tell you about?"

I spanned my hands along her waist. She curled her index fingers into the belt loops on the side of my jeans.

"Well, you've never talked about a sister," she accused. "And Mateo never said anything about another cousin."

"That's because she isn't related to Mateo. My mother left my dad. She had to." I swallowed the lump in my throat, thinking about how she'd left me behind too. For my own good as well as hers.

"Why?" she asked quietly, probably thinking I wouldn't answer.

What Violet didn't understand was that I'd tell her anything. I wanted her to know me, wanted to bind her to me in every way.

"My father had trouble controlling his temper. And his beast. He, uh, hurt her one too many times after shifting when he lost control."

I slid my hands under the hem of her loose button-down shirt, needing to feel her skin, needing it to ground me. I settled my palms on her waist again.

"When she left him, he agreed it was the best thing to do."

My poor father wasn't a perfect man, but he never could control his temper. For a wolf, that could be deadly for others. I didn't tell Violet that the last time he was violent, my mother was hospitalized with multiple lacerations and a broken arm.

"But how did you end up being raised with Mateo? Your mom—" She stopped, obviously realizing the truth.

"She had to leave me. A human woman can't raise a werewolf on her own. She had no idea how to teach me what to do, how to cover up what I was. She ended up moving to Florida and remarrying a good man. A human."

I couldn't keep the regret from my voice. Losing my mother had ruined my father, though he knew she had to leave. I remember him sitting on the back porch every afternoon, drinking a beer and staring off into space. He withdrew further and further until he went away one day on a trip to Montana. He didn't return home.

Mateo's dad and our grandfather found him deep in the woods in human form, naked. And dead. He had gashes all over, deep wounds on his stomach. He'd obviously gotten into a fight with a bear or wolves and had lost.

"And to be honest, I was afraid to go with her. I'd started shifting and understood the danger for her." I swallowed hard, my gaze sweeping her delicate collarbone. "I'd never forgive myself if I hurt my mother the way he had."

She slid her slender fingers under my shirt and swept them over my abdomen. I tightened at the sweet sensation.

"You did see her, though, right?"

I nodded.

"Of course. Till it was obvious to her family that I wasn't aging. And after she passed, I lost touch with her daughter."

"Layla's mother."

I nodded. "But then I get this call one day, and she tells me she's my mom's granddaughter. Apparently, my mother had pictures and letters of her and my father she'd passed down. Layla was happily married at the time with a baby girl and not much family still alive. But she'd wanted to meet me since I was almost all she had left except for her father. I suppose, technically, she's my niece, but I've always thought of her as a sister."

"Where does she live?"

"Baton Rouge."

"What? That's so close. Is that why you moved to New Orleans?"

I stared down at her, dumbfounded at that question. "No, Violet. She isn't the reason I came here." I wasn't hiding anymore. "But I guess it's another reason for me to stay."

She licked her lips and toyed with the button at the top of my shirt. "But you get to see her a lot more now, right?"

"Not as much as I'd like," I admitted, tucking a lock of her purple-blonde hair behind her ear.

"Because you're afraid you might shift or something? You don't have a hot temper, Nico. You're the coolest guy I know. As in calm and collected."

"Most of the time, yes. But there are times I've lost it."

Ty's terrified and bloody face flashed into my mind. I squeezed my eyes shut for a second.

"That boy in the Blood Moon pack?"

I nodded stiffly, ready to move away from this conversation. This wasn't what I had planned for our first date.

"Well, good thing you know a very crafty witch who's going to help you with that problem."

"Good thing," I agreed before leaning down to kiss those sweet lips.

I sampled her mouth for a long, lingering moment, tasting with just a little tongue. And that was all it took for me to reorganize our date night. I started unbuttoning her blouse.

She huffed. "Aren't we going to talk about this?"

Since our hard fuck in the supply closet, we hadn't exchanged a word besides the text she'd sent me.

"Do you want to talk?" I continued kissing and unbuttoning.

She pulled back, watching my hands descend. "Don't I even get dinner first?"

"I'll feed you after round one."

When I slid her arms out of the blouse, she noticed the setup on my dresser. Then she burst out laughing.

I grinned, not even glancing back as I unfastened and removed her bra, unable to look away from her beautiful body. I'd set out an array of items I'd picked up today, including a blindfold, fuzzy pink handcuffs, and a giant bottle of Hershey's syrup.

She turned her attention back to me since I already had her jeans halfway down her legs. She obliged and stepped out after I pulled off her socks and shoes.

"A man of action, wolfie. I like it."

I grabbed her waist and lifted. She immediately wrapped those long, sexy legs around me, and then I kissed the fuck out of her as I walked to the wall.

"Number three already?" she asked, all breathy.

Her pulse had quickened, and I could scent the wetness between her thighs. One thing I noticed in that supply closet was how well Violet responded to my dominant nature. With every command I ordered, she became more turned on. I also knew that I didn't want to hold back with her. Not in any possible way.

With a strong-willed woman like Violet, that meant pushing a few boundaries to show her I was no ordinary lay. I was going to be her only one from here on out. She just didn't know it yet.

"No," I finally answered, dropping her on her feet. Wrapping my hand around her nape, I slid my tongue along her lower lip, then bit it with a little force. "Number one."

I straightened as I gripped her shoulders and pressed her down. She followed my lead, sliding down the wall till she was on her knees. Those big blue eyes stared up at me with a little shock and a lot of arousal.

I cupped the side of her face, grazing my thumb across her cheekbone, her skin like silk. My wolf was already looking out from my eyes, siting his prey, wanting to bite and claim her in every way, but I held the leash. We were doing this my way, the only way to capture the heart of a witch like Violet. Her mouth was partly open, her pupils blown wide, black swamping her irises, leaving only a ring of vibrant blue.

"What are you waiting for?" My voice was gravel-deep, my question a command.

Her eyes fell to my crotch before she started unbuckling my belt with quick fingers. I brushed the pad of my thumb over her bottom lip, back and forth, as she panted lightly and pulled out my dick.

"You have any idea how long I've wanted to fuck this pretty mouth?"

She whimpered at my words, wasting no time in gripping the base of my dick and wrapping her lips around my head.

"Fuck." A feral groan rumbled deep in my chest.

Placing my palm under her chin, I held her jaw lightly, then eased her back till her head hit the wall. Then I started to slide deeper. She sunk her nails into my jeans at my thighs to hold on as I slowly pumped into her mouth, nice and shallow but going deeper with each thrust.

"Suck me."

She did. With enthusiasm, those gorgeous eyes looking up at me. I draped my forearm against the wall, still cupping her jaw in place with the other hand, then dropped my head to watch and spread my legs wider so I could fuck her mouth properly. No. Thoroughly.

"Can you take more of me?"

She nodded eagerly, never releasing that spine-tingling suction on my cock. I pumped deeper, hitting the back of her throat, groaning at the insane pleasure spiraling through my body.

I moved my hand from under her chin to the nape of her neck, her hair sliding between my fingers, then squeezed. She started to bob her head forward and pumped her hand on my dick in rhythm with her mouth.

"Good girl," I growled.

She reached her other hand between her legs.

I squeezed her neck tighter. "*No.*"

She glared up at me, defiant and frustrated. My cock got even harder. She rubbed her fingers over her panties. She was testing me. But I needed her to know that, in this, I needed, my wolf needed, full control. Full obedience.

"You heard me, Violet. *No.*" A rough command. I shook my head. "Touch your tits if you want, but that pussy is all mine tonight."

A glazed expression of pleasure swept across her eyes as she rolled her middle finger around one nipple. The sight made my balls squeeze tight, ready to blow.

Reaching back into my jeans pocket since they were barely off my hips, I pulled a condom out and dropped it between her spread knees. "Put it on me."

This time, she didn't hesitate. I pulled out, still only inches from her lips, sweeping her saliva over her mouth while she unwrapped the condom.

She was breathless and so silent. I'd never seen Violet without a smart-ass comeback. Even in the supply closet, she'd been mouthy. It was such a fucking turn-on.

My wolf liked her smart mouth. He also liked her lips swollen from sucking my cock. But there was something about her being reduced speechless—panting and frantic to get my dick inside her—that boosted my aggression to the next level.

As soon as she had the condom rolled on, I pulled her up and hoisted her with one arm under her ass, leveraging higher so I could suck her pretty tits. Her nails scraped my scalp as she ground herself against my abdomen.

I reached between us and tore open my shirt, buttons bouncing to the wood floor, needing to feel her on my naked skin. We managed to get my shirt off together. I sucked one nipple before coasting to the second, groaning at how pink and puckered they got for me.

"Please, Nico," she begged, grinding against me. "Please, please, please."

I lowered her, holding her up with one hand on her ass and my chest pressed to hers. Not that I had to do much; she had an iron grip around my neck. Licking into her mouth, I slid my dick back and forth between the folds of her pussy. She was so drenched it didn't take much to coat the condom.

"I could get used to hearing you beg," I whispered against her mouth, relishing the wild, pleasure-soaked look in her eyes.

She bit my bottom lip with a sharp sting and glared. "If you don't get your dick inside me now, I'm going to cut it off and take it home with me to use as I want."

I smiled then, lined myself up and gripped her ass with both hands before I drove inside her with one hard thrust.

Her head fell back to the wall and she arched her neck, offering me her throat. She probably had no idea what that meant to a werewolf. I didn't take her submission as truth, but my wolf bucked at the reins. I leaned forward and sucked her neck, biting a line down her throat as I fucked her hard and marked her up.

She made these desperate little sounds, a cross between a whimper and a moan, over and over again with each thrust of my hips. I moved my arms to hook under her knees and spread her wider, my palms on the wall, watching the insanely erotic motion of my dick pounding inside her soaking-wet pussy.

"Oh God!" She couldn't move her hips now that I had her pinned. "I'm gonna come."

"Fucking look at me," I growled.

She opened her eyes, an expression of near-pain creasing her brow. And then something else. Yes. Fucking right there.

That's what I wanted to see. Raw vulnerability as her body responded to mine, as I took her over the edge of pleasure into something deeper.

"Yes, baby," I whispered against her mouth before sliding my tongue inside and kissing her with aching tenderness. "You feel it too, don't you?"

I ground against her clit with each upward thrust, both of us groaning as she came apart, clenching around my cock.

I fucked her through her orgasm, following not too far behind, letting my head fall to her shoulder. We stayed just like that, trying to come back down from wherever we were. Because it sure as hell wasn't planet Earth.

Ghosting my lips up her neck, I finally lifted my eyes to hers. She stared at me, that vulnerable look fading behind a cocky smile. It didn't matter. I'd seen it, captured the moment, and stamped it on my heart. It was mine. Just like she was.

"Jesus, wolfie." She was still breathing hard. "You sure know how to fuck."

I chuckled, still buried deep inside her. "We took care of two on the list."

Her eyes narrowed. "Do you even know the definition of reciprocal?"

I couldn't help but laugh. "In the supply closet doesn't count?"

"Hell no. I may have to revoke your alpha male card if you can't take care of business."

I pressed a soft kiss to her lips. "Let me feed you. Then I'll eat dessert." I thrust up to make my point. "I'll check a few more off your list."

She grinned and kissed me sweetly. "Deal."

CHAPTER 19

~VIOLET~

HOLY HELL. WHAT A NIGHT. THAT WAS THE BEST SEX I'VE EVER HAD. And I've had my fair share.

I was curled on my side in his bed, having woken up when Fred crowed below the window at dawn. Nico was still sleeping. He lay on his back, one arm thrown over his eyes, the covers down to his waist.

I stared and admired. When I moved a little closer to him, I winced at the delicious soreness all over. We'd done our damnedest to knock quite a few off my list. I'd sent that list in jest, loving to tease Nico.

His playful side had me grinning. His sexy side made my insides liquefy. I tucked my knees a little higher, my hands beneath the pillow under my head, relishing the memory of him last night.

Let's be honest. I had no idea what I was in for. Whether he liked the label or not, we'd become friends over the past two years. His easygoing though broody nature had me imagining the same kind of lover. Slow and steady. I'd attributed our experience in the supply/sex closet to the buildup of unrequited lust. But I was wrong. So wrong. One-hundred percent alpha fucking male. And I loved it.

When I sighed contentedly, he roused and turned his head. His sleepy eyes took me in and then he smiled before rolling to his side and slipping his hand under the covers and over my bare hip.

"Good morning."

"Yeah, it is," I agreed.

"You feel okay?" His brow pinched a little as he glided his warm palm up to my waist, then back to my hip.

"Do I look okay?"

He chuckled, his hand sliding farther north, his thumb brushing over a nipple that responded immediately to his touch. Who was I kidding? My whole body was already humming with anticipation.

My gaze roamed over his broad, bronzed chest, the dappling of dark hair there, then down to the darker line on his lower abdomen that disappeared beneath the sheets.

"How long do your boyfriends usually last?" he asked casually.

"Hmm." I gave that some thought. "About a month. Two if they're lucky."

He grinned. "Challenge accepted."

I bit my lip, wanting to tell him that the reason no one ever lasted was because they weren't *the one* Aunt Beryl had told me about when I was sixteen. And I was still too embarrassed to tell him that I was fairly positive he was the one I'd been waiting for. That we should've been doing this a year ago when he came to New Orleans. But I just couldn't get the words out.

I let my gaze wander the width and breadth of his beautiful chest for a few seconds, while I enjoyed the slow caress of his hand. When I finally looked back up, he wore an expression of pure amusement.

"What are you thinking about?" I asked softly.

"Murphy's Outfitters."

"What?" I laughed, wondering what the hell he was talking about.

He smirked. "It's this great place in San Antonio. They have the best Stetson cowboy hats." His hand now completely covered one breast, mounding lightly, then plucking at my nipple between his thumb and forefinger. "I'm buying you one for your next birthday. You earned it last night."

"Never knew I had the skill to ride a bull like that," I teased, though my voice had already gone breathy and quiet.

"I did. I was just waiting for you to give me a chance and saddle up."

I spread my palm across his muscled chest, circling my own thumb over his nipple. Two could play at that game.

"Maybe we're all done," I kept taunting. "Maybe you fucked all the lust out of me last night."

His hand on my breast slid lower between my legs, one finger stroking my slit. "Doesn't feel like it."

"Not sure my body can handle another round."

He eased closer and rolled me over to face the window. I felt his body shift on the mattress, heard the crinkle of the condom wrapper before he put it on, then pulled me against him till my shoulders were pressed to his chest, his erection against my ass.

He dipped his mouth close to my ear, "I can be gentle too." He sucked on my earlobe and nipped lightly.

"Nico," I breathed, already desperate for him again. I clenched my nails into the side of his hip, whimpering with achy need.

What was this madness?

"Let me take care of you, baby." He lifted my top leg and draped it back over his, opening my legs wide before pushing slowly inside me.

I winced a little at the soreness. He stopped, sweeping tongue-laden kisses down my neck to my shoulder, then back up. I sighed, the slight pain giving way to languid pleasure.

He covered my mound with his palm, rubbing slow circles with just his middle finger as he pumped his dick with tender strokes, his mouth attentive to my neck, sweeping softly with lips and tongue. I dug my fingers in harder at his hip, rocking back with his tempo, trying to get him deeper.

"Goodness," I exhaled.

"It is," he whispered, sucking harder at the base of my neck. "So fucking good."

Then he lifted his palm away and slid his middle finger into my mouth. I sucked and twirled my finger around it, letting him pull it back out with a graze of my teeth. He growled, pumping a little harder but still nice and slow as he slicked that finger around my swollen nub.

"I know I'm a greedy bastard," he rumbled, still nipping and sucking right below my ear. "But I need to feel you come on my cock again before I can start the day." He placed a gentle kiss on my jaw. "Better than Wheaties."

I laughed, but then it was sucked right out of me as he stoked me higher with a deep, hard thrust. My brain started to haze. His finger left my clit, and I whimpered, but he gripped my inner thigh and hiked my leg higher so that he was stroking deeper than before, hitting me in that perfect sweet spot.

I released his hip and reached in front of me to grip the edge of the mattress, jutting my ass back for him.

"Deeper," I mumbled into the pillow.

He lifted onto his elbow, half folding on top of me and did just that, growling when my orgasm came swift and hard.

I was boneless beneath him as he kept his pace less punishing than last night, grinding in a circle when he was sheathed deep. With all my bravado, I was all ridden out, so I let him do all the work and take his pleasure at leisure, buzzing from the drunk-like endorphins rocketing through me.

When he finally groaned, falling near on top of me, his cock swelling and pulsing with release, I reached back haphazardly and patted his hip.

"Good boy," I whimpered, half into the pillow and breathless.

His laughter rumbled into my back. He pressed a soft kiss to my shoulder. "Let's get a shower."

I whipped my head around to look at him. "Are you crazy? I'm not ticking that one off the list right now."

"Just a shower." He smiled, a tender expression on his face.

"I can't move right now. Go take yours first."

He popped out of bed, holding himself to keep the condom on, completely unfazed by our sex marathon as he went into the bathroom. Freaking werewolves and their endurance. Guess the rumors were true.

I heard the shower turn on, then he was striding back in having disposed of the condom, all swagger and sinfully sexy.

"Ugh. Stop looking so hot. My body just can't take anymore right now." I shook my head as he dipped down to pick me up. "I can't believe I'm even admitting that. It's embarrassing, to tell the truth."

"Don't you worry. I'm going to take care of you."

Did he ever. He set me on my feet in the shower and proceeded to wash me clean with strong hands. He washed and conditioned my hair with languorous slowness.

His perfect hands slid over my sensitive skin but never sought to arouse me, even though I noticed he was semihard again. After he quickly washed his hair, he turned off the water and helped me out. Then dried me off.

"I could get used to this," I murmured as he ran a towel over my hair.

He wrapped the towel around my body, tucking the edge in at my breasts. He gripped my hips and pulled me against him. "Then get used to it," he said, coaxing my mouth apart and sliding his tongue inside.

I combed my fingers into the damp strands of his hair, clenching tighter when he sucked on my tongue. Now he was fully hard again. I pulled apart and glanced down at his impressive erection pressing into the terrycloth covering my belly.

"You have got to be kidding me. What are you made of?"

He cupped my face, bringing my attention back up to him. His expression so sweet as he brushed damp strands of hair away from my face. "Never dated a werewolf, I see."

"No one told me the stamina thing was for real."

"Now you know what you're in for." He arched a brow in challenge. "Unless you can't handle it."

I narrowed my gaze. "Don't even." I gripped his cock and gave it a stroke. "But we'll have to do this another way."

He smiled tenderly, wrapped his hand around my wrist, and gently pulled my hand away.

"No need to take care of it. He pretty much remains at attention when you're around."

Grinning, I slid my hands along his waist. "Really?"

"Why the hell you think I've been in a bad mood the past year since I moved here?" My laughter belted out.

He joined me, but a wash of sincerity flowed across those deep green eyes. He pressed a swift kiss to my lips. "Get dressed and come down for breakfast."

He patted my behind and slipped out of the bathroom. He pulled on a pair of sweatpants and a T-shirt before heading downstairs.

As I got dressed in last night's clothes, I figured there was no rush in telling him about Aunt Beryl's premonition. And my own stupidity. Because then I'd have to admit that my feelings for him were well beyond where they should be for a couple who'd just started dating.

I knew he'd wanted me for a long time; the sexual tension between us had attested to that.

But I also didn't know how much his heart was involved. Like mine.

Call me a coward, but I wanted to be sure he felt even close to what I felt before I admitted it. This wasn't dating. This was walking down your forever path. I needed to know he wanted to go with me.

๛

I was sitting in the big comfortable chair I had in my workspace, reading the addendums of Marigold Lord's book. There was actually one that spoke specifically to the ancient art of tattooing spells.

The part that interested me the most and had me riveted was the incantation of a Celtic druid named Cathbad who was also a powerful Divine Seer. It said that he would use the incantation to seal and activate the spell after it was put on the skin of the supernatural. It was in Gaelic but loosely translated to "Bind the elements to nature's power and magnify the magic within this host."

It wasn't poetic or pretty. Well, actually, in Gaelic it was, but the words themselves didn't spark me as riveting. Only the tingling sensation of my own magic humming under my skin as I read it told me this was significant.

The only thing was that this was the sort of incantation that seemed to match a warlock or witch. Even a vampire or grim. Because you would want to amplify their magic. But that wasn't exactly what we did want for a werewolf. We didn't want to increase his potency or strength, but to give him the power to wield it. Still, these words were close.

I typed the incantation in my notes section of my phone when Livvy came storming in, her expression tight as she stretched out in my client chair with a huff, then crossed both forearms over her eyes. "Looks like you have something to tend to."

I set aside the book and moved to sit on my stool and rolled up to the reclining chair.

"What's this about?"

She wrenched her arms away from her eyes, full lips pursed with aggravation. "Can you do one of your charmed tattoos that prevents the effect of grims?"

This was interesting. "What kind of effect?"

She snapped her gaze to mine. "You know what I mean. To block their grimness. That thing they do, making you think and feel things you don't want to."

Smirking, I pressed both palms onto the seat of my stool, propping my boots on the rungs. "The enchanted tattoos don't work that way. Besides, the grim aura just taps in to your darker feelings, ones that are already there under the surface. You know this."

Her glare escalated to a death stare before she looked at the ceiling in deep thought. "Maybe Clara or Isadora has something at Maybelle's that can help me."

She was an eclectic dresser, but today she wore a black pencil skirt, fitted mauve blouse that matched her lipstick, and strappy platform shoes. The one sign of her personality was the enamel pin of a gold dragon with ruby red eyes on her lapel.

"Where've you been?" I asked, thinking maybe this would give me more information on her current state of duress.

She shot up into a sitting position, blazing with anger. "To the last interview before they choose finalists for the contest. And that asshat grim did nothing but gloat, like he already knew he had it in the bag. If he makes the finals with me, he's going to need a serious attitude adjustment or I'm going to wipe that superior smile right off his face."

I couldn't help but laugh. This was *not* Livvy. She didn't get ruffled easily, if at all. "What does he do that bothers you so much?"

"Breathes." She narrowed her blue eyes, getting that far-off look as if imagining what she wanted to do to her enemy.

Oh hell. I think I knew what was going on. My psychic eye buzzed in agreement. "And what does this grim aura make you feel, sis?"

She snapped her gaze back to me. Then she zoned in on my neck, her demeanor shifting dramatically. "You little ho." She swung her legs over the side to face me, her expression positively gleeful. "You finally did the deed with Nico!"

"Can you say it louder? Because I don't think the whole building heard you."

"We did," Sean called from the front lobby.

She clapped her hands together, then reached over and grabbed my shoulders to shake me back and forth.

"What is this?" I laughed at her theatrics.

"I'm so excited!"

"Why?"

She stopped shaking me like a ragdoll, then rolled her eyes. "Why? Because you two have been circling each other for forever. The amount of pheromones you've both been putting off could impregnate a nunnery."

"Should I be worried that you think people can get pregnant from pheromones?" She batted my factual words away. Far be it from me to make some sense.

"Tell me," she whispered. "How was it?"

To say I couldn't stop the maniacal grin that creased my face was an understatement. It was a natural response to the mention of Nico and our sexathon last night.

"Yes! We should celebrate. Are you done for the day?" She glanced around as if waiting to find a client lurking in a corner.

"Yeah." I stood and put the book in my backpack to carry home. Jules would kill me if I left this book lying around. "Can we run by the house first so I can drop this off?"

"Of course. Then let's go to the pub."

"I should do some work on the inventory," I mumbled to myself, feeling like I should be working longer hours to be sure everything was perfect before the grand opening celebration.

"Nope." She popped off the reclining chair, linked her arm with mine, and hauled me off my stool. "Time for booze and details. Let's go."

I sighed while laughing as Livvy led the way because she wasn't a force you could stop once she set her mind on something.

CHAPTER 20

~NICO~

I'D SPENT THE ENTIRE AFTERNOON HELPING MATEO INSTALL ONE OF his new sculptures in the lobby of a downtown corporation. I hadn't seen Violet since she left my place after breakfast and I was starting to get fidgety. I was already going through withdrawal, needing a hit of my vicious addiction: Violet Savoie.

I wasn't kidding. My wolf paced my inner walls, wondering why the fuck we weren't glued to her all day long. Why we weren't buried deep inside her, night and day.

"You okay?" Mateo asked as we climbed into his vintage truck parked right off Canal Street.

"Mm-hmm."

He started the engine, gaze darting to my lap. I glanced down, noticing I was doing that guitar-strumming-on-my-pants-leg thing that I tended to do as a nervous habit. Right now, I was playing one of Eddie Van Halen's solos in my head, my fingers moving a hundred miles a minute.

Mateo pulled away from the curb and headed toward Magazine Street. Unable to help it any longer, I shot her a quick text to ask her what she was doing. Within ten seconds, I saw the dots moving as she answered.

Violet: Drinking whiskey.

Me: Jealous. Can I join you?

Violet: If you can stand being around my obnoxiously drunk sister and two other lovebirds.

What? I smiled at her odd, but very Violet, response.

Me: Where are you?

Violet: The Cauldron.

What is that goofy look about?" Mateo grinned as he glanced over before turning onto Magazine.

"Violet. You mind dropping me off at the Cauldron?"

"I'll come with you. Evie's working the afternoon shift. Should be off soon."

I let her know I was on my way and stared out at the neighborhood as the bars and restaurants' lights started popping on.

I loved this city at night, particularly where we lived. It had an energy that was both electric and intimate. Not that everyone knew each other, because it wasn't that small a neighborhood, but intimate in the way that we all belonged. And now that I finally had convinced Violet to date me, I never wanted to leave this place.

"Damn." Mateo huffed. "It took you two long enough."

He'd seen the signs a long time ago that I'd targeted Violet. "It took *her* long enough. But don't go talking out of your ass around her."

"What does that mean?" His voice came out a little growly. His wolf, Alpha, seemed to be tormenting him more than usual lately.

"That means she doesn't *know* how badly I want her." How badly I need her. "And I need to keep it that way for now."

Mateo regarded me with a flick of his eyes before turning to the road and nodding. "Good call. Might want to keep that under wraps for now. Violet doesn't seem to be the kind who'd like to be cornered."

"Well"—my mouth quirked up into a smile—"sometimes she does."

He laughed. He would be the only one I could joke with about that. Mateo was the brother I never had. We'd shared more than one secret over the years. When I struggled to leave the Blood Moon pack, he literally knocked some sense into me. We'd gotten into a brawl when I wasn't willing to leave.

Before that, I'd noticed that some of the pack lost control of their tempers and their beasts more and more often. It was infuriating. Both because I understood their pain but also because I wanted to turn wolf and tear into whichever asshole had lost his shit that day. Then I'd done just that—to a sixteen-year-old boy.

That's when I'd started to pull away from them slowly, realizing that it was safer for everyone if I lived alone.

I'd still spent time with Shane. He'd been my first friend in Austin and had introduced me on the music scene. I'd counted him as my best friend for a long while. But he'd started to notice how I was finding more excuses not to run with the pack, not to hang with them and stir up shit in bars.

Their idea of fun was to go looking for motorcycle gangs to pick a fight with and beat each other bloody. I was tired of giving in to my violent side. It was bad enough that the beast took over once a month, but their ways only amplified our natural aggression. Then that day with Ty.

He and his other teenage buddies, all werewolves, were horsing around in the clubhouse, an old mechanic shop turned into a hangout. Ty had spilled a beer on one of the newest members, who then immediately shifted. I jumped in, half-shifting, and pushed him away from the boys.

But then someone grabbed my arm. On pure, wild instinct, I turned and swiped a claw right across Ty's face and neck. The sight of that boy falling to the floor, his blood pooling on the concrete, had nearly broken me.

Thankfully, we had a warlock, a Conduit, who we paid to patch up our guys after brawls. Witches didn't normally help us. The stigma ran deep, and for good reason if you'd seen Ty's throat open and bleeding. But we paid the warlock well, so he came and saved Ty. The scars remained. After that, I fell into a foul mood. For months. Then Mateo punched the fuck out of me a couple of times and told me to wake up and get the hell away from that toxic pack.

I'd been looking for my moment to leave when we were invited to that New Year's Eve party. And the second I laid eyes on Violet Savoie, I knew when I was leaving, where I was going, and why. The pack became instant history, and she became my present and future.

I'd been patient for so long that I could hardly refrain from blurting out to her how I felt now that she'd opened herself up to me, to the idea of us. But no, the current course of action was the best one. Continue to seduce her body, then steal her heart when she wasn't looking.

Mateo turned onto the side street where the Savoie house was. It would be easier to park in their driveway and walk around the block to the Cauldron. One thing that was always limited in New Orleans was parking.

People buzzed from one pub or restaurant to the next. I waved to Clara as we passed Mystic Maybelle's. She was locking the front glass door, closing up shop. She gave us a friendly wave and sweet smile from the other side.

We strode quickly to the Cauldron next door and entered, hearing the trilling laughter from the bar the second we stepped inside. There weren't many customers but the music was turned up a tad louder than usual. Right now, "The Promise" by When In Rome was playing, which told me that Livvy had taken over the playlist. It was her laughter that echoed across the pub.

At the bar, my gaze zeroed in on Violet sitting next to Charlie with Livvy on the other side. I sidled toward them. Evie wove through the tables to deliver three beers to a four-top before stepping over to give Mateo a kiss hello. I moved quickly to Violet's side.

"Hey." I wrapped a hand around her waist and brushed a kiss against her cheek.

She twisted sideways on her stool, facing Charlie, and looked up at me. No, *beaming* up at me.

"Hey, yourself." She didn't have the glassy, tipsy look Livvy had. Or even Charlie propped on his stool, his blond hair disheveled as though he'd run his hand through it one too many times. "Nicooooo!" Livvy literally screamed. "You have to play with us! Come on, come on."

"What are we playing?"

Violet grinned, staring at her gregarious sister. "One of Livvy's drinking games."

"It's called Straight Face," declared Livvy, her s's slurring a bit.

Thank goodness she only had to walk home around the block from here.

"How do you play?" I asked, just then noticing a bunch of scraps of paper on the bar top.

Violet reached for a piece of paper and a pencil, but Livvy lunged across Charlie to grab one herself.

"No, no, no! I'm going to do Nico." Then she burst out laughing. "I mean, not do him, do him. Because that's Violet's job."

Violet's jaw dropped as she stared at Livvy. I simply basked in the open admission. Charlie turned toward me finally, giving me a sexy wink. "You devil. Finally got it in, eh?" Violet punched him on the arm.

"Ow!" He grimaced and rubbed the spot. "Be gentle, you barbarian."

"Everybody shut your drunken pieholes. What Nico and I do is none of the whole bar's business."

She glanced beyond my shoulder, but no one was paying attention to us.

I squeezed her hip where I hadn't let it go since the second I made it to her side. "So how do I play?"

"Easy peasy," said Livvy, scribbling something on her scrap of paper. "JJ!" she yelled down the bar where JJ was serving another customer. "We need a drink!" She pointed to me. Livvy was one of those fun-and-loud drunks. She turned to me and handed over the slip of paper. "All you have to do is read the slip of paper without laughing or smiling or reacting in any way."

"That's it?" I asked.

"That's it," she confirmed, grinning like a she-devil.

Just as I was opening the scrap of paper, JJ set a glass of whiskey over ice in front of me. I read the message Livvy had scribbled: *Violet said you made her come like a rocket at least five times.*

I'd been determined to keep a straight face, but there was no way in hell I could keep from grinning at that one.

"Drink!" yelled Livvy, shoving my whiskey closer to me.

"Like a rocket?" asked Charlie, peering sideways at the paper. "Not sure about that metaphor, Livvy. Maybe *he* came like a rocket."

I crumpled the paper and slipped it into my back pocket.

"Pfft." Livvy made a highly undignified noise through her lips with a drunken wave of her hand.

"What was it?" asked Violet, reaching around to my back pocket.

I let her slide her fingers along my ass to retrieve the message, ready to drag her out of here and back to my place three minutes ago.

When Violet read it, she gasped. "Livvy!" Then she grabbed another piece of paper and started scribbling something down. "My turn."

I moved up behind her, sliding both hands around her waist and leaning over to read her message for Livvy. I was confused at the message: *I bet that grim makes you cream in your panties every time you see him.*

She slid the piece of paper over with a superior look. I leaned down and whispered, "What grim?"

She waved me off as Livvy took the scrap of paper and opened it. Her stoic face turned mutinous before she let out a growl/scream of frustration. She snapped her fiery gaze to Violet.

"He in no way affects me in no possible way!"

"You said no way twice," chimed in Charlie, his gaze on JJ walking back toward us. "Is that a double negative?" He had that drunken confused look on his face that made him look quite young.

"Drink!" ordered Violet.

"Why? That wasn't funny. I didn't laugh at all."

"You said we couldn't react in any possible way. You definitely did *not* keep a straight face."

"Fine." She glared at Violet, tilting her drink back. Slamming the glass tumbler on the bar, she narrowed her gaze, looking off into space. "Did y'all know that grims are telepathic?" We all swiveled our attention to Livvy.

"I don't know *anything* about grims," I admitted. No one did. They were as silent as the grave when it came to their abilities. Or anything at all about them, quite frankly.

"No one does," said Violet before excitedly asking, "How do you know they're telepathic?" Livvy held up her empty glass for JJ to see down the bar, shaking it so that the glass clinked.

"Because he telepathed something to me."

"He who?" asked Charlie, frowning in confusion.

Violet grinned. "That guy in the contest with her. Gareth Blackwater. What did he say to you?"

"He didn't *say* anything." Her brows rose haughtily, but her face flushed pink.

"He sent an image?" I asked.

"Yes!" she snapped. "It was an accident, actually." She giggled and then she suddenly yell-whispered, framing her mouth with one hand as if to keep her voice from carrying, "And it wasn't appropriate."

"What was it?" asked Violet.

When Livvy's gaze whipped to Violet, my girl suddenly gasped, then burst out laughing. The sound filled me with a sweet emotion.

I squeezed her hip. "What?"

Violet craned her neck toward me so I leaned down. "Livvy is telepathic too. She sent me the image. Or ten-second video, rather." Violet waggled her eyebrows. "He's a naughty grim."

Livvy shook her glass in the air again for JJ, who finally headed our way. "Don't worry. I'm going to get him back." She gave me her Cruella smile, and I knew that poor man was in trouble.

JJ braced both hands wide on the bar in front of Charlie and Livvy. "Not sure you should drink anymore, Liv."

"One more! You and Charlie can walk me home."

"It would be my honor," said Charlie, placing a hand over his heart, his eyes as bleary as hers.

"So"—I leaned in close to Violet's ear—"what lovebirds were you talking about in your text?"

She pointed to Charlie and JJ.

"What? No way." I eyed the two men who I'd become friends with over the past year or so.

"But you told me they're just friends. Best friends."

"Yeah, well, friends can apparently turn into something else sometimes."

"They can." I squeezed my hands around her waist, hearing the insinuation in her expressive voice. "But are you sure?"

She snorted and nodded her head as JJ leaned forward to hear something Charlie was telling him. Then out of the blue, while Charlie was still talking, JJ grasped the back of Charlie's neck, then dragged him closer and planted a kiss on his lips. And it wasn't just a peck.

When Charlie made a little whimpering sound, JJ released him and turned back to the bar, but not before he gave Charlie a heated look that promised more later.

"Whoa," I whispered against her temple.

"Yeah," she said, grinning. "About fucking time." She said the last part louder, which got Charlie's attention.

"I could say the same about you," he snapped back, but his haughtiness was washed away by the significant pink blush high on his cheekbones.

Mateo finally ambled up next to us and raised a hand to JJ, who then pulled a longneck from the stand-up freezer and popped the top before handing it over.

"I missed something fun," he said, taking a swig of his beer.

"You so did," chimed in Livvy, still at that too-loud decibel. "FYI, Nico is banging Violet. And JJ is banging Charlie. Or Charlie is banging JJ. Well, both. Can Violet bang Nico?" Now she wore a drunk-and-confused expression. "Unsure if this term allows the girl to do the banging, since it seems to refer to penetration rather than just fucking."

"Right," said Mateo, taking another swig of his beer. "Be right back." Then he headed down the short hallway to the bathrooms.

Charlie started debating with Livvy over the semantics of the term banging, basically explaining that it's simply a synonym of fucking so there was no need for any discrimination on whether the person is the banger or bangee. It was nonsense, but I didn't care.

All I cared about was Violet's insane smile and sporadic laughter as she sipped her old-fashioned and watched the other two arguing.

I was so entranced by Violet, sweeping my hand up under her fall of silky hair to wrap around her neck, that I didn't catch the scent or shift in electrical currents in the air right away. It was actually Violet who stiffened first, her gaze moving from the bar to a booth in the back, a line creasing between her brows.

I followed her gaze, tensing immediately at the sight of Shane and two new guys to the pack who I hadn't liked before I left. Kyle and Rick, I think. Evie wound her way to the booth and started chatting, taking their order like any other customers.

"What the hell are they doing here?" asked Violet.

Then Mateo sauntered out from the area of the bathrooms and froze.

"Oh, fuck." Before I could do anything, his head had snapped to the booth, already zoning in on the enemy. "Shit. Stay here." I tore away and started to cross the bar, but he was too fast. Mateo was there in a millisecond, pulling Evie away from them and jabbing a finger in Shane's face, his voice guttural as he threw some nasty warnings their way.

Shane held his hands up in surrender, but the smirk on his face was not doing him any favors. Evie seemed to be trying to calm

Mateo with a hand on his chest, but suddenly he turned, tossed her over his shoulder like a caveman, and stormed off toward the kitchen, one hand possessively on her ass.

As we passed, I caught the fire-gold of his eyes. He didn't say a word, just bared his teeth and growled as Evie said rather calmly, her ponytail swinging, "Alpha, just put me down. I won't go near them. Promise."

I made my way to them, much calmer than Mateo, but that was probably because Violet had stayed next to the bar like I'd asked. If she moved any closer to them, I likely wouldn't be able to think clearly anymore, reverting to Neanderthal status like Mateo, solely because of who she was to me.

"What are you doing here?" I asked Shane.

"Just having a beer." He glanced beyond me. "If I can get some service, that is."

"There are lots of bars in New Orleans, Shane. What do you want?"

"Nothing," he said innocently. "From you, anyway." He'd zoned in on Violet at the bar, and I distinctly felt my blood pressure rise, a flame of rage percolating just beneath the surface.

"Look, I'm not sure what you think the spelled tattoos will do, but it doesn't work like a regular spell. So if you're trying to bulk up with magic or something to make your pack stronger"—and more violent—"then Violet can't help you."

"You don't know a fucking thing about what we want." He gave me a condescending huff.

"Or maybe you do since you fucked Ty up, then abandoned the pack."

I ground my teeth together, forcing my anger back, reasoning through his words. Frowning, I said, "If you're looking for help to control the wolf, Violet is working on it. When she has the spell, I'll let you know. Just go back to Austin. I know how to reach you."

"Yeah, I'm sure you'll be reaching out with open arms, won't you, *brother*?" Fuck, he was raging under the surface.

He sneered. "Witches are always so eager to help werewolves, aren't they?"

A shared memory of me and Shane popped into my mind. When one of the pack members had a nasty curse put on him that had made him violently sick, we'd gone to a hex-breaker in Austin. One look at us, and she'd hissed, *Like I'd help a goddamned werewolf. If he's cursed, then he deserves it.* Then she slammed the door in our faces. It wasn't the first or the last time we'd been subjected to that kind of treatment, merely because we were born werewolves.

"I can see that you and Mateo are the golden boys. The special snowflakes around here. But I'm well aware of how all these witches see *us*." He gestured to the guys in the booth. "Why else would you be trying so fucking hard to get us out of your city? It's a free fucking country, Nico. We aren't hurting anyone. We don't have to leave."

He was right. They hadn't hurt anyone. But I was very sure he was in a volatile state, his wolf making more of the decisions for the pack than the man. That made him dangerous.

"We know how it is," Kyle butted in. "Your witch won't do what we want. But she might help you because you're fucking that pretty pussy. Maybe if—"

Red rage hazed my vision a split second before I reached across the table, claws out, gripped him by the leather jacket, and dragged him over the table and out of the booth. Dropping him on his back, I put a knee on his chest, my hand around his throat. He didn't resist because he knew I'd slice through his jugular if he did. This was the way of werewolves in the midst of aggressive contact. If he wanted to keep his blood inside his body where it belonged, he needed to submit and deal with my fury right now.

I leaned close, not wanting to terrify the few customers gawking and looking on. I warned him in a low but lethal whisper, "Listen, motherfucker. If you touch a hair on her head, I'll eviscerate you. They'll never find the body."

Kyle didn't seem prone to fear, a young, cocky douchebag who didn't know when to keep his fucking mouth shut, but he glanced over at Shane for help.

"Nico," said Shane behind me. "We'll leave. No need for violence." He laughed as if it was a joke. He seemed to rather enjoy violence when we ran together. But he stood slowly from the booth, Rick with him.

I released Kyle but not before I swiped a claw under his chin, just enough to break the skin and draw blood. A small warning. I stood and glared at Shane, knowing good and well my beast shone through my eyes. "You need to get the fuck out of town," I told him.

Shane's reaction wasn't one of fear, but wary. Especially when Mateo strode back across the bar alongside JJ. Evie was nowhere to be seen. Violet still sat at the bar with the others, watching.

He didn't agree or disagree. Instead, he said something altogether worse. "Your new girl is pretty, Nico. Better watch her close."

When I took a step toward him, Mateo caught me with a fist in my shirt. Yeah, they were baiting us, but Shane knew right where to hit to send my wolf into a maddening spiral.

With that, he chuckled and sauntered slowly for the door, his lackeys right behind him. Once they were gone, I strode back to the bar and took Violet's hand. "Let's go." Rather than argue, she nodded.

"Should we close early?" asked JJ.

"Nah. They won't be back."

Mateo was in front of me before I could haul Violet through the kitchen door toward the back exit, my chest heaving.

"Are they leaving town?" he asked.

"I hope so" was all I could manage as I practically dragged Violet toward. "But that fucker was right."

"About what?" Mateo scowled.

"They haven't broken any law. If we're running them out of town for no reason, then we're no better than the other supernaturals who hate werewolves just for breathing the same air."

Mateo stared at me, considering. "That may be. But it doesn't mean we shouldn't keep an eye out. Packs are dangerous by nature, and he well fucking knows that."

"I'll report it to Jules and Ruben, but legally we can't do anything. Or we shouldn't do anything. I'm not going to discriminate against my own kind, but I sure as fuck will keep an eye on them."

Mateo nodded, then I hauled Violet behind me through the kitchen, needing to get her somewhere private. Immediately. Jules glanced up from a pot on one stove, frowning.

Evie was leaning against a counter, her arms crossed. "Can I come out now?"

I nodded, then kept marching out the back door. "Your place or mine?" I asked.

"Mine."

Their house was only half a block around the corner. By the time we made it to the stairs of the carriage house where she shared the loft with her sister, my labored breathing had escalated to near hyperventilation. I scooped her in my arms and charged up the stairs. As soon as I entered, I glanced around the small apartment.

"Where's your room?"

"That way." She pointed down a short hall past the kitchen, arms linked at my neck, staring intently. "What's going on?"

"I need you." A terse, gruff reply and nowhere close to matching the driving force propelling me toward her bed.

I slammed the door shut with my foot and spread her out on the white comforter, my mouth on hers with ferocity. Something about that encounter in the pub sparked a raging need for me to kiss and claim.

She moaned into my mouth before pulling back and stripping her shirt over her head. I paused, staring down at her red bra against milk-pale skin. My vision hazed for a second before sharpening to wicked clarity. My wolf was trying to come right out of my skin. Literally.

"Fuck, Violet," I murmured, mounding one breast with my hand before curling my fingers over the top of the cup and giving it a good yank. "So fucking beautiful."

She gasped when I leaned down and sucked her tight nipple into my mouth.

"God." She sunk her nails into my biceps. "Clothes. Get your fucking clothes off."

We tore and jerked and stripped till we were naked. I climbed on top of her, bracing my weight on one forearm. Holding her green-eyed gaze, I slid my fingers down her flat stomach, then between her legs. She spread her thighs on a breathy sound, arching her neck a little, eyes half closed in pleasure.

"How sore are you?" I murmured, finding her so wet and slick, my cock jerked.

She shook her head. "I saw Isadora today. Asked her to feed me a little healing energy."

Grinning, I swept my lips against hers, my hand gliding gently over her folds and slipping one finger inside her, then back out. "Did you tell her why?"

She had her nails on the rounded part of my shoulders, clenching and releasing as I stroked with little to no pressure, teasing.

"I told her we fucked each other's brains out, and I needed to heal fast so we could do it again."

I belted out a laugh, still sliding two fingers up and down her slit. When she rocked up to try to get more friction, I lifted away.

"Damn you, Nico. No more gentle."

"No?"

She must've seen a flash of wolf in my eyes because her eyes widened with excitement.

I bit her bottom lip. "You like him, don't you?"

"What's not to like?"

I flipped her over and shoved the pillows off the bed so that she was flat on the mattress.

"Reach up and hold on to the headboard." There were slats in her antique frame. "That headboard is perfect for fucking your brains out."

She laughed, turning her head to the side, breathing quicker. "Then get to it." She lifted her ass tauntingly.

"So pushy." I smacked her ass with a resounding *thwack*.

She laughed and moaned at the same time, then I bit and licked a trail down her spine. She wasn't laughing anymore. She whimpered when I reached her ass and licked the crease between thigh and cheeks.

"Mmm. Nico," she breathed on a slow exhale. "What are you doing to me?"

I spread her with my thumbs and licked her slit on a groan. Her scent was so necessary to life now, I wasn't sure how I was going to leave her alone for one second of the day.

I whispered against her cunt. "Can I just stay right here forever?"

She laughed but then stopped suddenly, sucking in a breath when I entered her with my tongue, mimicking what I'd be doing with my dick in short order.

"Be my guest," she mumbled into the mattress.

I gripped her thighs and opened her legs wider, continuing to fuck her with my tongue. When I slid one hand underneath her and rubbed her clit with insistent pressure, she came with a sharp cry. I lapped up her intoxicating juices before I opened and strapped on the condom I'd thought to toss on the bed before my jeans flew across the room earlier.

I crawled up her body, biting as I went. She shivered, still panting when I settled on top of her and used my knees to spread her legs wide for me.

Rather than pushing right in, I slid my dick along her slick folds, then along the crease of her ass, back and forth, while sucking on her neck. When she kept trying to push back with her ass to get me in, I chuckled.

"You're a total pussy-tease," she gritted out.

"You're so impatient."

"Fine then. I'll go find someone else who—"

I clamped down hard on her body, biting into her shoulder, and slammed into her with one hard thrust, jolting her body beneath me.

"Ah!" she cried out as I held myself deep, unmoving.

"You were saying?"

"Nothing. I wasn't saying anything."

"That's what I thought."

She laughed, knowing good and well she was just pushing my buttons till she got what she wanted.

I started to stroke, pulling almost all the way out, then pounding back in with a steady, slower tempo.

"Tell me you want no one else," I demanded in a silken whisper.

"No one else," she groaned as I pounded deep again.

"Tell me I'm the only one who can touch your body. Fuck this pussy."

She was getting lost in the sensations, gasping and moaning, her sex sucking me in deeper each time. I combed my fingers into her hair and tightened my grip to get her attention.

"Tell me, Violet." A primal demand I couldn't keep myself from making.

If I'd been able to think straight, I never would've said it. It was overly possessive and could've pushed her away. We might be monogamous, but she also wasn't the kind of woman to let herself be owned by anyone. Not yet anyway.

Still, the wolf needed it, choking on his desire to claim her as his own. My only hope was that Violet would think this all dirty talk and bed play because the next thing that came out of my mouth as I pounded her harder wasn't me at all. Pure wolf. My voice had gone Lycan-dark. "This body. This mouth. This pussy is mine. Only mine. Fucking say it." *Yield to me*, the wolf growled in my subconscious.

"Only yours," she whispered through panting breaths.

"Fucking right," I groaned.

I opened her thighs even wider with my knees and angled to go deeper, pounding with relentless force, flesh slapping and wet sex combined with the erotic sounds coming out of her mouth.

When her moans came closer together, and I knew she was going to come, I was suddenly desperate to see her face. I pulled out, almost smiling at her harsh protest, then flipped her over and slid back home with hardly a breath between.

"Yes," she crooned against my lips. "You even make vanilla sex feel good."

Grinning, I pinned her hands above her head, lacing our fingers together, then pumped in a steady rhythm, circling my pelvis at the end of each drive to give her clit some attention. She skated her heels up the backs of my thighs till she dug them into my ass and started rocking up to meet my thrusts.

When her mouth fell open, signaling her spiraling climax, and her sex clenched around my cock, the sight and sensation catapulted me toward my own release. There was something soft and tender in her eyes this time. An emotion I had caught only a glimpse of last time.

"Yes, baby," I murmured, feeling that intimate connection, too, that intangible emotion tying our hearts together with invisible, barely there thread.

My head fell forward, my mouth against her neck as I came hard, groaning deep and pumping through it with desperate strokes for more of her. Always more.

When my breathing started to even out, I finally lifted up onto my forearms to look at her beautiful, post-sex expression.

She was always beautiful, but something about her sated smile and the dreamy glimmer and wistful emotion in her eyes, knowing I was the one who put it there, made the wolf very happy.

And the man.

She tilted her head to the side, tracing a finger across one of my eyebrows, then over my cheek, down my jaw, and over my lips. There was a quiet, knowing expression on her face that made my pulse skip a beat. I was sure she was going to say something about what had just happened in that final climactic moment. Because it wasn't just an orgasm that put that tender expression on her face.

She opened her mouth but closed it. I waited. Then she finally said lightly, "You're super dominant in bed."

No, she wasn't brave enough yet to say it. But, hell, neither was I, so I shrugged a shoulder and said, "It's the same for a lot of men."

And honestly, I'd been staid today compared to our first couple of rounds.

"True. But there's something more there. Is it because of those other werewolves? Or is it just your wolf?"

I stiffened, glancing down to her kiss-swollen lips. "A little of both." Then I met her dark-eyed gaze again. "Does it bother you?"

She had no idea that she could cut me in two with the wrong response right now. She may not know what the wolf wanted. But I did. And her denial, in any way, would crush me. Break me.

She simply shrugged a shoulder, mimicking my movement a minute ago, and nonchalantly replied, "Your wolf likes me."

My wolf more than liked her. There were probably no words for what he felt. There were definite words for what I felt, but I couldn't say them yet. I had barely glimpsed the look in Violet's eyes that told me this was mutual, but I needed to be sure.

I was in so deep. My chest ached with all the words I wanted to say and couldn't. She must've seen some flicker of it across my face because her smile melted away.

"What is it?"

Rather than answer, I leaned down and pressed a lingering kiss to her lips, sliding my tongue inside for a gentle taste of her sweetness, but more to distract her. When I was able to withdraw my emotions and keep them off my face, I pulled back and gave her a smile.

"Be right back. Gotta take care of the condom."

I pulled out quickly. She hissed, and I felt her watching me walk into her bathroom.

"You say the most romantic things," she teased.

"I do my best," I shot back, tossing the condom, then washing my hands.

"Have you eaten?"

I braced one arm in the bathroom doorway. "Other than your pussy? No."

She threw a pillow at me, laughing. I caught it, watching her crawl on all fours, gloriously naked, toward the edge of her bed. "Definitely putting you up for *most romantic werewolf* award."

I shook my head, roving her gorgeous body, while my cock rose to semi-hardness again.

"You are the hottest fucking woman I've ever seen."

She slid off the bed with feline grace and walked toward me, the look in her eyes nearly bringing me to my knees. When she reached me, she slid her hands up my chest, brushing both her thumbs over my nipples, then watched as I became fully hard.

"Wow." She shook her head on a sigh, staring down at my dick. "I think I've finally met my match." She linked her arms around my neck and looked up, pressing her sweet body to mine.

I closed my eyes on a groan as I glided my palms down to cup her full ass. More than a handful. So perfect. I got even harder.

"What do you say," she whispered, "that we go tick shower sex off my list, then order some pizza?"

I smoothed my hands over her ass, squeezing and molding, pulling her against my erection.

"You're a woman after my own heart."

She laughed with delight, sliding away to go turn on the shower.

I wonder what she'd say if she knew that I wasn't joking. She already owned it.

CHAPTER 21

~VIOLET~

"L<small>IKE SPY LISTENING DEVICES?</small>" I <small>STARED AT</small> H<small>ENRY, A LITTLE ASTONISHED.</small>

Apparently, Sean's brother took it upon himself to do more than watch the shop. On instinct he'd said, he swept the shop for bugs.

"Found two here in the lobby and one right under the seat of your tattoo chair. We can talk freely. I deactivated them." He passed me one, a small, black innocuous-looking thing. "These have radio transmission, but I'm unsure of the reach. I'll have my cousin check them out."

"Where the hell would someone buy something like this?"

Sean laughed from the other side of the counter in the front lobby. "Everywhere."

Shocked, I looked up at him. "Really?"

"Best Buy. Amazon. You can even get them at Target and Walmart."

"Walmart sells spy-listening stuff?"

What the hell? What rock was I living under that I didn't know this?

The Blackwater brothers shared a smile between them at my expense.

"Like I said, I'll have my cousin check them out, see if we can get any telling information from tracking. But I'm pretty sure we can guess who put them there."

I remembered Shane paying me that visit on the first day in my workspace while his buddies stayed in the lounge. They all had easy access to place the devices that day.

"But why are they spying on us?"

"They're spying on you," said Henry emphatically.

This grim with his coal-black hair and eyes easily put most people on edge, but my psychic eye liked him. Trusted him.

"And I think you know why," he added. "They want that spelled tattoo."

I didn't ask how or how much Henry knew about my ability to spell tattoos. Grims seemed to know everything. Hell, they probably had the entire city bugged and on video surveillance. I didn't bother explaining to them that we still had no idea what Shane and the Blood Moon pack thought my tattoo could actually do. I suppose that's why they were listening in. Who the hell knew?

I tried to recall all the conversations I'd had in my workspace or the lobby since that day, and I remember talking to Nico and others about it. I mean, I wasn't trying to keep it a secret or anything.

"I better go tell Nico," I said offhandedly. "Is he in the back?" I asked Sean.

"Not sure."

He'd checked on the new electrical outlets earlier to be sure everything was working properly, so I wandered down the hall to see if he might be tinkering in the back.

In the kitchen, Tom and Lindsey sat close together at the table, their to-go bags from Red Dog Diner in front of them, burgers half eaten. Tom was pointing out some artistry of a tattoo he'd designed on his sketchpad while Lindsey looked on in total concentration. And admiration.

"Hey, guys. Y'all seen Nico?"

They both looked up, but it was Tom who said, "I think he said he had a project to work on at his place. But we should get him if we needed anything."

"Thanks." I nodded.

Immediately, Lindsey was again riveted to Tom's explanation of the technique he'd used in his design, and I was more than relieved to see there might be some sparks between those two. Not sure if Tom was aware of it because he seemed kind of clueless about personal matters. He was so deep and cerebral that he sometimes missed social cues. I might need to inform him if he couldn't figure out that Lindsey's admiring gazes meant more than she liked his tattoo designs.

I headed back down the hall toward the back door leading to Nico's courtyard but stopped in the lobby to tell Sean, "I'm going to step over to Nico's."

Sean gave me a head nod while talking to his brother at the door.

When I walked into Nico's courtyard, I certainly was not expecting what I found. Nico was in the grassy area of his yard, hammering away at a chicken coop. Fred was circling him and his construction, watching, perhaps critiquing, but not getting too close.

With mouth half ajar, I walked across the brick and onto the grass. "What's this?"

Nico glanced up from where he was crouched at the ramp into the coop, a lock of dark hair partially over one eye. "Thought it was pretty obvious."

Stunned, I braced my hands on my hips. "It is. You did this in one day?" I swallowed past the lump quickly forming in my throat.

He stood, hammer in his hand, his sleeves rolled up to expose his veiny forearms. The fact that I couldn't even focus on the hotness of the arm porn on display told me something was wrong with me; there was some other emotion besides lust welling up inside.

"It came mostly constructed. I just had to put all the parts together."

"Nico," I protested softly, "you didn't have to do this." And just like that, tears sprang into my eyes, threatening to spill. I blinked quickly, trying to make them go away, trying to get control of my swirling emotions.

What was wrong with me?

I never cried. For some reason, this sweet gesture had caught me by surprise, then squeezed my heart into a ball until I reacted.

He dropped the hammer in the grass, frowning as he strode right up to me. He cupped my face, his voice so tender. "Hey, hey, hey. What's wrong, baby?"

I tried to swallow the quiet sob, but the tears fell all the same. His frown turned into deep concern as he swept the tears away with his thumbs.

"What's this about?"

I tossed my hands in the air in exasperation before gripping his forearms. "What, you've never seen a girl cry over a chicken coop before?"

He smiled, tilting my head up and bridging the gap to press a tender kiss to my lips. "I have to be honest. I've never built a chicken coop for a girl before."

I slid my hands up over his long-sleeved shirt and laced my fingers at his nape. "I'd say this is getting pretty serious then," I whispered against his lips.

"Indeed."

Remembering why I came out here, I told him, "Henry just left. He found some eavesdropping devices in the shop."

Nico scowled, his hold on me tightening. He didn't ask who put them there. He knew. We both knew.

"Can Henry track them to the owner somehow?"

"He says he's bringing them to his cousin to see if he can. I imagine if anyone can, one of those grims could do it."

I tried for confident, but I heard the unsteadiness in my tone. Nico must've heard it too.

"Don't worry." He brushed a kiss to my temple.

My emotions were all over the place. Concerned about the bugs, stressed about the grand opening coming up, overwhelmed by Nico's kindness with Fred's new house, with everything he'd done for me, I clung tighter to him and kissed from his jaw to his perfect mouth.

He returned the kiss, gentle at first. Then his tenderness morphed into something ravenous as he crushed his mouth to mine, scooping one hand to the small of my back under my shirt where he pressed me tight against him. He tasted me with aggressive nips of teeth and strokes of his tongue, while his fingers glided gently over my skin along the top of my jeans. When a whimper slipped from between my lips, he clutched me tighter on a groan, breaking the kiss to nibble his way down my throat.

"Nico." I clenched both fists in his hair, pulling him closer. "What's happening between us?"

Rather than answer, he asked, "Can you stay?" Then licked along my collarbone.

"No. I have an appointment in a few minutes."

"What's a few?"

"Like eight."

"No problem." His hands went to my jeans where he unsnapped and unzipped.

Now he had me laughing where I was crying just a minute ago. I glanced around, but the brick walls were high and you had to have a key to open the door from the shop, which I happened to have. "Did you hear me?"

Then he was on his knees, and oh fuck, he was so beautiful on his knees in front of me, looking up through wolf-green eyes.

"All I need is five." He grinned, yanking my jeans and panties to my ankles.

The air was cold, but Nico's hands on my ass and thigh, his breath on my sex, were molten.

"I'm starting to see a trend here," I murmured right before he swiped his thumb over my clit, his eyes gone heavy. "You're in love with my pussy."

"We're deeply involved," he said without missing a beat, still stroking with his thumb. "I hope you're not jealous."

I held my breath as he eased closer, knowing the brain-hazing sensation I was about to experience.

"I'll share with her." My fingers sank into the dark locks of his hair. "But *only* her."

"So generous." He stared up at me, leaned forward, and licked his thick tongue right through my slit, then circled my swollen nub.

"That's me," I panted, bracing my hands on his shoulders now, nails sinking into the shirt-covered muscle. "Violet the Benevolent."

He grinned against my heated flesh. "And Lady V, the Conquering Werewolf Slayer." Another long, hard swipe.

"She's a lady?"

"Compliant, agreeable." Another long, hard lick. "Easy to please."

On a breathless exhale, I said, "Glad one of us is."

"Now be a good girl and let me suck you till you come on my tongue."

"Fuck, Nico," I breathed out harshly. "The things you say." I could already feel my sex clenching.

He lifted his palm and smacked my ass before grabbing a big handful and squeezing. "Quiet. I'm trying to concentrate."

I grinned and closed my eyes. "Shutting up."

Moving one hand to the back of his head, I held him harder against me. But it wasn't an orgasm I was chasing. It was that tender, raw emotion ever-present whenever Nico was near me now.

In these moments of ecstasy and intimacy, he drew it out of me like it had always been there. Waiting for him to weave his own magic and seduce not just my body but my soul too. My own magic sang to life, pumping through my blood, whispering the rightness of this. Of me and Nico. Of me finally opening my heart to the one who was meant to hold and cherish and care for it.

When his sweet mouth sent me over the edge, I sobbed at the realization that I was falling for him. Or I already had and didn't know it. I couldn't even help the tear that slipped with the overwhelming emotion that had been ripped out of me without my consent.

Nico caught me when my knees buckled, pulling me into his lap. He didn't say a word as he pressed his mouth to my temple and wiped the few tears that slipped down my cheeks with slow swipes of his thumb.

He didn't ask me what was wrong. He knew. He'd slipped into my jaded heart so fast. Or perhaps, it wasn't fast at all. He'd been doing it since the day I met him on the rooftop that New Year's Eve.

"Can I come to your place tonight?" he asked quietly a minute later, voice roughened as he swept another kiss to the crown of my head.

"Yes," I whispered, noting the vulnerability in my own voice.

He held me for another minute, simply caressing his mouth with chaste kisses along my forehead, seeming to recognize my need for comfort.

In true Nico fashion, he didn't demand to know what my tears were all about or insist that I tell him what I was feeling. He simply hugged me in his strong arms and let me be. Let me come to grips with what was between us. As if he already knew and was perfectly patient and willing to give me the time I needed to adjust.

When I could speak, I said, "It's the first night of the new moon, so I'm casting the werewolf charm." I combed my fingers tenderly through his hair, finally glancing up at him.

"Really hoping to get this right. For you. Do you want to come?"

His expression shone with deep affection. "Would me being there break the spell or something?"

"Not at all." I brushed my fingers along his hard jawline. "Someone watching has no effect on the spell."

He lifted me out of his lap and helped me slip my panties and jeans back on, then stood and angled my face to sweep another kiss to my lips.

I stared up into those beautiful, expressive eyes that had watched me for so long. I shivered at the thought of him wanting me all this time. Then a pang of regret followed in its wake, knowing we could've been together so much sooner.

"I'd like you to be there," I finally said, realizing in that moment that I wanted him to *always* be there. "Please."

"Then I will be," he said softly, tenderness shining in his eyes as I turned and walked back into the shop.

CHAPTER 22

~NICO~

"Just put me where I won't be in the way," I told Clara, now that I was standing in their private garden gated off from the rest of their courtyard. Ivy wove thickly around and through the wrought iron gate so that it felt very secluded.

Clara smiled and took my hand. "You won't be in the way. You're supposed to be here."

"Am I?"

Clara was Violet's twin, but also the opposite in every way. While Violet was direct and straightforward, Clara was enigmatic and puzzling. Where Violet was wild and untethered, Clara was sweet and nurturing. Like right now, she guided me gently around the witch's circle chalked onto the concrete slab at the center of the garden, making sure I was taken care of.

I'd texted Violet before I came over, just making sure it was still okay, unsure if her sisters would appreciate me there. She told me that after talking it over with Clara, her twin said it would be *better* for me to be there. Then she promised me there was nothing to be afraid of, especially since she'd had a talk with Clara, informing her that she couldn't dress up for the occasion and scare the hell out of me.

I wasn't sure what that meant, but Violet assured me that this wasn't like their monthly witch's round where they reenergized their magic. She would be leading the spell-casting and, finally, that I was wholeheartedly welcome.

Clara looked at me with a question in her eyes. "You're a Taurus, right?"

A little surprised, I turned to her on the other side of the chalked circle. "How'd you know?"

She just smiled. "I'm thinking end of April is your birthday."

"The twenty-seventh." She wasn't a psychic like Violet, so I was confused how and why she knew I was a Taurus.

"Have a seat near your birthday." She pointed to one spot near the wheel, then glanced over her shoulder and whispered to me, "I knew you'd eventually get to her. My sister's really smart but really slow when it comes to her own heart."

I'm sure my expression showed shock, but before I could react, she went on.

"You Taureans are always good at the long game." Then she gave me a playful wink.

"Um, thank you? How'd you—?"

She waved a hand like she was batting away an insect. "You did the right thing. Patience and planning. When I realized you were a Taurus, my money was immediately on you."

I shook my head at Violet's twin, who apparently knew I'd been infatuated with her sister all along. She just acknowledged my strategy to wait Violet out.

I wish I could've said it was a strategy. It had been more that I was unable to let go of my hard-core obsession. And then later, when my wolf recognized his other half, there was no way I was going anywhere. Still, I felt like it was new and tenuous and fragile, so I handled this precious baby with gentle hands. I sure as shit didn't want Violet to catch us talking about it when she came out here, so I switched subjects.

"I'm not a witch." As if she didn't know that. "How can my presence in the circle help?"

"You're a werewolf," said Violet, walking into the enclosure, holding a mason jar of what must've been black tattoo ink with Livvy right behind her holding two white pillar candles. "This spell is to help your kind, so having wolf magic present during the casting can only help. I'm just surprised I didn't think of it myself."

I nodded and took a seat outside the witch's wheel, which was intricately chalked onto the smooth stone pavement. With careful and decorative lettering, the wheel was labeled with the Celtic seasons—Beltane, Lughnasa, Yule, and Imbolc—as well as rune symbols. "Hey, Nico," said Livvy with a smile. "Welcome to our round."

"Thanks," I said uncomfortably.

I'd never seen witches cast spells. The only one I'd seen in action using his magic was the warlock Conduit who'd helped heal members of the pack when I was with the Blood Moon brothers.

Violet set the glass jar of ink in the middle of the wheel, directly on the smooth concrete, then she leaned over me, gripped my face, and pressed a kiss to my lips.

"Was that for luck?" I whispered when she pulled back, still holding my face.

"No. That's because I wanted to kiss your fine face."

I laughed a little nervously, glancing at her sisters sitting in their places around the wheel, simply smiling at the two of us.

"So I guess the secret's totally out." I sat at an angle, stretching my legs out behind Violet.

"Jules knows?"

"*Everybody* knows," Livvy chimed in with a laugh. "And I do mean everybody."

Clara's smile widened as she stood. Lighting the end of a sage bundle, she walked around us, smudging the space, whispering inaudible words. The smoky mixture of scents filled the space— cedar, lavender, sweet grass, and juniper. Violet arched a superior brow, seemingly proud of herself about something.

"What am I missing?" I asked.

"So apparently Violet had a really good afternoon yesterday." Livvy pulled her feet tighter beneath her crisscrossed legs. "And she decided to come have a few after-work drinks before she met you for dinner."

Violet had been happily tipsy when I showed up at her loft with Thai takeout last night.

"Do you want to tell him or can I?" asked Livvy, looking at Violet.

Clara set the smudge stick down in a wooden bowl filled with black sand next to the candles and ink, then took a seat next to Violet, who shrugged and said, "I'm not embarrassed. Go ahead."

"Right when she got your text about bringing dinner over, she set her phone down, then climbed on the bar and demanded JJ turn off the music so she could make an announcement. Just so you know, at this point, Jules, Isadora, and Clara were eating in the back corner since they had some bookkeeping questions about Maybelle's for Jules. It was a light crowd, but still, there were actual strangers present for this announcement. Anyway, Violet gets everyone's attention and shouts to the bar full of regulars since it was happy hour." Livvy braced both hands around her mouth, apparently mimicking Violet last night at the bar. "My boyfriend is Nico Cruz, local musician, business partner, and first-rate pussy-eater. I suggest the rest of you guys take lessons on how to do that proper if you wanna keep your girls happy."

I huffed out a laugh while the other three were already cackling. I turned to Violet. "You said that?"

"Sure did, and I don't regret it." She waggled her eyebrows at me.

"How drunk were you?"

She rolled her eyes. "I'd only had two Blood Orange Old-Fashioneds, though I think JJ might've put an extra shot in the second one. I was hounding him for details on him and Charlie, which he did not give to me."

Clara sighed heavily with a dreamy look. "They're so cute together."

"We can get the details out of Charlie later. He's much more likely to spill under pressure."

Livvy glanced up at the sky. "But we need to get this show on the road."

Violet glanced up. "Yeah. Let's move into the zone, ladies."

"What should I do?" I asked, suddenly feeling awkward. Nervous.

"Nothing." Violet smiled at me.

"Actually," interjected Clara, "when it feels right, I think it's best if you pull your wolf forward, almost into half-shift."

Now uncomfortable, I cleared my throat, glancing over at Violet. "That's not really a good idea."

Clara reached over and patted my hand, shooting me a wave of euphoria.

"Yes, it is. It's exactly what we need."

I turned back to Violet, wanting some sort of explanation for Clara's advice.

Violet shrugged. "If Clara says so, then she's right. Trust me."

"I do. I trust all of you. It's just . . . That could be dangerous."

All three of their faces slid into a smile at almost the exact same moment. It was a little disconcerting.

"We'll be fine," Violet assured me. "Even if you fully shift, nothing can hurt us in our round. Don't worry."

"And how will I know when it feels right?" I asked Clara.

"You just will." She smiled sweetly.

Licking my lips, I nodded and said nothing else. I still felt uncomfortable, but they were all completely confident in whatever was about to take place.

Violet picked up a piece of chalk and crawled on all fours to scratch a symbol in each corner. She chalked one directly in front of me. They seemed familiar, but still nothing I'd seen before in my studies of ancient runes. I spent one summer devouring everything on ancient civilizations, including the Romans, Gauls, and the Celts.

"Celtic?" I asked her.

She finished the strange symbol and smiled up at me. "Witch's runes. It's witch sign, to channel the right energy into the spell."

"Did you use them last time?" I asked.

She shook her head, a frown puckering her brow. "I hadn't thought about it till that vision I had with you. When I asked about your scar. Remember?"

"Of course." How could I forget? She'd gone into a sudden trance, her magic a soft hum cocooning me in palpable energy.

"Ever since then, I've been studying that rare book on witch sign that Ruben had gotten for Jules when Mateo had that curse put on him." Her expression was full of wonder and confidence. "And the book's been giving me everything I think we need. Other than the visions my magic has been sending me."

Surprised, I wondered if this was the first real step to help all my werewolf brethren. Because if this worked, it could fundamentally change the fabric of werewolf society. Possibly even the supernatural society. Over time, anyway.

The stigma of being the psychotic, violent race of supernaturals wouldn't go away anytime soon. It could still take decades, even centuries, depending how well the tattoo controlled our inner beasts.

I lifted a hand with crossed fingers, giving her a reassuring smile. Her frown faded, her expression shifting to one of resolve. Determination.

That's my girl.

Then she sat back into her place and set the chalk aside. The three of them braced their palms on their knees and closed their eyes. In an instant, I felt the sharp punch of magic filling our small space. It wasn't just ethereal, it was tangible. While I couldn't see anything, there was an undeniable energy weaving into the circle, their skin beaming with a luminous glow.

The three of them remained perfectly still, an otherworldly wind lifting their hair as it wove around us. But the strongest light beamed from Violet, a halo of power circling her. My wolf growled, sniffing the air at the foreign presence, then huffed as if to a friend. I'd never felt witch's magic like this. It was so different from wolf magic.

Werewolves were cursed. Our magic was heavy and oppressive and violent, then sometimes it flipped to tap in to the creative aspect, driving us like a freight train with artistic impulses. But it was always a lashing force, pushing against the skin. Hence, the reason werewolves were so dangerous. The beast could literally leap through our skin at any moment.

But this . . . this was so very different. It felt like being washed with power—both airy and fierce. No less powerful than that of the wolf, but elementally different. It felt like a soft ribbon skimming across my face, which could just as easily cut down to the bone. And still, I wanted to touch it, hold it, and swallow it down, let it absorb my entire being.

It was attractive by the very definition of that word. Magnetic. A force pulling me toward it, making me want more, then I felt and smelled a scent on the stream of magic.

Violet. This was *her*. Not all three of the witches' energies, but *her* essence whipping through the air, flowing around and through me. I swallowed the lump in my throat at the realization that I was inhaling and gulping deep breaths of my mate's magic. It was, in a word, magnificent.

My mate.

I needed to tell her. For us, the wolf was the one who chose. From the second he sniffed her out on that rooftop bar in Austin, Texas, I knew she had to be mine. The only problem was that now that I'd finally gotten her attention, and even though she was declaring our relationship on bar tops to the public, I was terrified she'd change her mind about us.

I wasn't sure that other supernaturals besides wolves felt that innate draw toward a mate. Her refusal to date me for two years told me that obviously she didn't. But the wolf wasn't wrong. And regardless of what he wanted, *I* wanted her. Body and soul.

Her voice echoed eerily in the circle, pulling me from my desperate thoughts.

"Goddess Divine, hear my call." Without opening her eyes, she lifted her hands, palms facing down over the jar of ink. "Black moon's power holds the key. Calling your singers by destiny. Give them the right that they should wield, their power, control, a solid shield."

Then her voice dropped to an almost inaudible whisper, a string of French words where I only made out *ecoutez* and *obéit.* Her mouth moved swiftly, the words no longer decipherable, then she clapped her hands together, punching the space with power. Two things happened in that second. The glyphs she'd chalked, the witch sign, electrified with light and my wolf surged to the surface of my skin.

I moved backward into a crouch, not completely outside the circle, but enough so that I could leap out of this enclosure if my beast took over. My nails extended into claws, my canines slid out, my jaw widened, and my bones stretched into an agonizing slow break. My legs lengthened without changing shape entirely. I could feel the fur wanting to push through my pores.

I heaved air in and out, a ghastly panting filling the round. But still Violet and her sisters didn't open their eyes or move a muscle. Only Violet's lips continued to move as I reached near-panic having her so close to *him*. A paralyzing fear I wasn't even aware existed sprouted to the forefront of my consciousness.

What would she do when she saw what I was? It was one thing to know that werewolves transformed into monsters. It was quite another to meet them in the flesh. I tried to resist the shift, to push him back. Just when I was sure he'd crush me under his will and burst fully through my skin, Violet whipped one hand through the air. A wind whirled in a torrent, snuffing the candles in one breath, and the sizzling magic vanished.

Staring at the ground, I let my head fall and gulped great lung-fuls of air as my wolf receded. My hands were splayed on either side of a glyph that looked like a winter tree. I stared down at it, noting the remnants of magic, like fine grains of airborne glitter, lifting away from the chalked symbol.

I wondered at the residue of Violet's power vanishing into the ether, thinking it felt like a loss of something beautiful. I wanted to capture it and store it in a vial. Carry it with me always.

It wasn't until I felt Violet's presence at my side, kneeling in front of me and coaxing me with gentle fingers in my hair, that I finally came back to myself. Looking inward, I knew that my wolf had receded, but the choking fear of rejection still hovered at the surface. A grimy, dirty sensation I didn't want to feel.

I'd never been ashamed of what I was. I was born this way, and I wouldn't apologize for it. But I also understood that we were considered the lowest in hierarchy among supernaturals. I'd never experienced the dread of Violet's rejection because I never thought she'd see *him*, be confronted with the monster that lived inside me.

"Hey." A whispered word of consolation, then soft lips on my brow. "You okay?"

I cringed at the sickening emotion welling inside me, at the shame of her seeing a part of me she might find repulsive. At the gutting fear of her rejection by her kind like what I'd experienced in Austin and other places.

"Yeah," I finally said, voice rough and raspy.

Her delicate hands cupped my face, lifting my downward head. I'd fallen to my knees at some point. Felt like I was still falling.

"Look at me." Gentle words.

Easing back onto my heels, I noticed that Clara and Livvy were gone, as were the candles and other things. Even the ink. I frowned, wondering how long I'd been sitting there. I hadn't heard them leave, and my senses were usually attuned to everything.

"Nico." Warm fingers stroked along my jaw.

When I finally met her gaze, there was genuine concern there. "What happened?"

Violet may have the dirty mouth of a sailor, but the truth was that she was a fucking angel straight down to her core. Her heart was encased in gold. A giving, caring soul I wanted to hold and cherish. And her beauty. I fucking ached to look at her. Those cerulean eyes—alert, watchful, compassionate. Would those eyes look at me differently if she saw what was underneath?

I swallowed hard. "Have you ever seen a werewolf in his beast form?"

"Not in real life." Her delicate fingers still brushed along my jaw, soothing me. I tried to turn my head away, but she held me firm and forced my face back to hers. "What's wrong?"

Licking my lips, I just told her, knowing this wasn't something I could avoid if we were going to be together. To stay together.

"The wolf is truly a monster."

"I've seen video footage on the SuperNet. And photos."

"It doesn't repulse you?"

She laughed. "No. Why should it?" *Why should it?*

This was Violet's unconcerned response. Unafraid, unapologetic. Not even remotely disturbed.

She scooted forward and lifted onto her knees, still stroking me with soft fingers. She arched a brow playfully, then whispered, "Actually, I think it would be kind of a turn-on to see him."

I huffed a disbelieving breath. "What?"

She played with the collar of my shirt, one finger tracing the line of my collarbone to the notch at the base of my throat.

"Nico," she said in a serious tone, all lightness fading away before she lifted her gaze to mine, "no part of you could be a monster. I don't care what you say. Your wolf is part of you, so I"—she stammered and cleared her throat—"I care for him as much as I do you."

Cupping her face, I dragged her against me and swept a rough kiss against her lips, drowning her in my emotions without saying a word. She whimpered into my mouth, which only drove me to go deeper, to devour.

Wolves were hungry creatures. Werewolves were ravenous. And the only flesh that could possibly sate my need was the witch I pulled onto my lap. But for some reason, it wasn't sex that I needed or even wanted right now. I just needed to hold her in my arms and feel her closeness, her warmth, her pounding pulse.

She straddled me on her knees and tilted her head, giving me perfect access to her throat. I groaned at her submission.

"Violet, do you know what that means to a wolf?"

She nuzzled her face against my neck, then whispered in my ear. "I've been reading a lot about your kind. When a woman or man offers their throat to an alpha wolf who is a lover, they're offering to be the wolf's one and only."

When offered by a mate to an alpha, it means even more. But I bit my tongue.

"Do you want to be my one and only?" I asked, voice rumbling rough as rock.

She pulled back, her face inches from mine. Her heart beat wildly in her chest, like a panicked bird's wings. "Yes." She licked her lips nervously. "And I want you to be mine."

Staring intently, I held this moment in my memory, wanting it to burn through flesh and into the marrow of my bones. Finally, I kissed her softly, melding our mouths with gentle sweeps.

"Then I'm yours, and you're mine."

She exhaled a heavy breath and buried her face in my neck, hugging me tightly. I did the same, stroking slow circles on her back, feeling my woman so sweetly tucked in my arms. The magic from the round still lingered in the air, encircling the two of us with ethereal essence.

It felt like a blessing.

And our beginning.

CHAPTER 23

~VIOLET~

"If you're done murdering me with your eyeballs, go tell Sean to come here," Mateo, or rather Alpha, ordered Nico.

Nico sat in the only extra chair in my workspace, his arms crossed, and yes, a murderous scowl aimed at his cousin in my reclining chair. I almost laughed but didn't think that would put Nico in a better mood. And something really was urging me to soothe him. But I couldn't do that until I finished this tattoo in the crook between Mateo's shoulder and pectoral.

I wasn't giving him a spelled tattoo yet. I'd given Nico his yesterday, and we decided to wait and see how it went first. Mateo didn't have trouble controlling his wolf ever since Evie had broken his curse. He also seemed to like having his wolf, Alpha, in his head. And since we weren't sure yet whether my spell might send Alpha away permanently, Mateo had declined getting the spelled one.

So I was giving Mateo a tattoo as a Valentine's Day present for Evie. He wanted a scene rather than just one object. It still made me smile as I stared down at the intricately detailed X-wing fighter flying toward a Death Star in the distance.

Yes. Mateo had wanted a Star Wars tattoo. After he told me that he knew Evie would like it, I reminded him that this was permanent and it wasn't a good idea to get a tattoo to please someone else. Then the strangest thing happened. Mateo blushed and mumbled that he'd become a fan himself, and he wanted it.

Mateo was a unique guy. Typically, he was quiet with an easy smile. He had the whole tenderhearted artist thing down to a tee. He was completely and utterly devoted to my sister Evie, which made him one of my favorite people in the world.

But then there were times when Alpha pushed to the forefront, and his personality switched to aggressive, sarcastic, and quite Neanderthal-ish. Lately, Alpha seemed to be hanging around more than Mateo. I'd asked Nico about it, and he said it was because those other werewolves were in town.

Nico heaved an exasperated sigh from against the wall, then unfolded out of the chair and strode to the front lobby.

"What's his problem?" Mateo huffed.

I glanced up at him, his eyes shimmering gold. Definitely Alpha hanging with me this morning. "I think he's a little territorial," I admitted, knowing full well why Nico needed to sit there while I gave shirtless Mateo a tattoo.

Nico was jealous and possessive, and it turned me the fuck on, which was the exact opposite reaction I usually had when men behaved this way with me. But this wasn't just any man. This was Nico. My heart thumped a little harder, telling me what I already knew.

The werewolf in my tattoo chair grinned lasciviously, his wolf-gold eyes gleaming from half-slits.

"It's all right, Violet. I'm a mated man. You have nothing to worry about."

"I know," I said, head down while I finished the detailing of the Death Star, biting my bottom lip so I wouldn't laugh.

An arrogant sigh. Yes, his sigh was arrogant. "They can't help it," he whispered conspiratorially.

"Help what?" I glanced up, definitely recognizing the vain expression of Alpha.

"I am the superior male," he said with such a straight face, pitying the rest of male-kind. "All others are threatened by me."

"Yeah." I cleared my throat, shifting back to put the needle down, then wiping away the excess ink. "I can see how you'd have to deal with that a lot."

He patted my shoulder with a knowing look, like we now shared the same secret.

Nico strode back in with Sean on his heels. The teenager had decided to shave his head into a faux-hawk. And somehow, it looked really good on him.

"You can take a look," I told Mateo, wheeling back to put my tools away and gesturing toward the mirror.

He hopped up and checked it out, grinning at his Star Wars ink. He was such a conundrum. But so was Nico. I'd thought I had him all figured out. Boy, was I wrong.

I went to finish up dressing Mateo's tattoo while he looked over at Sean. "What's the latest from your brother?"

I hadn't tuned in much because I really wasn't as concerned as the men around here, but Nico had told me that they had Henry doing regular sweeps of the neighborhood for Shane and any of his pack buddies. We might not be able to run them out of the city, but we sure as shit could keep tabs on them.

Sean watched me doing the dressing while answering him. "Henry said we've been clear for a week now. They're not around."

"You're all set," I told Mateo.

Nico picked up Mateo's T-shirt and tossed it to the werewolf, whose eyes had dimmed to the normal warm shade of brown they usually were.

Rather than look irritated, though, Nico seemed relieved. "That makes me feel better about having the grand opening celebration now."

"What do you mean?" I asked while spraying down the chair. "You considered canceling it because of them?"

"I was planning on it," he said with finality.

Removing my latex gloves, I tossed them in the trash and asked, "Without asking me? Because if I recall, this is half my business too."

He didn't respond to my spike of temper the way I'd thought. He eased closer and gripped my hips, pulling me against him and effectively maneuvering me farther away from Mateo. He brushed a kiss between my brows, which I knew was his ineffective attempt at wiping away my frown.

He dipped his head close to my ear and whispered, "I was planning on coaxing you into my plan to postpone it." He bit my earlobe.

Gripping his biceps, I said, "I suppose you think you have good enough coaxing skills."

"According to you and Livvy, you already announced it to half the neighborhood."

"Pffft. I was exaggerating to entertain the masses," I protested, even as I felt my middle melting at the thought of his skills.

"No, you weren't." He pressed his thumb between my brows, rubbing softly. "Stop frowning. I wasn't going to do anything without your permission."

"My permission?" I stared up at him, thinking about permission and giving orders. The way he gave orders in the bedroom. My irritation derailed toward wayward thoughts. "I think I know something we need to add to the list."

"Yeah?" He was still speaking low, even though Mateo and Sean had left to the lobby where Evie was hanging out. Mateo wouldn't let her come in since he wanted this to be a surprise.

"I want to be on top," I told him.

His mouth tipped up on one side. "You've been on top lots of times."

"Yeah, but not really. You're always in charge, even when I am. I want to be in charge." His brow arched in challenge.

I laughed. "Yep. It's going on the list. I want to see how long you can stand taking my orders."

His grip tightened on my hips a second before he slanted his mouth over mine, stroking in aggressively, his hands sliding down to cup my ass. Yeah, not so sure I was going to get to tick that off the list.

One hand came up to wrap around my nape possessively as he swept in with hungry strokes. He nipped my bottom lip, then my top before coming inside again. Meanwhile, I already had a leg wrapped around his hip and was getting ready to climb him when we were rudely interrupted. "Hey! Love bunnies!" Livvy was obviously standing in the doorway, but I couldn't take my eyes or lips off Nico. "We've got a lot of fucking work to do. Chop chop!"

A growl rumbled in his chest, sparking my arousal even more, but I dropped away and pressed my forehead to his shoulder. "She'll only come back in if we're not out in one minute."

He dipped his head to my ear again, nuzzling the sensitive skin right below. "I only need five."

My thighs clenched at the memory of the last time he said that. Laughing, I stepped away on a weary sigh and took his hand. "No, seriously. Livvy is relentless when she's in manager mode. She will legit come back in sixty seconds."

"Fine." He heaved a sigh and followed me through the lobby area and out in front of the shop.

Mateo, Evie, and Sean were already assisting two big muscly guys unloading the back of a U-Haul truck full of tables and chairs. Livvy stood off to the side with a clipboard, counting tables as they came out and checking her list.

She wore casual Livvy attire—black jeans, a mauve sweetheart-cut blouse with matching lipstick. Even in what she'd consider her shabby clothes, she was a knockout. The two poor guys unloading the truck couldn't help but ogle her every time they came down the ramp. But like I said, when Livvy was in manager mode, she stayed in the zone, not veering for anything. Not even two hot guys who could barely keep their tongues from hanging out of their mouths.

I assisted in unloading the chairs and stacked them on the sidewalk for now. Livvy was pointing out where she wanted the tables placed in a semicircle around the stage, leaving room for dancing.

"You know," I told her, stopping and propping my hands on my hips, "when I first told you I wanted to do a grand opening street party, I'd imagined getting a DJ, asking JJ to sell beer, and have a table for Empress Ink merch to sell."

Livvy gave me her best side-eye, tapping her pen on the clipboard. "Really, Violet." She snorted with something akin to disgust. "It's like you don't even know me."

"We're here!" said Clara, popping up out of nowhere with a perky smile as she surveyed the activity, Isadora right next to her.

"What can we do?" asked Isadora, checking out Livvy's list over her shoulder.

"Don't worry, Is. Even you would be proud of my thoroughness." Livvy spun and pointed to two boxes right off the curb. "The linens and votive candles are in there, and I've got the Empress Ink coasters and napkins in that one. Would you set them out in the way I showed y'all last night?"

"On it!" Clara went right to work with Isadora in her wake.

There was an elevated stage set up right in front of the wooden fence that marked the end of our dead-end street, but the band wouldn't be here for hours.

"The food trucks are still coming?" I asked.

"Don't worry." Livvy scribbled something on her list. "I've taken care of everything. Trust me. Jules is having Mitch, who's the chef tonight, shut down the Cauldron early so JJ and Finnie can serve drinks here at the party."

Jules had a regional meeting in Houston with the covens of Mississippi, Louisiana, and south Texas. I was sorry she'd miss the grand opening, but there was no way she couldn't be there to represent New Orleans.

I peered around the U-Haul to see JJ and Finnie setting up a wide tent. It was generous of them to help out before their shift at the pub, then to come here and serve at the party. I owed them both, big time.

JJ's Ford F-150 was parked with the huge rolling cooler in the bed of his truck.

"Damn. Livvy, don't we need a permit for something of this size?"

"Yes. And done. All you need to do is show up, make your big welcome speech, and enjoy the launch of your dreams."

She turned to me, her business expression slipping to caring sister mode.

I wrapped an arm around her shoulders and gave her a tight squeeze. "You really are awesome."

"Yes, I know."

"What can I do?"

"Glad you asked. Look over in that box there. I've included extension cords, but I want the white fairy lights strung up in a square around the dance floor. Nico can help you put up the selfstanding poles to string them from one to the other."

"That's going to be so pretty," piped in Clara from the table closest to us that she was currently dressing with cracked-glass votive candles.

"It really is," I breathed on a whisper, my heart fluttering that this was really happening.

What Livvy had planned would draw the kind of attention we needed to put us on the map in New Orleans. I took a moment to bask on the precipice of success, relishing that moment of hopeful possibility and buoyant potential.

"Hey," a deep voice rumbled in my ear. Strong arms wrapped around my waist, and a warm, hard body pressed against my back.

"Hey," I whispered back, wrapping my arms alongside his.

"You seem deep in thought over here. Everything okay?"

"More than okay." I turned in his arms, linked my hands around his neck, and pulled him down so I could bury my face against his throat and hug him hard. "Thank you for helping make this happen."

His arms tightened around me as he rocked me softly back and forth, his mouth at my temple. "Anything for you, Violet."

He brushed a kiss there, and I thought my heart might burst with joy.

You know those moments in life when everything seems absolutely perfect and you're filled with this insurmountable happiness? I tried to grab on to it and hold on, wishing I could freeze this moment in time. It was a culmination of two things. Obviously, the fact that I was kicking off Empress Ink with what would no doubt be a fabulous party, thanks to Livvy and my sisters and friends. The second was that the man in my arms was more than my friend. More than my lover. And I was finally ready to tell him exactly how I felt.

I gave him a squeeze. "Come on. Let's get this all set up so we can rest before we get dressed for the party."

He pressed a kiss to my neck and released me. I took his hand and pulled him toward the stage area where the box of lights and poles were stacked.

"What are you wearing tonight?" Nico asked, picking up one of the poles and setting it in its stand.

"I don't know. You have something in mind?"

He slid a devilish grin my way. "A dress."

"A dress?" Like that was foreign to me. Because it kind of was. I rarely, if ever, wore dresses. Only if I had a wedding or a formal occasion like the Witch's Guild Summit we had to attend annually.

Nico tightened the pole into place and shoved it over to the first spot, which apparently Livvy had marked with taped Xs. When his gaze swung back to me, his eyes glittered that electric green.

"Please," he whispered, a sexy plea in his smoldering gaze.

I smiled and winked. "Anything for you."

CHAPTER 24

~VIOLET~

"You're nervous."

"I know I'm nervous!" I screamed back at Clara standing in our loft living room.

She grinned wider. "Why? You look gorgeous. I told you my dress would look fantastic on you."

We were twins, so of course we had the same coloring, but our styles were so different. Still, this dress looked more like me than Clara.

I glanced down at the deep purple fabric hugging my torso with long sleeves and a deep vee. Smoothing my hands over my hips, I admired how the soft fabric didn't hug my thighs but fell perfectly straight, ending a few inches above my knees. It wasn't looking-for-a-hookup hot but sexy with understated lines, accentuating my curves with elegant tapering rather than tightness.

"I've never seen you wear this dress," I realized aloud.

"I bought it, thinking I'd have some occasion. But that occasion hasn't come up. Maybe I bought it for you, actually." She stared at the dress thoughtfully.

"You really do have more psychic ability than you know," I told her, glancing at her in a silvery minidress with matching cardigan.

With her hair falling in long waves down to her waist and pastel shades of makeup, she looked every inch the fairy queen. I'd gone for a heavier, smoky look for makeup tonight. Along with the dress, the lavender shade in my hair, and the way the sleeves cut at an angle, exposing most of my shoulder and my colorful orchid tattoo, I looked the part of co-owner of Empress Ink.

I wondered, not for the second or third time, what Nico would think of this dress. A burst of butterflies launched in my stomach. I pressed my hand over my belly, glancing around for those black flats. The dress I didn't mind, but I wasn't a heel girl. Ever.

"Stop worrying," said Clara, handing over my little black clutch with my phone in it. "This is going to be fantastic."

I exhaled a deep breath, then released a laugh. "You're right."

Clara suddenly reached over and pulled me into her arms. I was a little stiff. Clara and I were affectionate. All of my sisters and I were, but out-of-the-blue hugs weren't the norm. Still, this was Clara, and she rarely walked inside the confines of *normal*. That's why I loved her so much. She was her own person, no matter what others thought of her.

"I'm so proud of you," she said.

Hugging her tight, I relaxed into the comfort and praise of my sweet twin sister. "Thank you, Sissy. Love you."

"Love you."

Then suddenly I was feeling misty and weepy. What the hell? That's not how this night was supposed to go. I needed my badass, business-owner persona in full swing.

"Come on." I laughed, breaking our hug. "You'll make my mascara run."

"And that would be a shame. Especially before Nico gets a look at you. That werewolf is going to pass out."

We laughed and hurried to the Jeep Cherokee in the drive. My other sisters would be meeting us when the party started, but I wanted to get there a little early just to make sure there was nothing else that needed to be done. I'd left once we got the fairy lights up and the place was still coming together. Now that the sun had set, I was anxious to see the full effect of all our efforts.

We had to park farther up the block, but even from here it took my breath away.

"Oh wow," said Clara before hopping out with me.

We walked right through the barricades that the city had put up for us to keep people from parking close to the venue. This was all due to Livvy's exceptional planning and getting the appropriate permits and such. I swear, I think I owed her way more than the fee she charged me for her time.

"It's so beautiful, isn't it?"

We ambled dreamily through the tables, the candle votives already lit, watching as the band set up and warmed up their instruments. The singer strummed a few strings, keying his guitar. The bass player did the same, while the drummer tested with a string of random beats. I couldn't help but beam as I crossed under the lights Nico and I had set up earlier. Now, it cast the whole dance floor in a soft glow, along with the tables, the ambience inviting and fun.

A catcall whistle pulled both my and Clara's attention toward the tent set up to the right of the stage where JJ stood with Finnie, both of them grinning at us. We walked over.

"Damn, look at you," said JJ, his arms crossed as he shook his head.

I put a little more sway into my strut just to make him laugh. It did.

"You're one fine-looking business owner, Violet."

"Thank you, JJ." I rounded their portable bar and practically leaped into his arms.

He lifted me off the ground in one of those JJ bear hugs.

I'd been working at the Cauldron for so many years with JJ that he'd become more than a friend, closer to a brother. And he was the one I had secretly told about this little venture. Well, him and Charlie, before I'd even told my sisters. JJ had always encouraged me to reach for what I wanted, to show no fear.

"Thank you," I whispered into his neck.

"For what, love?" He palmed the back of my head, a gentle touch.

"For just being you. Telling me what I needed to hear."

He set me on the ground, big hands on my shoulders. "Always, Vi. You know that."

"God, y'all are all going to make me cry tonight." I blinked away the tears before they could fall, refusing to fuck up my makeup before Nico saw me.

"This is going to be one kick-ass party," said Finnie. "I've got all my friends from UNO coming."

"Perfect," I said excitedly, swiveling around to admire the place. College kids loved getting tattoos. "Be sure to tell them they get fifteen percent off their first tattoo. Not that it isn't on every table already."

Livvy had made sure to advertise with these cool artistic pop-ups on each table. A cutout of the logo, promoting our first-timer discount, was on a swivel that turned slowly like a music box. I thought she'd created it with magic, but she said no; it was a simple techie thing she'd seen recently.

"Hey, hotties!" Evie headed toward us with Mateo in tow. They were more dressed up too. Mateo wore dark jeans and a gray button-down while Evie wore a blue wrap dress with long sleeves. This was dressing up for Evie since her regular attire was almost always jeans and a novelty T-shirt with some sarcastic expression or something from one of the fandoms she adored.

We were fortunate that the weather was mild this weekend. Louisiana weather was notoriously bipolar. One day she thought she was spring, forcing open May-blooming plants in the middle of January. Then the next day, she said nah, how about a pipe-freezing rain? And dropped the temp into the twenties. Then two days later, we'd be back to pleasant fall weather. This was why our plants never knew what the fuck to do and leaves started falling in October, stopping and starting, all the way through February. Today, she was being kind, giving us that California-cool breeze in the lower sixties.

"This place looks fantastic," Evie practically squealed, running up and giving me a tight hug. "You did it!"

"Well, actually, Livvy did all this."

Evie laughed, which made Mateo grin where he stood behind her. "I mean the shop." She hooked her arm with Mateo's and peered up at him. "And thanks for that kick-ass Star Wars tattoo."

"I'm glad you like it."

"Love it," she said, still beaming up at Mateo. "He said he couldn't wait till Valentine's Day because there was no way we weren't getting naked before then, so . . ." She shrugged, as if fill in the details.

So apparently the raging libido thing wasn't exclusive to Nico.

Without a word, Mateo leaned down and pressed a sweet kiss to her mouth. That man worshipped the ground she walked on. It made my insides warm and melty and had me wishing my man was here already.

Another flutter of nerves shot through my body. Tonight was momentous in that it was the official opening of Empress Ink to the public, but also because I had some questions for Nico. I also had a few things to say to him. One in particular that had my heart doing somersaults at random.

"Holy hell," came the muttered words in a familiar deep voice behind us.

I turned to find the devil himself devouring me with his gaze. They'd gone wolf-green in a flash, brightening further as I walked toward him, my smile broadcasting how that look made me feel.

He was devastatingly handsome in black slacks and black button-down, cuffs rolled up to his forearms, his hair messily styled. He was the kind of handsome you'd expect in an expensive cologne commercial that was cut with a montage of hot scenes and overlaid by some obscure French narration.

He stood at the edge of the dance floor under one of the strings of lights, which cast his bronze skin and the sharp angles of his face with a warm glow. He crooked his finger at me.

"Come here."

Whoa. His voice had rumbled low and deep. Far be it from me to keep a hot werewolf waiting. I walked over, taking my time as his gaze wandered down my bare legs, back up to my breasts, skating over the exposure of my chest and neck due to the deep vee of the dress, then finally landed back on my eyes when I stopped right in front of him.

"You look—"

His mouth was on mine, my body pressed to his in a heartbeat. One of his hands skimmed across my back to my opposite hip. The other was under my hair, wrapping my nape, while he kissed the living fuck out of me.

I'm not lying. I'd felt him being possessive in the past, but his teeth and tongue were marking me, stroking into my mouth, nipping at my lips, and then back inside again. All the while, a growl rumbled from his chest, vibrating against my own. So arousing.

I whimpered when he finally drew back, breaking the kiss on a wet suction. He stared at me, both of us a little breathless before he pressed his forehead to mine and closed his eyes.

"Violet."

I had my hands at his waist, my nails curled into his shirt, probably wrinkling it.

"What was that for?" I asked.

"You look"—he swallowed, licking his lips—"edible."

"Well, hell, I would've worn a dress for you sooner if I knew it would get that kind of reaction."

He chuckled. "Sorry."

"No apologies necessary. Now I expect that level of greeting every day, though."

"Hey, Nico."

We both turned toward the stage to the singer who was speaking into the mic.

"How about we get started with something sweet for your girl?" He winked, then looked back at the bass player, who played the beginning chords of "Perfect" by Ed Sheeran.

Nico laced his fingers with mine and led me onto the dance floor. Once he swung me into his arms, a hand at the small of my back, one in the middle of my shoulder blades, he went back to admiring my dress, my face. I laced my fingers at his neck and did the same to him, both of us smiling and not saying a word.

The second I thought about the conversation I wanted to have with him, that unbidden rush of nerves flooded my bloodstream.

He frowned, probably hearing my accelerated heartbeat. "What's wrong?"

"Nothing." I cleared my throat, trying to remember how I'd wanted to say this. It was the perfect moment: romantic ambience, soulful song, hot guy in my arms. "I wanted to talk to you tonight."

"Yeah?" He tilted his head in a curious expression, that frown still scrunching his brow.

"Mm-hmm. I wanted to tell you something." I inhaled a deep breath, staring at his chest to avoid his gaze.

A tight squeeze, then his mouth was at my temple while we swayed softly. "Tell me."

It took me a solid minute to get my courage up, but Nico waited patiently, holding me tightly in his arms.

"So I'm good at divining for other people. But apparently I'm total shit at seeing my own future."

He didn't say anything. Just watched me, our faces close, our bodies closer. Wrapped in his warmth and affection, I found the courage to finally tell him.

"When you first came here last year, I did my own reading about you. About us. And um, I read the cards wrong." I glanced up to find that infinite patience still on his face. "I thought we'd be bad together. Like really bad, according to my interpretation."

One hand wrapped my neck under my hair, and then he gave me a gentle squeeze. "Then what happened?"

"That night you came home from your full moon trip, it hit me. I finally saw in the cards what I was supposed to see."

"And what was that?"

I swallowed hard, staring into the most beautiful face I'd ever seen. My heart tripped faster because those were the thoughts of someone completely and utterly in love.

"That you and I are meant to be," I whispered.

His comforting hold on my nape tightened as he grazed his lips against mine. "Yeah, baby. We are." He kissed me a little deeper, then—"Violet!"

We both looked over to see Livvy, dressed to the nines in a black minidress and thigh-high, high-heeled boots, signature red lipstick on. "I need you!"

She waved me over in a hurry. Sighing, I pulled Nico down for a quick kiss on his perfect mouth. He looked a little frustrated, like he wanted to tell me something else.

"Hold that thought," I told him with a smile, completely believing we'd have at least one more quiet minute before things got crazy. Boy, was I wrong.

Three hours later, and the party was kicking ass, so I didn't get back to that conversation with Nico as I'd hoped. Tonight in private at his place would work better anyway. I wanted to continue that conversation. For the first time in my life, I wanted to pour my heart out to a guy. It had me a little giddy.

Looking around at our street party, I was sure that every bar on Magazine must be empty, because our party had extended well beyond the barricades and rolled all the way down our side street.

I'd been making the rounds all night to make sure everything was running smoothly. Right now, I was pushing a dolly with another box of T-shirts from the shop out to the merch table where Sean, Lindsey, and Tom had been hanging most of the night. Not just to sell the T-shirts—which we'd been selling super cheap at cost under Livvy's advisement to get people wearing and promoting around town—but to meet potential customers and hand out business cards.

I set the dolly upright on the curb right behind Sean.

"I've got it," he said, leaning over and picking up the box.

The band was rocking, and the laughter and chatter of everyone filled the street with lively energy. It was a huge success.

As if to confirm my thoughts, Tom walked over with brows raised. "I've booked ten clients for this coming month tonight, and at least twenty more said they'd come to look at my portfolio soon."

"Yes," beamed Lindsey on my other side. "I haven't gotten quite as many as Tom, but it looks like I'll be booked pretty solid the next few weeks."

I didn't miss the charged look the two gave one another, and I sighed with relief that Lindsey wasn't hung up or hurt about Nico. It was a brief crush, and who could blame her? But I sure didn't want that to mess up having a very talented artist working for me.

I threw my arms around both their shoulders. "Thank you both for taking a chance with me. Together, we'll have this business booming."

Tom patted my back and sighed in that droll way of his before easing out of my embrace. He really wasn't the hugging type. "Woman, you knew this was going to be a success."

"Not really. But now I do."

A trill of familiar laughter drew my gaze beyond the merch table to the outside of the shop where Clara was leaning next to Henry Blackwater. He had both hands in his jeans pockets, his back to the brick building, one foot propped on the wall, his gaze fixed on Clara. She faced him, gesturing toward something in the crowd of people, then said something animatedly before laughing again. The grave grim who I'd never seen smile at any time quirked up one side of his mouth as he watched and listened intently.

I patted Tom and Lindsey on the shoulder, then meandered up to Sean, who was all business, this kid, folding shirts and setting them on display with rapid movements.

"Hey. What's going on over there?" I pointed casually to Clara and Henry.

Sean tilted his devious grin my way and arched his brow. "Looks pretty obvious to me."

"Does it?"

"Your sister is flirting with my brother." He shrugged. "Girls can't help it really. He's got that bad-boy magnetism. Runs in the family."

I refrained from rolling my eyes and telling Sean that he wasn't a bad boy, but my eyes were too fixed on Henry Blackwater. I didn't know him well, only of him in the neighborhood.

There was definitely an aura of darkness around the guy, and I didn't mean his grim reaper magic that they all wore like a cloak. Something else. Something not quite right or normal. It had pinged on my psychic level more than once, but it was still too elusive to grab hold of and define what it meant.

And what was Clara doing? I watched her more closely, recognizing that there was a subtle flush to her cheeks when she glanced back at the crowd. There was also a sparkle of excitement in her eyes.

"Shit."

She was definitely flirting. I made a mental note to interrogate her later. But now, I needed to find Nico. The night had run away from us. He'd been socializing with everyone and playing the good host like me, helping out Finnie and JJ when needed. I glanced across the dance floor and saw him standing next to Mateo, both of them taller than most people in the crowd.

"Text me if y'all need anything," I told Sean, making my way through the thick cluster of people near the stage.

The band had been doing a great job of keeping to upbeat classics most of the night but were now slowing it down a little. Southern Sun had the couples on the floor, so I had to do a little dodging to maneuver my way through.

I was halfway across when a hand wrapped around my wrist. I looked over my shoulder right as someone jerked me back, spinning my body to face him. I landed into a hard chest. Shane. In complete shock, I pushed off his chest, but he held tight. I could knock him on his ass with telekinesis, but since we were surrounded by humans, that wouldn't be a wise move. Besides, he wouldn't actually hurt me or anyone here in this crowd. I hoped not anyway.

"What do you want?"

His mischievous grin held that same hint of malice as the last time we'd had a conversation in my shop.

"I want a lot of things, Miss Savoie."

He stared down at me, his gaze flicking up and around the crowd stealthily as though he was keeping tabs on multiple places. Probably checking out exits so he wouldn't get his face pummeled by Nico, because that's what was going to happen pretty damn soon.

His grip was merciless as he kept me tight against his body, both my arms pinned between us as I tried to keep some distance. And failed.

I glared up at him, voice still steady. "Why don't you share your thoughts and tell me a few of those things?"

His gaze, bright and laced with wolf magic, swung back down to me. "Don't worry, beautiful. You're going to know all about it soon. Whether you want to or not."

"That doesn't sound ominous at all."

Dipping his head to my ear, he said, "It doesn't need to be unpleasant. Just go along, and you'll be perfectly fine."

"You might want to get your mouth away from my neck before my boyfriend finally sees you and rips out your tongue."

"That's what I'm hoping for."

"So you're not only psychotic, you're suicidal?"

He lifted his head away and laughed, an amused expression on his face. "I actually like you." Then he glanced back across the crowd and smiled wide, revealing his sharp extended canines. "Looks like your boyfriend's coming to rip out my throat as we speak."

Careening my neck over my shoulder, I could see Nico and Mateo storming this way, murder in their eyes.

Shane gripped my jaw and forced my head back around to face him. "See you soon, beautiful." Then he planted a kiss on my lips, nipping my lip enough to sting.

"Ow! What the hell?" I reached up and touched the dab of blood on my lip.

He pushed me out of his arms and tore off through the crowd in the opposite direction. A couple of people shouted "hey, man" and "watch it" as Shane booked it on the sidewalk. Mateo was fast on his heels, while Nico came straight to me. He cupped my face, hands shaking, and brushed his thumb over my lip where I'd been bitten, his pad coming away streaked with blood.

"Are you okay?"

Holy fuck! His wolf was 100 percent in his voice, his eyes blazing with eerie energy, and I could see his canines sliding out as he partially shifted. If anyone looked him dead-on right now, they'd know he wasn't human.

"I'm fine, fine! Go help Mateo."

I knew that's what he needed to do anyway. Without another word, he was gone, faster than I'd ever seen a man run, leaping over the barricade like an Olympic champion. Then another streak of black was right behind Nico. Henry Blackwater. Before I could take three breaths, the three of them disappeared around the corner of Magazine Street.

The band had faltered for a minute when there was sudden violence in the crowd, but I walked over and leaned up to the singer from the edge of the stage. "Something upbeat please. To get the crowd going again."

He nodded with a wink. "Sure thing."

"Hey, guys. How about an oldie but a goodie?" he yelled into the mic, launching into something fun and fast-tempo.

Needing a drink, I moved around to walk behind the stage to avoid the crowd, the quickest route to where JJ and Finnie were still serving. The second I rounded the stage, stepping between it and the wooden fence, two things happened at once. The empress on my forearm burned like a demon had snapped his whip, slapping me to alertness with stinging pain, then giant burly arms wrapped around me from behind.

"Gotcha," whispered a deep, growly voice.

"Wha—?"

Before I could even get the word out, a sharp pain struck my head, and I slipped into the black.

CHAPTER 25

~NICO~

I WAS GOING TO KILL THAT MOTHERFUCKER.

He was half a block ahead of Mateo, who was only a few yards ahead of me now, my wolf pushing to the surface, urging me to catch my prey and fuck him up beyond recognition.

Even so, I hadn't fully shifted, and I'd managed to keep my cool long enough to check on Violet. When my wolf had wanted to rip through my skin, I'd somehow quelled the beast long enough to ensure she was all right before joining the chase, keeping him calm enough to think straight. Barely.

A car pulled out from a side street as Shane crossed, leaping up and running over the hood, not losing stride. The owner of the car stared as the three of us maneuvered into the street itself, right behind Shane, so we could avoid sidewalk traffic and pick up speed. He was headed for the French Quarter, and we had to get him before he melded with the Mardi Gras tourist crowd.

He'd definitely get lost in that sea of madness.

While rage scraped against my rib cage, my mind remained calm. I knew it was Violet's spelled tattoo. Magic tingled outward from the point on my ribs where I'd had her tattoo a Celtic knot on me yesterday, washing me with a coolness that bled into my bones. Violet's tattoo charm was the only way I was able to think straight after seeing Shane grab, then forcibly kiss my mate.

What the hell was Shane playing at? Why was he taunting me? I couldn't wait to find out after I beat him bloody.

A horn blared at us as it passed. I'm sure we were freaking out drivers. It was full dark, and I doubt we looked close to sane tearing down the street after Shane.

"He's almost to Canal!" yelled Henry, speeding past me. Damn, he was fast! I had no idea grims could move like that.

Shane banked right when Magazine intersected with Canal, grinning over his shoulder at us. Mateo's growl echoed back to me. When we rounded the corner in the same direction, the streets packed with cars and people meandering the sidewalks, I almost careened right into a Lucky Dog street vendor.

"Where is he?" yelled Mateo, slowing but not stopping.

I couldn't find him as I scanned the tops of heads. "Fuck!"

Henry passed me. "There!" Leading the way, he pointed toward the river. "He's heading toward the water."

We took off again, weaving through people, accidentally knocking a few.

"Watch out, asshole!" some suit yelled after us.

I moved back into the street. It was easier to weave through and around cars than people. Likely, Shane was headed to the moonwalk on the levee, a less populated place for people to stroll along the river. He could get away faster that way and also head straight into the chaos of the Quarter and lose us.

At the very end of Canal, I ran across the circular cobblestone parking entrance of the Hilton and toward the steps beyond leading to the moonwalk.

"Where's that fucker going?" asked Mateo, running at my side now, neither of us even winded.

This was when werewolf genes came in handy.

"Gotta be heading to Jackson Square. It'll be a nightmare of tourists right now."

"As soon as we're out of sight of the populace, I'll catch him," assured Henry.

Mateo and I shared a questioning glance. Just how fast were grims?

It was a rule that supernaturals couldn't do anything in front of humans that revealed our superhuman abilities. And while anyone could see that we were running faster than almost any human, it wasn't outside the realm of reality, which was why Henry mentioned that we were almost out of sight of people on the street.

We pushed on up onto the moonwalk. Only a couple or two in the distance. Shane's scent came stronger; we were gaining on him. My wolf rumbled a deep growl in my chest.

"We're close." Mateo's voice had dropped into wolf-range too.

His scent was so strong now. Near the water.

Then Henry blurred past us, basically disappeared in a streak of black. We saw him materialize and scale down out of sight. When we caught up a few seconds behind him, he stood right down at the edge of the water lapping against the rocks of the levee.

"What the fuck?" I stared down the embankment, a pile of jagged rocks.

Shane was in a speedboat, some other werewolf driving, already too far offshore for me to leap to him if I tried.

"What the fuck are you doing?" I called out to him.

His grin and golden eyes lit up under the moonlight.

"Don't worry, brother!" he called out, sarcasm reeking in every syllable. "We'll take good care of your girl before we give her back." Then he laughed as the boat vanished, speeding into the darkness.

My blood chilled in my veins. "*No.*" This was a fucking decoy.

I reached for my phone in my back pocket, but Henry already had his in his hand, answering a call. "Talk."

His coal-black eyes skated to mine with something I'd never seen in the obsidian gaze of that grim. Concern.

My stomach plummeted. He listened for five more seconds, then clicked off, holding my gaze. I knew what he was going to say before he said it, but it didn't diminish the lacerating pain of hearing the words.

"Violet is gone."

CHAPTER 26

~VIOLET~

Waking with a jolt, I noted two things immediately. My head ached like the devil, and I was laying on an old sofa I didn't recognize. I touched my fingers to the top of my forehead near the hairline where the pain radiated through my skull. There I could feel the edge of wiry stitches.

Goddamn, they had hit me hard.

"Sorry about that." I finally glanced around, finding Shane sitting in a wooden chair a few feet from me, hands clasped loosely, elbows on his thighs. "Rick shouldn't have hit you quite so hard. He doesn't know his own strength." He leaned in as if to tell me a secret. "He's not the brightest bulb in the box." His smile did nothing to disarm me.

The warehouse was mostly empty except for some scattered shelves, wall-size toolboxes, and a rusted-out car with no wheels up on blocks. Grease stains throughout and the double garage doors—currently closed—told me I was in an old mechanic shop.

The place was cold, but Shane had set up a small space heater near the sofa where I lay, keeping me relatively warm. Several werewolves stationed against the walls were watching us.

The two I'd seen at the Cauldron weren't there; most likely they were outside guarding the place.

I was still in my dress, my shoes gone. I wasn't sure if they'd fallen off when they'd snatched me or if they'd taken them to keep me from running too far on bare feet.

When I sat up, I winced from a sharp pain on my hip, drawing my attention down to where the dress was torn open right above my pantie line, the white satin of my underwear showing. There was a scrape about three inches wide that had dried over with crusted blood. Not too deep, but it stung.

"I'd have taken care of that, too, but I thought maybe you'd want to tend to that one yourself."

Shane was calmer and more cordial than I'd ever seen him. The hardness was still there, but the menace was gone. "Again. I apologize." His gaze was on the opening of my dress and the angry-looking scratch. "Rick wasn't so gentle getting you over that wooden fence." He stood and held out two capsules of Advil and a glass of water. "Take this."

Without having Isadora nearby to help me out, I was grateful to have something for the pain.

I sat up completely and drank the pills down, then held the glass with both hands in my lap. "Sorry about that too." He tapped the edge of his lip, motioning to me.

The sting of his bite still throbbed a little. "No. You're not sorry for that one."

He grinned. "You're right. I'm not." Deep laughter rumbled in his chest. "I thought Nico's head was going to explode."

He'd kissed and bitten me just so Nico would be so enraged he'd chase after him. Which of course led him and Mateo away from me, leaving me more vulnerable. No one would've thought these guys would abduct me from a large crowd right under their noses.

"Now that you have me, what is it you want?"

"You already know that, but since I was sure you weren't going to give it willingly, I took matters into my own hands."

For a millisecond, my heart rate skipped, wondering if this was some sort of werewolf gang bang situation, but my instincts and, more importantly, my psychic magic told me otherwise. The violence radiating from the werewolves in this room wasn't directed at me. It was more of a sliver of viciousness focused inward.

Shane stood and walked to a table next to the sofa and lifted a duffel bag and a smaller bag that looked like what a doctor might carry in the 1940s for house calls. He opened the duffel bag, revealing my cordless tattoo machine, charger, antiseptic wipes, latex gloves, and clear tape from my shop.

Basically, my entire drawers had been emptied and carefully placed within. Then he opened the doctor's bag where every bottle of ink I had stored in my cabinets had been wrapped carefully and placed. Most of them were regular ink, but there was also the vial labeled NMW for the New Moon Werewolf serum.

"I want you to give us the same spelled tattoo you gave Nico."

"Do you even know what the spell does?"

He dipped his head in one nod. "From what I gathered from pieces of conversation at your shop and at the Cauldron, it will help us control the wolf."

"You bugged our pub too?"

"That was especially helpful when your sisters had dinner at that table near the kitchen. A routine they seem to stick to. Chatty bunch."

Wow. He'd been spying pretty damn good.

"So you kidnapped me, banged my head and body around, to make me give you guys tattoos." I might've sounded a tad put out.

"Again, sorry about Rick's rough handling."

"I don't even know that it works yet."

Partially true. My psychic eye had told me that it would. If I were to trust my magic, then I was 90 percent sure I had the right spell. The vision was so strong with the witch sign, the magic so potent the night of the new moon.

"After you give us the tattoo," he went on as if I hadn't protested, "I'll deliver you safely back to your family." He cleared his throat before adding, "To Nico." *Nico.*

I licked my dry lips and took another gulp of water, wondering what kind of agony my werewolf was in right now. He was undoubtedly shredding from the inside out over this.

"It's going to take some time."

He shrugged. "Whatever it takes."

"You know, you could've just asked."

"I did that."

"No." I stared him down. "You came into my place of business and made demands for something I wasn't sure I could deliver at the time. It was rude."

He sneered. "I'm used to having to use force to get what I want with other supernaturals." He sat back in his chair, amber eyes fixed and adamant. "Werewolves have to take what they need from your kind. Or go without." He flicked a hand down to the open bags. "It's obvious you now have what I need. What we need. And you're gonna give it to us."

Ah, now there was the menace that had been hidden and tucked away. But behind all of that anger was a sheet of pain blanketing the man. I was only able to see it with my psychic eye, delving in and discovering that there was more than the malicious front he showed me now.

Then it hit me like a tornado-lobbed brick. What he was demanding was something anyone would want—control over their baser instincts to maim and hurt and harm. For a werewolf, that meant power over an uncontrollable impulse that could force him to kill someone in a blink without meaning to.

My anger over being abducted and wounded by these asshats melted behind a need to help them. They were like Nico. Like Mateo. In need of something, peace and healing, that I could possibly give them.

Holding Shane's hostile gaze, his jaw clenching, I set my glass of water aside on the table and stood. "Okay."

He narrowed his disbelieving gaze. "Okay?"

"Let's get to work." I stood and moved the bags back to the table. "Who's up first?" I started to set out my instruments. "I need an extension cord for my charger." Met with silence, I glanced over my shoulder at Shane's widened, surprised gaze. "As lovely as it is to be in your friendly company, I'd rather not be here longer than necessary, so let's get started."

With the first genuine smile I'd seen on the man since the first time we'd met on that Austin rooftop, he stood and removed his leather jacket.

"Ty!" he called out. "Get that extension cord from my trunk."

"Ty?" I mumbled, watching a younger werewolf head out through a door into the night.

Shane shoved up the long sleeve of his gray Henley. "Nico told you about him?"

"Yeah." I busied myself, setting out everything I needed, then retrieved the bottle marked NMW. I'd even drawn a cute crescent moon on the label.

"He told you his wolf almost killed Ty?"

I turned, pointedly giving him my sincerest of expressions. "Why the hell do you think I was working so hard to find the right spell for werewolves?"

"You mean for him."

"Yes." I gulped hard, turning back to my supplies. "Anything for him."

Ty rushed up, all wide eyes, carrying the extension cord. I smiled at him, which caused streaks of red to appear high on his cheekbones. I couldn't help but observe the scarred claw marks running under his chin and down one side of his throat into his T-shirt.

"Thank you," I said sweetly, which made him blush harder. "Could you plug it in for me?"

While he zipped off to do that, I dragged the table closer to the sofa. Then I pulled the wooden chair Shane had been sitting in closer to the sofa. I angled the lamp on the table as best I could to get the most light. He had rolled up his sleeve past the elbow, revealing one patch of bare skin not inked with other roping tattoos.

"Um, actually, that's not going to work."

"What do you mean?" That ice-man demeanor was back in a flash. Obviously, he thought I was refusing to give him the tattoo again. Damn, this guy was temperamental. But he was a fucking werewolf. What did I expect? "I can't explain it, but my psychic ability tells me this one needs to be close to the heart. So"—I flicked a hand toward his chest—"take off your shirt."

The lascivious grin he gave me rivaled anything I'd seen Nico or Mateo wear time and again. A deep roll of laughter rumbled out of him as he pulled off his shirt and tossed it on the back of the sofa.

"I'm all yours, baby." That wicked grin was aimed directly at me. "Right on top of my heart is fine by me." He tapped a finger over the left pec of his broad chest.

I popped on my latex gloves, which they'd thankfully included when they'd somehow robbed my office space during the gallery opening celebration. Thankfully, they'd packed my razor as well. I shaved the spot I needed to tattoo and cleaned the area with antiseptic wipes.

"What do you want? I usually have a stencil copied on transfer paper to outline the tattoo, but I'll have to freestyle something so keep it simple."

"How about that? Turn around, Ty."

I glanced over to see that not only was Ty standing close and watching but several others had moved in for a better view.

The back of Ty's jacket bore *Blood Moon* in jagged lettering with a symbol of a stylized wolf's head. It was made with sharp lines, filled in with black, the white of an almond-shaped eye, the wolf's mouth open and revealing sharp canines. It was a cool design. Pretty, even. And simple enough.

"It would be easier with a stencil, but I can do that. Just no bitching if it isn't perfect."

"None at all. It's the ink I'm after more than the tat."

"Give me your jacket, Ty." I held out my hand for it.

"You can use mine," said Shane, pointing to the one he'd draped on the table.

Some chestnut-haired guy passed it over with a dimpled smile. Jeesh. Was it a requirement that all werewolves be smoking hot?

"Thanks." I draped the jacket over Shane's bare abs so that I could see the wolf's head as I worked.

"Trying to cover me up?" Shane asked playfully, bending the arm closest to me behind his head.

"Be still," I ordered, setting to work with my cordless tattoo machine.

"Whatever you say, Miss Savoie."

After a few minutes of working in silence, I glanced up at him. Those wolf-gold eyes were half-lidded and staring at me.

"Nico is going to kill you," I informed him matter-of-factly.

"Oh yeah," he agreed. "He's going to try to gut me, I have no doubt." The others were silently watching from behind us.

"As long as you're prepared for the fallout."

We were silent again for several minutes. My tattoo machine was silent, so the only noise in the place was the creak of the wind against the steel roof outside and the shuffle of feet when someone moved around.

"I knew that night, you know," he said so low it was a whisper.

"What do you mean?"

"New Year's Eve. In Austin."

I glanced up at him, his expression no longer playful or stern—the two expressions he wore the most. Now, it was rather sad.

"What is it you knew exactly?"

By now, my hand was glowing with magic, the ethereal shimmer shining in the darkened room, lit only by a few lights left whose bulbs weren't busted by vandals. Most likely by teenagers who used this place for drinking or sex or both.

"That you were it for him. That you would drag him away from us."

A little shock and a little anger sparked my emotional response. "So you're blaming me for Nico leaving your boy band over here?"

"No." His voice was soft and steady. "It was fate. I see that now."

"Fate? You believe in that?"

"I'm a werewolf." He gave me a sardonic look. "Cursed by a witch who hexed every male descendant of the original witch hunter till the end of time. Her blood hex hasn't lost its luster or potency, and it's been a couple of centuries, so, yeah, I believe in fate."

True. Witches and warlocks were born with innate magic. Vampires were either born or made with their gifted abilities. Who knew how grims came into being? But werewolves were cursed by birth. Their magic wasn't a gift. It was an affliction they couldn't escape. One very malicious witch facing her hunter decided the fate of hundreds of his descendants. For eternity.

I suppose he did believe in fate. Because it was sealed by the pain of their monster within and all the harm that beast could unleash on those they loved and cared about. There was no pain or accompanying dread or heartache that came with being one of the other supernaturals. And no one really seemed to notice. Or care about the troubles of the outcasts of the otherworld. The werewolves.

But I did. I hoped that I could help change their fate. Though I couldn't do it alone.

"Back then, I just didn't want to acknowledge it." His voice dropped even lower. "Or accept it."

"I'm sorry, what?"

"That he had to leave," he clarified. "He was my brother. My best friend. Then he left, and I was angry."

I tried to assuage the obvious pain he still felt over Nico. "He felt like he had no choice. After Ty, that is."

"I know." He paused before adding, "I know all of that now. It doesn't make it hurt any less."

"I suppose not." Understanding the source of pain and grief doesn't alleviate it.

I'd finished the wolf's head, choosing to keep it around two inches in diameter all the way around. "What color do you want the eye to be?" It was the only vacant space within the tattoo. "Yellow?"

He flashed me those amber eyes again. "That works."

"Seems only natural," I said, standing to change out the ink and needle for color.

"Whoever's next, get ready."

"I'll go next," said the auburn-haired one with the dimples, flashing them to me again.

"There should be a warning label with your kind," I mumbled to myself when I sat back down to fill in the almond-shaped eye of the wolf's head.

"Why's that?" asked Shane.

Sighing, I laughed a little. "I forget that werewolves can hear and smell everything."

"Yeah. And we can smell Nico all over you," remarked Dimples teasingly.

"He's definitely under the skin," another remarked with what seemed like admiration.

I settled and finished adding the final ink to Shane's tattoo, though this was for aesthetics, not the spell. The spell was now etched into his skin along with my whisper of magic. It would seal to his own spirit of magic once I'd chanted the incantation.

"His scent *should* be all over her," said another barrel-chested guy I didn't know.

I shivered with excitement and hope, knowing full well what scent marking meant for a werewolf. That was fine by me. I wanted to be his as much as I wanted him to be mine.

"Okay, sit still a minute, and everyone be quiet please."

The low murmuring and chatter stopped at once. Placing both palms at the center of Shane's chest, not touching the tattoo but needing direct contact with him, I closed my eyes and concentrated.

Whispering *"Venez à moi,"* calling my magic to me, I tapped in to my psychic eye. The response was violent in its swiftness.

The witch sign I'd seen in that vision when I first touched Nico's scar swam in my mind. I honestly didn't have to do any of the work. It was like the magic itself longed to right this wrong, the channel opening like a floodgate of pulsing power, pouring right through my fingers into Shane.

It was the exact same when I did this for Nico's tattoo just a few days ago. I was positive it was the universe using me as a vessel to correct the error of that first witch, my ancestor, so long ago. The Divine Goddess, the persona we called to embody all magic, seemed to be wielding me to do her will. All I had to do was open up and let it go. So I did.

After only a moment or two, the gate closed, and the light glowing from my skin dimmed. I sat up and pulled my hands away from Shane. The circle of werewolves was silent. The crackle of magic buzzed in the air.

He sat up, breathing heavy as he stared down at his skin. It didn't look any different other than the faint ghostly glow as the magic dissipated.

"Be still," I said, wiping the area once more with antiseptic. Then I covered it with the clear tape.

"Thank you," he said quietly.

The sincere look of appreciation on his face made me smile. "You're welcome."

Shane stood to be replaced by yet another hot, shirtless werewolf reclining back on the sofa. I settled next to Dimples, who'd adopted Shane's position, curling one forearm behind his head so I could lean over him with ease.

"Lucky fucking guy, that Nico," rumbled Dimples, flashing me his pretty smile.

Rather than comment on his flirtiness, I simply said, "So am I, big guy. I just hope I can finish these tats and get back to him before he finds all of you."

"Worried about us?" asked Shane.

Knowing the depth of Nico's feelings for me because I was positive his matched my own, my response was one simple word but heavy with an ominous promise.

"Very."

CHAPTER 27

~NICO~

IT WAS FOUR A.M. AND I SAT WHERE I'D BEEN FOR THE PAST FEW HOURS— on the sofa of our shop lobby with my phone in my fucking hands, waiting for Shane to call.

I'd called his cell number, which he hadn't changed, 172 times. He'd let every single one go to voice mail. I'd sent some heinous, life-threatening texts with explicit details of how he would come to his imminent demise. All had been left on *read*. Then not even that. Presumably, he'd turned his phone off so it couldn't be traced.

"Here, Nico." Clara sat next to me, offering a cup of coffee. Not that there was a chance of me falling asleep. My body was riddled with so much anxiety-laced adrenaline that there was no way I would nod off for even a second. Not until I found her.

Clara smiled while patting my shoulder and urging me to take the cup.

"Thanks," I muttered, my heart cracking at seeing Violet's twin, her features a lovely mirror of her sister's.

I took a gulp, glancing around the room. Mateo and Evie were curled up on the other side of the L-shaped sofa, whispering to each other. Isadora was making tea in the kitchen. Jules was still out of town, apparently hightailing it back here.

Livvy sat behind the computer at the reception desk, tapping away, trying to find help through the SuperNet. Devraj and Ruben had taken the small amount of information that we had and then left to rally the local vampire covens to search. Sean had left with Henry the second we'd returned from that wild fucking goose chase Shane had led us on. If I could've throttled myself for being so stupid, I would have.

Shane had understood my depth of affection for Violet the moment he'd met her face-to-face here in the shop. He'd used my insane level of protectiveness against me, knowing full well that touching and kissing her would have only one result. Me coming after him. Which is what I'd done back at the Cat's Meow.

He was testing my attachment to Violet that night. And I'd done exactly what he'd wanted tonight, leaving Violet behind without protection from his lackey assholes who'd snatched her right underneath everyone's noses.

We'd had to slowly shut down the party without terrifying the locals. We had let them know that my co-owner of Empress Ink had been kidnapped from the event, but no one had seen anything. Not a soul. Evie had to force JJ and Finnie to go home, both of them feeling guilty they hadn't seen anything or been able to help. JJ had wanted blood, which I 100 percent empathized with. But there was nothing to do. Not yet. And when there was, it would be a matter between me and Shane. Humans shouldn't be present when I got my hands around that fucker's throat.

Shifting on the sofa, I turned to look at Clara, who had that worried look on her face. She'd been trying to pump me with her happy spell, but it had rebounded almost as soon as she'd touched me.

"You're not worried?" I asked her.

She gave me a small smile. "She's okay. I promise."

"How do you know? Are you psychic like Violet?" I knew that all witches had one leading power, but they also carried secondary magical gifts. But Clara shook her head, then pressed her palm to the middle of her chest. "I can feel it."

I wondered if that was hopeful thinking, like when you say you just know someone is going to be all right, but you honestly have no idea. She seemed to see where my thoughts ran.

"As an Aura, I can read people's emotions, which I'm sure you know. But I don't have to be in the room with someone I have an intimate connection with to know how they're feeling. I'm closer to Violet than anyone in the world, and I can sense her right now." She glanced up, tapping in to her magic. In to Violet. "She isn't afraid or in pain." Her gaze swiveled back to me. "I can promise you that."

"Will you tell me if that changes?" She gave me a nod.

"I just can't believe how calm you are," I admitted.

Her smile widened. "This is Violet. Those werewolves have no idea who they've kidnapped. It'll be fine."

I wish I could've been as confident as Clara. If Violet were as safe as she'd implied, then why hadn't she found a way to reach out to us? I'd already drilled Livvy to death to use her telepathic link to send Violet messages that we were looking for her and would find her soon. I was pissed as hell that Livvy's telepathic link didn't work in reverse. What's worse, Livvy had said that she didn't have the sense that Violet had received her messages. That told me one thing—she was unconscious, which was also why Clara hadn't sensed her afraid or in pain.

If that asshole hurt her in any way, I'd make him regret ever being born. If this was his way of getting back at me for abandoning the Blood Moon pack, then I'd say he'd done his job well. I felt the pain of it acutely. Sharply. Deeply.

The door whooshed open. I leaped to my feet. Henry and Sean strode in with another guy I didn't recognize right behind them. Oh, wait. Yes I did. He was that guy we saw at the Brat Pack. He was of similar build to Henry and wore the same attire. Dark. Though he seemed slightly more polished than Henry, wearing a black cable sweater and slacks. An indecipherable tattoo filled the back of his left hand. Same black hair and obsidian eyes, pale complexion.

Definitely a grim with a powerful punch of darkness pulsing off him.

His gaze swept the room coolly until it landed on Livvy behind the receptionist desk. He tensed.

Her typically casual demeanor had fallen, her eyes wide as she yelped, "*Gareth*. What are you doing here?"

His hands went to his hips, his mannerisms holding an air of authority as he stared at her for a heartbeat more before giving her a casual nod. "Lavinia."

Lavinia? That must be her full name, which I'd never heard anyone speak before.

His gaze swept away from her. He scowled as he scanned the room till he found me. When Henry whispered in his ear and gestured toward me, he walked over and extended his hand for me to shake.

Touching a grim, especially one who held an intensely powerful aura like this guy, wasn't something I should do in my fractured state. I shook my head.

"No offense, man. But that's not a good idea right now." He must've heard the deep gruffness of my voice because he only nodded.

"No problem. I'm Gareth Blackwater. I know where they've got your girl."

An audible sigh of relief swept over several people, including Isadora, who'd run up to the lobby, an unopened tea bag in hand.

"Where is she?" asked Livvy, having rounded the reception desk closer to where we were standing.

"The West Bank," he answered her before turning to me. "On the outskirts of Belle Chasse."

"Let's go." I glanced at Mateo, who was already on his feet, whispering to Evie to stay put.

"Wait!" Livvy stepped closer. "Jules is on her way back from Houston. She should be home in about two hours."

"I'm not waiting." Even if Jules had the power to walk into a room and null every supernatural, which would obviously give us an advantage to take down human-level strength as opposed to werewolves, I wasn't waiting a fucking second to get Violet back.

"Ugh. Fine! How the hell did you find her anyway?" Livvy looked both impressed and perturbed at Gareth.

He grinned down at her. "It's easy if you have the means."

"The grim data network, I suppose?" She arched a brow.

"No need for that." When he shifted slightly toward her, she took a step back. He grinned before saying, "Tracking phones isn't that difficult."

"Seriously?" she scoffed. "You didn't even know their names or have SIM card info or anything."

Apparently, Shane hadn't shut his phone down quickly enough then. Grims were famously fast at any and all tech work.

He shrugged a shoulder. "That's easy to get. For me."

Clara stepped up to her side and whispered rather loudly, "Guess you can't call him *cockwaffle* anymore."

Henry smiled like the devil himself before adding in his deep tenor, "You can definitely keep calling him that."

Gareth tossed a scowl at Henry.

"Are y'all brothers?" asked Mateo, glancing between the three grims, their features so similar, fair skin with black hair and eyes.

"Cousins," said Gareth.

"Can we do introductions later?" I snapped out, my wolf pulling at the leash. My canines were already fully extended. "I'll drive."

"Wait, let me get my shoes," said Livvy, running back to the reception desk.

"You're not coming," said Gareth, his gaze sweeping down her body, which was no longer in a dress but black jeans and a casual red top.

"*What?*" She stormed back over and propped a hand on her hip. "You can't make decisions for me, Mr. Blackwater. You might be group leader in our contest finals, but you have no pull here."

"How can you possibly help?" he asked. And while the question might sound condescending, his tone was even and calm.

"I can—"

"You're an Influencer with light telekinesis ability, not heavy like Violet and Jules. An Influencer planting thoughts only works with subtle persuasion. This will be a brute force mission. No time for mind games. You have one-way telepathy. With your sisters." The way he added that last bit made Livvy scowl. "What good does that do? You'll be a liability more than a help. We'll have to protect you while trying to get Violet out. So the wisest course of action is for you to stay here."

Livvy's face flushed pink with obvious anger. Whether that was because the grim spoke sense or that she just hated this guy giving her orders, or perhaps both, I wasn't quite sure.

Clara squeezed Livvy's arm. "He's right. The only one of us equipped to go up against a pack of werewolves is Jules. And Violet." Clara faced Gareth and Henry. "We'll stay. But I honestly don't think it's necessary. Violet is totally fine."

While Gareth and Sean looked at her like she might be a little off-center, Henry kept smiling. Seems someone else might be under the Savoie sisters' spell, but I didn't have time for this.

"Let's go."

Isadora stepped closer. "We'll be at our house when you return. In case you need me." In case someone needs healing. In case someone comes back wounded.

We'd stationed ourselves at the shop, staying near the scene of the crime. But now we had to prepare for the possibility of injuries. As long as they were on me and not Violet, I'd be fine. I couldn't even think about her being hurt without wanting to maim and claw and be violently sick all at the same time.

I gave Isadora a nod before storming out the door. Mateo and the grims were on my heels, following me out to my Jeep parked right outside.

"You go up front," said Mateo, gesturing to Gareth. "You know where we're going."

With a nod, Gareth hopped in the front passenger seat. I gunned it before seat belts were even clicked, speeding dangerously down Magazine toward the interstate. The streets were mostly clear now since it was closing in on five in the morning. Now was the time drinkers were well in bed or searching for an all-night diner like Daisy Dukes in the Quarter for a greasy cheeseburger or French dip po'boy to soak up the alcohol.

I wished this night had ended how I'd planned. With Violet in my bed, in my arms, me worshipping her body as we celebrated tonight's success. Of our business. Of our beginning.

Because whether she knew it or not, this was just the beginning for us.

Then Shane and my past crashed the party and fucked it all up. He had some kind of vendetta against me, and I was going to make fucking sure that shit ended tonight. Whatever unresolved issues we had, we'd be fighting them out once and for all.

"Do you have information on how many of the pack are there?" I asked, needing to focus on the task at hand, my fingers white-knuckling around the steering wheel.

Gareth glanced at me with that dismissive look grims liked to give other supernaturals. It was basically an eye roll without the eye roll. He stared straight as I veered onto the on-ramp and toward the West Bank across the Mississippi River.

"There are twelve werewolves holding her at the location. Ten adults. Two adolescents. It's a small warehouse building made entirely of corrugated steel that was once a mechanic's shop. It's just south of Belle Chasse Navy Base off a gravel road. Head toward the base when we're across the bridge, and I'll tell you where to turn from there."

Mateo asked from the back seat right behind me, "So what exactly are grims capable of in a situation like this?"

"You mean, a situation of brutal violence," clarified Henry, not a question.

Gareth kept his eyes forward, his head resting casually against the headrest.

"We can—" Sean started but Henry slapped his chest with the back of his hand.

I glared in my rearview mirror at him. "Look. I know you assholes are super secretive, but I need to know if you're going to get in the fucking way or are you actually capable of doing something besides collect data when we get there."

My wolf filled the space with threat and warning. Mateo's growl rumbled, echoing my sentiments exactly. It's not like we lived in covens, or even organized packs, where we could spread their hidden abilities. Grims were odd supernaturals. No one had documented what they were able to do. Anytime something was written down somewhere, the books disappeared, the digital documents vanished. Whatever people knew was only by word of mouth, and I'd never been able to acquire one single piece of information besides what we all knew about their auras.

And the dark halos around the three in my car were urging me to shift and eviscerate anything I could get my hands on. The impulse was a palpable shove against my skin, willing my bones to break and re-form into the shape of my beast so that I could do real damage.

And yet, both Mateo and I remained in man form with the exception of our eyes and canines. The telltale pulse of magic radiated from the tattoo on my ribs. If I wasn't sure before, I was now absolutely positive that Violet's spell had worked. If I hadn't had this tattoo, I would already be in full werewolf form, scouring the city for any clue to her whereabouts. And I never would've found her. Not like these fucking grims who seemed to have everything they needed at their fingertips. But what I needed to know was, could they handle themselves in a fight?

I was about to snap out another nasty question when Gareth said smoothly, "You won't have to worry about us. We can handle ourselves." He aimed those dark eyes at me. "And yes, we'll be able to help."

"Even him?" asked Mateo, practically sneering at Sean. Well, it was really Alpha now, who didn't much care for Sean since he'd taken up flirting with Evie incessantly.

Sean grinned like a fiend. "Even me, Alpha." He winked at my cousin.

Mateo narrowed his gaze, then huffed before turning back toward the window.

Gareth guided us through the small town of Belle Chasse. We all fell into silence as we passed the navy base, the lights disappearing as we crossed into the shadowy outskirts where Violet was being held in who knows what kind of condition. Heaven help Shane if he'd hurt her, because nothing on this earth or in hell would stop me from killing him if he did.

CHAPTER 28

~VIOLET~

Ty slipped his shirt back on while I pulled off my latex gloves. We'd kept to small talk while I tattooed him. One reason was because I was getting tired and really needed to concentrate. The other was that every question I wanted to ask him related to Nico, and I was afraid that might be an invasion of privacy. For Nico.

As I put my tattoo machine on the charger, I knew I needed food and sleep before I started on the next round. I'd only done three tattoos, but after the long day and night for the grand opening party, then being kidnapped and knocked over the head, I'd say I was doing a stellar job.

"I forgive him, you know."

I snapped my head around to look at Ty, the shy young werewolf who could barely hold my gaze. He gave me a small smile as he picked up his jacket.

Turning back to the table to straighten my ink bottles unnecessarily, I asked, "Does he know that?"

"I told him so. Many times before he left. But somehow I don't think it's about my forgiveness."

Facing him, I crossed my arms—to ward off the chill, not to be defensive. "What is it about then?"

"Nico needs to forgive himself."

The teenager had a kindness in his eyes despite weathering some rough times in his short life. From what I understood, the only reason he and his brother were a part of this pack was because their parents hadn't wanted them.

"You're pretty smart for someone so young."

His shy smile widened into a true one. Yet again, I was shaken by the fact that all werewolves seemed to have this magnetism that was inescapable. This one would be a heartbreaker one day.

"Anyway . . ." He glanced toward the door as Shane reentered, carrying take-out bags of fast food. "Maybe you can help him move on. He deserves it."

Returning his smile, I agreed. "He definitely deserves to move on, find some peace."

"Oh yeah." He shook his head. "That too. But what I really meant was that he deserves you."

"Me?" I laughed. "How do you mean?"

"Well, you're—" He glanced down my body, then blushed and looked away. "Um, really beautiful and kind. And Nico, he's a good guy. A great guy. He deserves someone like you."

Okay, now I was positive this kid was going to one day collect hearts and leave them in broken shards in his wake, all the while apologizing with that tender look, making them still want him despite their heartache.

"Thank you, Ty. Don't worry. I'm going to take care of him." He held out his jacket. "If you're cold, you can use my jacket." As I slipped it on, I shook my head with a laugh.

"What?" he asked.

"Oh, Ty. I feel so sorry for every girl in your future."

His brow furrowed in confusion but then Shane was there, opening up the first bag and taking out wrapped burgers.

"Not much was open but a joint around the corner, but I figured you might be hungry."

"Thanks." I took a burger and fell onto the sofa, tucking my legs underneath me. "I need to get some rest anyway." This side of the room had been in a perpetual glow from the magic I was emitting, but the light had dimmed to almost nothing as soon as I'd finished up with Ty. My energy was depleted, my body exhausted.

Shane observed my face, likely seeing the bags under my eyes before he nodded. "I figured. Eat up and take the couch."

I took a seat and opened the wrapper on my lap, so damn hungry I didn't even care what was on it. Not that I was all that picky anyway.

"You should let me call Nico and let him know I'm okay. He's likely going out of his mind, trying to find me."

Shane seemed to consider it for a split second before shaking his head. "Too risky. He may have access to cell tower locations and find us quicker."

"Your funeral," I said, biting into my burger.

"Probably. But Nico can't think clearly where you're concerned. As soon as you finish the tattoos, I'll bring you back safe and sound."

I didn't mention to him that Livvy had sent me frantic telepathic messages a few times while I was tattooing, letting me know they were looking for me and not to worry. I wasn't worried.

Besides, if they listened to Clara, they'd know I was perfectly fine. I might've eschewed her "twin bubble" idea from time to time, but it was true that she'd be able to detect my well-being and could relay that to them.

I hoped that she was able to calm Nico down because he was surely unraveling over all this.

"You know, I'm still not even sure if this spelled ink will work," I told Shane around a mouthful.

He devoured half his burger in one bite, staring down at the floor. When he swallowed, he said, "You gave a tattoo to Nico with the ink, though."

"How'd you know?"

He arched a brow.

"Oh, right. The bugs." I stared up at him, rather impressed with his devious ways. "Huh." I took another bite, trying to remember all the clients that came through and what else they may have overheard.

He cleared his throat after he polished off his burger. "Our tech was really good." He wore such a devious smile that I expected devil's horns to sprout out of his dirty-blond hair. "Even detected sound through the closed door of your supply closet."

This asshole had listened in when Nico and I had first had sex? A flush of heat swept up my neck from both embarrassment and fury. "Not cool."

Several werewolves close by laughed, but not more than Rhett. That was Dimples' real name, I'd found out after a very flirty tattoo session.

Shane chuckled too. "The intel actually helped, believe it or not."

"How so?" I glared daggers at him, running back through that volcanic sex session with Nico in my mind.

"It told me exactly how fixated Nico was on you. And that if I gave him the right incentive, I could easily lure him away long enough to snatch you. And that you were making breakthroughs with the werewolf tattoo."

I dropped my hands in my lap over the wrapper, still holding the burger in both hands.

"Huh. You're right."

"Don't worry," he whispered. "I deleted the audio once we had what we needed." He winked at me and gestured toward the sofa. "Get some sleep."

"You know, you don't have to hold me here. I'll do the tattoos without force."

He observed me a minute, biting his lip in concentration. "I know that now. But Nico's going to want blood. Best we do this all in one swoop and get our asses back to Texas."

He was probably right. I finished the burger, then lay down as the lights went off in the warehouse. I could still see the outline of figures near the door and a few settling onto the floor on the opposite wall. My eyes were drifting closed when I felt a blanket spread over me.

Opening my eyes, I caught the slender silhouette of Ty walking away.

Smiling to myself, I mumbled, "Poor girls," before closing my eyes again.

Right as I felt myself slipping into sleep, the outside door burst open. I didn't have the heightened senses that werewolves did, but I recognized the hulking figure and voice of Rick when he said, "We've got company coming up the gravel road."

"Fuck," cursed Shane before heaving an aggravated sigh. "Get ready for one fucking insane werewolf, guys."

CHAPTER 29

~NICO~

"Do you know how far ahead the warehouse is?" My voice had gone gravel-deep, nothing but pure wolf.

"One point three miles," said Gareth. "Pull over. They'll already know we're here. Let's go on foot through the woods so we can circle to the back."

Perfectly fine with that, I pulled over. I needed to shift anyway. There was no holding back the full beast now. He would have none of my chains as we stalked to the lair where they'd taken our mate.

"Is there another exit?" asked Mateo.

"No. They'd have to carry her on foot, which would be risky. We'd catch up to them before they got far."

"Me and Nico would anyway," he clarified with a snort.

"No," said Henry, who rarely spoke. "We'd catch up faster than you, most likely."

I remembered for a split second the moonwalk near the river earlier tonight when he blurred past us. I wondered what grims truly were and what they could do. But now wasn't the time. I didn't give a shit as long as they didn't get in the way. And so far, all they'd been was completely honest and helpful so I wasn't second-guessing them.

I parked and pulled the emergency brake. As we hopped out, I started stripping.

"Hey." Mateo had stripped off his shirt and tossed it on the hood and was shoving off his boots. "Don't kill anyone until we find out exactly what's going on."

"Are you fucking kidding me right now? *You're* trying to be the voice of reason? What if they had Evie?"

I got nothing but a spine-chilling growl in response.

"That's what I thought." I shoved off my jeans and boxer briefs, tossing them on the front seat. "Don't worry. I'm only going to fuck him up a little bit at first. Unless they did something to Violet." I popped my neck, getting ready for the shift. "Then he's a dead man."

Another growl in response as Mateo shifted. Bones broke and realigned until he was towering behind me.

I honestly didn't believe Shane would harm Violet. He had to know what she meant to me.

And even if she hadn't been my mate, he'd never been violent toward another woman. He'd beat the shit out of plenty of guys in bars for fun, but he didn't crave hurting women. At least, he hadn't when we'd been best friends. Then again, I'd never seen that menacing glare that he'd directed at me in the Cauldron. He blamed me for leaving. How far would he go to make me pay for it?

With a flare of rage, I shifted, the painful rip through my skin a cathartic release that I craved as much as my next breath. My awareness of every sight and sound and smell heightened triple-fold. I huffed a misty breath into the cold night air, glancing down at the three grims watching us.

While Henry and Gareth observed all of this with perfect poise, Sean took a decided step backward, eyes widening. I almost smiled. He was lucky he wasn't my prey. The wolf sometimes latched on to whatever nearby creature showed fear. But tonight, my target was very clear, even with my wolf driving my instincts.

"Follow me," said Gareth, turning and blurring into the woods.

What the fuck? They could trace almost as fast as vampires?

Then I remembered how fast Henry moved when we chased Shane on the streets. He was obviously holding back even then. He could've caught Shane.

I turned my head toward him and bared my teeth, releasing an eerie growl.

What did that fucker do?

He smiled, tilting his head. "I can't trace in front of humans. It's part of our code."

Gareth reappeared in a blink. "What the fuck are y'all waiting on?"

Right. I took off through the woods with Alpha at my side, my cousin's fierce wolf shining from his golden eyes. Our size and speed allowed us to move as fast as the tracing grims.

Tracing. Unbelievable. I had no idea they could move like vampires. What else could they do? I had a feeling I was going to find out.

Find our woman.

My wolf was present in both mind and body.

We skirted the property, but I could hear the werewolves off to our right about half a mile, moving around and barking orders.

They were stalking away from the warehouse to the perimeter of the woods to try to stop us before we could get there. Once they saw us, they'd be shifting, too, and it would be a nasty, all-out brawl, which is exactly what I wanted right now.

My craving for violence reared up, needing to release the rage that had rooted itself in my soul the second I heard that Violet was gone. We maneuvered to the northern perimeter on the exact opposite side of the gravel road that led into the property.

Henry signaled for me to come alongside him, completely unaffected by my monstrous form, and then whispered to me, "You and Mateo go straight in from this side. We'll go another quarter mile that way and come in from behind and sneak into the warehouse to get Violet. They won't expect grims, and they won't detect us."

I glanced at him, unable to speak in this form, but I was wondering how the werewolves couldn't detect them.

His dark eyes glinted under the half-moon. "We don't smell like werewolves. Or vampires. But we can move as fast as them."

And apparently, they were also telepathic and could read minds. With a nod, I crept straight toward the edge of the woods with Alpha right at my side, our beasts larger than the average werewolves.

All werewolves were gargantuan beasts, but the alpha blood that ran through both our wolves made us bigger than the norm. And stronger. Shane would know this, him being the only alpha that I knew of among his pack now that I was gone.

Alpha's growl rumbled like a tangible ripple in the woods, shivering into the wind, his electric yellow eyes mere slits as he spotted the men at the edge. But they hadn't shifted. They were still in human form. What were they playing at? Didn't they understand the threat at their door?

Fucking cowards!

I agreed with my wolf.

Alpha and I shared a look of understanding. He seemed to feel the same way my wolf did, curling his lip at the men. I huffed out an angry breath before stalking forward on all fours.

As we exited the edge of the woods, I reared up onto my hind legs and walked forward, knowing my nearly ten-foot-tall stance would intimidate the fuck out of them. There were two men, unarmed, standing there and walking backward with hands up.

What the fuck were they doing? They weren't shifting, and it pissed me off.

Kill them anyway.

Alpha's rumbling growl reverberated with my own. I fell back to all fours and moved slowly forward, glaring at their puny human forms. Even as my wolf was ready to rake a claw out and slice them to ribbons, it hit me with blunt force. The fact that they hadn't shifted was their surrender.

A human was no match for a werewolf. They knew it. And Shane also knew that I wouldn't kill a man unless it was warranted. Right now, I wasn't quite sure if it was warranted.

Of course, this could be some sort of stalling maneuver, to keep me placated while they tried to sneak Violet out another way.

Slit their throats. Gut them good.

It was hard to think clearly with him in my head. I almost listened to him.

With the enraging thought that they might be trying to escape with Violet out the back, I leaped over the men and charged toward the building. A few other werewolves sprinted out of my way when I reached the double garage and gouged through the corrugated steel to get inside.

Alpha was right there with me, clawing and ripping away the metal like it was paper.

When I stormed inside, I wasn't prepared for what I saw. Violet stood next to Shane, holding on to his arm and wearing a Blood Moon jacket. His hand was apparently on her back. Something primal clicked inside me that wasn't human. It was a lashing red fury at my senses, roaring at this other man trying to take my mate.

Fucking *kill* him.

The reasoning man inside me was shoved behind bars as the beast took full control and charged toward his goal and target. To eliminate the competitor. To kill Shane.

Yes.

~VIOLET~

"Oh, fuuuck." At the sound of huffing beasts outside the garage doors, I grabbed Shane's arm to keep him near me so I could protect him. If I could calm Nico down long enough to explain what was going on before he got to him, then we'd be fine. Right?

Then the screeching rip of metal gave way to the deafening snarl of two seriously pissed-off werewolves leaping through the holes they'd created in the building. I knew which one was Nico right away, his electric green eyes so familiar.

I swallowed but had no saliva left in my mouth as I stared at Nico in werewolf form. There were no words to describe the sheer power and aggression pumping off his massive body, made of nothing but muscle and fur and sharp fucking teeth.

"My God," I whispered.

I had no idea what he'd look like. I'd seen plenty of pictures in books and even videos on the SuperNet. But nothing had prepared me for seeing my boyfriend in beast form. Breathtaking didn't quite cover it.

"Don't shift!" shouted Shane as Rhett and some other guy were heaving breaths, canines extended.

But it didn't matter. Nico's beast narrowed his eyes on Shane, and I realized in that split second what he was seeing. Me, his woman, clinging to another alpha male. I suddenly released Shane and took a step forward. But it was too late.

Nico charged on all fours across the concrete slab, his finger-size claws scratching and clacking on the surface as he came at full gallop.

"No!" I screamed, running forward. "Wait!"

He shoved me aside with the back of his paw, which sent me sliding across the floor till the sofa stopped me.

"Ow," I hissed in pain. My hip would be bruised from that.

Shane shifted in a millisecond, the only way he could defend himself since it was obvious Nico planned to gut him no matter what.

"Are you okay?" Ty was there, helping me up.

I looked down at my scraped knee, growing angrier by the second.

Nico and Shane were going at each other, teeth snapping, claws slicing, bodies colliding and rolling across the warehouse to bang into the side of the building. Alpha had corralled the rest of the men into one corner, none of whom had shifted.

"These motherfuckers." I huffed out an angry breath and hobbled toward the two idiots tearing each other to pieces.

"Uh, Violet, that might not be a good idea," said Ty behind me.

"They wanna play rough? Fucking *fine*."

I might be tired, but the fury in my blood snapped my magic to attention with blinding speed. When those two idiots tumbled apart, I reached out with my telekinesis and lifted the old car on blocks and tossed it through the air to slide into Nico, shoving and pinning him to the wall. He snuffed and looked down at the car in wolfie confusion.

Shane was getting ready to leap over the car, so I latched on to the wall-size toolbox and yanked it from the wall, bolts and all, then waved my hand, sending it to knock into Shane's chest and shove him to the opposite wall. The toolbox creaked and fell onto its side, partly blocking Shane.

I limped forward and pointed at both of them. "Not another fucking move, you jackasses." Total silence in the room except for the heaving pants of Nico and Shane.

When Nico's gaze swept past me to Shane, he started to growl. I lobbed a sphere of TK—telekinesis—to knock his head back against the warehouse wall, which echoed with a loud clang. Hard-ass head, that man.

"I said, stop it, Nico."

He shook his head as I marched, hobbled rather, over to him in the most dignified way possible with my knee scratched up and bleeding.

"I have had a seriously shitty night, and I need you to listen to me."

For the first time since he'd ripped his way into the warehouse and charged Shane, he looked at me. His ears fell as he snuffed the air, his gaze sweeping to my leg. No doubt taking in the injuries he caused me when he bulldozed his way in here.

Hands on my hips, I sighed and stared up at him. I'd never imagined seeing a remorseful werewolf, but I was looking at one.

"Stop this, Nico. I'm safe. Just shift back so we can talk."

I wondered if he even understood me, because his gaze kept flitting beyond me to Shane, then to Alpha and the others in the corner, then to . . . wait, was that Henry and Sean? And who was that other guy? Wait a second. A hazy memory tried to emerge, but I'd deal with that later.

"Nico, please." I stepped closer and dropped my voice to a soothing tone rather than the biting one I was using at first. "Shift back, baby. I'm fine."

After a few seconds more, he tilted his head down, chin close to his chest, and shifted back. It took all of three seconds, but the snapping noise of bones breaking and realigning was not pretty.

I winced at the pain evident in his expression before he smoothed it away when he looked at me. He went to push the car back, but probably should've done that before he shifted. I lifted a hand to move it with my TK, struggling now that I was nearly zapped out with my magic, but then the car lifted in the air and fell back three feet off to the side.

When I turned my head over my shoulder, the three grims were watching casually. I wasn't sure which one used TK to move the car, but for a second I was stunned stupid. I had no idea grims had that level of telekinetic power. Then I felt strong hands on my shoulders.

Nico skated his hands down my waist, noticed the gash in my dress. He cupped my face, staring angrily at the cut near my hairline. His hands were shaking as he took inventory of my entire body, and I was sure he was on the verge of wanting to shift back.

"Before you go all nuts again, let me say that my injuries were accidental. And my knee is scratched because of you."

Well, that took some wind out of his sails. His anger morphed into pain. I felt a twinge of guilt, but I needed to shift his emotions away from rage as quickly as possible. He jerked me into his arms, crushing me to his body. His naked body.

If we didn't have an audience and I wasn't beat to hell, I'd be able to appreciate it a bit more.

"Are you okay?" he mumbled into my hair, voice rusty with emotion.

"Yes. I'm completely fine." Except for the bumps and bruises these brutes had put on me, that was.

"What did they do to you?" Fuck, he was back to ragey again.

"Nothing that I didn't want to give."

He flinched, his arms tightening around me.

"Oh, for fuck's sake, Nico. Not sex or anything. It was the tattoos." I pushed back enough to press my hand over his heart where the spelled tattoo of the Celtic tree was. "They want the same thing you want." I smoothed my palm in a circle over the tattoo, over his heart. "Peace."

He swallowed hard, letting me ease out of his embrace a little. Like maybe six inches. I took hold of his hand.

"Come on. You need to have a civil conversation with Shane. If possible."

When I turned, everyone was watching our exchange. Including a very nude Mateo and Shane. Not that I didn't enjoy the show because, holy wow, were they beautiful male specimens, but it was a little jarring to say the least.

"Whoa. Can y'all—?"

Suddenly, Nico spun me back around and pressed my head to his chest before barking, "Go put some fucking pants on."

"With what?" asked Mateo, or Alpha rather, that smug lilt in his voice.

"Here" came the voice of the teenager I'd gotten to know in the past few hours, the one who'd haunted my man for far too long.

"Ty?" whispered Nico, staring over my shoulder, his heart so evidently in his throat.

Hearing the rasp of denim against skin behind me, I took Nico's hand. "Come on. Let's go talk."

Nico swallowed hard, glancing back down at me, then he laced our fingers and tugged me close, leading the way.

CHAPTER 30

~NICO~

My emotions were running riot through my blood, but the most prominent at this very second was fury at the asshole in front of me.

"What the fuck were you thinking?" I grated out through my teeth, canines still sharp just in case I decided he needed another bite to prove my point.

I wouldn't even pretend I wasn't proud of the claw marks running from his shoulder down his chest. Werewolves healed from superficial wounds relatively quickly, even without a witch to heal them. We were almost indestructible in werewolf form, but it still made me smile at the blood dripping down his chest. He deserved it, the prick.

"No witch was going to give us what we needed by asking nicely," said Shane, his voice dripping with acid. "We learned that shit back in Austin."

"If you'd just waited, Violet would've given you the tattoos," I snapped back.

"Really? You would've let us within five feet of her shop?" I ground my teeth together, unable to answer that rationally.

"That's what I fucking thought." Then he mumbled lower, "Not with what she is to you."

Violet didn't respond to that last part, so maybe she didn't hear him. I glared at Shane, thinking about punching him again.

He just grinned back, knowing Violet and I were still on the precipice of the mating bond. That's why I wouldn't, I couldn't, allow another werewolf male near her without losing my mind.

"Anyway," he continued, "we knew the only option was to take Violet and get the tattoos the only way we've ever gotten shit we needed. By force."

"But it shouldn't be that way." Violet stood beside me, her hand still in mine.

Even as she spoke, she never broke that contact, as if she knew I needed grounding right now. And I did. I needed to know she was here and with me and safe, needed touch to assure my inner wolf that all was going to be okay.

"That's the way it's always been," said Rhett, a packmate who'd joined not long before I left. It seemed like so many who'd been a part of the pack were no longer here.

"What happened to everyone else?" I asked Shane.

His frown softened to one of sorrow. "They all left. You know how it is. They battle their inner wolves, fight alongside us to release the aggression when we rumble with other gangs, but the beast keeps coming." Wearing only jeans, he propped both hands low on his hips. "He keeps coming till they're on the verge of maiming a friend. Or they accidentally do it anyway. Then they leave. You know this cycle better than anyone."

My gaze went to Ty, standing off to the side beside his brother, both of whom had remained completely silent. Even when he handed me a pair of jeans to slip on, he barely looked at me. The choking guilt rushed back tenfold. I barely swallowed the whimper of pain trying to climb up my throat.

Violet squeezed my hand and smiled up at me. "Well," she said, turning back to the group, "I'm going to change that. Not just me, but my sister Jules is, too. *All* of my sisters."

"What?" Shane spat the word like it was a filthy lie.

She looked at me. "Is the spell working? Have you noticed a difference? I mean, I know that you both came barreling in here in a fury, but do you feel a difference otherwise?"

"Absolutely," I said, blowing out a breath. "To be honest, without it, I would've sliced them up the second we arrived. It didn't matter to me that they weren't showing aggression by shifting, I would've normally let loose and cut them up."

"Agreed." Shane rubbed a hand across his chest.

I hadn't really paid attention to the tattoo that was covered in gauze tape and plastic wrap when I'd come in here. It had all ripped away when he'd shifted. Now that he was back in human form, I could see the red swollen lines around the tattooed emblem of the Blood Moon pack.

"Normally, I would've shifted the second they came in here, but I was able to control it longer. Till it was obvious this dickhead meant to try to kill me."

I rolled my eyes. "You deserved it, asshole."

"Maybe. But I don't regret it. I got what I wanted. Plus she was really pretty to look at when she was giving me that tattoo."

Growling, I took a big step forward. Violet let go of my hand and stood in front of me, pushing at my chest.

"Dammit, Shane. Shut the hell up! I'm already about to drown in the level of testosterone in this damn warehouse."

Shane laughed, so did a few others, but I didn't find any of this fucking funny. I knew he was baiting me, but it didn't keep me from wanting to throttle him.

So far, the grims hadn't said a damn word. Silent as the grave, which wasn't shocking. Except for Sean, who typically had the loudest mouth in the room. Something about being with his brother and cousin had mellowed him. Or maybe it was being in a room full of testy werewolves, I wasn't sure. They were probably just collecting as much intel as they could to upload to whatever data system they kept all their info on.

"What did you mean your sister Jules would help us?" Ty had eased forward, arms crossed, still avoiding my gaze. That familiar pinprick of pain tightened in my chest at the sound of his voice. "Your sister is an Enforcer. How can she help?"

"Good question," added Shane.

"I understand that you've had to take what you need because of how you're viewed, how you're treated by the supernatural community." Violet turned to face the men circled around in a staggered horseshoe. "But that has to stop."

All of them glared at me like I was the enemy, which didn't bother me one bit. I wasn't the only one who'd left the pack. But for some reason, Shane, and obviously others, blamed me for it. One glance at Ty reminded me why I'd left, and for good reason.

But with Violet's help, there was a sliver of possibility that things could change for werewolves. Not just me and the Blood Moon pack. But for all of us.

"Are you saying," I began cautiously, "that Jules could help all werewolves?"

She turned her beautiful face back to me. "More than that even." Her voice was soft, but easily heard by those in this room with our extrasensory hearing. "It's not just hurting the werewolves. It's hurting all of us, the entire supernatural community, whether they realize it or not. It's not right that this stigma exists. Yes, I get it how your ancestor was first cursed and how this all began. But that was hundreds of years ago, for Christ's sake!" Ty winced. Violet's righteous anger permeated the air. "And you're still paying for *his* crimes. *His* sins against a powerful witch who cast a blood spell that tainted the lives of so many. That wasn't her right. Just like it's not the right of witches and warlocks and vampires today to be prejudiced against werewolves." She turned to the three grims. "I'd include you guys in that list, but honestly no one knows where you all stand on anything. And you seem to avoid *all* of us, not just werewolves."

"We're here now." Gareth stood like stone, an immovable force next to his cousins. Grims were an entity unto themselves.

"True," she added. "And though I have no idea why you're here, I want to thank you for helping Nico."

That earned her a slight nod from Gareth.

"So where do we go from here?" asked Shane.

"First things first, I'm going home," she said with force. "Tomorrow morning, you'll call Sean—that's this guy over there—at the shop and set up appointments for this week so I can tattoo the rest of your pack."

Shane's eyes glinted with distrust.

"Seriously?" she snapped at him. "I'm giving you my word. The trust goes both ways. And it's not like I'm not leaving regardless because my boyfriend here is still humming with murderous rage beneath his docile veneer."

Shane snorted as he glanced at me, my fists coiled at my sides, teeth gritted.

"Docile?"

"Fuck off."

"Fine then." Shane finally glanced around, seeming to notice something. "Where's Rick, Kyle, and Drake?"

"Sleeping," said Henry.

"As in, you knocked them unconscious?"

"No permanent damage," he said without remorse.

"Hell. Rhett, take the guys and check on them."

Mateo heaved out a sigh. "I'll help," he added begrudgingly.

Glad that these grims were on our side, I actually smiled as Gareth walked my way. "We'll get the Jeep and swing it around here."

"Thanks."

"I'll take you back, Mateo," said Shane, shooting me one of his trademark grins. "I'm pretty sure Nico will insist on having Violet ride back with him."

"Got that fuckin' right," I told him.

The grims jogged slowly out of the warehouse, obviously waiting to trace until they were out of sight. The woods were gray as dawn swept away the night.

Interesting that they trusted me and Mateo enough to use their abilities when no one that I knew had a clue grims could move like vampires and use telekinesis like witches.

"Hey," whispered Violet.

I cupped her face and pressed my forehead to hers, not moving or thinking. Just feeling. "I was afraid for you," I admitted softly.

"I know. I'm sorry."

"Not your fault."

"In a way it is, though." She pulled back, her blue eyes glittering by the morning light. "I could've been more understanding the first time Shane came to me. Not that he gave me much reason since he was being a total ass that day, but all of this stems from something greater. An intolerance that needs to be eradicated."

If you'd asked me what had suddenly made my heart constrict and my breath falter, I'm not sure I could pinpoint or define the emotion. What I knew was that Violet had voiced an old pain, an old injustice, which we'd lived with always, thinking we deserved. That the foul deeds of our ancestor had rightfully cursed us all.

But then there was Violet. Ready to stand up against the cruelty and the violation of it all.

For me. For my brothers.

Combing my fingers into her hair, I cradled her cheeks in my palms, breathless at how beautiful she was. Not just her face, but her courage and her heart too.

"Christ, woman. I'm so fucking in love with you."

Before she could say a word, I slanted my mouth over hers, delving in deep. She didn't respond at first, seemingly in shock, but then her tongue stroked against mine, meeting my passion.

All I could think about from the second she'd been taken was that the woman I loved was missing, out of reach, possibly hurt.

I poured my emotions into that kiss, trying not to frighten her with my intensity. When I bit her bottom lip and licked the tiny drop of blood, she moaned into my mouth. My body trembled, needing to get her home—*my* home. To mark her, make her mine. She broke the kiss, breathing heavily. "Nico. Let's get out of here."

"Right." Grabbing her hand, I headed toward the opening.

"Wait. My tattoo machine." She pulled me back toward the table where Ty was packing some things in a duffel bag. "And you need to talk to him," she whispered vehemently.

Funny that it hadn't even dawned on me that I hadn't wondered how she'd tattooed Shane.

Apparently, those fuckers were wilier than I'd realized.

Nodding, because she was right of course, I strode over with her, ready to finally talk to the kid I'd scarred for life. What brilliant words did I come up with when I finally mustered the courage to speak? "Hey."

Ty glanced up, surprise in his eyes, then he smiled. Fucking smiled. Somehow, that made me more nervous.

"Hey yourself."

Then he went back to wrapping Violet's tools in bubble wrap while she joined him. Well, we were off to a brilliant start.

"You know, Ty," I said quietly, "I really am sorry for what happened."

"For an incredibly intuitive werewolf, you're kind of an idiot." He said it with a smile, no malice whatsoever.

"Huh?"

"I agree," said Violet, tilting her pretty smile up at me.

"I'm sorry, but what does that mean exactly?" I tried not to sound aggravated, but the kid just called me an idiot.

Ty stopped wrapping and stood straight, shoulders back. He was more filled out than the last time I'd seen him. Broader chest but with muscle still left to fill in. Must be almost eighteen by now. He was just over six feet, not quite as tall as me, but could still grow a few more inches.

And yet, his gaze was as steady as any grown man's.

"I never blamed you for this." He pointed to the scars along his jaw. "You never gave me a chance to say so, but I know it wasn't your fault. It wasn't your intention. So do us both a favor and drop the guilt trip you've been giving yourself."

His brown eyes held mine, a gentleness in the young man. It had always been there, but there was also something more now. Confidence. Self-assurance. What comes from knowing yourself and liking who you are. No sadness. No regret. No trace of malice toward another.

Toward me.

Finally, I held out my hand for him to shake. His stern expression loosened into one of relief as he shook my hand.

I jerked him into a hug and whispered, "Thank you, Ty."

"How about you thank me by keeping in touch?" He pulled back, and I caught the first glimpse of sorrow in his eyes. "You were my friend before that all happened."

Glancing at Violet, who watched our exchange with obvious joy, I cleared my throat. "Give me your phone." I held out my hand to him.

He paused for just a second before pulling his phone out of his back pocket and handing it over. I'd changed my phone number when I left Austin, trying to cut all ties like the stubborn asshole I was. In my attempt to protect myself from emotional harm, I'd told the pack they didn't matter anymore. I'd thought I was doing them and myself a favor when I was really just hurting them more. No wonder Shane believed the only way to get what he needed was by taking Violet.

This whole shitshow was as much my fault as his.

After taking Ty's phone, I added my name and number to his contacts, then passed it back.

"Call or text me anytime."

"Thanks." In a flash of memory, I saw the happy-go-lucky kid when he'd first started to come around the pack and follow me around like a puppy.

"Come by the shop while y'all are still in town."

He nodded, his Adam's apple bobbing as he tried to hold back his smile. "I will."

I wanted to ruffle his hair like I used to, but he was becoming too much of a man for that so I patted him on the shoulder, then hefted the duffel bag onto my shoulder. Violet grabbed the smaller bag and tucked her hand back in mine.

As we hustled toward the exit, the Jeep already out front, I leaned down to Violet. "When we get in the car, I need you to call your sisters and tell them you're all right."

"I planned on it."

"Then I need you to tell them you're not coming home."

"Oh?"

We walked through the gouged-out garage doors. Tugging her against my body, I wrapped my hand around her nape, giving her a firm squeeze. "I need you at my house."

"But I really need a shower and—"

"I'll take care of that. At *my* house." Sweeping down, I nipped at her lip again. "I'll take care of you, Violet."

At the slow rumble of her name that poured out of a growl from my lips, she whimpered.

"Just say yes," I commanded.

"Yes," she said softly, looking at me with the most submissive expression I'd ever seen on her face.

It annihilated me. Decimated me. And filled me with the insatiable need to tuck her close and hold her in my arms until I was sure she was indeed *mine*.

As if sensing my sudden desperate desire, she stepped closer, cupped my jaw, and whispered gently, "Take me home, Nico."

Without another word to anyone, I did just that.

CHAPTER 31

~VIOLET~

"I THINK I LIKE THIS MODE OF TRANSPORTATION."

I swung my legs back and forth that were dangling over one of his arms, my own linked tightly around his neck as he carried me like a bride through his courtyard. He arched a brow at me, still quiet. He'd gone super silent on the way home, simply keeping hold of my hand in his lap as he drove. Fred's clucking caught my attention.

"Oh, Fred. Is he hungry, you think?"

"You can tend to him later," he said gruffly, shoving open his door and slamming it shut with his foot, all while keeping me in his arms and barely jostling me.

"You need tending to first?" I queried with my own arched brow.

"No." He stared down, his expression intense yet tender. "You do."

I wasn't going to argue. When we hit the top of his stairs, I expected him to toss me on the bed and strip me naked, but he strode directly into his bathroom instead. After setting me on my feet, I went to unzip the dress on the side, but he pushed my hand away.

"Let me do it," he whispered low and serious. So serious.

Just like that, all levity evaporated. The nearness of our bodies, the heating of our blood, the ever-present magnetism sluicing through our bones, coupled with being separated by force, charged the room with a sudden and jarring spark.

Still, he slid my zipper down with care, then gently pulled my dress over my head. His hands tracked my body, sliding over my skin as if to ascertain any bruises or marks he hadn't cataloged yet. He was careful not to touch the scratch at my hip. It wasn't deep and had just a little dried blood caked there. With gentle fingers, he removed my bra and panties, then put a hand on my hip to keep me in place while he reached over and turned on the shower.

"Get in," he urged me when the steam started to billow behind the glass door.

The hot water felt like heaven pouring over my body. I stood under the stream, letting it wet my hair as I watched him remove his clothes and step inside with me. Being confined in the space of his shower reminded me how big of a man he was. And how beautiful.

"Nico—?"

His mouth was on mine, firm but gentle licks, coaxing my lips wider apart so he could invade. His big hands slid over my slick skin, down my back, over the curve of my ass, squeezing, then trailing back up my waist, my hips, my breasts. And yet, his hands weren't seeking sexual pleasure or arousal, but more like simply seeking me instead. Gripping and holding and caressing, making sure I was real and here and safe. With him.

"Fuck, fuck, fuck," he grated out against my lips, his hands back on my waist where he squeezed hard and held me against the tiles so I couldn't move as he pulled away.

The wreck in his eyes made me pause. "Hey. What's going on?"

He swallowed hard, his Adam's apple bobbing, the water dripping over his black hair that stuck in whorls to his cheekbones and down over his face. His hands cupped my face gently, a tremor shivering through his body. He shook his head and closed his eyes tight, the words seeming to have lodged in his throat.

"Look at me, Nico." I cupped his jaw, mirroring his hold on me, demanding that he open his eyes.

When he finally did, my breath caught. The devastation there sliced through my flesh and rib cage, right down to my heart.

"Baby," I whispered, "what's wrong?"

He brushed his thumbs along my cheeks, then one hand curled into my wet hair, fisting tightly, almost to pain. His voice was sandpaper and jagged nails. "You're so precious to me, Violet." He swallowed hard again, water dripping from his beautiful, perfect mouth saying beautiful, perfect things. "When I thought you could be hurt, I nearly died from the agony." Shaking his head, water droplets dripped from his chin. As he swept his thumb over the wetness of my bottom lip, he added, "I can't live without you."

"Oh, baby," I soothed, dragging his face closer so he could see me clearly when I said, "I love you too." I pressed a kiss to his wet lips, whispering against them. "I so do."

His eyes fell closed on a groan, his lips trembling as they pressed against my mouth. But when his tongue slipped inside and licked against mine, it was with the gentlest care.

He showed me with languorous sweet kisses how precious I was to him. When my happy tears mingled with the water and his desperation faded, he simply held me close underneath the shower, his heart beating wildly against mine.

After some time, he shut off the water and wordlessly dried me off, then himself. He dressed me in one of his T-shirts and slipped on some boxers, then carried me not to bed but downstairs.

He then tucked me on his sofa with a warm, cushy blanket and left me there.

I didn't say anything, drowsing slightly as I heard pans clanking as he moved around the kitchen. He nudged me awake I'm not sure how much later, helped me sit up, and made me eat a burger he'd whipped up with sauteed onions and mushrooms with a side of jalapeno cheese fries.

The heavy carbs and protein tasted like heaven.

"I really do love you," I muffled around a bite of delicious burger.

He chuckled, watching me eat while he did the same. "Is it just my talent in the kitchen?"

"All your talents." I grinned as I swiped a glob of cheesy fries in ketchup.

After we ate, I took his feet into my lap and massaged them, yet again admiring them. Let's be honest. Every part of Nico utterly fascinated me.

"Foot fetish, Vi?"

He had his hands linked behind his head at the head of the sofa while he watched me with those wolf-green eyes. I liked that he was calmer now. His panic was gone, now that I was safe at home.

Home? When had I thought of his home as mine?

A ping of magic flashed through my mind, like deja vu. This was the vision I saw that day when I did his reading with the tarot cards. I smiled.

"And if I do have a foot fetish?" I arched a brow at him.

"You can play with anything of mine to your heart's delight." Then he wiggled his toes.

I tickled the bottom of his feet. He jerked them away with a bark of laughter.

"This is a fascinating discovery." I crawled up the sofa and over his body till I could tickle his ribs.

"No, Violet!" he yelled and laughed at the same time.

I kept going till he twisted and moved my body beneath him, wrangled my wrists with one hand and pinned them above my head. We panted, both still chuckling. His gaze drifted up to the injury on my forehead.

"I'm sorry about that." He traced the line of my jaw with a gentle stroke. "I should've punched Shane one more time for that."

"It wasn't his fault, to be honest, but that guy Rick. And if we're keeping score, then I should punch you for banging up my knee."

He winced, a slight groan rumbling in his chest.

"Jeesh, I'm fine. I'm tougher than I look. I can handle a few bruises."

"I don't want you to ever be bruised again. I forbid it." He pressed a kiss to my lips, a chaste but pleasant one.

"Well, if you forbid it, then"—I yawned—"I suppose that makes it final."

He smiled. "Let's get some sleep." He stood and lifted me into his arms and carried me up to his bed.

"I do have working legs, you know."

"I know."

"Though I could get used to getting carted around."

"Just let me do this without all your sass."

"Yes, sir."

He groaned. "Once you're well rested, I'm going to get you to say that a lot."

"Yes, sir."

He narrowed his gaze on me as he slipped me into his bed. I laughed, utterly content, as he slid in underneath the covers with me. I curled onto my side, and he spooned his body around mine, the warmth and luxury of it feeling like heaven.

My eyelids were already drooping when I said, "We need to talk about the werewolf issue."

"Tomorrow." He kissed the crown of my head, banding my waist and pulling me flush to him. "It'll wait."

"'Kay." I yawned again. "Night, Nico. I love you."

Funny how easy it was and how natural it felt slipping from my mouth now. A heartbeat passed. And another. A heavy sigh huffed against the back of my neck as he nuzzled into my hair.

"I love you too."

Then I fell into the most blissful sleep of my whole life.

CHAPTER 32

~NICO~

I STARED AT THE SCRIBBLED WRITING IN MY JOURNAL ON MY LAP. TRYING TO focus was a Herculean effort after last night. I'd woken next to the love of my life, my mate, and couldn't stop grinning like a fiend. I'd snuggled closer, contemplating ways I could wake her that might put the same smile on her face.

But she was so tired after that long ordeal. It would've been selfish to wake her just so I could see that look in her eyes when I made her come. My need to know she was rested and cared for overrode my need to bury myself inside her. Another reminder of how absolutely she'd ensnared my heart.

I'd cooked chocolate chip pancakes and fried bacon for her, thinking she'd be up by nine or ten a.m. I was wrong. It was approaching eleven and the woman was still out. But there was something beguiling about having her asleep and safe in my home. A warm contentment seeped through flesh to my bones, rapping out a gentle reminder that she was exactly where she was meant to be. With me.

Knock, knock.

Setting my journal on the coffee table, I meandered to the door. I'd wondered how long it would take for a Savoie to show up at my house. By the scent, it was Clara who'd finally broken down.

"Good morning." She beamed brightly, her voice chipper as always.

"I'm surprised you or your sisters weren't banging on my door at dawn." I stepped aside for her to come in.

Laughing, she removed her fuchsia peacoat and set it on the back of a chair in my living room. "I told them she was perfectly well and fine, and they believed me. Especially after Mateo showed up and recounted events for Jules." She walked over to my bookshelf and perused the books and photographs. "Of course, Jules wants a full personal account as soon as she's up."

"I expected that." After taking a seat on the sofa, I leaned forward, elbows on my knees, my nerves jacking up. "Clara, I wanted to tell you something. Ask you something, really."

She turned away from the shelf and plopped down in the cushy chair opposite me. "How can I help?"

"Do I seem to need help?"

"Your anxiety spiked to alarming levels three seconds ago, so I think that you do."

"You're right. But not in the way you might think. I don't need an Aura spell or anything like that. I wanted to tell you that Violet and I are together."

She blinked her bright blue eyes, identical in shade to Violet's but holding none of the aggressiveness Violet's usually held. "Yes, I know. And?"

"And, well, we're very together. In a permanent way." That sounded a little creepy. "What I mean is that she's my mate and, for wolves, that's as good as marriage. Not that she's agreed to marriage or anything." I laughed nervously, wondering how to say this without sounding like a fool. Too late. "But I suspect or hope she will at some point. Either way, what I'm doing a terrible job of explaining is that I love her. And since you're her closest sister, her twin, I wanted your approval. Of us being together."

Her smile grew from serene to blinding, then she launched herself around the coffee table and into my arms, hugging the hell out of me. "Of course I approve," she said into my ear, squeezing me tight. "I've always known you were soul mates."

"You have?" I chuckled, confused.

She eased back and squeezed my shoulders in a very maternal way. "Your auras have matched since the first time I saw you together."

"Matching auras means we're soul mates?"

"Of course not." She laughed and let me go, then took a seat on the sofa.

I settled beside her. "I'm confused."

"Hmm. It's hard to explain exactly. My magic is extremely intuitive. It wasn't just the matching auras. It was that you matched *all* the time. Within seconds if there was a shift. If your aura turned blue, so did Violet's. If hers turned red, so did yours. And then there was the whole lust-field."

"Lust-field?"

"Big time." She nodded her head vigorously, her blonde tendrils sliding in front of one shoulder, then she leaned forward and whispered, "Like y'all were sexually in sync." She straightened again and said matter-of-factly, "But, of course, you weren't."

"We weren't?" I was so fucking muddled I had no idea what she was talking about.

"It wasn't your fault." She patted my knee in that maternal way again. "It was Violet's. She's the most stubborn person I know. Except Jules maybe."

"I can believe that." Finally, something that made sense.

"So you see, even though I knew you two were fated to be together, it didn't matter. Violet has to see things for herself. If you tell her to do something, she'll only run in the opposite direction and reject whatever it is. Bit of a rebel."

"Just a bit."

"And a dummy if you ask me. I wouldn't have made you wait that long."

Wow. Clara was . . . something else. The most forthright, direct person I'd ever met. I almost felt sorry for the man who finally snagged her because he probably would have no idea how to handle her insanely honest nature.

"Oh, you wouldn't, would you?" Violet stood in the arched entry to the living room from the hallway.

She was wearing my Rolling Stones T-shirt, which hit her mid-thigh, her hair looked like a rat's nest, and the stitched cut at her hairline had turned blue from the faded bruising. She looked like hell, but still my stomach somersaulted and my mouth went dry.

I stood and went to her, then gently cupped her jaw and tilted her face up to get a look at the cut. "How do you feel? Want some Advil?"

"Meh." She shrugged. "A visit to Isadora will do the trick better actually."

"I'll go feed Fred," Clara called out to us before disappearing.

"Smart sister. Giving us privacy." Leaning down, I pressed a kiss to her sweet mouth.

She kissed me back, then slipped her hands around my waist and burrowed her cheek into the middle of my sternum. "Why did you leave me in bed all alone?"

"Because you were sleeping like the dead, and I didn't want to wake you." I smoothed my palms in circles on her back.

"You should've."

"You needed sleep."

"What smells so good? Did you cook?"

"That would be bacon and pancakes from three hours ago."

"Pancakes?" She lurched back and gave me her wide-eyed excited face.

"Chocolate chip."

"Aww! You remembered?"

"I remember everything you say."

She doesn't respond, just looks at me. I'm perfectly content with that smug expression on her face. I have no problem that she knows how twisted I am around her little finger.

"I'll go heat up a plate if you want to tell Clara she can come inside."

Right then, Clara opened the door and stepped into the entryway off the kitchen. "I forgot to tell you, Devraj figured out Archie's escape trick."

"No way." Violet turned to the side so she could see Clara. "How was he doing it?"

"A jump to an upturned bucket, then to the recycling bin, then to the garbage, then over the fence. Quite the acrobat, that Archie. Anyway, Fred can come home now."

I tightened my hold on Violet. "I kind of like having him here. It'll make you visit more often."

"Or I could just move in with you. He loves his new house you made him."

I was stuck on the moving in with me part. "Seriously?"

She scoffed. "It's better than the one he has at our house."

"No, I mean about you moving in."

She shrugged one shoulder. "Why not? I know what I want now. Plus, I like the idea of getting sex on demand."

Stunned. This woman had put me off for so long, and now was perfectly fine to move in.

"What has made you so agreeable?"

She arched a brow and slid her bare leg forward between my jeans. "I think you know."

"Noted."

"Nico, I love that statue you have of Violet," interrupted Clara, her voice coming from the kitchen. "Did Mateo make it for you?"

My pulse skittered ahead as Violet's head swiveled toward the kitchen, then back to me.

"*Whaaaat?*"

"Okay, I know it seems weird—"

Violet took off running outside with no pants and in bare feet.

Heaving a sigh, I gave Clara a disgruntled look after walking over to the entryway. "You *were* my favorite sister. Now she's going to be impossible."

"You mean she didn't know?" Clara rolled her eyes, tearing off a piece of chocolate chip pancake and eating it cold. "For a witch, and a psychic, she's so clueless."

Following Violet out to the courtyard, I found her standing in front of the fairy on the far side of the fountain, grinning like the cat who got the cream. She propped her hands on her hips.

"You were so in love with me the *whole* time."

"She bears a slight resemblance to you."

"She's me. Exactly me. She's even got a smirky smile that looks like me, not Clara."

Crossing my arms, I pretended nonchalance. "You're delusional."

"Admit it." She hopped from one foot to the other.

"It's fucking freezing out here, Violet. Come here." I started toward her around the fountain. She maneuvered away from me, circling to the other side.

"Just say I'm right."

"I'm not saying that." I juked her and ran around the other side. She squealed and yelled, "Say I'm right!"

I caught her around the waist and swept her off her feet, tossed her into the air, then caught her in both arms, knees dangling over my left arm. She cackled with laughter, flinging her head back with unfettered joy. The sound lit something inside me, rekindling that deeply rooted warmth we'd found in the bedroom last night.

I leaned down and nipped her exposed neck, smiling against her tender skin while striding toward the house.

She wrapped her hands around my neck and singsonged, "Just say it!"

"Okay, fine, fine," I whined begrudgingly. I stopped on the stoop right in front of the door and hauled her closer till I could press my forehead to hers, then I whispered, "I was so in love with you." I closed my eyes, admitting words that had terrified me months ago and now only made my heart soar with bliss. "The whole time." I opened my eyes to make sure she heard me. "And it might've taken you two years to figure out what I already knew, but I would've waited longer for you."

She sucked in a shuddering breath. "Well . . ." She swallowed hard and pulled on a longer lock of hair at my nape. "I might be as clueless as my sister says I am, but my eyes are wide open now."

"Yeah?" I set her gently on the welcome mat and rested my hands on her hips. "And what do you see?"

"I see . . ." She tilted her head, her crazy bed-hair so wild and untamed like the woman herself that it made my heart hurt. Her hands skated up my shoulders to rest on the sides of my neck.

"My man."

"That's right, you do." I opened the door, then popped her behind. "Now go eat breakfast before you earn another spanking."

She marched through the door, then tossed me a sexy look over her shoulder with a low, "Yes, sir."

When I growled, she jumped right back into my arms and cupped a hand against my ear to whisper, "I really want breakfast because I'm starving. But I want another spanking later too."

Then she was swishing back toward the kitchen, my T-shirt just barely covering her fine ass. That woman could twist my heart and my dick into knots so fast, I never knew what I wanted to do more, cuddle her or fuck her. What I did know was that now we had plenty of time for both.

And no matter what happened from here on out, what trials and tribulations life threw at us, one truth would never change. She was mine. I was hers. And that's all that mattered.

CHAPTER 33

~VIOLET~

"You've got us all here. Now tell us what this is about."

Jules was on edge, and I didn't blame her. When I told her I wanted all of these people assembled, she demanded to know why. I'd told her I wasn't going to tell her until we all met and she just needed to do this for me.

There were a few reasons I wanted to handle things this way.

One, Jules might've used the time leading up to this meeting to contemplate and create a counterargument without the presence of all those here. Particularly Ruben. Whether she wanted to admit it or not, the thing between these two a decade ago had caused a rift that made her want to avoid him at all costs. But for this to work, we needed Ruben.

Ruben had offered the use of his bookshop lounge for the meeting. It was an elegant blend of art deco design and luxurious comfort with velvet seating and Tiffany lamps on side tables. Devraj sat next to Isadora with their hands entwined and on his thigh. Clara and Livvy were curled on a blue velvet chaise, delicate coffee cups and saucers in their laps. Jules was in a chair next to them. Mateo was in another plush chair to Jules's right, Evie sitting on his lap, his hand wrapped around her abdomen.

"Wait," I told her. "We're waiting on one more."

The outer door opened and closed, then in stepped Henry. As usual, he was decked out in all black. Scanning the room, his gaze lingered on my twin. That familiar ping of magic buzzed along my skin, then he wound through the seating to lean against the wall next to Ruben, who had remained standing, hands in his pants pockets. I could see Jules wanted to ask why a grim was here, but thankfully she held her tongue.

To be honest, I wasn't sure of Henry's role within his community of grim reapers, but I did know that he had influence and held some power. The display at my so-called rescue, along with what Nico had told me about their abilities, meant that grims weren't just Gothic decoration in the supernatural world. And apparently, the Blackwaters were not only powerful grims, they had access to invaluable data as well as the ability to pass information through the Supernatural Net. And whatever other secretive paths they held in their hands. They'd also proven themselves to be allies with my family. That family now included Nico and his friends and brothers in the Blood Moon pack.

Nico stood next to me at the front of the assembly, arms crossed as he leaned back against a bookshelf.

"Right. As you are aware, I was recently kidnapped. The recent incident with the Blood Moon pack has taught me something that I was too stubborn to realize before." Honestly, I was expecting some sarcastic remarks at this point, but no one said a word.

All were intently listening. "Shane and his pack did what they did out of desperation. Not desperation to hurt or harm me, but to receive the magic they needed the only way they knew how. This magic, my spells, has the ability to calm their volatile impulses. Nico can attest that my most recent charmed tattoo has had the positive effect on them that we'd hoped." I glanced at Nico by my side. He nodded to show agreement and gave me a small smile of encouragement. "I'll be giving the entire pack the spelled ink that they need over the next week or so, but that isn't enough."

"That isn't the full pack?" asked Devraj, one arm on the sofa back, his fingers casually playing with Isadora's hair.

"That's not what I mean. The problem is that all werewolves need this kind of charm. It's more than a spell to keep their beast in check. Am I right?" I turned to Nico again.

Holding my gaze, he addressed everyone loud so they could hear, "It's a healing charm. For in here." He tapped his chest.

"Then that's great," said Livvy. "You can help all the werewolves in our region then."

Shaking my head, I added, "I don't want to help just the werewolves here where we live. I want to help all of them."

"All?" Jules understood the enormity of what I was saying.

"All."

Mateo held Evie close, tucked tenderly against him. In turn, she had her hand resting on his stomach beneath his shirt. Skin to skin contact was a comfort to werewolves. I smiled at the two of them, understanding now the zinging through my bones.

"You know, there aren't many mixed couples with werewolves. And we all know why. It's not just the fact that the werewolf race has had a history of violent behavior. It's the prejudice that was created against them a long time ago because of this. I'm sure that the first werewolf, Diego Ortega, created by the witch Ethelinda"—yes, I did my research before coming today—"deserved his punishment. But do every descendant beyond him, innocent men only guilty by birth alone, do they deserve the intolerance of the entire supernatural world against them?"

Jules's usual stoic veneer faltered. Her brow furrowed to one of concern. She'd been taught by our mother what every witch and Enforcer before her had been taught: Beware of werewolves. Keep them away for your own safety. But then, she also made an exception when she saw Mateo in trouble, when he needed the help of a good witch to break the hex put on him. "What I want," I declared with emphasis, "is a revolution against the too-long discrimination of an entire race of supernaturals." I reached beside me without looking at Nico. He took my hand immediately and squeezed with reassurance. "It may have taken me falling in love with a werewolf to see this, but the problem isn't just to help them with a spell. We need to help our world to see that they're one of us. The fact that they've been suffering for centuries when one witch could've created a spell to help them all along honestly makes me sick."

"But Violet . . ." Clara straightened, looking off to the side, a frown marring her usually tranquil face. I felt the tug of magic as it flowed through the room from her and hummed along my skin with familiarity. She was tapping in to her psychic eye. "You were the only witch who would've thought to use the permanent charm for werewolves. And you were the only witch powerful enough to cast it."

She said it not as a compliment or as a means of support for her twin sister, but as a fact. She'd read the otherworld for knowledge and had been told by the Spirit. The effervescent glow of her skin proved it.

"It won't be easy," said Jules, concern still etched in her brow.

"I know," I agreed softly. "Which is why we'll need help." I looked at Ruben and Henry. "It isn't just a witch problem anyway."

Ruben's mouth tipped up with his devilish, crooked smile. "I'll do whatever you ask in the vampire community."

Henry didn't say anything, but he nodded alongside Ruben. I suppose that's all I'd get from a grim as far as compliance.

"I think it needs to be a group effort," I told him. "Actually, it's the witches and vampires who are most outspoken in their discrimination against the werewolves so I was hoping to work with you and Jules to figure out how we can take this all the way to the top." Jules glanced nervously at Ruben, but I went on. "Clara may be right, and it may be only my spell that can help them, but I'm in no way capable of tattooing every werewolf in the world. But I can spell enough ink and train other willing witches, other powerful Seers, to cast the spell."

"That would require a lot of organization," agreed Devraj.

"And open-minded Enforcers to allow the practice in their covens," Jules added.

"Not to mention the regions run by vampire overlords who would need to agree to the same." Ruben's voice was gruff, but I think it was at the thought of dealing with arrogant vampire overlords in other territories who wouldn't take it kindly to be told to play nice with werewolves.

"So you see," I said, "I need your help." Then I stepped closer to Nico's side. He wrapped an arm around me and tucked me close, pressing a kiss to my temple. "*We* need your help."

Without a second thought, Ruben dipped his chin. "Given."

Jules actually smiled at him, and I thought the earth might open up with the onslaught of the apocalypse. Then she turned her smile to me, pride in her eyes. "You have my full support. And I know you'll have our parents, as well."

"And Maybelle's," added Livvy with a chuckle. Maybelle was our wild grandmother who had been spending her time traveling the world and trying out foreign lovers in every port. "If I recall, she's had more than one love affair with a werewolf and would certainly support this venture."

Isadora piped up then. "I'm not sure what I can do, but if you need me for anything, I'm at your disposal, Vi."

"Thanks, Is. So I guess everyone is with me on this?"

"I'm always up for a revolution." Livvy winked.

Clara glanced around before settling back on me. "We're all with you. Nico and Mateo are our family now. It's our responsibility to show the world that we can't shun a race simply because our ancestors did. What's wrong is wrong."

"Agreed," said Jules, standing. "Ruben, I'll email you with some meeting times on this. We'll need a detailed plan moving forward."

"As you wish," he said with a bow of his head.

For some reason, that had her frowning harder than normal before she headed for the door. Everyone else started to stand and make their way toward the exit. Clara stopped Henry as he passed to tell him something. They walked, and he listened as they left the lounge. Evie and Mateo headed straight for us instead.

Evie grinned so hard I thought her face might break, then I saw the glassy look in her eyes.

She blinked back the tears and swept me into a tight hug. "Fuck, Evie, I can't breathe."

She laughed, and I could hear her fighting the tears. "You're the bestest, Vi. Such a softie."

"Shut up. Don't tell anyone."

"It's our secret." Then she smacked a kiss on my cheek, took Mateo's hand, and tugged him toward the door.

But not before Mateo chucked me on the chin. "Thank you."

I swallowed the lump in my throat, unable to respond, so I just gave a little wave. I wasn't the mushy kind of girl, but all this teary-eyed gratitude had my emotions running amuck.

Big, strong arms wrapped around me from behind, then Nico dipped his mouth close to my ear. "She's right. You're the bestest."

"You're not biased at all."

"Not at all."

I turned in his arms. "Let's go home. I have something I want to add to the list."

"Oh yeah?"

"Let's just say Isadora sent me a list of her favorite toys."

"Isadora?"

I laughed at his shocked expression. Isadora didn't appear to be the adventurous type to the outside world, but that girl knew her sex toys better than anyone. I'd seen the packages she'd ordered when she lived with us in the house. So I knew she'd be the one to give me some tips.

"And I had a notification that my package was delivered while we've been out."

He grabbed my hand and led me toward the exit, pressing a kiss to my inner wrist. "Let's go home."

Home. A stirring of warmth filled my chest because I knew now that my home was with him. Clara was right. Nico was family. He was my better half, and I had no problem admitting that. I might be slow on the uptake, as I was when I left him high and dry in Austin two years ago and when I pretended we were just friends after he moved here to New Orleans to pursue me, but I can tell you something about myself that's always been true. I learn from my mistakes, and I don't waste time.

So I skipped ahead of him and dragged my fine-ass werewolf toward our home so I could have my wicked way with him. Another thing I was 100 percent positive about. I was going to do my damnedest to never let that list end. Thankfully, Nico seemed to have the same idea. I knew I was right when we walked past an alley.

"Alley sex," he whispered.

"Really? That could be gross."

"Not if I hold you up." He glanced my way, a flash of wolf-green taking my breath away. "It could be hot."

Nodding, I said, "It's going on the list."

Then we sauntered home, happy in our little bubble of love and prospects of pleasure, even if we had a long road ahead with my revolution. With him by my side, nothing was impossible.

EPILOGUE

~VIOLET~

"Stay right here." Nico stood between my thighs where my butt was planted on the stool, my back leaning against the bar. He brushed a lingering, closed-mouth kiss to my lips, then sauntered back toward the stage where he'd been playing for most of the night.

I'd gotten gussied up, even put on a dress at his request, for a late dinner and who knows what else. It was date night, and I didn't care where we were going. He'd insisted that I meet him at the Cauldron at the end of his gig. When I told him Jules would've understood if he wanted out of tonight's gig, which he'd scheduled over a month ago, he said no, he wanted to work it.

And he wanted me here before he finished.

So here I was, sitting next to Charlie, who was waiting for JJ, his boyfriend, to get off work.

His boyfriend! I turned to look at Charlie, who'd spun around to watch with me.

"I still can't get over the two of you." I waggled my eyebrows at Charlie.

His usual smirk lacked the sharp edge because of the ridiculously obvious bliss sparkling in his baby-blue eyes. "You were the one who said I needed to go for it with him." He glanced behind him where JJ was serving Flaming Gin Dragons—our newest and most popular cocktail—to three giggling girls at the end of the bar.

"So you were the one to make the first move?"

He opened his mouth, then snapped it shut again and smiled. "Sort of."

"No more of this cryptic shit! Who kissed who first?"

His smile widened to Joker-levels. "He did."

"That's it. You and I have a date tomorrow afternoon. At Tea Witch Café. I need all of the details."

"It's not like I've been hiding from you. You've just been way too busy for me."

"Charles. I had like a dozen werewolves to tattoo. And I have more coming in almost every day, seems like. Sean can barely fit them in fast enough."

"I thought that pack was from Austin."

"They are. But apparently, they decided to stick around here. And they've been telling friends about the shop. Which is fine by me, but I'm glad Nico made me take the day off." Smiling wickedly to myself, I said, "Actually, I think Nico needed me to take a night off as well."

"Why? What's that look for?"

"See, this werewolf charm works best when it's tattooed close to the heart. So I've been spending every day with hot, bare-chested werewolves."

"Poor you," he said sarcastically. His attention swiveled to the stage. "Poor Nico." Charlie grinned as Nico lifted the guitar strap over his shoulder, saying something to a customer down front. "I'm sure he had other ulterior motives. He wanted you well rested."

"I have no problems with that because I always get lots of orgasms from his ulterior motives."

Then Nico spoke into the mic. "How are all our lovers this Valentine's Day?"

Catcalls and whoops echoed through the bar. Evie yelled louder than most from her spot on the other side of Charlie, standing between Mateo's legs and facing the stage. Livvy said something to them that made them both laugh.

My attention snapped back to Nico when he said, "Here's hoping you all get some love tonight." More catcalls, laughter, and applause. "This last song goes to my sweetheart. It's called 'Sapphire River.'"

I gulped hard, barely feeling the nudge of Charlie's elbow in my rib cage. His *sweetheart*. Something about those words proclaimed so publicly sent an eruption of shivery tingles along my skin.

As he strummed the first chords, looking down at his fingers moving over the strings, my heart rate picked up. Wearing dark jeans, a black button-down, his hair casually messy, a little scruff on his sharp jaw that gave him a sexy edge, he was the most beautiful man I'd ever seen.

And now he was singing a song for me.

When he started singing slow and sensuous, I blocked out every soul in the room. This wasn't another artist's work he'd used to tell me how he felt. These were his own words. Written for me.

He'd explained that he didn't like the spotlight. He liked to blend into the background, even as he loved singing and using his creative gift. I could barely hold in the swelling of love, knowing that he had put his words to music for me.

He sang about being lost in the deep, dark woods. A half-man without a home. Then his voice became more intense, deeper, rougher as he sang about being swept away by a river, nearly drowning in an abyss of despair and longing. But then the intense strumming suddenly stopped with his palm over the strings. He hummed deep and low into the mic before beating his hand on the hollow of the guitar, a slow tempo slowly gaining speed, like a heartbeat coming back to life.

Then his eyes landed on me across the Cauldron, a shimmer of electric green in his eyes as he picked a tender, sweet melody from the strings, singing about an angel with sapphire eyes, pulling him out of the dark and delivering him onto a shore of paradise with purple skies and warm, warm nights. He strummed the last few chords of the sweet melody in unison with his rumbling masculine hum.

When he finished, the crowd erupted into a frenzy of applause and whistles. He modestly stood and gave them a little wave, unhooking his guitar and setting it in the case. I was moving without even knowing it, my heart in my fucking throat as I pushed through the crowd and around tables to get to him. By the time he'd turned and took a few steps toward me, a sweet smile on his face and love in his eyes, I was on him, leaping into his arms. He caught me, bracing an arm under my ass when I wrapped my legs around him, not giving a shit that my loose skirt rode up my thighs. I pressed my face into his neck, and he held me, swaying back and forth with comforting strokes up and down my spine.

"I've got you, baby."

Like he knew I needed those words, needed him to soothe and calm me as emotions swelled and poured out of me. I barely heard the crowd cheering us on, and I knew this was probably driving him crazy with everyone watching us. Even so, he held me in the middle of the bar, crooning sweet reassurances into my ear, his big hands sweeping gentle strokes until I managed to loosen my death grip and slide my feet to the ground.

"That was—" I shook my head, swallowing the lump choking my vocal cords.

He lifted his hands and cupped my face, brushing away tears on my cheeks that I hadn't realized I'd cried.

"Just wanted you to know how much I love you," he whispered.

I gripped his nape and pulled him down to me. "You're going to get the best blow job of your life tonight."

He laughed, even as I kissed him.

"Now that I know what it takes, I'll start writing another song for you for my birthday."

Both of us laughing, I tugged him back to the bar where JJ, Charlie, Livvy, Evie, Mateo, and Clara clapped vigorously. For Nico. And why shouldn't they? He was insanely talented. I might've been biased and thought his song was the most beautiful ever created, but the truth was, it was absolutely amazing. He was amazing. And he was mine.

"Man, you've been holding out on us," said JJ, sliding a Witch's Brew longneck to him across the bar.

He shrugged. "Thanks, guys."

Livvy eyed him with serious calculation. "You know, if you've got more songs like that, I could totally help you create a social media presence."

Nico's eyes widened in fright. Before he could answer, I said, "No, Livvy! He doesn't want that. He already makes money on his songs. He doesn't want to be famous or anything."

"Damn shame." Livvy shook her head. "Looking like you do and with a voice and talent like that, you could sell a million albums."

"And then I'd have to live in a gated community with body-guards, imprisoned in my own house. Thank you, Livvy, but no thank you." He swept a kiss to the crown of my head. "I love my life just the way it is."

"Hmph. You have a point."

Finnie walked up, carrying an empty tray of drinks. "JJ, can I get four more Spider Bite Martinis? Extra olives."

"Sure thing." JJ turned back to the bar to make the order.

"Finnie, you got a hot date later?" asked Livvy. "I'll bet those college girls are lining up for your cute face." She pinched his cheeks.

He chuckled. "Yeah. A seriously hot date with my Organic Chemistry textbook. Can't wait."

"Where are you two headed?" asked Mateo to me and Nico.

"I don't know." I glanced up at the man wrapped around me from behind. "Where are we headed?"

"Drago's. I know how much my girl loves raw oysters."

He squeezed his banded arms around my middle. Honestly, the two of us didn't need an aphrodisiac, but I really did love oysters. Raw, chargrilled, fried. Any old way. And Drago's had the best in town.

"Yum!" I wiggled in place, then suddenly noticed Evie's face going white.

"You okay?" Mateo asked her with a hand at her hip.

She didn't answer, even when JJ slid Finnie's tray across the bar with fresh martinis, olives galore. He picked it up, passing it right under Evie's nose.

"Oh God." She clutched her stomach and sprinted toward the hallway where the bathrooms were.

"Oh no!" Clara circled into our group, worry etched in the lines of her face. "Her aura is gray."

Mateo seemed completely unconcerned. Actually, he was smiling.

"What the hell, asshat?" Livvy scowled at him. "Why are you happy that Evie is sick?"

A sharp pulse vibrated in my bones, my psychic eye sending me a clear message. "Holy fuck," I whispered. All eyes swiveled to me. "Evie's pregnant."

No one said a word, all of us stunned silent. Then we all looked at Mateo, who was grinning even wider.

"Explain yourself," Livvy demanded in a high, shrieky voice.

His eyes went molten gold and his voice was rumbly dark when he spoke in Alpha's voice. "I'm very potent."

Charlie laughed but Livvy slapped him in the stomach with the back of her hand.

"But Evie was on the pill," said Clara, not quite believing this herself. "Wasn't she?" Alpha shrugged with all the smugness of a championship-winning underdog football team. Evie wandered back out of the bathroom, her face pale. Then she caught all of us staring and froze.

Before she could utter a word, Livvy said, "I thought you were on the pill."

She looked nervously from one of us to the next. "I was."

"Did you miss a pill or something?"

"Not one," she said.

"Isn't the pill ninety-nine percent effective?" asked Clara.

"I'm the one percent." Alpha exhaled a satisfied, manly breath. "My seed is strong."

"Are you okay?" asked Clara, reaching out a hand to Evie.

Then Evie unfroze and beamed a smile at Mateo. "Very." Clara pulled her into a hug.

"Damn," said Livvy. "A baby."

"Likely more than one," pointed out Alpha with a heavy dose of arrogance. "A small litter, at least."

A shot of magic simmered along my skin. I gulped, looking at Evie. "He's right." I reached out and put a hand on top of her flat stomach, still not even a bump. "Triplets."

"What!" Evie's question came out breathless on a laugh. Then her joy morphed back to anxiety.

But Mateo reached through the circle of sisters and hauled her close, pressing his mouth to her ear. "I'll take care of you. Don't worry about anything." That was more Mateo's voice than Alpha's.

She wrapped her arms around him as the rest of us looked at each other, completely shell-shocked.

"Well, Jules is going to have to find a new waiter," I said. "She won't be able to work too long. She'll be on bed rest in a few months."

Everyone talked excitedly at once, letting the reality sink in. Our family was growing, and as happy as I was, I was also terrified. When Mateo insisted on getting his pregnant mate home, who couldn't have been more than six weeks or so along, we dispersed, Nico leading me out to his Jeep, holding my hand.

We were both quiet, obviously trying to assimilate to the reality that we'd have nieces and/or nephews by next Christmas.

"Nico?"

"Yeah, babe."

"If werewolves are that fucking potent, we may be going back to condoms."

He chuckled and pulled me into his chest next to the passenger door of his Jeep. "That's fine. Whatever you want."

"What does that mean?" I frowned up at him.

He tucked my hair behind both ears, contentment written all over his face. "Just what I said. Whatever you want."

"Are you implying that you'd be fine taking a chance in getting me pregnant right now?"

"If you want to wait, that's fine with me. But having a baby, many babies with you, is something I hope we do one day. I'd be just as happy as Mateo so obviously is."

"You want babies with me?" I grinned like the devil, having never thought much about having kids in the past.

"Of course I do." He lowered his head, kissing the corner of my mouth. "A little wild Violet running around would melt my heart."

Sighing, I gripped the lapels of his black peacoat. "Or a little hellion Nico."

"I was never a hellion."

"Liar! Mateo has told me stories."

He chuckled. "I'm fine waiting, Violet. But I hope you want them at some point."

Huffing out a breath, I said, "I actually think I will." Then my thoughts wandered to Evie. I'd definitely read the word three along my psychic eye, but I wasn't sure about the sex of her babies. "So will she have werewolves or witches?"

Nico's brow furrowed, his mouth thinning a little before he answered. "Every male offspring of a werewolf carries the werewolf gene. As for mixed blood with witches, I don't know. I've actually never met a mixed couple who had more than a one-night stand. I guess we'll find out."

"It doesn't matter," I said, allowing the joy of being an aunt sink in. "We'll love them no matter what."

"Of course we will." He pressed his lips to mine, sliding his tongue along the seam till I opened for him. He licked in with a tender stroke, his hand at my back, sliding down to my ass. Giving me a squeeze, he grunted as he pulled back. "Now, let's go to dinner, then go home and practice making babies."

"Practice makes perfect, they say."

"Then we need to get started." He spanked my behind and urged me into the Jeep.

I hopped in and buckled up. When he'd gotten behind the wheel and pulled out into traffic, I put my hand on his thigh. "Thank you for my present. For the song. I loved it."

He slid me a tender expression, putting his hand over mine and curling his fingers under my palm. "I'm glad you did, baby."

"Although," I said playfully, "a traditional love poem would've sufficed. For Valentine's Day and all."

"It would, huh?" His mouth quirked with a wicked smile as he made the next turn toward mid-city. He remained silent for about thirty seconds. "There once was a werewolf in love. Who was sent an angel from above."

"Oh my God, stop!" We both knew I wasn't an angel. The fact that he saw me that way had me laughing hysterically.

He chuckled, then went on. "But her halo was bent from her constant descent." He arched a brow at me. "Even so, the wolf loved her the more."

My head back on the headrest, I beamed over at him. "I hate to be the bearer of bad news, wolfie, but that wasn't a perfect limerick."

"Doesn't matter." He lifted my hand, our fingers laced, and pressed a kiss to the back of my hand. "My girl's perfect."

I didn't correct him because we both knew that I wasn't perfect. But our love was. We were perfect for each other.

"Your turn," he said, squeezing my hand in his lap.

"Oh no! I'm so horrible at this."

"Which is why I love hearing you come up with them." He laughed with complete joy, and it was heady hearing it, filling my chest to bursting. "Let's hear it."

"Ugh!" I complained, coming up with something quick and absolutely ridiculous. "There once was a girl who was horny, who wrote poems that were hopelessly corny. But her man didn't care, he just wanted her bare, so he could try all his moves that were porny."

"Got that fuckin' right." He pulled into a parking spot across from the Hilton. "Now let's go get you fed so I can get you into my bed."

"Stop rhyming!"

"Let's be quick. So I can show you my hard dick."

He unbuckled me and pulled me, laughing, into his lap, my hip scrunched against the steering wheel.

"You are so fucking ludicrous." I giggled as he pressed his smiling mouth to mine.

"As long as you're laughing, or moaning, I'm a happy man."

"Same, baby."

Then we made out like teenagers, making it to second base before we calmed down enough to go into dinner. It was the best Valentine's Day I'd ever had. Perhaps because it was the first I'd spent with a man I loved.

Jules and Ruben had called a cease-fire and agreed to work together to present my plan, now our plan, to the regional Witches Coven Guild and to the Vampires Guild. That would be step one. We also had babies on the way. *Babies!* I couldn't wait to meet my little nieces or nephews. Or according to Alpha, nieces *and* nephews.

Squeezing Nico's hand, I looked up at him. I could see our future clearly now, my psychic eye tingling. Chaos and love, wolf babies and little witches, heartache and happiness. And I knew for a fact, as I stared at the tall, fine man—my best friend—at my side, that one day we'd have our own. Without a single sliver of fear about our future, I let him lead me on.

Acknowledgments

A huge thank-you to my beta readers, Cherie Lord and Christina Gwin, for paying so much attention to detail. And to Jessen Judice and Nilika Mistry, your feedback was imperative in making Nico and Violet their absolute best. I might've spent a full month in heavy revisions on the first draft, but it was well worth it.

I also owe my editor, Corinne DeMaagd, for her superior editing skills and for handing me my ass when I needed it. Much appreciated as always. I also want to thank the readers of the Stay a Spell series for continuing to follow the Savoie sisters' journey. It's not over yet, and there's lots more to tell. Happy reading and keep dreaming.

About the Author

JULIETTE CROSS is a multi-published author of paranormal and fantasy romance and is the co-host of the podcast *Smart Women Read Romance*. She is a native of Louisiana, living in the heart of Cajun land with her husband, four kids, her dogs, Kona and Jeaux, and kitty, Betty. When she isn't working on her next project, she enjoys binge-watching her favorite shows with her husband and a glass (or two) of red wine.